NEBULA AWARD STORIES SEVEN

Nebula Award Stories Seven

EDITED BY LLOYD BIGGLE, JR.

HARPER & ROW, PUBLISHERS

NEW YORK

EVANSTON

SAN FRANCISCO

LONDON

Acknowledgment is made for permission to reprint the following material:

"The Queen of Air and Darkness" by Poul Anderson. Copyright © 1971, by Mercury Press, Inc. First published in *The Magazine of Fantasy and Science Fiction*, April 1971. Reprinted by permission of the author and the author's agents, Scott Meredith Literary Agency, Inc.

"The Last Ghost" by Stephen Goldin. Copyright © 1971, by Ballantine Books, Inc. First published in *Protostars*, edited by David Gerrold. Reprinted by permission of the author and the author's agent, Virginia Kidd.

"The Encounter" by Kate Wilhelm. Copyright © 1970, by Damon Knight. First published in *Orbit 8*, edited by Damon Knight and published by G. P. Putnam's Sons. Reprinted by permission of the author.

"Sky" by R. A. Lafferty. Copyright © 1971, by Robert Silverberg. First published in *New Dimensions 1*, edited by Robert Silverberg and published by Doubleday Co., Inc. Reprinted by permission of the author and the author's agent, Virginia Kidd.

"Mount Charity" by Edgar Pangborn. Copyright © 1971, by Terry Carr. First published in *Universe 1*, edited by Terry Carr and published by Ace Books. Reprinted by permission of the author and the author's agent, Robert P. Mills, Ltd.

"Good News from the Vatican" by Robert Silverberg. Copyright © 1971, by Terry Carr. First published in *Universe 1*, edited by Terry Carr and published by Ace Books. Reprinted by permission of the author and the author's agents, Scott Meredith Literary Agency, Inc.

"Horse of Air" by Gardner R. Dozois. Copyright © 1970, by Damon Knight. First published in *Orbit 8*, edited by Damon Knight and published by G. P. Putnam's Sons. Reprinted by permission of the author and the author's agent, Virginia Kidd.

continued on next page

FIRST EDITION

STANDARD BOOK NUMBER: 06-010328-0

LIBRARY OF CONGRESS CATALOG CARD NUMBER: 66-20974

To Lawrence P. Ashmead,
who made the beginning possible . . .

Contents

Introduction

Each of the stories in this collection has been published in a book or magazine labeled "Science Fiction." Each of them was nominated for a Nebula Award by members of Science Fiction Writers of America and appeared on one or both of the ballots in the awards voting. All of them are, therefore, illustrious examples of contemporary science fiction,* and as a special favor I am asking those who read them to complete the following sentence in 25,000 words or less: "Science fiction is . . ." Send your responses to me. There are no prizes, but I'll be grateful to have a stack of answers ready for those who persist in asking me to define science fiction.

The fact is that science fiction, in this summation of 1971's best writing, defies definition. Each of these stories reveals a dazzlingly different facet of a literary genre whose facets are infinite. The settings span the universe, the times range from remote beginnings to ultimate endings, and the themes probe man's environment within and without and test his ethics and values with problems as old as human consciousness and as new as the millennium beyond tomorrow. The literary styles and narrative techniques of these eleven authors are as varied as their subject

---

*Inasmuch as works of fantasy are also eligible for the Nebula Awards, this is a controversial statement. Next year's readers will be invited to distinguish between science fiction and fantasy—in 25,000 words or more.

matters. For the reader who is asking of this book, as Theodore Sturgeon suggests, "Tell me a story," here is science fiction in all of its infinite variety.

In the months during which this book was planned and finally assembled, I managed to become deeply indebted to a startling number of people. Damon Knight, Poul Anderson and Theodore Sturgeon, busy men with their own presses of responsibilities and deadlines, took on an additional one of each in order to provide this book with special features. The authors, each and every one of them, bore up under my onslaught of forms and questionnaires with splendid patience, as did their various editors, publishers and agents. Howard DeVore furnished his usual invaluable assistance in supplying copies of books and magazines; Dean McLaughlin did the same, and also permitted me to bombard him, guinea pig fashion, with alpha and beta particles of ideas, scraps of copy and potential contents pages, without snarling—much. Edward Wood and George Price, of Advent:Publishers; Diane Cleaver, of Doubleday; Judy-Lynn del Rey, of Galaxy/If; Edward Ferman, of F&SF; Betty Ballantine, of Ballantine Books; editors Terry Carr, Robert Silverberg, David Gerrold and Damon Knight; Fred Marcotte, the staffs of the Ypsilanti Area Public Library and the Lincoln Library of Springfield, Illinois—all took the time to provide the obvious answer or help track down the elusive fact. I offer a special word of thanks to the Los Angeles Convention Committee and its Publicity and Publications Director, Fred Patten, for assistance in a project that at this date (April 17) is without predictable consequence: making available for this book, in time for publication, the results of this year's Hugo Awards balloting (which won't be known until mid-August). At least we have, collectively, tried.

Nebula Award Stories Seven represents, to M. S. Wyeth and Victoria Schochet of Harper & Row, an introduction to the strange people of SFWA, and they have managed to conceal their astonishment with commendable grace and humor. The phrase "This will hurt me more than it hurts you" has acquired an unfortunate flavor of hypocrisy, but it does have application to one of the most difficult tasks imposed on any editor—deciding what, or whom, to leave out. Inevitably he must leave out much that he would like to include, and sometimes that does, indeed, hurt.

Finally, as is appropriate with any volume of a series, I wish to acknowledge my indebtedness to my distinguished predecessors who edited volumes one through six: Damon Knight, Brian Aldiss and Harry Harrison, Roger Zelazny, Poul Anderson, James Blish and Clifford D. Simak—each of whom may be surprised to note what I have learned from his experience.

LLOYD BIGGLE, JR.

Ypsilanti, April 17, 1972

DAMON KNIGHT

1971: The Year in Science Fiction

Nineteen seventy-one was a year of changes. Interest in science fiction was plainly on the increase: *Publishers Weekly* reported a total of 304 sf books in 1971 as against 269 in 1970.* Courses on science fiction proliferated in high schools and colleges. *Time*, in its March 29 issue, ran a long and favorable report on modern sf. The Tolkien boom continued: *Lord of the Rings* was read aloud over WRVR-FM in New York, a bit every weekday at midnight. The first tower of the World Trade Center in New York City reached its full height, and the sf newsmagazine *Locus* announced a contest with a free lifetime subscription to the first gorilla to climb it.

John W. Campbell, who had dominated the sf magazine field for more than thirty years, died July 11 of a heart ailment. He was sixty-one. Campbell, who began writing science fiction when he was a student at MIT in the twenties, became editor of *Analog* (then *Astounding Stories*) in 1937, and in the next few years introduced the work of Isaac Asimov, Robert A. Heinlein, L. Sprague de Camp, L. Ron Hubbard, Lester del Rey and others. His abrasive and controversial editorials became a feature of the magazine in

---

*PW's figures are widely thought to be low; Joanne Burger, who publishes an annual checklist, reported 784 sf books published in 1971.

the late forties and continued to his death. In October Ben Bova
was appointed his successor.

Campbell's death altered the balance of the field noticeably, and
so did some other editorial changes. In April Terry Carr left Ace
Books, "with mutual acrimony"; later Ace announced it would
drop the Ace Specials line which Carr had originated and edited.
Carr also severed his connection with the annual *World's Best
Science Fiction*, which he had edited in collaboration with Donald
A. Wollheim, but announced that he would edit another year's-
best series for Ballantine Books. Later in the year, Wollheim re-
signed as editor-in-chief of Ace to form his own publishing company, Daw Books, which will publish science fiction paperbacks
exclusively. His place was taken by Frederik Pohl, formerly editor
of *Galaxy*.

In the November issue of *English Journal*, Sheila Schwartz
wrote: "Before World War II, science fiction writing speculated
about the world of the future. Today, all a writer need do to qualify
as a science fiction writer is to record the present with such details
as napalm, self-cleaning ovens, pep pills, pollution, birth control
pills, thought control, dream research, or tranquillizers. Science
fiction reflects our world as accurately, spiritually and factually, as
the work of Charles Dickens reflected the Victorian world, or the
work of Alexander Pope the world of the eighteenth century."
Evidences such as this of sf's new academic respectability were
greeted with pleasure by some. Others, like Poul Anderson (writing in the March *Science Fiction Review*), agreed with the anony-
mous wit who wrote on a blackboard at the Secondary Universe
Conference in 1970: "GET SCIENCE FICTION OUT OF THE CLASS-
ROOM AND BACK IN THE GUTTER WHERE IT BELONGS."

In 1971 most sf magazine circulations dropped; the only excep-
tion was *If*, which rose from 35,000 to 42,000 copies, while two of
its companion magazines, *Worlds of Fantasy* and *Worlds of Tomorrow*, were suspended, and the third, *Galaxy*, went from
monthly to bimonthly publication. Six other magazines, not considered important markets, were also suspended during the year.

Five were edited by Robert A. W. Lowndes: *Magazine of Horror, Startling Mystery Stories, Weird Terror Tales, Bizarre Fantasy Tales* and *Exploring the Unknown*. The sixth was *Forgotten Fantasy*, published in Hollywood. *Amazing Stories* and *Fantastic* phased out their reprint policy, but in spite of Ted White's intelligent editing, sales continued to slide.

Quark, the quarterly paperback edited by Samuel R. Delany and his wife, Marilyn Hacker, was suspended in April after four issues, but to balance this there were four new original-anthology series in 1971—*Universe*, edited by Terry Carr, *New Dimensions*, edited by Robert Silverberg, *Clarion*, edited by Robin Scott Wilson, and *Protostars*, edited by David Gerrold.

Sf conventions and conferences, too many to list, included the Noreascon, the annual World S.F. Convention, held in Boston over the Labor Day weekend (guest of honor, Clifford D. Simak); Secondary Universe 4 in Toronto, October 8–11 (principal guest, Ursula K. Le Guin); the Balticon in Baltimore, February 12–24 (Harry Harrison); the Mondocon in New York City, January 22–24 (Hal Clement); the Disclave in Washington, D.C., May 28–31 (Terry Carr); the SFancon 2 in Antwerp, Belgium, April 17–18; the Gothcon in Göteborg, Sweden, May 20–23; and the Eastercon in Worcester, England, April 9–11 (Anne McCaffrey). The Eastercon program booklet was enlivened by a last-minute ad taken by "the Rare SF Mail Order Book Co." in New York City. The ad contained a jigsaw puzzle and a picture which purported to represent the puzzle when put together. When actually put together, the puzzle turned out to be obscene. Writer Charles Platt was accused of the prank, but denied it.

Lester del Rey, recently converted to Judaism, married Judy-Lynn Benjamin, managing editor of the *Galaxy* group, March 21 in a religious ceremony. Ed Emshwiller, sf illustrator turned avant-garde filmmaker, won the prize for the most original film with his *Image, Flesh, Voice* at the Mannheim Internationale Filmwoche. "The Best of SF," an international exhibition of sf literature, was held in London, May 17–31, as part of the National

Book Exhibition. The Apollo astronauts named a Moon crater "Dune," after the Nebula- and Hugo-winning novel by Frank Herbert—and in Tucson, Arizona, a school board dismissed the teacher of a class on witchcraft and the occult on the grounds that she was practicing witchcraft.

The Clarion Workshop in Science Fiction and Fantasy Writing was held for the third year, this time at Tulane University in New Orleans under the direction of James Sallis. Two other sf workshops were also held: the Washington Writers' Workshop at the University of Washington, directed by Vonda N. McIntyre, and the Guilford Gafia in Baltimore, March 26–28. New American Library, publisher of the anthology *Clarion*, announced the winners of its first annual prize contest: first prize, "Wheels" by Robert Thurston; second, "Spectra" by Vonda N. McIntyre; third (tie), "Silent Hands" by Gerard F. Conway and "An Uneven Evening" by Steve Herbst.

At the Vancouver, sf convention, April 9–11, "Elrons" were awarded for the worst sf of 1971. The trophies, each consisting of a bronzed lemon on a plywood base, were given in absentia to Robert Moore Williams ("least promising new writer"), Robert A. Heinlein ("worst novel"), *Beneath the Planet of the Apes* ("worst melodramatic presentation") and Lin Carter ("consistent standard of poor writing").

The Nebula Awards banquets were held, as usual, in New York City, Berkeley and New Orleans on April 3. A day-long conference was held in Berkeley in conjunction with the banquet. Featured speakers in New York were Lester del Rey, Marvin Minsky of MIT and Alan Ravage of Bantam Books; in New Orleans, Jerry Page of *Witchcraft and Sorcery*, and James Sallis; in Berkeley, George Clayton Johnson, coauthor of *Logan's Run*. Toastmaster Avram Davidson, in Berkeley, presented the Nebulas to Theodore Sturgeon, Fritz Leiber and Larry Niven. (Later in the year, the World S.F. Convention awarded its Hugos to the same authors for the same stories.)

For SFWA, under presidents Gordon R. Dickson and James E.

Gunn (who succeeded Dickson in June), it was a year of consolidation after the previous year's debate over policy. Gunn inaugurated a series of filmed interviews with science fiction editors and writers, produced by the Extramural Independent Study Center of the University of Kansas. Vice-President Tom Purdom organized a large traveling library display focused on the Nebula and Hugo winners. Fred Saberhagen was assigned the task of writing an article on science fiction for the 1973 edition of the *Encyclopaedia Britannica*. The changes are continuing; next year's summary of events should include some surprises. Indeed, "The future isn't what it used to be."

Nebula Awards, 1972

The awards were presented at the annual Nebula banquets held on April 29 in New York City (Les Champs Restaurant), Los Angeles (the Airport-Marina Hotel), and New Orleans (Le Pavillon Hotel). Associated business meetings, panels and cocktail parties were held on both coasts, and the winners of the SFWA elections were announced: Poul Anderson, president; Norman Spinrad, vice-president; Robert Coulson, secretary; Joe W. Haldeman, treasurer. Toastmasters were Harlan Ellison in New York, Norman Spinrad in Los Angeles, and Don Walsh, Jr., in New Orleans.

The principal speaker in New York was Leslie Fiedler, who argued that the old distinctions between "high" and "low" fiction are no longer valid, and that critics must now distinguish between works that are inherently good or bad, whether they are mainstream or science fiction. He pointed out that only science fiction has kept the short story alive in recent decades, and expressed the hope that academia will not smother it with "deadly dissertations." Other speakers included Isaac Asimov and James E. Gunn (New York), and Theodore Sturgeon (Los Angeles).

Voting for the Nebula Awards was as follows:

NOVEL

Winner: *A Time of Changes* by Robert Silverberg (New American Library; serialized in *Galaxy*)

Runners-up: *The Lathe of Heaven* by Ursula K. Le Guin (Scribner; serialized in *Amazing*); *The Devil Is Dead* by R. A. Lafferty (Avon); *Margaret and I* by Kate Wilhelm (Little, Brown); *The Byworlder* by Poul Anderson (New American Library; serialized in *Fantastic*); *Half Past Human* by T. J. Bass (Ballantine; serialized in *Galaxy*)

NOVELLA

Winner: "The Missing Man" by Katherine MacLean (*Analog*)

Runners-up: "The Infinity Box" by Kate Wilhelm (*Orbit 9*); *Being There* by Jerzy Kosinski (Harcourt Brace Jovanovich); "The God House" by Keith Roberts (*New Worlds Quarterly 1*); "The Plastic Abyss" by Kate Wilhelm (*Abyss*, Doubleday)

NOVELETTE

Winner: "The Queen of Air and Darkness" by Poul Anderson (*The Magazine of Fantasy and Science Fiction*)

Runners-up: "Mount Charity" by Edgar Pangborn (*Universe 1*); "Poor Man, Beggar Man" by Joanna Russ (*Universe 1*); "The Encounter" by Kate Wilhelm (*Orbit 8*); "A Special Kind of Morning" by Gardner R. Dozois (*New Dimensions 1*)

SHORT STORY

Winner: "Good News from the Vatican" by Robert Silverberg (*Universe 1*)

Runners-up: "The Last Ghost" by Stephen Goldin (*Protostars*); "Horse of Air" by Gardner R. Dozois (*Orbit 8*); "Heathen God" by George Zebrowski (*The Magazine of Fantasy and Science Fiction*)

NEBULA AWARD STORIES

POUL ANDERSON

The Queen of Air
and Darkness

POUL ANDERSON was born November 25, 1926, in Bristol, Pennsylvania, of Scandinavian parents. Part of his youth was spent in Denmark. He returned to the United States before World War II, and he sold his first story while a student at the University of Minnesota. When he graduated with distinction, in 1948, he decided to try to support himself for a time with his writing before seeking employment in his area of specialization, physics. That *for a time* is approaching twenty-five years with the end happily not in sight. In 1953 Anderson married Karen Kruse, herself an author of fiction and poetry. They have one daughter, Astrid. They make their home in Orinda, California.

Anderson's dazzling versatility as a writer is reflected in James Blish's description of him as ". . . the scientist, the technician, the stylist, the bard, the humanist and the humorist—a non-exhaustive list." He ranks as one of the most prolific science fiction writers of all times (a recently compiled bibliography, published in the April 1971 issue of *The Magazine of Fantasy and Science Fiction,* fills seven pages!). From poetry to novels to short stories to nonfiction books and articles on a variety of subjects, he brilliantly combines the saga and song of his Scandinavian heritage with the searching mind and speculative science of the scholar. He also finds time for such varied activities as houseboat building, sailing, mountain climbing, gardening, chess, poker, Science Fiction Writers of America, Mystery Writers of America, and the Society for

Creative Anachronism (where he is known as Béla of Eastmarch in its medieval tourneys)—another non-exhaustive list.

Under his own name and his two pseudonyms, Winston P. Sanders and Michael Karageorge, he is the author of some fifty books and perhaps two hundred shorter items. His stories "No Truce with Kings," "The Longest Voyage" and "The Sharing of Flesh" won Hugo Awards. His mystery novel *Perish by the Sword* won the Cock Robin Award. Well-known science fiction novels are *Brain Wave, The High Crusade, Three Hearts and Three Lions, Earthman's Burden* (with Gordon R. Dickson), *The Broken Sword, After Doomsday* and *Tau Zero*. Recently anthologized stories are "Call Me Joe" (selected for inclusion in the SFWA *Hall of Fame,* Volume 2), "The Man Who Came Early," "Sam Hall," "Kings Who Die" and "Journeys End." His Time Patrol series was collected in *Guardians of Time.* Other series concern Nicholas van Rijn, the interstellar trader, Dominic Flandry and Trygve Yamamura.

Anderson's novel *The Byworlder* was a finalist in the balloting for the 1971 Nebula Awards; and his novelette "The Queen of Air and Darkness" won a Nebula Award.

The last glow of the last sunset would linger almost until midwinter. But there would be no more day, and the northlands rejoiced. Blossoms opened, flamboyance on firethorn trees, steelflowers rising blue from the brok and rainplant that cloaked all hills, shy whiteness of kiss-me-never down in the dales. Flitteries darted among them in iridescent wings; a crownbuck shook his horns and bugled. Between horizons the sky deepened from purple to sable. Both moons were aloft, nearly full, shining frosty on leaves and molten on waters. The shadows they made were blurred by an aurora, a great blowing curtain of light across half heaven. Behind it the earliest stars had come out.

A boy and a girl sat on Wolund's Barrow just under the dolmen it upbore. Their hair, which streamed halfway down their backs, showed startlingly forth, bleached as it was by summer. Their bodies, still dark from that season, merged with earth and bush and rock, for they wore only garlands. He played on a bone flute and she sang. They had lately become lovers. Their age was about sixteen, but they did not know this, considering themselves Outlings and thus indifferent to time, remembering little or nothing of how they had once dwelt in the lands of men.

His notes piped cold around her voice:

> "Cast a spell,
> weave it well
> of dust and dew
> and night and you."

A brook by the grave mound, carrying moonlight down to a hill-hidden river, answered with its rapids. A flock of hellbats passed black beneath the aurora.

A shape came bounding over Cloudmoor. It had two arms and two legs, but the legs were long and claw-footed and feathers covered it to the end of a tail and broad wings. The face was half human, dominated by its eyes. Had Ayoch been able to stand wholly erect, he would have reached to the boy's shoulder.

The girl rose. "He carries a burden," she said. Her vision was not meant for twilight like that of a northland creature born, but she had learned how to use every sign her senses gave her. Besides the fact that ordinarily a pook would fly, there was a heaviness to his haste.

"And he comes from the south." Excitement jumped in the boy, sudden as a green flame that went across the constellation Lyrth. He sped down the mound. "Ohoi, Ayoch!" he called. "Me here, Mistherd!"

"And Shadow-of-a-Dream," the girl laughed, following.

The pook halted. He breathed louder than the soughing in the growth around him. A smell of bruised yerba lifted where he stood.

"Well met in winterbirth," he whistled. "You can help me bring this to Carheddin."

He held out what he bore. His eyes were yellow lanterns above. It moved and whimpered.

"Why, a child," Mistherd said.

"Even as you were, my son, even as you were. Ho, ho, what a snatch!" Ayoch boasted. "They were a score in yon camp by Fallowwood, armed, and besides watcher engines they had big ugly dogs aprowl while they slept. I came from above, however, having spied on them till I knew that a handful of dazedust—"

"The poor thing." Shadow-of-a-Dream took the boy and held him to her small breasts. "So full of sleep yet, aren't you?" Blindly, he sought a nipple. She smiled through the veil of her hair. "No, I am still too young, and you already too old. But come, when you wake in Carheddin under the mountain, you shall feast."

"Yo-ah," said Ayoch very softly. "She is abroad and has heard and seen. She comes." He crouched down, wings folded. After a moment Mistherd knelt, and then Shadow-of-a-Dream, though she did not let go the child.

The Queen's tall form blocked off the moons. For a while she regarded the three and their booty. Hill and moor sounds withdrew from their awareness until it seemed they could hear the northlights hiss.

At last Ayoch whispered, "Have I done well, Starmother?"

"If you stole a babe from a camp full of engines," said the beautiful voice, "then they were folk out of the far south who may not endure it as meekly as yeomen."

"But what can they do, Snowmaker?" the pook asked. "How can they track us?"

Mistherd lifted his head and spoke in pride. "Also, now they too have felt the awe of us."

"And he is a cuddly dear," Shadow-of-a-Dream said. "And we need more like him, do we not, Lady Sky?"

"It had to happen in some twilight," agreed she who stood above. "Take him onward and care for him. By this sign," which she made, "is he claimed for the Dwellers."

Their joy was freed. Ayoch cartwheeled over the ground till he reached a shiverleaf. There he swarmed up the trunk and out on a limb, perched half hidden by unrestful pale foliage, and crowed.

Boy and girl bore the child toward Carheddin at an easy distance-devouring lope which let him pipe and her sing:

"Wahaii, wahaii!
Wayala, laii!
Wing on the wind
high over heaven,
shrilly shrieking,
rush with the rainspears,
tumble through tumult,
drift to the moonhoar trees and the dream-heavy
    shadows beneath them,
and rock in, be one with the clinking wavelets of
    lakes where the starbeams drown."

*   *   *

As she entered, Barbro Cullen felt, through all grief and fury, stabbed by dismay. The room was unkempt. Journals, tapes, reels, codices, file boxes, bescribbled papers were piled on every table. Dust filmed most shelves and corners. Against one wall stood a laboratory setup, microscope and analytical equipment. She recognized it as compact and efficient, but it was not what you would expect in an office, and it gave the air a faint chemical reek. The rug was threadbare, the furniture shabby.

This was her final chance?

Then Eric Sherrinford approached. "Good day, Mrs. Cullen," he said. His tone was crisp, his handclasp firm. His faded gripsuit didn't bother her. She wasn't inclined to fuss about her own appearance except on special occasions. (And would she ever again have one, unless she got back Jimmy?) What she observed was a cat's personal neatness.

A smile radiated in crow's feet from his eyes. "Forgive my bachelor housekeeping. On Beowulf we have—we had, at any rate—machines for that, so I never acquired the habit myself, and I don't want a hireling disarranging my tools. More convenient to work out of my apartment than keep a separate office. Won't you be seated?"

"No, thanks. I couldn't," she mumbled.

"I understand. But if you'll excuse me, I function best in a relaxed position."

He jackknifed into a lounger. One long shank crossed the other knee. He drew forth a pipe and stuffed it from a pouch. Barbro wondered why he took tobacco in so ancient a way. Wasn't Beowulf supposed to have the up-to-date equipment that they still couldn't afford to build on Roland? Well, of course old customs might survive anyhow. They generally did in colonies, she remembered reading. People had moved starward in the hope of preserving such outmoded things as their mother tongues or constitutional government or rational-technological civilization. . . .

Sherrinford pulled her up from the confusion of her weariness. "You must give me the details of your case, Mrs. Cullen. You've simply told me your son was kidnapped and your local constabulary did nothing. Otherwise, I know just a few obvious facts, such as your being widowed rather than divorced; and you're the daughter of outwayers in Olga Ivanoff Land who, nevertheless, kept in close telecommunication with Christmas Landing; and you're trained in one of the biological professions; and you had several years' hiatus in field work until recently you started again."

She gaped at the high-cheeked, beak-nosed, black-haired and gray-eyed countenance. His lighter made a *scrit* and a flare which seemed to fill the room. Quietness dwelt on this height above the city, and winter dusk was seeping through the windows. "How in cosmos do you know that?" she heard herself exclaim.

He shrugged and fell into the lecturer's manner for which he was notorious. "My work depends on noticing details and fitting them together. In more than a hundred years on Roland, tending to cluster according to their origins and thought habits, people have developed regional accents. You have a trace of the Olgan burr, but you nasalize your vowels in the style of this area, though you live in Portolondon. That suggests steady childhood exposure to metropolitan speech. You were part of Matsuyama's expedition, you told me, and took your boy along. They wouldn't have allowed any ordinary technician to do that; hence, you had to be valuable enough to get away with it. The team was conducting ecological research; therefore, you must be in the life sciences. For the same reason, you must have had previous field experience. But your skin is fair, showing none of the leatheriness one gets from prolonged exposure to this sun. Accordingly, you must have been mostly indoors for a good while before you went on your ill-fated trip. As for widowhood—you never mentioned a husband to me, but you have had a man whom you thought so highly of that you still wear both the wedding and the engagement ring he gave you."

Her sight blurred and stung. The last of those words had brought Tim back, huge, ruddy, laughterful and gentle. She must turn from this other person and stare outward. "Yes," she achieved saying, "you're right."

The apartment occupied a hilltop above Christmas Landing. Beneath it the city dropped away in walls, roofs, archaistic chimneys and lamplit streets, goblin lights of human-piloted vehicles, to the harbor, the sweep of Venture Bay, ships bound to and from the Sunward Islands and remoter regions of the Boreal Ocean, which glimmered like mercury in the afterglow of Charlemagne. Oliver was swinging rapidly higher, a mottled orange disc a full degree wide; closer to the zenith which it could never reach, it would shine the color of ice. Alde, half the seeming size, was a thin slow crescent near Sirius, which she remembered was near Sol, but you couldn't see Sol without a telescope—

"Yes," she said around the pain in her throat, "my husband is about four years dead. I was carrying our first child when he was killed by a stampeding monocerus. We'd been married three years before. Met while we were both at the University—'casts from School Central can only supply a basic education, you know—We founded our own team to do ecological studies under contract—you know, can a certain area be settled while maintaining a balance of nature, what crops will grow, what hazards, that sort of question—Well, afterward I did lab work for a fisher co-op in Portolondon. But the monotony, the . . . shut-in-ness . . . was eating me away. Professor Matsuyama offered me a position on the team he was organizing to examine Commissioner Hauch Land. I

thought, God help me, I thought Jimmy—Tim wanted him named
James, once the tests showed it'd be a boy, after his own father and
because of 'Timmy and Jimmy' and—oh, I thought Jimmy could
safely come along. I couldn't bear to leave him behind for months,
not at his age. We could make sure he'd never wander out of camp.
What could hurt him inside it? *I* had never believed those stories
about the Outlings stealing human children. I supposed parents
were trying to hide from themselves the fact they'd been careless,
they'd let a kid get lost in the woods or attacked by a pack of satans
or— Well, I learned better, Mr. Sherrinford. The guard robots
were evaded and the dogs were drugged and when I woke, Jimmy
was gone."

He regarded her through the smoke from his pipe. Barbro Eng-
dahl Cullen was a big woman of thirty or so (Rolandic years, he
reminded himself, ninety-five percent of Terrestrial, not the same
as Beowulfan years), broad-shouldered, long-legged, full-breasted,
supple of stride; her face was wide, straight nose, straightforward
hazel eyes, heavy but mobile mouth; her hair was reddish-brown,
cropped below the ears, her voice husky, her garment a plain
street robe. To still the writhing of her fingers, he asked skepti-
cally, "Do you now believe in the Outlings?"

"No. I'm just not so sure as I was." She swung about with half
a glare for him. "And we have found traces."

"Bits of fossils," he nodded. "A few artifacts of a neolithic sort.
But apparently ancient, as if the makers died ages ago. Intensive
search has failed to turn up any real evidence for their survival."

"How intensive can search be, in a summer-stormy, winter-
gloomy wilderness around the North Pole?" she demanded.
"When we are, how many, a million people on an entire planet,
half of us crowded into this one city?"

"And the rest crowding this one habitable continent," he
pointed out.

"Arctica covers five million square kilometers," she flung back.
"The Arctic Zone proper covers a fourth of it. We haven't the
industrial base to establish satellite monitor stations, build aircraft

we can trust in those parts, drive roads through the damned dark-lands and establish permanent bases and get to know them and tame them. Good Christ, generations of lonely outwaymen told stories about Graymantle, and the beast was never seen by a proper scientist till last year!"

"Still, you continue to doubt the reality of the Outlings?"

"Well, what about a secret cult among humans, born of isolation and ignorance, lairing in the wilderness, stealing children when they can for—" She swallowed. Her head dropped. "But you're supposed to be the expert."

"From what you told me over the visiphone, the Portolondon constabulary questions the accuracy of the report your group made, thinks the lot of you were hysterical, claims you must have omitted a due precaution, and the child toddled away and was lost beyond your finding."

His dry words pried the horror out of her. Flushing, she snapped, "Like any settler's kid? No. I didn't simply yell. I consulted Data Retrieval. A few too many such cases are recorded for accident to be a very plausible explanation. And shall we totally ignore the frightened stories about reappearances? But when I went back to the constabulary with my facts, they brushed me off. I suspect that was not entirely because they're undermanned. I think they're afraid too. They're recruited from country boys, and Portolondon lies near the edge of the unknown."

Her energy faded. "Roland hasn't got any central police force," she finished drably. "You're my last hope."

The man puffed smoke into twilight, with which it blent, before he said in a kindlier voice than hitherto: "Please don't make it a high hope, Mrs. Cullen. I'm the solitary private investigator on this world, having no resources beyond myself, and a newcomer to boot."

"How long have you been here?"

"Twelve years. Barely time to get a little familiarity with the relatively civilized coastlands. You settlers of a century or more—what do you, even, know about Arctica's interior?"

Sherrinford sighed. "I'll take the case, charging no more than I must, mainly for the sake of the experience," he said. "But only if you'll be my guide and assistant, however painful it will be for you."

"Of course! I dreaded waiting idle. Why me, though?"

"Hiring someone else as well qualified would be prohibitively expensive, on a pioneer planet where every hand has a thousand urgent tasks to do. Besides, you have a motive. And I'll need that. I, who was born on another world altogether strange to this one, itself altogether strange to Mother Earth, I am too dauntingly aware of how handicapped we are."

Night gathered upon Christmas Landing. The air stayed mild, but glimmer-lit tendrils of fog, sneaking through the streets, had a cold look, and colder yet was the aurora where it shuddered between the moons. The woman drew closer to the man in this darkening room, surely not aware that she did, until he switched on a fluoropanel. The same knowledge of Roland's aloneness was in both of them.

One light-year is not much as galactic distances go. You could walk it in about 270 million years, beginning at the middle of the Permian Era, when dinosaurs belonged to the remote future, and continuing to the present day when spaceships cross even greater reaches. But stars in our neighborhood average some nine light-years apart, and barely one percent of them have planets which are man-habitable, and speeds are limited to less than that of radiation. Scant help is given by relativistic time contraction and suspended animation en route. These make the journeys seem short, but history meanwhile does not stop at home.

Thus voyages from sun to sun will always be few. Colonists will be those who have extremely special reasons for going. They will take along germ plasm for exogenetic cultivation of domestic plants and animals—and of human infants, in order that population can grow fast enough to escape death through genetic drift. After all, they cannot rely on further immigration. Two or three times a century, a ship may call from some other colony. (Not from Earth. Earth has long ago sunk into alien concerns.) Its place of origin will be an old settlement. The young ones are in no position to build and man interstellar vessels.

Their very survival, let alone their eventual modernization, is in doubt. The founding fathers have had to take what they could get, in a universe not especially designed for man.

Consider, for example, Roland. It is among the rare happy finds, a world where humans can live, breathe, eat the food, drink the water, walk unclad if they choose, sow their crops, pasture their beasts, dig their mines, erect their homes, raise their children and grandchildren. It is worth crossing three-quarters of a light-century to preserve certain dear values and strike new roots into the soil of Roland.

But the star Charlemagne is of type F9, forty percent brighter than Sol, brighter still in the treacherous ultraviolet and wilder still in the wind of charged particles that seethes from it. The planet has an eccentric orbit. In the middle of the short but furious northern summer, which includes periastron, total insolation is more than double what Earth gets; in the depth of the long northern winter, it is barely less than Terrestrial average.

Native life is abundant everywhere. But lacking elaborate machinery, not yet economically possible to construct for more than a few specialists, man can only endure the high latitudes. A ten-degree axial tilt, together with the orbit, means that the northern part of the Arctican continent spends half its year in unbroken sunlessness. Around the South Pole lies an empty ocean.

Other differences from Earth might superficially seem more important. Roland has two moons, small but close, to evoke clashing tides. It rotates once in thirty-two hours, which is endlessly, subtly disturbing to organisms evolved through gigayears of a quicker rhythm. The weather patterns are altogether unterrestrial. The globe is a mere 9500 kilometers in diameter; its surface gravity is $0.42 \times 980 \text{ cm/sec}^2$; the sea level air pressure is slightly above one Earth atmosphere. (For actually Earth is the freak, and

man exists because a cosmic accident blew away most of the gas
that a body its size ought to have kept, as Venus has done.)

However, Homo can truly be called sapiens when he practices
his specialty of being unspecialized. His repeated attempts to
freeze himself into an all-answering pattern or culture or ideology,
or whatever he has named it, have repeatedly brought ruin. Give
him the pragmatic business of making his living, and he will usually do rather well. He adapts, within broad limits.

These limits are set by such factors as his need for sunlight and
his being, necessarily and forever, a part of the life that surrounds
him and a creature of the spirit within.

Portolondon thrust docks, boats, machinery, warehouses into
the Gulf of Polaris. Behind them huddled the dwellings of its five
thousand permanent inhabitants: concrete walls, storm shutters,
high-peaked tile roofs. The gaiety of their paint looked forlorn
amidst lamps; this town lay past the Arctic Circle.

Nevertheless Sherrinford remarked, "Cheerful place, eh? The
kind of thing I came to Roland looking for."

Barbro made no reply. The days in Christmas Landing, while he
made his preparations, had drained her. Gazing out the dome of
the taxi that was whirring them downtown from the hydrofoil that
brought them, she supposed he meant the lushness of forest and
meadows along the road, brilliant hues and phosphorescence of
flowers in gardens, clamor of wings overhead. Unlike Terrestrial
flora in cold climates, Arctican vegetation spends every daylit hour
in frantic growth and energy storage. Not till summer's fever gives
place to gentle winter does it bloom and fruit; and estivating
animals rise from their dens and migratory birds come home.

The view was lovely, she had to admit: beyond the trees, a
spaciousness climbing toward remote heights, silvery-gray under
a moon, an aurora, the diffuse radiance from a sun just below the
horizon.

Beautiful as a hunting satan, she thought, and as terrible. That
wilderness had stolen Jimmy. She wondered if she would at least

be given to find his little bones and take them to his father.

Abruptly she realized that she and Sherrinford were at their hotel and that he had been speaking of the town. Since it was next in size after the capital, he must have visited here often before. The streets were crowded and noisy; signs flickered, music blared from shops, taverns, restaurants, sports centers, dance halls; vehicles were jammed down to molasses speed; the several-stories-high office buildings stood aglow. Portolondon linked an enormous hinterland to the outside world. Down the Gloria River came timber rafts, ores, harvest of farms whose owners were slowly making Rolandic life serve them, meat and ivory and furs gathered by rangers in the mountains beyond Troll Scarp. In from the sea came coastwise freighters, the fishing fleet, produce of the Sunward Islands, plunder of whole continents further south where bold men adventured. It clanged in Portolondon, laughed, blustered, swaggered, connived, robbed, preached, guzzled, swilled, toiled, dreamed, lusted, built, destroyed, died, was born, was happy, angry, sorrowful, greedy, vulgar, loving, ambitious, human. Neither the sun's blaze elsewhere nor the half year's twilight here—wholly night around midwinter—was going to stay man's hand.

Or so everybody said.

Everybody except those who had settled in the darklands. Barbro used to take for granted that they were evolving curious customs, legends and superstitions, which would die when the outway had been completely mapped and controlled. Of late, she had wondered. Perhaps Sherrinford's hints, about a change in his own attitude brought about by his preliminary research, were responsible.

Or perhaps she just needed something to think about besides how Jimmy, the day before he went, when she asked him whether he wanted rye or French bread for a sandwich, answered in great solemnity—he was becoming interested in the alphabet—"I'll have a slice of what we people call the F bread."

She scarcely noticed getting out of the taxi, registering, being

conducted to a primitively furnished room. But after she un-
packed, she remembered Sherrinford had suggested a confiden-
tial conference. She went down the hall and knocked on his door.
Her knuckles sounded less loud than her heart.

He opened the door, finger on lips, and gestured her toward a
corner. Her temper bristled until she saw the image of Chief
Constable Dawson in the visiphone. Sherrinford must have
chimed him up and must have a reason to keep her out of scanner
range. She found a chair and watched, nails digging into knees.

The detective's lean length refolded itself. "Pardon the interruption," he said. "A man mistook the number. Drunk, by the
indications."

Dawson chuckled. "We get plenty of those." Barbro recalled his
fondness for gabbing. He tugged the beard which he affected, as
if he were an outwayer instead of a townsman. "No harm in them
as a rule. They only have a lot of voltage to discharge, after weeks
or months in the backlands."

"I've gathered that that environment—foreign in a million major and minor ways to the one that created man—I've gathered
that it does do odd things to the personality." Sherrinford tamped
his pipe. "Of course, you know my practice has been confined to
urban and suburban areas. Isolated garths seldom need private
investigators. Now that situation appears to have changed. I called
to ask you for advice."

"Glad to help," Dawson said. "I've not forgotten what you did
for us in the de Tahoe murder case." Cautiously: "Better explain
your problem first."

Sherrinford struck fire. The smoke that followed cut through the
green odors—even here, a paved pair of kilometers from the nearest woods—that drifted past traffic rumble through a crepuscular
window. "This is more a scientific mission than a search for an
absconding debtor or an industrial spy," he drawled. "I'm looking
into two possibilities: that an organization, criminal or religious or
whatever, has long been active and steals infants; or that the
Outlings of folklore are real."

"Huh?" On Dawson's face Barbro read as much dismay as surprise. "You can't be serious!"

"Can't I?" Sherrinford smiled. "Several generations' worth of reports shouldn't be dismissed out of hand. Especially not when they become more frequent and consistent in the course of time, not less. Nor can we ignore the documented loss of babies and small children, amounting by now to over a hundred, and never a trace found afterward. Nor the finds which demonstrate that an intelligent species once inhabited Arctica and may still haunt the interior."

Dawson leaned forward as if to climb out of the screen. "Who engaged you?" he demanded. "That Cullen woman? We were sorry for her, naturally, but she wasn't making sense, and when she got downright abusive—"

"Didn't her companions, reputable scientists, confirm her story?"

"No story to confirm. Look, they had the place ringed with detectors and alarms, and they kept mastiffs. Standard procedure in country where a hungry sauroid or whatever might happen by. Nothing could've entered unbeknownst."

"On the ground. How about a flyer landing in the middle of camp?"

"A man in a copter rig would've roused everybody."

"A winged being might be quieter."

"A living flyer that could lift a three-year-old boy? Doesn't exist."

"Isn't in the scientific literature, you mean, Constable. Remember Graymantle; remember how little we know about Roland, a planet, an entire world. Such birds do exist on Beowulf—and on Rustum, I've read. I made a calculation from the local ratio of air density to gravity, and, yes, it's marginally possible here too. The child could have been carried off for a short distance before wing muscles were exhausted and the creature must descend."

Dawson snorted. "First it landed and walked into the tent where mother and boy were asleep. Then it walked away, toting

him, after it couldn't fly further. Does that sound like a bird of
prey? And the victim didn't cry out, the dogs didn't bark!"

"As a matter of fact," Sherrinford said, "those inconsistencies
are the most interesting and convincing features of the whole
account. You're right, it's hard to see how a human kidnapper
could get in undetected, and an eagle type of creature wouldn't
operate in that fashion. But none of this applies to a winged intelligent being. The boy could have been drugged. Certainly the dogs
showed signs of having been."

"The dogs showed signs of having overslept. Nothing had disturbed them. The kid wandering by wouldn't do so. We don't need
to assume one damn thing except, first, that he got restless and,
second, that the alarms were a bit sloppily rigged—seeing as how
no danger was expected from inside camp—and let him pass out.
And, third, I hate to speak this way, but we must assume the poor
tyke starved or was killed."

Dawson paused before adding: "If we had more staff, we could
have given the affair more time. And would have, of course. We
did make an aerial sweep, which risked the lives of the pilots, using
instruments which would've spotted the kid anywhere in a fifty-
kilometer radius, unless he was dead. You know how sensitive
thermal analyzers are. We drew a complete blank. We have more
important jobs than to hunt for the scattered pieces of a corpse."

He finished brusquely. "If Mrs. Cullen's hired you, my advice is
you find an excuse to quit. Better for her, too. She's got to come
to terms with reality."

Barbro checked a shout by biting her tongue.

"Oh, this is merely the latest disappearance of the series," Sherrinford said. She didn't understand how he could maintain his easy
tone when Jimmy was lost. "More thoroughly recorded than any
before, thus more suggestive. Usually an outwayer family has
given a tearful but undetailed account of their child who vanished
and must have been stolen by the Old Folk. Sometimes, years
later, they'd tell about glimpses of what they swore must have
been the grown child, not really human any longer, flitting past in

murk or peering through a window or working mischief upon them. As you say, neither the authorities nor the scientists have had personnel or resources to mount a proper investigation. But as I say, the matter appears to be worth investigating. Maybe a private party like myself can contribute."

"Listen, most of us constables grew up in the outway. We don't just ride patrol and answer emergency calls; we go back there for holidays and reunions. If any gang of . . . of human sacrificers was around, we'd know."

"I realize that. I also realize that the people you came from have a widespread and deep-seated belief in nonhuman beings with supernatural powers. Many actually go through rites and make offerings to propitiate them."

"I know what you're leading up to," Dawson fleered. "I've heard it before, from a hundred sensationalists. The aborigines are the Outlings. I thought better of you. Surely you've visited a museum or three, surely you've read literature from planets which do have natives—or damn and blast, haven't you ever applied that logic of yours?"

He wagged a finger. "Think," he said. "What have we in fact discovered? A few pieces of worked stone; a few megaliths that might be artificial; scratchings on rock that seem to show plants and animals, though not the way any human culture would ever have shown them; traces of fires and broken bones; other frag- ments of bone that seem as if they might've belonged to thinking creatures, as if they might've been inside fingers or around big brains. If so, however, the owners looked nothing like men. Or angels, for that matter. Nothing! The most anthropoid reconstruc- tion I've seen shows a kind of two-legged crocagator.

"Wait, let me finish. The stories about the Outlings—oh, I've heard them too, plenty of them. I believed them when I was a kid —the stories tell how there're different kinds, some winged, some not, some half human, some completely human except maybe for being too handsome—It's fairyland from ancient Earth all over again. Isn't it? I got interested once and dug into the Heritage

Library microfiles, and be damned if I didn't find almost the identical yarns, told by peasants centuries before spaceflight.

"None of it squares with the scanty relics we have, if they are
relics, or with the fact that no area the size of Arctica could spawn
a dozen different intelligent species, or . . . hellfire, man, with the
way your common sense tells you aborigines would behave when
humans arrived!"

Sherrinford nodded. "Yes, yes," he said. "I'm less sure than you
that the common sense of nonhuman beings is precisely like our
own. I've seen so much variation within mankind. But, granted,
your arguments are strong. Roland's too few scientists have more
pressing tasks than tracking down the origins of what is, as you put
it, a revived medieval superstition."

He cradled his pipe bowl in both hands and peered into the tiny
hearth of it. "Perhaps what interests me most," he said softly, "is
why—across that gap of centuries, across a barrier of machine
civilization and its utterly antagonistic world view—no continuity
of tradition whatsoever—why have hardheaded, technologically
organized, reasonably well-educated colonists here brought back
from its grave a belief in the Old Folk?"

"I suppose eventually, if the University ever does develop the
psychology department they keep talking about, I suppose eventually somebody will get a thesis out of your question." Dawson
spoke in a jagged voice, and he gulped when Sherrinford replied:

"I propose to begin now. In Commissioner Hauch Land, since
that's where the latest incident occurred. Where can I rent a
vehicle?"

"Uh, might be hard to do—"

"Come, come. Tenderfoot or not, I know better. In an economy
of scarcity, few people own heavy equipment. But since it's
needed, it can always be rented. I want a camper bus with a
ground-effect drive suitable for every kind of terrain. And I want
certain equipment installed which I've brought along, and the top
canopy section replaced by a gun turret controllable from the
driver's seat. But I'll supply the weapons. Besides rifles and pistols

of my own, I've arranged to borrow some artillery from Christmas Landing's police arsenal."

"Hoy? Are you genuinely intending to make ready for . . . a war . . . against a myth?"

"Let's say I'm taking out insurance, which isn't terribly expensive, against a remote possibility. Now, besides the bus, what about a light aircraft carried piggyback for use in surveys?"

"No." Dawson sounded more positive than hitherto. "That's asking for disaster. We can have you flown to a base camp in a large plane when the weather report's exactly right. But the pilot will have to fly back at once, before the weather turns wrong again. Meteorology's underdeveloped on Roland; the air's especially treacherous this time of year, and we're not tooled up to produce aircraft that can outlive every surprise." He drew breath. "Have you no idea of how fast a whirly-whirly can hit, or what size hailstones might strike from a clear sky, or—? Once you're there, man, you stick to the ground." He hesitated. "That's an important reason our information is so scanty about the outway and its settlers are so isolated."

Sherrinford laughed ruefully. "Well, I suppose if details are what I'm after, I must creep along anyway."

"You'll waste a lot of time," Dawson said. "Not to mention your client's money. Listen, I can't forbid you to chase shadows, but—"

The discussion went on for almost an hour. When the screen finally blanked, Sherrinford rose, stretched and walked toward Barbro. She noticed anew his peculiar gait. He had come from a planet with a fourth again of Earth's gravitational drag, to one where weight was less than half Terrestrial. She wondered if he had flying dreams.

"I apologize for shuffling you off like that," he said. "I didn't expect to reach him at once. He was quite truthful about how busy he is. But having made contact, I didn't want to remind him overmuch of you. He can dismiss my project as a futile fantasy which I'll soon give up. But he might have frozen completely, might even have put up obstacles before us, if he'd realized through you how determined we are."

"Why should he care?" she asked in her bitterness.

"Fear of consequences, the worse because it is unadmitted—fear of consequences, the more terrifying because they are unguessable." Sherrinford's gaze went to the screen, and thence out the window to the aurora pulsing in glacial blue and white immensely far overhead. "I suppose you saw I was talking to a frightened man. Down underneath his conventionality and scoffing, he believes in the Outlings—oh, yes, he believes."

The feet of Mistherd flew over yerba and outpaced windblown driftweed. Beside him, black and misshapen, hulked Nagrim the nicor, whose earthquake weight left a swath of crushed plants. Behind, luminous blossoms of a firethorn shone through the twining, trailing outlines of Morgarel the wraith.

Here Cloudmoor rose in a surf of hills and thickets. The air lay quiet, now and then carrying the distance-muted howl of a beast. It was darker than usual at winterbirth, the moons being down and aurora a wan flicker above the mountains on the northern world-edge. But this made the stars keen, and their numbers crowded heaven, and Ghost Road shone among them as if it, like the leafage beneath, were paved with dew.

"Yonder!" bawled Nagrim. All four of his arms pointed. The party had topped a ridge. Far off glimmered a spark. "Hoah, hoah! 'Ull we right off stamp dem flat, or pluck dem apart slow?"

We shall do nothing of the sort, bonebrain, Morgarel's answer slid through their heads. *Not unless they attack us, and they will not unless we make them aware of us, and her command is that we spy out their purposes.*

"Gr-r-rum-m-m. I know deir aim. Cut down trees, stick plows in land, sow deir cursed seed in de clods and in deir shes. 'Less we drive dem into de bitterwater, and soon, soon, dey'll wax too strong for us."

"Not too strong for the Queen!" Mistherd protested, shocked.

Yet they do have new powers, it seems, Morgarel reminded

him. *Carefully must we probe them.*

"Den carefully can we step on dem?" asked Nagrim.

The question woke a grin out of Mistherd's own uneasiness. He slapped the scaly back. "Don't talk, you," he said. "It hurts my ears. Nor think; that hurts your head. Come, run!"

Ease yourself, Morgarel scolded. *You have too much life in you, human-born.*

Mistherd made a face at the wraith, but obeyed to the extent of slowing down and picking his way through what cover the country afforded. For he traveled on behalf of the Fairest, to learn what had brought a pair of mortals questing hither.

Did they seek that boy whom Ayoch stole? (He continued to weep for his mother, though less and less often as the marvels of Carheddin entered him.) Perhaps. A birdcraft had left them and their car at the now-abandoned campsite, from which they had followed an outward spiral. But when no trace of the cub had appeared inside a reasonable distance, they did not call to be flown home. And this wasn't because weather forbade the farspeaker waves to travel, as was frequently the case. No, instead the couple set off toward the mountains of Moonhorn. Their course would take them past a few outlying invader steadings and on into realms untrodden by their race.

So this was no ordinary survey. Then what was it?

Mistherd understood now why she who reigned had made her adopted mortal children learn, or retain, the clumsy language of their forebears. He had hated that drill, wholly foreign to Dweller ways. Of course, you obeyed her, and in time you saw how wise she had been. . . .

Presently he left Nagrim behind a rock—the nicor would only be useful in a fight—and crawled from bush to bush until he lay within man-lengths of the humans. A rainplant drooped over him, leaves soft on his bare skin, and clothed him in darkness. Morgarel floated to the crown of a shiverleaf, whose unrest would better conceal his flimsy shape. He'd not be much help either. And that was the most troublous, the almost appalling thing here. Wraiths were among those who could not just sense and send thoughts, but cast illusions. Morgarel had reported that this time his power seemed to rebound off an invisible cold wall around the car.

Otherwise the male and female had set up no guardian engines and kept no dogs. Belike they supposed none would be needed, since they slept in the long vehicle which bore them. But such contempt of the Queen's strength could not be tolerated, could it?

Metal sheened faintly by the light of their campfire. They sat on either side, wrapped in coats against a coolness that Mistherd, naked, found mild. The male drank smoke. The female stared past him into a dusk which her flame-dazzled eyes must see as thick gloom. The dancing glow brought her vividly forth. Yes, to judge from Ayoch's tale, she was the dam of the new cub.

Ayoch had wanted to come too, but the Wonderful One forbade. Pooks couldn't hold still long enough for such a mission.

The man sucked on his pipe. His cheeks thus pulled into shadow while the light flickered across nose and brow, he looked disquietingly like a shearbill about to stoop on prey.

"—No, I tell you again, Barbro, I have no theories," he was saying. "When facts are insufficient, theorizing is ridiculous at best, misleading at worst."

"Still, you must have some idea of what you're doing," she said. It was plain that they had threshed this out often before. No Dweller could be as persistent as she or as patient as he. "That gear you packed—that generator you keep running—"

"I have a working hypothesis or two, which suggested what equipment I ought to take."

"Why won't you tell me what the hypotheses are?"

"They themselves indicate that that might be inadvisable at the present time. I'm still feeling my way into the labyrinth. And I haven't had a chance yet to hook everything up. In fact, we're really only protected against so-called telepathic influence—"

"What?" She started. "Do you mean . . . those legends about how they can read minds too . . ." Her words trailed off and her gaze sought the darkness beyond his shoulders.

He leaned forward. His tone lost its clipped rapidity, grew earnest and soft. "Barbro, you're racking yourself to pieces. Which is no help to Jimmy if he's alive, the more so when you may well be badly needed later on. We've a long trek before us, and you'd better settle into it."

She nodded jerkily and caught her lip between her teeth for a moment before she answered, "I'm trying."

He smiled around his pipe. "I expect you'll succeed. You don't strike me as a quitter or a whiner or an enjoyer of misery."

She dropped a hand to the pistol at her belt. Her voice changed; it came out of her throat like knife from sheath. "When we find them, they'll know what I am. What humans are."

"Put anger aside also," the man urged. "We can't afford emotions. If the Outlings are real, as I told you I'm provisionally assuming, they're fighting for their homes." After a short stillness he added: "I like to think that if the first explorers had found live natives, men would not have colonized Roland. But too late now. We can't go back if we wanted to. It's a bitter-end struggle, against an enemy so crafty that he's even hidden from us the fact that he is waging war."

"Is he? I mean, skulking, kidnapping an occasional child—"

"That's part of my hypothesis. I suspect those aren't harassments, they're tactics employed in a chillingly subtle strategy."

The fire sputtered and sparked. The man smoked awhile, brooding, until he went on:

"I didn't want to raise your hopes or excite you unduly while you had to wait on me, first in Christmas Landing, then in Portolondon. Afterward we were busy satisfying ourselves that Jimmy had been taken further from camp than he could have wandered before collapsing. So I'm only now telling you how thoroughly I studied available material on the . . . Old Folk. Besides, at first I did it on the principle of eliminating every imaginable possibility, however absurd. I expected no result other than final disproof. But I went through everything, relics, analyses, histories, journalistic accounts, monographs; I talked to outwayers who happened to be in town and to what scientists we have who've taken any interest in the matter. I'm a quick study. I flatter myself I became as expert as anyone—though God knows there's little to be expert on. Furthermore, I, a comparative stranger to Roland, maybe looked on the problem with fresh eyes. And a pattern emerged for me.

"If the aborigines had become extinct, why hadn't they left more remnants? Arctica isn't enormous, and it's fertile for Rolandic life. It ought to have supported a population whose artifacts ought to have accumulated over millennia. I've read that on Earth, literally tens of thousands of paleolithic hand axes were found, more by chance than archaeology.

"Very well. Suppose the relics and fossils were deliberately removed, between the time the last survey party left and the first colonizing ships arrived. I did find some support for that idea in the diaries of the original explorers. They were too preoccupied with checking the habitability of the planet to make catalogues of primitive monuments. However, the remarks they wrote down indicate they saw much more than later arrivals did. Suppose what we have found is just what the removers overlooked or didn't get around to.

"That argues a sophisticated mentality, thinking in long-range terms, doesn't it? Which in turn argues that the Old Folk were not mere hunters or neolithic farmers."

"But nobody ever saw buildings or machines or any such thing," Barbro objected.

"No. Most likely the natives didn't go through our kind of metallurgic-industrial evolution. I can conceive of other paths to take. Their full-fledged civilization might have begun, rather than ended, in biological science and technology. It might have developed potentialities of the nervous system, which might be greater in their species than in man. We have those abilities to some degree ourselves, you realize. A dowser, for instance, actually senses variations in the local magnetic field caused by a water table. However, in us, these talents are maddeningly rare and tricky. So we took our business elsewhere. Who needs to be a telepath, say, when he has a visiphone? The Old Folk may have seen it the other way around. The artifacts of their civilization may have been, may still be unrecognizable to men."

"They could have identified themselves to the men, though," Barbro said. "Why didn't they?"

"I can imagine any number of reasons. As, they could have had a bad experience with interstellar visitors earlier in their history. Ours is scarcely the sole race that has spaceships. However, I told you I don't theorize in advance of the facts. Let's say no more than that the Old Folk, if they exist, are alien to us."

"For a rigorous thinker, you're spinning a mighty thin thread."

"I've admitted this is entirely provisional." He squinted at her through a roil of campfire smoke. "You came to me, Barbro, insisting in the teeth of officialdom that your boy had been stolen, but your own talk about cultist kidnappers was ridiculous. Why are you reluctant to admit the reality of nonhumans?"

"In spite of the fact that Jimmy's being alive probably depends on it," she sighed. "I know." A shudder. "Maybe I don't dare admit it."

"I've said nothing thus far that hasn't been speculated about in print," he told her. "A disreputable speculation, true. In a hundred years, nobody has found valid evidence for the Outlings being more than a superstition. Still, a few people have declared it's at least possible that intelligent natives are at large in the wilderness."

"I know," she repeated. "I'm not sure, though, what has made you, overnight, take those arguments seriously."

"Well, once you got me started thinking, it occurred to me that Roland's outwayers are not utterly isolated medieval crofters. They have books, telecommunications, power tools, motor vehicles; above all, they have a modern science-oriented education. Why *should* they turn superstitious? Something must be causing it." He stopped. "I'd better not continue. My ideas go further than this; but if they're correct, it's dangerous to speak them aloud."

Mistherd's belly muscles tensed. There was danger for fair, in

that shearbill head. The Garland Bearer must be warned. For a
minute he wondered about summoning Nagrim to kill these two.
If the nicor jumped them fast, their firearms might avail them
naught. But no. They might have left word at home, or— He came
back to his ears. The talk had changed course. Barbro was murmuring, "—why you stayed on Roland."

The man smiled his gaunt smile. "Well, life on Beowulf held no
challenge for me. Heorot is—or was; this was decades past,
remember—Heorot was densely populated, smoothly organized,
boringly uniform. That was partly due to the lowland frontier, a
safety valve that bled off the dissatisfied. But I lack the carbon
dioxide tolerance necessary to live healthily down there. An expedition was being readied to make a swing around a number of
colony worlds, especially those which didn't have the equipment
to keep in laser contact. You'll recall its announced purpose, to
seek out new ideas in science, arts, sociology, philosophy, whatever might prove valuable. I'm afraid they found little on Roland
relevant to Beowulf. But I, who had wangled a berth, I saw oppor-
tunities for myself and decided to make my home here."

"Were you a detective back there, too?"

"Yes, in the official police. We had a tradition of such work in
our family. Some of that may have come from the Cherokee side
of it, if the name means anything to you. However, we also
claimed collateral descent from one of the first private inquiry
agents on record, back on Earth before spaceflight. Regardless of
how true that may be, I found him a useful model. You see, an
archetype—"

The man broke off. Unease crossed his features. "Best we go to
sleep," he said. "We've a long distance to cover in the morning."

She looked outward. "Here is no morning."

They retired. Mistherd rose and cautiously flexed limberness
back into his muscles. Before returning to the Sister of Lyrth, he
risked a glance through a pane in the car. Bunks were made up,
side by side, and the humans lay in them. Yet the man had not
touched her, though hers was a bonny body, and nothing that had

passed between them suggested he meant to do so.

Eldritch, humans. Cold and claylike. And they would overrun the beautiful wild world? Mistherd spat in disgust. It must not happen. It would not happen. She who reigned had vowed that.

The lands of William Irons were immense. But this was because a barony was required to support him, his kin and cattle, on native crops whose cultivation was still poorly understood. He raised some Terrestrial plants as well, by summerlight and in conservatories. However, these were a luxury. The true conquest of northern Arctica lay in yerba hay, in bathyrhiza wood, in pericoup and glycophyllon, and eventually, when the market had expanded with population and industry, in chalcanthemum for city florists and pelts of cage-bred rover for city furriers.

That was in a tomorrow Irons did not expect that he would live to see. Sherrinford wondered if the man really expected anyone ever would.

The room was warm and bright. Cheerfulness crackled in the fireplace. Light from fluoropanels gleamed off hand-carven chests and chairs and tables, off colorful draperies and shelved dishes. The outwayer sat solid in his high seat, stoutly clad, beard flowing down his chest. His wife and daughters brought coffee, whose fragrance joined the remnant odors of a hearty supper, to him, his guests and his sons.

But outside, wind hooted, lightning flared, thunder bawled, rain crashed on roof and walls and roared down to swirl among the courtyard cobblestones. Sheds and barns crouched against hugeness beyond. Trees groaned, and did a wicked undertone of laughter run beneath the lowing of a frightened cow? A burst of hailstones hit the tiles like knocking knuckles.

You could feel how distant your neighbors were, Sherrinford thought. And nonetheless they were the people whom you saw oftenest, did daily business with by visiphone (when a solar storm didn't make gibberish of their voices and chaos of their faces) or in the flesh, partied with, gossiped and intrigued with, inter-

married with; in the end, they were the people who would bury
you. The lights of the coastal towns were monstrously further
away.

William Irons was a strong man. Yet when now he spoke, fear
was in his tone. "You'd truly go over Troll Scarp?"

"Do you mean Hanstein Palisades?" Sherrinford responded,
more challenge than question.

"No outwayer calls it anything but Troll Scarp," Barbro said.

And how had a name like that been reborn, light-years and
centuries from Earth's Dark Ages?

"Hunters, trappers, prospectors—rangers, you call them—
travel in those mountains," Sherrinford declared.

"In certain parts," Irons said. "That's allowed, by a pact once
made 'tween a man and the Queen after he'd done well by a
jack-o'-the-hill that a satan had hurt. Wherever the plumablanca
grows, men may fare, if they leave man-goods on the altar boulders in payment for what they take out of the land. Elsewhere"
—one fist clenched on a chair arm and went slack again—" 's not
wise to go."

"It's been done, hasn't it?"

"Oh, yes. And some came back all right, or so they claimed,
though I've heard they were never lucky afterward. And some
didn't; they vanished. And some who returned babbled of won-
ders and horrors, and stayed witlings the rest of their lives. Not for
a long time has anybody been rash enough to break the pact and
overtread the bounds." Irons looked at Barbro almost entreat-
ingly. His woman and children stared likewise, grown still. Wind
hooted beyond the walls and rattled the storm shutters. "Don't
you."

"I've reason to believe my son is there," she answered.

"Yes, yes, you've told and I'm sorry. Maybe something can be
done. I don't know what, but I'd be glad to, oh, lay a double
offering on Unvar's Barrow this midwinter, and a prayer drawn in
the turf by a flint knife. Maybe they'll return him." Irons sighed.
"They've not done such a thing in man's memory, though. And he

could have a worse lot. I've glimpsed them myself, speeding mad-cap through twilight. They seem happier than we are. Might be no kindness, sending your boy home again."

"Like in the Arvid song," said his wife.

Irons nodded. "M-hm. Or others, come to think of it."

"What's this?" Sherrinford asked. More sharply than before, he felt himself a stranger. He was a child of cities and technics, above all a child of the skeptical intelligence. This family *believed*. It was disquieting to see more than a touch of their acceptance in Bar-bro's slow nod.

"We have the same ballad in Olga Ivanoff Land," she told him, her voice less calm than the words. "It's one of the traditional ones —nobody knows who composed them—that are sung to set the measure of a ring dance in a meadow."

"I noticed a multilyre in your baggage, Mrs. Cullen," said the wife of Irons. She was obviously eager to get off the explosive topic of a venture in defiance of the Old Folk. A songfest could help. "Would you like to entertain us?"

Barbro shook her head, white around the nostrils. The oldest boy said quickly, rather importantly, "Well, sure, I can, if our guests would like to hear."

"I'd enjoy that, thank you." Sherrinford leaned back in his seat and stoked his pipe. If this had not happened spontaneously, he would have guided the conversation toward a similar outcome.

In the past he had had no incentive to study the folklore of the outway, and not much chance to read the scanty references on it since Barbro brought him her trouble. Yet more and more he was becoming convinced that he must get an understanding—not an anthropological study, but a feel from the inside out—of the rela-tionship between Roland's frontiersmen and those beings which haunted them.

A bustling followed, rearrangement, settling down to listen, coffee cups refilled and brandy offered on the side. The boy ex-plained, "The last line is the chorus. Everybody join in, right?" Clearly he too hoped thus to bleed off some of the tension. Cathar-

sis through music? Sherrinford wondered, and added to himself:
No; exorcism.

A girl strummed a guitar. The boy sang, to a melody which beat
across the storm noise:

> "It was the ranger Arvid
> rode homeward through the hills
> among the shadowy shiverleafs,
> along the chiming rills.
> *The dance weaves under the firethorn.*
>
> "The night wind whispered around him
> with scent of brok and rue.
> Both moons rose high above him
> and hills aflash with dew.
> *The dance weaves under the firethorn.*
>
> "And dreaming of that woman
> who waited in the sun,
> he stopped, amazed by starlight,
> and so he was undone.
> *The dance weaves under the firethorn.*
>
> "For there beneath a barrow
> that bulked athwart a moon,
> the Outling folk were dancing
> in glass and golden shoon.
> *The dance weaves under the firethorn.*
>
> "The Outling folk were dancing
> like water, wind and fire
> to frosty-ringing harpstrings,
> and never did they tire.
> *The dance weaves under the firethorn.*
>
> "To Arvid came she striding
> from where she watched the dance,
> the Queen of Air and Darkness,
> with starlight in her glance.
> *The dance weaves under the firethorn.*

> "With starlight, love and terror
> in her immortal eye,
> the Queen of Air and Darkness—"

"No!" Barbro leaped from her chair. Her fists were clenched and tears flogged her cheekbones. "You can't—pretend that—about the things that stole Jimmy!"

She fled from the chamber, upstairs to her guest bedroom.

But she finished the song herself. That was about seventy hours later, camped in the steeps where rangers dared not fare.

She and Sherrinford had not said much to the Irons family, after refusing repeated pleas to leave the forbidden country alone. Nor had they exchanged many remarks at first as they drove north. Slowly, however, he began to draw her out about her own life. After a while she almost forgot to mourn, in her remembering of home and old neighbors. Somehow this led to discoveries—that he, beneath his professional manner, was a gourmet and a lover of opera and appreciated her femaleness; that she could still laugh and find beauty in the wild land around her—and she realized, half guiltily, that life held more hopes than even the recovery of the son Tim gave her.

"I've convinced myself he's alive," the detective said. He scowled. "Frankly, it makes me regret having taken you along. I expected this would be only a fact-gathering trip, but it's turning out to be more. If we're dealing with real creatures who stole him, they can do real harm. I ought to turn back to the nearest garth and call for a plane to fetch you."

"Like bottommost hell you will, mister," she said. "You need somebody who knows outway conditions, and I'm a better shot than average."

"M–m–m . . . it would involve considerable delay too, wouldn't it? Besides the added distance, I can't put a signal through to any airport before this current burst of solar interference has calmed down."

Next "night" he broke out his remaining equipment and set it up. She recognized some of it, such as the thermal detector. Other items were strange to her, copied to his order from the advanced apparatus of his birthworld. He would tell her little about them. "I've explained my suspicion that the ones we're after have telepathic capabilities," he said in apology.

Her eyes widened. "You mean it could be true, the Queen and her people can read minds?"

"That's part of the dread which surrounds their legend, isn't it? Actually there's nothing spooky about the phenomenon. It was studied and fairly well defined centuries ago, on Earth. I daresay the facts are available in the scientific microfiles at Christmas Landing. You Rolanders have simply had no occasion to seek them out, any more than you've yet had occasion to look up how to build power beamcasters or spacecraft."

"Well, how does telepathy work, then?"

Sherrinford recognized that her query asked for comfort as much as it did for facts and he spoke with deliberate dryness: "The organism generates extremely long-wave radiation which can, in principle, be modulated by the nervous system. In practice, the feebleness of the signals and their low rate of information transmission make them elusive, hard to detect and measure. Our prehuman ancestors went in for more reliable senses, like vision and hearing. What telepathic transceiving we do is marginal at best. But explorers have found extraterrestrial species that got an evolutionary advantage from developing the system further, in their particular environments. I imagine such species could include one which gets comparatively little direct sunlight—in fact, appears to hide from broad day. It could even become so able in this regard that, at short range, it can pick up man's weak emissions and make man's primitive sensitivities resonate to its own strong sendings."

"That would account for a lot, wouldn't it?" Barbro said faintly.

"I've now screened our car by a jamming field," Sherrinford told her, "but it reaches only a few meters past the chassis. Beyond, a scout of theirs might get a warning from your thoughts, if you knew precisely what I'm trying to do. I have a well-trained subconscious which sees to it that I think about this in French when I'm outside. Communication has to be structured to be intelligible, you see, and that's a different enough structure from English. But English is the only human language on Roland, and surely the Old Folk have learned it."

She nodded. He had told her his general plan, which was too obvious to conceal. The problem was to make contact with the aliens, if they existed. Hitherto, they had only revealed themselves, at rare intervals, to one or a few backwoodsmen at a time. An ability to generate hallucinations would help them in that. They would stay clear of any large, perhaps unmanageable expedition which might pass through their territory. But two people, braving all prohibitions, shouldn't look too formidable to approach. And . . . this would be the first human team which not only worked on the assumption that the Outlings were real but possessed the resources of modern, off-planet police technology.

Nothing happened at that camp. Sherrinford said he hadn't expected it would. The Old Folk seemed cautious this near to any settlement. In their own lands they must be bolder.

And by the following "night," the vehicle had gone well into yonder country. When Sherrinford stopped the engine in a meadow and the car settled down, silence rolled in like a wave.

They stepped out. She cooked a meal on the glower while he gathered wood, that they might later cheer themselves with a campfire. Frequently he glanced at his wrist. It bore no watch—instead, a radio-controlled dial, to tell what the instruments in the bus might register.

Who needed a watch here? Slow constellations wheeled beyond glimmering aurora. The moon Alde stood above a snowpeak, turning it argent, though this place lay at a goodly height. The rest of the mountains were hidden by the forest that crowded around. Its trees were mostly shiverleaf and feathery white plumablanca,

ghostly amidst their shadows. A few firethorns glowed, clustered
dim lanterns, and the underbrush was heavy and smelled sweet.
You could see surprisingly far through the blue dusk. Somewhere
nearby, a brook sang and a bird fluted.

"Lovely here," Sherrinford said. They had risen from their supper and not yet sat down again or kindled their fire.

"But strange," Barbro answered as low. "I wonder if it's really
meant for us. If we can really hope to possess it."

His pipestem gestured at the stars. "Man's gone to stranger
places than this."

"Has he? I . . . oh, I suppose it's just something left over from
my outway childhood, but do you know, when I'm under them I
can't think of the stars as balls of gas, whose energies have been
measured, whose planets have been walked on by prosaic feet. No,
they're small and cold and magical; our lives are bound to them;
after we die, they whisper to us in our graves." Barbro glanced
downward. "I realize that's nonsense."

She could see in the twilight how his face grew tight. "Not at
all," he said. "Emotionally, physics may be a worse nonsense. And
in the end, you know, after a sufficient number of generations,
thought follows feeling. Man is not at heart rational. He could stop
believing the stories of science if those no longer felt right."

He paused. "That ballad which didn't get finished in the house,"
he said, not looking at her. "Why did it affect you so?"

"I couldn't stand hearing *them*, well, praised. Or that's how it
seemed. Sorry for the fuss."

"I gather the ballad is typical of a large class."

"Well, I never thought to add them up. Cultural anthropology
is something we don't have time for on Roland, or more likely it
hasn't occurred to us, with everything else there is to do. But—
now you mention it, yes, I'm surprised at how many songs and
stories have the Arvid motif in them."

"Could you bear to recite it?"

She mustered the will to laugh. "Why, I can do better than that
if you want. Let me get my multilyre and I'll perform."

She omitted the hypnotic chorus line, though, when the notes rang out, except at the end. He watched her where she stood against moon and aurora.

"—the Queen of Air and Darkness
cried softly under sky:

" 'Light down, you ranger Arvid,
and join the Outling folk.
You need no more be human,
which is a heavy yoke.'

"He dared to give her answer:
'I may do naught but run.
A maiden waits me, dreaming
in lands beneath the sun.

" 'And likewise wait me comrades
and tasks I would not shirk,
for what is ranger Arvid
if he lays down his work?

" 'So wreak your spells, you Outling,
and cast your wrath on me.
Though maybe you can slay me,
you'll not make me unfree.'

"The Queen of Air and Darkness
stood wrapped about with fear
and northlight flares and beauty
he dared not look too near.

"Until she laughed like harpsong
and said to him in scorn:
'I do not need a magic
to make you always mourn.

" 'I send you home with nothing
except your memory
of moonlight, Outling music,
night breezes, dew and me.

" 'And that will run behind you,
   a shadow on the sun,
   and that will lie beside you
   when every day is done.

" 'In work and play and friendship
   your grief will strike you dumb
   for thinking what you are—and—
   what you might have become.

" 'Your dull and foolish woman
   treat kindly as you can.
   Go home now, ranger Arvid,
   set free to be a man!'

 "In flickering and laughter
   the Outling folk were gone.
   He stood alone by moonlight
   and wept until the dawn.
      The dance weaves under the firethorn."

She laid the lyre aside. A wind rustled leaves. After a long quietness Sherrinford said, "And tales of this kind are part of everyone's life in the outway?"

"Well, you could put it thus," Barbro replied. "Though they're not all full of supernatural doings. Some are about love or heroism. Traditional themes."

"I don't think your particular tradition has arisen of itself." His tone was bleak. "In fact, I think many of your songs and stories were not composed by human beings."

He snapped his lips shut and would say no more on the subject. They went early to bed.

Hours later, an alarm roused them.

The buzzing was soft, but it brought them instantly alert. They slept in gripsuits, to be prepared for emergencies. Sky-glow lit them through the canopy. Sherrinford swung out of his bunk, slipped shoes on feet and clipped gun holster to belt. "Stay inside," he commanded.

"What's here?" Her pulse thuttered.

He squinted at the dials of his instruments and checked them against the luminous telltale on his wrist. "Three animals," he counted. "Not wild ones happening by. A large one, homeothermic, to judge from the infrared, holding still a short ways off. Another . . . hm, low temperature, diffuse and unstable emission, as if it were more like a . . . a swarm of cells coordinated somehow . . . pheromonally? . . . hovering, also at a distance. But the third's practically next to us, moving around in the brush; and that pattern looks human."

She saw him quiver with eagerness, no longer seeming a professor. "I'm going to try to make a capture," he said. "When we have a subject for interrogation—Stand ready to let me back in again fast. But don't risk yourself, whatever happens. And keep this cocked." He handed her a loaded big-game rifle.

His tall frame poised by the door, opened it a crack. Air blew in, cool, damp, full of fragrances and murmurings. The moon Oliver was now also aloft, the radiance of both unreally brilliant, and the aurora seethed in whiteness and ice-blue.

Sherrinford peered afresh at his telltale. It must indicate the directions of the watchers, among those dappled leaves. Abruptly he sprang out. He sprinted past the ashes of the campfire and vanished under trees. Barbro's hand strained on the butt of her weapon.

Racket exploded. Two in combat burst onto the meadow. Sherrinford had clapped a grip on a smaller human figure. She could make out by streaming silver and rainbow flicker that the other was nude, male, long-haired, lithe and young. He fought demoniacally, seeking to use teeth and feet and raking nails, and meanwhile he ululated like a satan.

The identification shot through her: A changeling, stolen in babyhood and raised by the Old Folk. This creature was what they would make Jimmy into.

"Ha!" Sherrinford forced his opponent around and drove stiffened fingers into the solar plexus. The boy gasped and sagged. Sherrinford manhandled him toward the car.

Out from the woods came a giant. It might itself have been a tree, black and rugose, bearing four great gnarly boughs; but earth quivered and boomed beneath its leg-roots, and its hoarse bellowing filled sky and skulls.

Barbro shrieked. Sherrinford whirled. He yanked out his pistol, fired and fired, flat whipcracks through the half light. His free arm kept a lock on the youth. The troll shape lurched under those blows. It recovered and came on, more slowly, more carefully, circling around to cut him off from the bus. He couldn't move fast enough to evade it unless he released his prisoner—who was his sole possible guide to Jimmy—

Barbro leaped forth. "Don't!" Sherrinford shouted. "For God's sake, stay inside!" The monster rumbled and made snatching motions at her. She pulled the trigger. Recoil slammed her in the shoulder. The colossus rocked and fell. Somehow it got its feet back and lumbered toward her. She retreated. Again she shot, and again. The creature snarled. Blood began to drip from it and gleam oilily amidst dewdrops. It turned and went off, breaking branches, into the darkness that laired beneath the woods.

"Get to shelter!" Sherrinford yelled. "You're out of the jammer field!"

A mistiness drifted by overhead. She barely glimpsed it before she saw the new shape at the meadow edge. "Jimmy!" tore from her.

"Mother." He held out his arms. Moonlight coursed in his tears. She dropped her weapon and ran to him.

Sherrinford plunged in pursuit. Jimmy flitted away into the brush. Barbro crashed after, through clawing twigs. Then she was seized and borne away.

Standing over his captive, Sherrinford strengthened the fluoro output until vision of the wilderness was blocked off from within the bus. The boy squirmed beneath that colorless glare.

"You are going to talk," the man said. Despite the haggardness in his features, he spoke quietly.

The boy glared through tangled locks. A bruise was purpling on his jaw. He'd almost recovered ability to flee while Sherrinford chased and lost the woman. Returning, the detective had barely caught him. Time was lacking to be gentle, when Outling reinforcements might arrive at any moment. Sherrinford had knocked him out and dragged him inside. He sat lashed into a swivel seat.

He spat. "Talk to you, man-clod?" But sweat stood on his skin, and his eyes flickered unceasingly around the metal which caged him.

"Give me a name to call you by."

"And have you work a spell on me?"

"Mine's Eric. If you don't give me another choice, I'll have to call you . . . m-m-m . . . Wuddikins."

"What?" However eldritch, the bound one remained a human adolescent. "Mistherd, then." The lilting accent of his English somehow emphasized its sullenness. "That's not the sound, only what it means. Anyway, it's my spoken name, naught else."

"Ah, you keep a secret name you consider to be real?"

"She does. I don't know myself what it is. She knows the real names of everybody."

Sherrinford raised his brows. "She?"

"Who reigns. May she forgive me, I can't make the reverent sign when my arms are tied. Some invaders call her the Queen of Air and Darkness."

"So." Sherrinford got pipe and tobacco. He let silence wax while he started the fire. At length he said:

"I'll confess the Old Folk took me by surprise. I didn't expect so formidable a member of your gang. Everything I could learn had seemed to show they work on my race—and yours, lad—by stealth, trickery and illusion."

Mistherd jerked a truculent nod. "She created the first nicors not long ago. Don't think she has naught but dazzlements at her beck."

"I don't. However, a steel-jacketed bullet works pretty well too, doesn't it?"

Sherrinford talked on, softly, mostly to himself: "I do still believe the, ah, nicors—all your half-humanlike breeds—are intended in the main to be seen, not used. The power of projecting mirages must surely be quite limited in range and scope as well as in the number of individuals who possess it. Otherwise she wouldn't have needed to work as slowly and craftily as she has. Even outside our mind-shield, Barbro—my companion—could have resisted, could have remained aware that whatever she saw was unreal . . . if she'd been less shaken, less frantic, less driven by need."

Sherrinford wreathed his head in smoke. "Never mind what I experienced," he said. "It couldn't have been the same as for her. I think the command was simply given us, 'You will see what you most desire in the world, running away from you into the forest.' Of course, she didn't travel many meters before the nicor waylaid her. I'd no hope of trailing them; I'm no Arctican woodsman, and besides, it'd have been too easy to ambush me. I came back to you." Grimly: "You're my link to your overlady."

"You think I'll guide you to Starhaven or Carheddin? Try making me, clod-man."

"I want to bargain."

"I s'pect you intend more'n that." Mistherd's answer held surprising shrewdness. "What'll you tell after you come home?"

"Yes, that does pose a problem, doesn't it? Barbro Cullen and I are not terrified outwayers. We're of the city. We brought recording instruments. We'd be the first of our kind to report an encounter with the Old Folk, and that report would be detailed and plausible. It would produce action."

"So you see I'm not afraid to die," Mistherd declared, though his lips trembled a bit. "If I let you come in and do your man-things to my people, I'd have naught left worth living for."

"Have no immediate fears," Sherrinford said. "You're merely bait." He sat down and regarded the boy through a visor of calm. (Within, it wept in him: *Barbro, Barbro!*) "Consider. Your Queen can't very well let me go back, bringing my prisoner and telling about hers. She has to stop that somehow. I could try fighting my way through—this car is better armed than you know—but that wouldn't free anybody. Instead, I'm staying put. New forces of hers will get here as fast as they can. I assume they won't blindly throw themselves against a machine gun, a howitzer, a fulgurator. They'll parley first, whether their intentions are honest or not. Thus I make the contact I'm after."

"What d' you plan?" The mumble held anguish.

"First, this, as a sort of invitation." Sherrinford reached out to flick a switch. "There. I've lowered my shield against mind-reading and shape-casting. I daresay the leaders, at least, will be able to sense that it's gone. That should give them confidence."

"And next?"

"Next we wait. Would you like something to eat or drink?"

During the time which followed, Sherrinford tried to jolly Mistherd along, find out something of his life. What answers he got were curt. He dimmed the interior lights and settled down to peer outward. That was a long few hours.

They ended at a shout of gladness, half a sob, from the boy. Out of the woods came a band of the Old Folk.

Some of them stood forth more clearly than moons and stars and northlights should have caused. He in the van rode a white crown-buck whose horns were garlanded. His form was manlike but unearthly beautiful, silver-blond hair falling from beneath the antlered helmet, around the proud cold face. The cloak fluttered off his back like living wings. His frost-colored mail rang as he fared.

Behind him, to right and left, rode two who bore swords whereon small flames gleamed and flickered. Above, a flying flock laughed and trilled and tumbled in the breezes. Near them drifted a half-transparent mistiness. Those others who passed among trees after their chieftain were harder to make out. But they moved in quicksilver grace and as it were to a sound of harps and trumpets.

"Lord Luighaid." Glory overflowed in Mistherd's tone. "Her master Knower—himself."

Sherrinford had never done a harder thing than to sit at the main control panel, finger near the button of the shield generator, and not touch it. He rolled down a section of canopy to let voices travel. A gust of wind struck him in the face, bearing odors of the roses in his mother's garden. At his back, in the main body of the vehicle, Mistherd strained against his bonds till he could see the oncoming troop.

"Call to them," Sherrinford said. "Ask if they will talk with me."

Unknown, flutingly sweet words flew back and forth. "Yes," the boy interpreted. "He will, the Lord Luighaid. But I can tell you, you'll never be let go. Don't fight them. Yield. Come away. You don't know what 'tis to be alive till you've dwelt in Carheddin under the mountain."

The Outlings drew nigh.

Jimmy glimmered and was gone. Barbro lay in strong arms, against a broad breast, and felt the horse move beneath her. It had to be a horse, though only a few were kept any longer on the steadings and they only for special uses or love. She could feel the rippling beneath its hide, hear a rush of parted leafage and the thud when a hoof struck stone; warmth and living scent welled up around her through the darkness.

He who carried her said mildly, "Don't be afraid, darling. It was a vision. But he's waiting for us and we're bound for him."

She was aware in a vague way that she ought to feel terror or despair or something. But her memories lay behind her—she wasn't sure just how she had come to be here—she was borne along in a knowledge of being loved. At peace, at peace, rest in the calm expectation of joy . . .

After a while the forest opened. They crossed a lea where boulders stood gray-white under the moons, their shadows shifting in the dim hues which the aurora threw across them. Flitteries danced, tiny comets, above the flowers between. Ahead gleamed a peak whose top was crowned in clouds.

Barbro's eyes happened to be turned forward. She saw the horse's head and thought, with quiet surprise: Why, this is Sambo, who was mine when I was a girl. She looked upward at the man. He wore a black tunic and a cowled cape, which made his face hard to see. She could not cry aloud, here. "Tim," she whispered.

"Yes, Barbro."

"I buried you—"

His smile was endlessly tender. "Did you think we're no more than what's laid back into the ground? Poor torn sweetheart. She who's called us is the All Healer. Now rest and dream."

"Dream," she said, and for a space she struggled to rouse herself. But the effort was weak. Why should she believe ashen tales about . . . atoms and energies, nothing else to fill a gape of emptiness . . . tales she could not bring to mind . . . when Tim and the horse her father gave her carried her on to Jimmy? Had the other thing not been the evil dream, and this her first drowsy awakening from it?

As if he heard her thoughts, he murmured, "They have a song in Outling lands. The Song of the Men:

"The world sails
to an unseen wind.
Light swirls by the bows.
The wake is night.

But the Dwellers have no such sadness."

"I don't understand," she said.

He nodded. "There's much you'll have to understand, darling, and I can't see you again until you've learned those truths. But meanwhile you'll be with our son."

She tried to lift her head and kiss him. He held her down. "Not yet," he said. "You've not been received among the Queen's people. I shouldn't have come for you, except that she was too merciful to forbid. Lie back, lie back."

Time blew past. The horse galloped tireless, never stumbling, up the mountain. Once she glimpsed a troop riding down it and thought they were bound for a last weird battle in the west against . . . who? . . . one who lay cased in iron and sorrow. Later she would ask herself the name of him who had brought her into the land of the Old Truth.

Finally spires lifted splendid among the stars, which are small and magical and whose whisperings comfort us after we are dead. They rode into a courtyard where candles burned unwavering, fountains splashed and birds sang. The air bore fragrance of brok and pericoup, of rue and roses, for not everything that man brought was horrible. The Dwellers waited in beauty to welcome her. Beyond their stateliness, pooks cavorted through the gloaming; among the trees darted children; merriment caroled across music more solemn.

"We have come—" Tim's voice was suddenly, inexplicably a croak. Barbro was not sure how he dismounted, bearing her. She stood before him and saw him sway on his feet.

Fear caught her. "Are you well?" She seized both his hands. They felt cold and rough. Where had Sambo gone? Her eyes searched beneath the cowl. In this brighter illumination, she ought to have seen her man's face clearly. But it was blurred, it kept changing. "What's wrong, oh, what's happened?"

He smiled. Was that the smile she had cherished? She couldn't completely remember. "I—I must go," he stammered, so low she could scarcely hear. "Our time is not ready." He drew free of her grasp and leaned on a robed form which had appeared at his side. A haziness swirled over both their heads. "Don't watch me go . . . back into the earth," he pleaded. "That's death for you. Till our time returns— There, our son!"

She had to fling her gaze around. Kneeling, she spread wide her arms. Jimmy struck her like a warm, solid cannonball. She rumpled his hair; she kissed the hollow of his neck; she laughed and wept and babbled foolishness; and this was no ghost, no memory that had stolen off when she wasn't looking. Now and again, as she turned her attention to yet another hurt which might have come upon him—hunger, sickness, fear—and found none, she would glimpse their surroundings. The gardens were gone. It didn't matter.

"I missed you so, Mother. Stay?"

"I'll take you home, dearest."

"Stay. Here's fun. I'll show. But you stay."

A sighing went through the twilight. Barbro rose. Jimmy clung to her hand. They confronted the Queen.

Very tall she was in her robes woven of northlights, and her starry crown and her garlands of kiss-me-never. Her countenance recalled Aphrodite of Milos, whose picture Barbro had often seen in the realms of men, save that the Queen's was more fair and more majesty dwelt upon it and in the night-blue eyes. Around her the gardens woke to new reality, the court of the Dwellers and the heaven-climbing spires.

"Be welcome," she spoke, her speaking a song, "forever."

Against the awe of her, Barbro said, "Moonmother, let us go home."

"That may not be."

"To our world, little and beloved," Barbro dreamed she begged, "which we build for ourselves and cherish for our children."

"To prison days, angry nights, works that crumble in the fingers, loves that turn to rot or stone or driftweed, loss, grief, and the only sureness that of the final nothingness. No. You too, Wanderfoot who is to be, will jubilate when the banners of the Outworld come flying into the last of the cities and man is made wholly alive. Now go with those who will teach you."

The Queen of Air and Darkness lifted an arm in summons. It halted, and none came to answer.

For over the fountains and melodies lifted a gruesome growling. Fires leaped, thunders crashed. Her hosts scattered screaming before the steel thing which boomed up the mountainside. The pooks were gone in a whirl of frightened wings. The nicors flung their bodies against the unalive invader and were consumed, until their Mother cried to them to retreat.

Barbro cast Jimmy down and herself over him. Towers wavered and smoked away. The mountain stood bare under icy moons, save for rocks, crags, and farther off a glacier in whose depths the auroral light pulsed blue. A cave mouth darkened a cliff. Thither folk streamed, seeking refuge underground. Some were human of blood, some grotesques like the pooks and nicors and wraiths; but most were lean, scaly, long-tailed, long-beaked, not remotely men or Outlings.

For an instant, even as Jimmy wailed at her breast—perhaps as much because the enchantment had been wrecked as because he was afraid—Barbro pitied the Queen who stood alone in her nakedness. Then that one also had fled, and Barbro's world shivered apart.

The guns fell silent; the vehicle whirred to a halt. From it sprang a boy who called wildly, "Shadow-of-a-Dream, where are you? It's me, Mistherd. Oh, come, come!"—before he remembered that the language they had been raised in was not man's. He shouted in that until a girl crept out of a thicket where she had hidden. They stared at each other through dust, smoke and moonglow. She ran to him.

A new voice barked from the car, "Barbro, hurry!"

Christmas Landing knew day: short at this time of year, but sunlight, blue skies, white clouds, glittering water, salt breezes in busy streets, and the sane disorder of Eric Sherrinford's living room.

He crossed and uncrossed his legs where he sat, puffed on his pipe as if to make a veil, and said, "Are you certain you're recovered? You mustn't risk overstrain."

"I'm fine," Barbro Cullen replied, though her tone was flat. "Still tired, yes, and showing it, no doubt. One doesn't go through such an experience and bounce back in a week. But I'm up and about. And to be frank, I must know what's happened, what's going on, before I can settle down to regain my full strength. Not a word of news anywhere."

"Have you spoken to others about the matter?"

"No. I've simply told visitors I was too exhausted to talk. Not much of a lie. I assumed there's a reason for censorship."

Sherrinford looked relieved. "Good girl. It's at my urging. You can imagine the sensation when this is made public. The authorities agreed they need time to study the facts, think and debate in a calm atmosphere, have a decent policy ready to offer voters who're bound to become rather hysterical at first." His mouth quirked slightly upward. "Furthermore, your nerves and Jimmy's get their chance to heal before the journalistic storm breaks over you. How is he?"

"Quite well. He continues pestering me for leave to go play with his friends in the Wonderful Place. But at his age, he'll recover—he'll forget."

"He may meet them later anyhow."

"What? We didn't—" Barbro shifted in her chair. "I've forgotten too. I hardly recall a thing from our last hours. Did you bring back any kidnapped humans?"

"No. The shock was savage as it was, without throwing them straight into an . . . an institution. Mistherd, who's basically a sensible young fellow, assured me they'd get along, at any rate as regards survival necessities, till arrangements can be made." Sherrinford hesitated. "I'm not sure what the arrangements will be. Nobody is, at our present stage. But obviously they include those people—or many of them, especially those who aren't full-grown—rejoining the human race. Though they may never feel at home in civilization. Perhaps in a way that's best, since we will need some kind of mutually acceptable liaison with the Dwellers."

His impersonality soothed them both. Barbro became able to say, "Was I too big a fool? I do remember how I yowled and beat my head on the floor."

"Why, no." He considered the big woman and her pride for a few seconds before he rose, walked over and laid a hand on her shoulder. "You'd been lured and trapped by a skillful play on your deepest instincts, at a moment of sheer nightmare. Afterward, as that wounded monster carried you off, evidently another type of being came along, one that could saturate you with close-range neuropsychic forces. On top of this, my arrival, the sudden brutal

abolishment of every hallucination, must have been shattering. No
wonder if you cried out in pain. Before you did, you competently
got Jimmy and yourself into the bus, and you never interfered
with me."

"What did you do?"

"Why, I drove off as fast as possible. After several hours, the
atmospherics let up sufficiently for me to call Portolondon and
insist on an emergency airlift. Not that that was vital. What chance
had the enemy to stop us? They didn't even try—But quick transportation was certainly helpful."

"I figured that's what must have gone on." Barbro caught his
glance. "No, what I meant was, how did you find us in the backlands?"

Sherrinford moved a little off from her. "My prisoner was my
guide. I don't think I actually killed any of the Dwellers who'd
come to deal with me. I hope not. The car simply broke through
them, after a couple of warning shots, and afterward outpaced
them. Steel and fuel against flesh wasn't really fair. At the cave
entrance, I did have to shoot down a few of those troll creatures.
I'm not proud of it."

He stood silent. Presently: "But you were a captive," he said. "I
couldn't be sure what they might do to you, who had first claim
on me." After another pause: "I don't look for any more violence."

"How did you make . . . the boy . . . cooperate?"

Sherrinford paced from her, to the window, where he stood
staring out at the Boreal Ocean. "I turned off the mind-shield,"
he said. "I let their band get close, in full splendor of illusion.
Then I turned the shield back on, and we both saw them in
their true shapes. As we went northward, I explained to Mistherd how he and his kind had been hoodwinked, used, made
to live in a world that was never really there. I asked him if he
wanted himself and whomever he cared about to go on till
they died as domestic animals—yes, running in limited freedom
on solid hills, but always called back to the dream-kennel." His
pipe fumed furiously. "May I never see such bitterness again.

He had been taught to believe he was free."

Quiet returned, above the hectic traffic. Charlemagne drew nearer to setting; already the east darkened.

Finally Barbro asked, "Do you know why?"

"Why children were taken and raised like that? Partly because it was in the pattern the Dwellers were creating; partly in order to study and experiment on members of our species—minds, that is, not bodies; partly because humans have special strengths which are helpful, like being able to endure full daylight."

"But what was the final purpose of it all?"

Sherrinford paced the floor. "Well," he said, "of course the ultimate motives of the aborigines are obscure. We can't do more than guess at how they think, let alone how they feel. But our ideas do seem to fit the data.

"Why did they hide from man? I suspect they, or rather their ancestors—for they aren't glittering elves, you know; they're mortal and fallible too—I suspect the natives were only being cautious at first, more cautious than human primitives, though certain of those on Earth were also slow to reveal themselves to strangers. Spying, mentally eavesdropping, Roland's Dwellers must have picked up enough language to get some idea of how different man was from them, and how powerful; and they gathered that more ships would be arriving, bringing settlers. It didn't occur to them that they might be conceded the right to keep their lands. Perhaps they're still more fiercely territorial than we. They determined to fight, in their own way. I daresay, once we begin to get insight into that mentality, our psychological science will go through its Copernican revolution."

Enthusiasm kindled in him. "That's not the sole thing we'll learn, either," he went on. "They must have science of their own, a nonhuman science born on a planet that isn't Earth. Because they did observe us as profoundly as we've ever observed ourselves; they did mount a plan against us, one that would have taken another century or more to complete. Well, what else do they know? How do they support their civilization without visible agriculture or aboveground buildings or mines or anything? How can they breed whole new intelligent species to order? A million questions, ten million answers!"

"*Can* we learn from them?" Barbro asked softly. "Or can we only overrun them as you say they fear?"

Sherrinford halted, leaned elbow on mantel, hugged his pipe and replied, "I hope we'll show more charity than that to a defeated enemy. It's what they are. They tried to conquer us, and failed, and now in a sense we are bound to conquer them since they'll have to make their peace with the civilization of the machine rather than see it rust away as they strove for. Still, they never did us any harm as atrocious as what we've inflicted on our fellow men in the past. And, I repeat, they could teach us marvelous things; and we could teach them, too, once they've learned to be less intolerant of a different way of life."

"I suppose we can give them a reservation," she said, and didn't know why he grimaced and answered so roughly:

"Let's leave them the honor they've earned! They fought to save the world they'd always known from that"—he made a chopping gesture at the city—"and just possibly we'd be better off ourselves with less of it."

He sagged a trifle and sighed, "However, I suppose if Elfland had won, man on Roland would at last—peacefully, even happily —have died away. We live with our archetypes, but can we live in them?"

Barbro shook her head. "Sorry, I don't understand."

"What?" He looked at her in a surprise that drove out melancholy. After a laugh: "Stupid of me. I've explained this to so many politicians and scientists and commissioners and Lord knows what, these past days, I forgot I'd never explained to you. It was a rather vague idea of mine, most of the time we were traveling, and I don't like to discuss ideas prematurely. Now that we've met the Outlings and watched how they work, I do feel sure."

He tamped down his tobacco. "In limited measure," he said, "I've used an archetype throughout my own working life. The rational detective. It hasn't been a conscious pose—much—it's simply been an image which fitted my personality and professional style. But it draws an appropriate response from most people, whether or not they've ever heard of the original. The phenomenon is not uncommon. We meet persons who, in varying degrees, suggest Christ or Buddha or the Earth Mother, or, say, on a less exalted plane, Hamlet or d'Artagnan. Historical, fictional and mythical, such figures crystallize basic aspects of the human psyche, and when we meet them in our real experience, our reaction goes deeper than consciousness."

He grew grave again. "Man also creates archetypes that are not individuals. The Anima, the Shadow—and, it seems, the Outworld. The world of magic, of glamour—which originally meant enchantment—of half-human beings, some like Ariel and some like Caliban, but each free of mortal frailties and sorrows—therefore, perhaps, a little carelessly cruel, more than a little tricksy; dwellers, in dusk and moonlight, not truly gods but obedient to rulers who are enigmatic and powerful enough to be— Yes, our Queen of Air and Darkness knew well what sights to let lonely people see, what illusions to spin around them from time to time, what songs and legends to set going among them. I wonder how much she and her underlings gleaned from human fairy tales, how much they made up themselves, and how much men created all over again, all unwittingly, as the sense of living on the edge of the world entered them."

Shadows stole across the room. It grew cooler and the traffic noises dwindled. Barbro asked mutedly, "But what could this do?"

"In many ways," Sherrinford answered, "the outwayer *is* back in the Dark Ages. He has few neighbors, hears scanty news from beyond his horizon, toils to survive in a land he only partly understands, that may any night raise unforeseeable disasters against him and is bounded by enormous wildernesses. The machine civilization which brought his ancestors here is frail at best. He could lose it as the Dark Ages nations had lost Greece and Rome, as the whole of Earth seems to have lost it. Let him be worked on, long, strongly, cunningly, by the archetypical Outworld, until he has come to believe in his bones that the magic of the Queen of Air and Darkness is greater than the energy of engines; and first his faith, finally his deeds will follow her. Oh, it wouldn't happen fast. Ideally, it would happen too slowly to be noticed, especially by self-satisfied city people. But when in the end a hinterland gone back to the ancient way turned from them, how could they keep alive?"

Barbro breathed, "She said to me, when their banners flew in the last of our cities, we would rejoice."

"I think we would have, by then," Sherrinford admitted. "Nevertheless, I believe in choosing one's destiny."

He shook himself, as if casting off a burden. He knocked the dottle from his pipe and stretched, muscle by muscle. "Well," he said, "it isn't going to happen."

She looked straight at him. "Thanks to you."

A flush went up his thin cheeks. "In time, I'm sure somebody else would have— What matters is what we do next, and that's too big a decision for one individual or one generation to make."

She rose. "Unless the decision is personal, Eric," she suggested, feeling heat in her own face.

It was curious to see him shy. "I was hoping we might meet again."

"We will."

Ayoch sat on Wolund's Barrow. Aurora shuddered so brilliant, in such vast sheafs of light, as almost to hide the waning moons. Firethorn blooms had fallen; a few still glowed around the tree roots, amidst dry brok which crackled underfoot and smelled like woodsmoke. The air remained warm but no gleam was left on the sunset horizon.

"Farewell, fare lucky," the pook called. Mistherd and Shadow-of-a-Dream never looked back. It was as if they didn't dare. They trudged on out of sight, toward the human camp whose lights made a harsh new star in the south.

Ayoch lingered. He felt he should also offer good-bye to her who had lately joined him that slept in the dolmen. Likely none would meet here again for loving or magic. But he could only think of one old verse that might do. He stood and trilled:

> "Out of her breast
> a blossom ascended.
> The summer burned it.
> The song is ended."

Then he spread his wings for the long flight away.

STEPHEN GOLDIN

The Last Ghost

STEPHEN GOLDIN was born February 28, 1947, in Philadelphia, Pennsylvania. He began writing at the age of thirteen and first sold a story when he was eighteen. He received his bachelor's degree in astronomy from UCLA in 1968 and then was employed for almost three years as a physicist/space scientist for Navy Space Systems. He left the Navy's employment to become, in his words, "a full-time, starving writer." He is a member of Science Fiction Writers of America, World Future Society, Astronomical Society of the Pacific, and the SFWA Speakers' Bureau. His hobby is zookeeping, and the current inventory of his ménage lists cats, mice, chipmunks, fish, snakes, a rat, an iguana, a chameleon, a land crab, a hamster, a parrot and an alligator.

Goldin edited the forthcoming collection *The Alien Condition,* and he assisted editor David Gerrold with the collections *Protostars* and *Generation.* He has two novels in progress.

His short story "Sweet Dreams, Melissa," concerning a new-generation computer brought up to think it's a little girl, was anthologized in *Best SF: 1968,* edited by Harry Harrison and Brian Aldiss, and also in *The Eleventh Galaxy Reader,* edited by Frederik Pohl.

"The Last Ghost" was a finalist in the balloting for the 1971 Nebula

Awards. It is a reminder that the ultimate loneliness is not the experience of the last man alive, but the last man dead.

Eternity is a terrible place to endure alone.

He is the last of his kind, if he is a "he." (Gender is an arbitrary difference. All things are eventually the same—and in eternity, eventually equals always.) He must once have had a name, a handle to his soul, but that was back before the eternity/instant when he had existed in corporeal form. He tries to think about things as he had known them, and finds he can't. He tries to think about things as they are, and finds he can't quite manage that, either. The will-be is far beyond his powers of contemplation.

He exists (if that's the word) in an everlasting now, as a state of nothingness less substantial than a vacuum, smaller than infinity, larger than thought. Eternity lies as far behind him as it does ahead. He drifts through this lack of anything at infinitely greater than no speed at all. He sees with non-eyes. He hears without ears. He thinks thoughtless thoughts that revolve in circles and make little eddies of emptiness in the not-quite-nothing of his mind.

He searches for
He wants a
He desires some
He loves to

No objects remain within his mental grasp. The words have been corroded by the gentle acid of time. All that's left is the search; the want; the desire; the love.

She began to appear slowly, a flicker at the limits of his nonperception. (Why he considered her a "she" could not be explained. There was just an aspect about her that was complementary to him.) His unthoughts raced in puzzlement. She was a newness in his stale cosmos, where nothing ever changed. He watched her as she took on a form even less substantial than his own. He watched with his crumbling mind at a crossroad, afraid to approach, even more afraid to run from her in fear. (If, that is, there were anyplace to run in eternity.)

She gained awareness suddenly, and started at the alien strangeness of her new environment. The eerie infinitude produced within her a wave of awe commingled with fear. She could, as yet, perceive only herself and the barren continuum around her.

She spoke. (What came out was not sound, but could be interpreted as communication.) "Where am I?"

The action was a simple one. It seemed utterly new to him, but down somewhere among the shards of his memory it was all tantalizingly familiar. He trembled.

She perceived his being, and turned her attention toward him. "What are you? What's happened to me?"

He knew the answers—or rather, he had known them. As it had with everything else, infinity had eaten away at these chunks of information too in what was left of his mind. It had all been so important once. So important! That was why he was what he was, and why he wasn't what he wasn't.

"Please!" she begged him. Hysteria edged her voice. "Tell me!"

Through mists that swirled down dusty corridors of memory, the words came out unbidden. "You are dead."

"No! That's impossible! I can't be!"

Loud silence.

"I can't be," she repeated. "Death was conquered more than five thousand years ago. After our minds were transferred into computer banks, we became immortal. Our bodies may fail, but our minds go on. Nobody dies anymore...." Her voice trailed off.

"You are dead," he repeated emotionlessly.

"Are ... are you a ghost?" she asked.

Though the meaning of the word had been stolen from him, that shred of identity remained: "Yes."

She brooded, and large quantities of non-time elapsed. He waited. He became accustomed to her existence. No longer was she an alien thing in his empty universe. She was now a half presence, and he accepted her as he had come to accept everything else—without comment.

"I suppose," she said at last, "some sort of equipment failure might have temporarily dislodged my personality pattern from the memory banks. But only temporarily. I'm only half dead so far. As soon as the trouble is fixed, I'll be all right again. I will be all right, won't I?"

He didn't answer. He knew nothing about equipment failures —or had forgotten if he ever had known.

"Equipment failures are supposed to be impossible," she prattled on, trying desperately to convince herself that her comfortable reality would return again. "Still, in thousands of years even a trillion-to-one shot might happen. But they'll fix it soon. They've got to. They must. Won't they? *Won't they?*"

She stared at her impassive companion with non-eyes widened by panic. "Don't just stand there! Help me!"

Help. That word found a niche somewhere in the haunted cavern of his mind. He was supposed to help . . . to help . . .

The who, or what, or how he was supposed to help eluded him. That is, if he had ever known.

They drifted on through the void together, side by side, ghost and almost-ghost. The unthoughts of the elder spirit were tangled more than usual, owing to the presence of another after such a lonely period of timelessness. But it was not a bad tangle; in fact, it was rather nice to share the universe with someone else again. She was a pleasant aura beside him in an otherwise insensate world.

They had both existed for over five thousand years. He was undoubtedly the older of the pair; but the real difference between them was that, while he had existed alone for so long that solitude had nibbled away at his Swiss cheese mind, she had lived those centuries with other people, other minds—a situation that either cracks one completely or produces near-total stability. The latter was the case with her, and so eventually her initial panic subsided and the clinical attitude she had held for thousands of years returned.

"Well, it appears I'm going to be here for a while, so I might as well get acquainted with this place. And since you're the only thing around, I'll start with you. Who are you?"

"Dead."

"Obviously." Her non-voice managed to handle even sarcasm nicely. "But don't you have some kind of a name?"

"No."

"Just for a moment she lost her patience. "That's impossible, Gabby. You must have had a name sometime. What was it?"

"I don't . . . I don't . . . I don't . . ." His broken-record attempt to answer was so pathetic that it touched the maternal instincts that she had thought long-dead within her.

"I'm sorry," she said a bit more tenderly. "Let's talk about something else. Where are we?"

"We are . . ."

"Dead," she finished with him. *Oh Lord, help me have patience with him. He's worse than a child.* "Yes, I know that. But I mean our physical location. Does it have a name?"

"No."

Stymied again. Her companion was obviously not inclined to conversation, but her analytical mind felt an urgent need to talk, to try to hold on to her sanity under such adverse conditions. "'All right, then, if you don't want to talk, do you mind if I do?"

"No."

So she did. She told him about her earliest life, when she had had a body, and about the things she had done and the children she had had. She spoke of the mind-transferral breakthrough that had finally enabled Man to conquer Death. She told him about the first thousand or so years she had spent in the computer bank when, exhilarated by the thrill of immortality, she had occupied animated robot bodies and engaged in "Death-defying" sports and exciting activities. And she related how even this had paled with time, and how she had passed into the current, mature phase of her life, the search for knowledge and wisdom. She told how ships had been built to take these computerized people to the stars, and what strange and wonderful things they had found there.

He listened. Most of it was incomprehensible to him, for the words were either unfamiliar or forgotten. His sievelike mind retained very little of what she said. But he listened, and that was important. He soaked in the experience, the thrill, of another pseudobeing communicating with him.

At last she paused, unable to think of anything else to say. "Would you like to talk now?" she asked.

Something burned within him. "Yes."

"Good," she said. "What would you like to talk about?"

He tried hard to think of something, anything, but once again his brain failed him.

She sensed his difficulty. "Tell me something about yourself," she prompted.

"I am dead."

"Yes, I know that. But what else?"

He thought. What was "himself" that he could tell something about?

"I search for

"I want a

"I desire some

"I love to . . ."

"What, what, what, what?" she insisted. But there was no answer. Frustrated, she continued. "Let's try something else. Does . . . did everyone who died become a ghost like you?"

"Yes."

"Where are they all, then?"

"Gone."

"Gone where?"

"Away."

Almost, she lost her patience again, but her millennia of training saved her. "They *all* went away?"

"Yes."

"All except you?"

"Yes."

"How long has it been?"

"Long."

She hadn't felt closer to crying in nearly five thousand years, both out of sympathy for this pathetic creature and frustration at being unable to solve his riddle. "Why didn't you go with them?"

"I . . . I was left behind."

"Why?"

His answer came much more slowly this time, dredged from the silt at the bottom of his pool of consciousness. "To . . . to . . . to point the way for Those Who Follow."

"You're a guide, then?" she asked incredulously.

"Yes."

"To where?"

"To . . . to . . . away."

"Can you show me where?"

For the first time, sadness was in his voice. "No."

Slowly, very slowly, using all the powers of patience and logical reasoning she had developed over the centuries, she extracted from him the pieces necessary to complete the puzzle. Long ago (how long was indeterminate; time has no meaning in eternity), the ghosts had discovered a new and higher level of existence. All of them had gone over to this new evolutionary state; all except one. One last ghost to show the way up for all the new ghosts who would be coming along.

Only, the mind-transferral breakthrough had changed all that. Suddenly, there were no new ghosts. And the last ghost was left alone. Duty confined him to ghostdom, and solitude condemned him to stagnation.

Her pity exploded like a pink nova, even while some analytical portion of her mind noted that the maternal instinct does not fade through disuse. She cradled his pathetic non-being deep within her own shadowy self and whispered words of tender concern.

And suddenly he felt warm with a glow he hadn't felt in eons. His null senses tingled deliciously with the nearness of this glorious other. Happily, he nestled himself against her.

A shock ripped through her. And another. And another. "Oh dear. They're repairing the equipment failure. Soon they'll be fixing the memory circuit, and I'll go back to being alive again."

In the sad stillness that followed, he uttered one word. "Don't."

She was startled. This was the first time he had initiated a thought, the first time he had expressed a preference for something. "What did you say?"

"Don't be alive."

"Why not?"

"I need"

"What?" She could feel herself beginning to fade from this non-place.

"I need"

"Yes? Tell me. Tell me what you need."

"I need"

"*What?*" She was fading quickly. "I don't have much time left here. Please, tell me what!"

"I need"

She disappeared forever from his non-universe, without a trace.

The last ghost wanders. He is a signpost with nowhere to point. He is a guide with no one to lead. So he drifts on with an empty mind and a half-forgotten, unfulfillable purpose. And occasionally:

I NEED
I NEED
I NEED

As always, the object eludes him.

KATE WILHELM

The Encounter

KATE WILHELM was born June 8, 1929, in Toledo, Ohio. She sold her first story in 1957, and she has been writing and selling steadily ever since. It is fashionable to say of our feminine celebrities, "In real life she is Mrs. John Blank." Kate Wilhelm is married to author, editor and critic Damon Knight, which makes her Mrs. Damon Knight; but in real life she is Kate Wilhelm, her husband and three sons notwithstanding, and her individuality is as distinctive as her writing.

A Charter Member of Science Fiction Writers of America, she provided the original sketch from which the Nebula Award Trophy was designed. She was codirector of the Milford Science Fiction Writers' Conference from 1963 to 1969 and lecturer at the Clarion Writers' Workshop from 1969 to 1972.

In addition to magazine appearances she has contributed stories to Volumes 1 through 12 of the *Orbit* series. She has had two collections of short stories published, *The Mile Long Spaceship* (1963) and *The Downstairs Room* (1968). *More Bitter than Death* (1962) is a mystery novel. Her four science fiction novels are *The Killer Thing* (1965), *The Nevermore Affair* (1967), *Let the Fire Fall* (1969), and *Margaret and I* (1971). Two more science fiction novels were written in collaboration with Ted Thomas: *The Clone* (1965), and *The Year of the Cloud*

(1970). *Abyss* (1971) contains two novellas, "The Plastic Abyss" and "Stranger in the House."

She has been a Nebula Awards finalist four of the seven years the awards have been presented. Her story "The Planners" received the Nebula Award as the best short story of 1968, and in the 1971 balloting her name appeared on the final ballot a record four times: with her novel *Margaret and I;* with her novellas "The Infinity Box" and "The Plastic Abyss"; and with her novelette "The Encounter."

The bus slid to an uneasy stop, two hours late. Snow was eight inches deep, and the white sky met the white ground in a strange world where the grubby black bus station floated free. It was a world where up and down had become meaningless, where the snow fell horizontally. Crane, supported by the wind and the snow, could have entered the station by walking up the wall, or across the ceiling. His mind seemed adrift, out of touch with the reality of his body. He stamped, scattering snow, bringing some feeling back to his legs, making himself feel the floor beneath his feet. He tried to feel his cheek, to see if he was feverish, but his hands were too numb, his cheek too numb. The heating system of the bus had failed over an hour ago.

The trouble was that he had not dressed for such weather. An overcoat, but no boots, no fur-lined gloves, no woolen scarf to wind and wind about his throat. He stamped and clapped his hands. Others were doing the same.

There had been only nine or ten people on the bus, and some of them were being greeted by others or were slipping out into the storm, home finally or near enough now. The bus driver was talking to an old man who had been in the station when they arrived, the ticket agent, probably. He was wearing two sweaters, one a heavy, hip-length green that looked home-knit; under it, a turtleneck gray wool with too-long sleeves that hung from beneath the green sleeves. He had on furry boots that came to his knees, with his sagging pants tucked tightly into them. Beyond him, tossed over one of the wooden benches, was a greatcoat, fleece-lined, long enough to hang to his boot tops. Fleecy gloves bulged from one of the pockets.

"Folks," he said, turning away from the bus driver, "there won't be another bus until sometime in the morning, when they get the roads plowed out some. There's an all-night diner down the road, three, four blocks. Not much else in town's open this time of night."

"Is there a hotel?" A woman, fur coat, shiny patent boots, kid gloves. She had got on at the same station that Crane had; he remembered the whiff of expensive perfume as she had passed him.

"There's the Laughton Inn, ma'am, but it's two miles outsida town and there's no way to get there."

"Oh, for God's sake! You mean this crummy burg doesn't even have a hotel of its own?"

"Four of them, in fact, but they're closed, open again in April. Don't get many people to stay overnight in the wintertimes."

"Okay, okay. Which way's the diner?" She swept a disapproving glance over the bleak station and went to the door, carrying an overnight bag with her.

"Come on, honey, I'm going there, too," the driver said. He pulled on gloves and turned up his collar. He took her arm firmly, transferred the bag to his other hand, then turned to look at the other three or four people in the station. "Anyone else?"

Diner. Glaring lights, jukebox noise without end, the smell of hamburgers and onions, rank coffee and doughnuts saturated with grease. Everyone smoking. Someone would have cards probably, someone a bottle. The woman would sing or cry, or get a fight going. She was a nasty one, he could tell. She'd be bored within an hour. She'd have the guys groping her under the table, in the end booth. The man half turned, his back shielding her from view, his hand slipping between her buttons, under the blouse, under the slip, the slippery smooth nylon, the tightness of the bra, unfastening it with his other hand. Her low laugh, busy hands. The hard nipple between his fingers now, his own responsive hardness. She had turned to look at the stranded passengers when the driver spoke, and she caught Crane's glance.

"It's a long wait for a Scranton bus, honey," she said.

"I'd just get soaked going to the diner," Crane said, and turned his back on her. His hand hurt, and he opened his clenched fingers and rubbed his hands together hard.

"I sure as hell don't want to wait all night in this rat hole," someone else said. "Do you have lockers? I can't carry all this gear."

"Lock them up in the office for you," the ticket agent said. He pulled out a bunch of keys and opened a door at the end of the room. A heavy-set man followed him, carrying three suitcases. They returned; the door squeaked. The agent locked it again.

"Now, you boys will hold me up, won't you? I don't want to fall down in all that snow."

"Doll, if you fall on your pretty little ass, I'll dry you off personally," the driver said.

"Oh, you will, will you?"

Crane tightened his jaw, trying not to hear them. The outside door opened and a blast of frigid air shook the room. A curtain of snow swept across the floor before the door banged again, and the laughing voices were gone.

"You sure you want to wait here?" the ticket agent asked. "Not very warm in here. And I'm going home in a minute, you know."

"I'm not dressed to walk across the street in this weather, much less four blocks," Crane said.

The agent still hesitated, one hand on his coat. He looked around, as if checking on loose valuables. There was a woman on one of the benches. She was sitting with her head lowered, hands in her lap, legs crossed at the ankles. She wore a dark cloth coat, and her shoes were skimpier than Crane's, three crossing strips of leather attached to paper-thin soles. Black cloth gloves hid her hands. She didn't look up, in the silence that followed, while the two men scrutinized her. It was impossible to guess her age in that pose, with only the dark clothes to go by.

"Ma'am, are you all right?" the agent asked finally.

"Yes, of course. Like the gentleman, I didn't care to wade through the snow. I can wait here."

She raised her head and with a touch of disappointment Crane saw that she was as nondescript as her clothing. When he stopped looking at her, he couldn't remember what she looked like. A woman. Thirty. Thirty-five. Forty. He didn't know. And yet. There was something vaguely familiar about her, as if he should remember her, as if he might have seen her or met her at one time or another. He had a very good memory for faces and names, an invaluable asset for a salesman, and he searched his memory for this woman and came up with nothing.

"Don't you have nothing with you that you could change into?" the agent asked peevishly. "You'd be more comfortable down at the diner."

"I don't have anything but some work with me," she said. Her voice was very patient. "I thought I'd be in the city before the storm came. Late bus, early storm. I'll be fine here."

Again his eyes swept through the dingy room, searching for something to say, not finding anything. He began to pull on his coat, and he seemed to gain forty pounds. "Telephone under the counter, back there," he said finally. "Pay phone's outside under a drift, I reckon."

"Thank you," she said.

The agent continued to dawdle. He pulled on his gloves, checked the rest rooms to make sure the doors were not locked, that the lights worked. He peered at a thermostat, muttering that you couldn't believe what it said anyways. At the door he stopped once more. He looked like a walking heap of outdoor garments, a clothes pile that had swallowed a man. "Mr.—uh—"

"Crane. Randolph Crane. Manhattan."

"Uh, yes. Mr. Crane, I'll tell the troopers that you two are up here. And the road boys. Plow'll be out soon's it lets up some.

They'll keep an eye open for you, if you need anything. Maybe drop in with some coffee later on."

"Great," Crane said. "That'd be great."

"Okay, then. I wouldn't wander out if I was you. See you in the morning, then. Night."

The icy blast and the inrushing snow made Crane start to shake again. He looked over at the woman, who was huddling down, trying to wrap herself up in the skimpy coat.

His shivering eased and he sat down and opened his briefcase and pulled out one of the policies he had taken along to study. This was the first time he had touched it. He hoped the woman would fall asleep and stay asleep until the bus came in the morning. He knew that he wouldn't be able to stretch out on the short benches, not that it would matter anyway. He wasn't the type to relax enough to fall asleep anywhere but in bed.

He stared at the policy, a twenty-year endowment, two years to go to maturity, on the life of William Sanders, age twenty-two. He held it higher, trying to catch the light, but the print was a blur; all he could make out were the headings of the clauses, and these he already knew by heart. He turned the policy over; it was the same on the back, the old familiar print, and the rest a blur. He started to refold the paper to return it to the briefcase. She would think he was crazy, taking it out, looking at it a moment, turning it this way and that, and then putting it back. He pursed his lips and pretended to read.

Sanders, Sanders. What did he want? Four policies, the endowment, a health and accident, a straight life, and mortgage policy. Covered, protected. Insurance-poor, Sanders had said, throwing the bulky envelope onto Crane's desk. "Consolidate these things somehow. I want cash if I can get it, and out from under the rest."

"But what about your wife, the kids?"

"Ex-wife. If I go, she'll manage. Let her carry insurance on me."

Crane had been as persuasive as he knew how to be, and in the end he had had to promise to assess the policies, to have figures to show cash values, and so on. Disapprovingly, of course.

"You know, dear, you really are getting more stuffy every day," Mary Louise said.

"And if he dies, and his children are left destitute, then will I be so stuffy?"

"I'd rather have the seven hundred dollars myself than see it go to your company year after year."

"That's pretty shortsighted."

"Are you really going to wear that suit to Maggie's party?"

"Changing the subject?"

"Why not? You know what you think, and I know what I think, and they aren't even within hailing distance of each other."

Mary Louise wore a red velvet gown that was slit to her navel, molded just beneath her breasts by a silver chain, and almost completely bare in the back, down to the curve of her buttocks. The silver chain cut into her tanned back slightly. Crane stared at it.

"New?"

"Yes. I picked it up last week. Pretty?"

"Indecent. I didn't know it was a formal thing tonight."

"Not really. Optional anyway. Some of us decided to dress, that's all." She looked at him in the mirror and said, "I really don't care if you want to wear that suit."

Wordlessly he turned and went back to the closet to find his dinner jacket and black trousers. How easy it would be, a flick of a chain latch, and she'd be stripped to her hips. Was she counting on someone's noticing that? Evers maybe? Or Olivetti! Olivetti? What had he said? Something about women who wore red in public. Like passing out a dance card and pencil, the promise implicit in the gesture?

"Slut!" he said, through teeth so tightly pressed together that his jaws ached.

"What? I'm sorry."

He looked up. The woman in the bus station was watching him across the aisle. She still looked quite cold.

"I am sorry," she said softly. "I thought you spoke."

"No." He stuffed the policy back in his case and fastened it. "Are you warm enough?"

"Not really. The ticket agent wasn't kidding when he said the thermostat lies. According to it, it's seventy-four in here."

Crane got up and looked at the thermostat. The adjustment control was gone. The station was abysmally cold. He walked back and forth for a few moments, then paused at the window. The white world, ebbing and growing, changing, changeless. "If I had a cup or something, I could bring in some snow and chill the thermostat. That might make the heat kick on."

"Maybe in the rest room . . . " He heard her move across the floor, but he didn't turn to look. There was a pink glow now in the whiteness, like a fire in the distance, all but obscured by the intervening clouds of snow. He watched as it grew brighter, darker, almost red; then it went out. The woman returned and stood at his side.

"No cups, but I folded paper towels to make a funnel thing. Will it do?"

He took the funnel. It was sturdy enough, three thicknesses of brown, unabsorbent toweling. "Probably better than a cup," he said. "Best stand behind the door. Every time it opens, that blizzard comes right on in."

She nodded and moved away. When he opened the door the wind hit him hard, almost knocking him back into the room, wrenching the door from his hand. It swung wide open and hit the woman. Distantly he heard her gasp of surprise and pain. He reached out and scooped up a funnel full of snow and then pushed the door closed again. He was covered with snow. Breathless, he leaned against the wall. "Are you all right?" he asked after a few moments.

She was holding her left shoulder. "Yes. It caught me by surprise. No harm done. Did you get enough snow?"

He held up the funnel for her to see and then pushed himself away from the wall. Again he had the impression that there was no right side up in the small station. He held the back of one of the benches and moved along it. "The wind took my breath away," he said.

"Or the intense cold. I think I read that breathing in the cold causes as many heart attacks as overexertion."

"Well, it's cold enough out there. About zero by now, I guess." He scooped out some of the snow and held it against the thermostat. "The furnace must be behind this wall, or under this area. Feel how warm it is."

She put her hand on the wall and nodded. "Maybe we can fasten the cup of snow up next to the termostat." She looked around and then went to the bulletin board. She removed several of the notices and schedules there and brought him the thumbtacks. Crane spilled a little snow getting the tacks into the paper towel and then into the wall. In a few minutes there was a rumble as the furnace came on and almost immediately the station began to feel slightly warmer. Presently the woman took off her coat.

"Success," she said, smiling.

"I was beginning to think it had been a mistake after all, not going to the diner."

"So was I."

"I think they are trying to get the snowplows going. I saw a red light a couple of minutes ago. It went out again, but at least someone's trying."

She didn't reply, and after a moment he said, "I'm glad you don't smoke. I gave it up a few months ago, and it would drive me mad to have to smell it through a night like this. Probably I'd go back to them."

"I have some," she said. "I even smoke once in a while. If you decide that you do want them . . . "

"No. No. I wasn't hinting."

"I just wish the lights were better in here. I could get in a whole night's work. I often work at night."

"So do I, but you'd put your eyes out. What—"

"That's all right. What kind of work do I do? An illustrator for Slocum House Catalogue Company. Not very exciting, I'm afraid."

"Oh, you're an artist."

"No. Illustrator. I wanted to become an artist, but . . . things didn't work out that way."

"I'd call you an artist. Maybe because I'm in awe of anyone who can draw, or paint, or do things like that. You're all artists to me."

She shrugged. "And you're an insurance salesman." He stiffened and she got up, saying, "I saw the policy you were looking over, and the briefcase stuffed full of policies and company pamphlets and such. I knew an insurance salesman once."

He realized that he had been about to ask where she was going, and he clamped his jaw again and turned so that he wouldn't watch her go into the ladies' room.

He went to the window. The wind was still at gale force, but so silent. With the door closed, the station seemed far removed from the storm, and looking at it was like watching something wholly unreal, manufactured to amuse him perhaps. There were storm windows, and the building was very sturdy and probably very well insulated. Now, with the furnace working, it was snug and secure. He cupped his hands about his eyes, trying to see past the reflections in the window, but there was nothing. Snow, a drift up to the sill now, and the wind-driven snow that was like a sheer curtain being waved from above, touching the windows, fluttering back, touching again, hiding everything behind it.

She was taking a long time. He should have gone when she left. Now he had the awkward moment to face, of excusing himself or not, of timing it so that she wouldn't think he was leaving deliberately in order to dodge something that one or the other said or hinted. She had done it so easily and naturally. He envied people like her. Always so sure of themselves.

"Which face are you wearing tonight, Randy?" Mary Louise reached across the table and touched his cheek, then shook her head. "I can't always tell. When you're the successful salesman, you are so assured, so poised, charming, voluble even."

"And the other times? What am I those times?"

"Afraid."

Drawing back from her hand, tight and self-contained again, watchful, he said, "Isn't it lucky that I can keep the two separated, then? How successful a salesman would I be if I put on the wrong face when I went to work?"

"I wonder if mixing it up a little might not be good for you. So you wouldn't sell a million dollars' worth of insurance a year, but you'd be a little happier when you're not working."

"Like you?"

"Not like me, God forbid. But at least I haven't given up looking for something. And you have."

"Yeah. You're looking. In a bottle. In someone else's bed. In buying sprees."

"*C'est la vie.* You can always buzz off, you know."

"And add alimony to my other headaches? No, thanks."

Smiling at him, sipping an Old Fashioned, infinitely wise and infinitely evil. Were wise women always evil? "My poor Randy. My poor darling. You thought I was everything you were not, and instead you find that I am stamped from the same mold. Number XLM 119543872—afraid of life, only not quite afraid of death. Someone let up on the pressure there. Hardly an indentation even. So I can lose myself and you can't. A pity, my darling Randy. If we could lose ourselves together, what might we be able to find? We are so good together, you know. Sex with you is still the best of all. I try harder and harder to make you let go all the way. I read manuals and take personalized lessons, all for your sake, darling. All for you. And it does no good. You are my only challenge, you see."

"Stop it! Are you crazy?"

"Ah. Now I know who you are tonight. There you are. Tight mouth, frowning forehead full of lines, narrowed eyes. You are not so handsome with this face on, you know. Why don't you look at me, Randy?" Her hands across the table again, touching his cheeks, a finger trailing across his lips, a caress or mockery. "You never look at me, you know. You never look at me at all."

He leaned his forehead against the window, and the chill roused

him. Where was the woman? He looked at his watch and realized
that she had been gone only a few minutes, not the half hour or
longer that he had thought. Was the whole night going to be like
that? Minutes dragging by like hours? Time distorted until a lifetime could be spent in waiting for one dawn?

He went to the men's room. When he returned, she was sitting
in her own place once more, her coat thrown over her shoulders,
a sketch pad in her lap.

"Are you cold again?" He felt almost frozen. There was no heat
in the men's room.

"Not really. Moving about chilled me. There's a puddle under
the funnel, and the snow is gone, but heat is still coming from the
radiator."

"I'll have to refill it every half hour or so, I guess."

"The driver said it's supposed to go to ten or fifteen below
tonight."

Crane shrugged. "After it gets this low, I don't care how much
farther it drops. As long as I don't have to be out in it."

She turned her attention to her pad and began to make strong
lines. He couldn't tell what she was drawing, only that she didn't
hesitate, but drew surely, confidently. He opened his briefcase and
got out his schedule book. It was no use, he couldn't read the small
print in the poor lighting of the station. He rummaged for something that he would be able to concentrate on. He was grateful
when she spoke again.

"It was so stupid to start out tonight. I could have waited until
tomorrow. I'm not bound by a time clock or anything."

"That's just what I was thinking. I was afraid of being snowed
in for several days. We were at Sky Mount Ski Lodge, and everyone else was cheering the storm's approach. Do you ski?"

"Some, not very well. The cold takes my breath away, hitting
me in the face like that."

He stared at her for a moment, opened his mouth to agree, then
closed it again. It was as if she was anticipating what he was going
to say.

"Don't be so silly, Randy. All you have to do is wear the muffler around your mouth and nose. And the goggles on your eyes. Nothing is exposed then. You're just too lazy to ski."

"Okay, lazy. I know this—I'm bored to death here. I haven't been warm since we left the apartment, and my legs ache. That was a nasty fall I had this morning. I'm sore. I have a headache from the glare of the snow, and I think it's asinine to freeze for two hours in order to slide down a mountain a couple of times. I'm going back to the city."

"But our reservation is through Saturday night. Paid in advance."

"Stay. Be my guest. Have yourself a ball. You and McCone make a good pair, and his wife seems content to sit on the sidelines and watch you. Did you really think that anemic blonde would appeal to me? Did you think we'd be too busy together to notice what you were up to?"

"Tracy? To tell the truth I hadn't given her a thought. I didn't know she didn't ski until this afternoon. I don't know why Mac brought her here. Any more than I know why you came along."

"Come on home with me. Let's pack up and leave before the storm begins. We can stop at that nice old antique inn on the way home, where they always have pheasant pie. Remember?"

"Darling, I came to ski. You will leave the car here, won't you? I'll need it to get the skis back home, and our gear. Isn't there a bus or something?"

"Mary Louise, this morning on the slope, didn't you really see me? You know, when your ski pole got away from you."

"What in the world are you talking about? You were behind me. How could I have seen you? I didn't even know you had started down."

"Okay. Forget it. I'll give you a call when I get to the apartment."

"Yes, do. You can leave a message at the desk if I don't answer."

The woman held up her sketch and narrowed her eyes. She ripped out the page and crumpled it, tossed it into the wastecan.

"I think I'm too tired after all."

"It's getting cold in here again. Your hands are probably too cold." He got up and took the funnel from the wall. "I'll get more snow and see if we can't get the furnace going again."

"You should put something over your face, so the cold air won't be such a shock. Don't you have a muffler?"

He stopped. He had crushed the funnel, he realized, and he tried to smooth it again without letting her see what he had done. He decided that it would do, and opened the door. A drift had formed, and a foot of snow fell into the station. The wind was colder, sharper, almost deliberately cutting. He was blinded by the wind and the snow that was driven into his face. He filled the funnel and tried to close the door again, but the drift was in the way. He pushed, trying to use the door as a snowplow. More snow was being blown in, and finally he had to use his hands, push the snow out of the way, not outside, but to one side of the door. At last he had it clear enough and he slammed the door, more winded this time than before. His throat felt raw, and he felt a constriction about his chest.

"It's getting worse all the time. I couldn't even see the bus, nothing but a mountain of snow."

"Ground blizzard, I suspect. When it blows like this you can't tell how much of it is new snow and how much is just fallen snow being blown about. The drifts will be tremendous tomorrow." She smiled. "I remember how we loved it when this happened when we were kids. The drifts are exciting, so pure, so high. Sometimes they glaze over and you can play Glass Mountain. I used to be the princess."

Crane was shivering again. He forced his hands to be steady as he pushed the thumbtacks into the funnel to hold it in place next to the thermostat. He had to clear his throat before he could speak. "Did the prince ever reach you?"

"No. Eventually I just slid back down and went home."

"Where? Where did you live?"

"Outside Chicago, near the lake."

He spun around. "Who are you?" He grabbed the back of a bench and clutched it hard. She stared at him. He had screamed at her, and he didn't know why. "I'm sorry," he said. "You keep saying things that I'm thinking. I was thinking of that game, of how I never could make it to the top."

"Near Lake Michigan?"

"On the shores almost."

She nodded.

"I guess all kids play games like that in the snow," he said. "Strange that we should have come from the same general area. Did your milk freeze on the back steps, stick up out of the bottle, with the cap at an angle?"

"Yes. And those awful cloakrooms at school, where you had to strip off snowsuits and boots, and step in icy water before you could get your indoors shoes on."

"And sloshing through the thaws, wet every damn day. I was wet more than I was dry all through grade school."

"We all were," she said, smiling faintly, looking past him.

He almost laughed in his relief. He went to the radiator and put his hands out over it, his back to her. Similar backgrounds, that's all, he said to himself, framing the words carefully. Nothing strange. Nothing eerie. She was just a plain woman who came from the same state, probably the same county that he came from. They might have gone to the same schools, and he would not have noticed her. She was too common, too nondescript to have noticed at the time. And he had been a quiet boy, not particularly noteworthy himself. No sports besides the required ones. No clubs. A few friends, but even there, below average, because they had lived in an area too far removed from most of the kids who went to his school.

"It's only two. Seems like it ought to be morning already, doesn't it?" She was moving about and he turned to see what she was doing. She had gone behind the counter, where the ticket agent had said there was a telephone. "A foam cushion," she said, holding it up. "I feel like one of the Swiss Family Robinson, salvaging what might be useful."

"Too bad there isn't some coffee under there."

"Wish you were in the diner?"

"No. That bitch probably has them all at each other's throats by now, as it is."

"That girl? The one who was so afraid?"

He laughed harshly and sat down. "Girl!"

"No more than twenty, if that much."

He laughed again and shook his head.

"Describe her to me," the woman said. She left the counter and sat down on the bench opposite him, still carrying the foam cushion. It had a black plastic cover; gray foam bulged from a crack. It was disgusting.

Crane said, "The broad was in her late twenties, or possibly thirties—"

"Eighteen to twenty."

"She had a pound of makeup on, nails like a cat."

"Fake nails, chapped hands, calluses. Ten-cent-store makeup."

"She had expensive perfume, and a beaver coat. I think beaver."

She laughed gently. "Drugstore spray cologne. Macy's Basement fake fur, about fifty-nine to sixty-five dollars, unless she hit a sale."

"And the kid gloves, and the high patent leather boots?"

"Vinyl, both of them." She looked at him for an uncomfortable minute, then examined the pillow she had found. "On second thought, I'm not sure that I would want to rest my head on this. It's a little bit disgusting, isn't it?"

"Why did you want me to describe that woman? You have your opinion of what she is; I have mine. There's no way to prove either of our cases without having her before us."

"I don't need to prove anything. I don't care if you think you're right and I'm wrong. I felt very sorry for the girl. I noticed her."

"I noticed her, too."

"What color was her hair, her eyes? How about her mouth—big, small, full? And her nose? Straight, snub, broad?"

He regarded her bitterly for a moment, then shrugged and turned toward the window. He didn't speak.

"You can't describe what she really was like because you didn't see her. You saw the package and made up your mind about the contents. Believe me, she was terrified of the storm, of those men, everything. She needed the security of the driver and people. What about me? Can you describe me?"

He looked, but she was holding the pillow between them and he could see only her hands, long, pale, slender fingers, no rings.

"This is ridiculous," he said after a second. "I have one of those reputations for names and faces. You know, never forget a name, always know the names of the kids, the wife, occupation and so on."

"Not this side of you. This side refuses to see anyone at all. I wonder why."

"What face are you wearing tonight, Randy?" Mary Louise touching him. "Do you see me? Why don't you look at me?"

Wind whistling past his ears, not really cold yet, not when he was standing still anyway, with the sun warm on him. But racing down the slope, trees to his right, the precipice to his left, the wind was icy. Mary Louise a red streak ahead of him, and somewhere behind him the navy and white blur that was McCone. Holding his own between them. The curve of the trail ahead, the thrill of the downward plummet, and suddenly the open-mouthed face of his wife, silent scream, and in the same instant, the ski pole against his legs, tripping him up, the more exciting plunge downward, face in the snow, blinded, over and over, skis gone now, trying to grasp the snow, trying to stop the tumbling, over and over in the snow.

Had his wife tried to kill him?

"Are you all right, Mr. Crane?"

"Yes, of course. Let me describe the last man I sold insurance to, a week ago. Twenty-four, six feet one inch, a tiny, almost invisible scar over his right eyebrow, crinkle lines about his eyes, because he's an outdoor type, very tanned and muscular. He's a professional baseball player, incidentally. His left hand has larger knuckles than the right. . . ."

The woman was not listening. She had crossed the station and was standing at the window, trying to see out. "Computer talk," she said. "A meaningless rundown of facts. So he bought a policy for one hundred thousand dollars, straight life, and from now on you won't have to deal with him, be concerned with him at all."

"Why did you say one hundred thousand dollars?"

"No reason. I don't know, obviously."

He chewed his lip and watched her. "Any change out there?"

"Worse, if anything. I don't think you'll be able to use this door at all now. You'd never get it closed. It's half covered with a drift."

"There must be a window or another door that isn't drifted over."

"Storm windows. Maybe there's a back door, but I bet it opens to the office, and the ticket agent locked that."

Crane looked at the windows and found that she was right. The storm windows couldn't be opened from inside. And there wasn't another outside door. The men's room was like a freezer now. He tried to run the water, thinking that possibly cold water would work on the thermostat as well as snow, but nothing came out. The pipes must have frozen. As he started to close the door, he saw a small block-printed sign: "Don't close door all the way, no heat in here, water will freeze up." The toweling wouldn't hold water anyway.

He left the door open a crack and rejoined the woman near the window. "It's got to be this door," he said. "I guess I could open it an inch or two, let that much of the drift fall inside and use it."

"Maybe. But you'll have to be careful."

"Right out of Jack London," he said. "It's seventy-two on the thermometer. How do you feel?"

"Coolish, not bad."

"Okay, we'll wait awhile. Maybe the wind will let up."

He stared at the puddle under the thermostat, and at the other larger one across the room near the door, where the snowdrift had entered the room the last time. The drift had been only a foot high then, and now it was three or four feet. Could he move that much snow without anything to work with, if it came inside?

He shouldn't have started back to town. She had goaded him into it, of course. Had she suspected that he would get stranded somewhere, maybe freeze to death?

"Why don't you come right out and say what you're thinking?" Red pants, red ski jacket, cheeks almost as red.

"I'm not thinking anything. It was an accident."

"You're a liar, Randy! You think I guessed you were there, that I let go hoping to make you fall. Isn't that what you think? Isn't it?"

He shook his head hard. She hadn't said any of that. He hadn't thought of it then. Only now, here, stranded with this half-mad woman. Half-mad? He looked at her and quickly averted his gaze. Why had that thought come to him? She was odd, certainly, probably very lonely, shy. But half-mad?

Why did she watch him so? As if aware of his thoughts, she turned her back and walked to the ladies' room. He had to go too, but he remembered the frozen pipes in the men's room. Maybe she'd fall asleep eventually and he'd be able to slip into her rest room. If not, then he'd wait until morning. Maybe this night had come about in order to give him time to think about him and Mary Louise, to really think it through all the way and come to a decision.

He had met her when he was stationed in Washington, after the Korean War. He had been a captain, assigned to Army Intelligence. She had worked as a private secretary to Senator Robertson of New York. So he had done all right without her up to then. She had introduced him to the president of the company that he worked for now. Knowing that he wanted to become a writer, she had almost forced him into insurance. Fine. It was the right choice. He had told her so a thousand times. But how he had succeeded was still a puzzle to him. He never had tested well on salesmanship on aptitude tests. Too introverted and shy.

"You make other people feel stupid, frankly," she had said once. "You are so tight and so sure of yourself that you don't allow anyone else to have an opinion at all. It's not empathy, like it is with so many good salesmen. It's a kind of sadistic force that you apply."

"Oh, stop it. You're talking nonsense."

"You treat each client like an extension of the policy that you intend to sell to him. Not like a person, but the human counterpart of the slick paper with the clauses and small print. You show the same respect and liking for them as for the policies. They go together. You believe it and make them believe it. Numbers, that's what they are to you. Policy numbers."

"Why do you hang around if you find me so cold and calculating?"

"Oh, it's a game that I play. I know there's a room somewhere where you've locked up part of yourself, and I keep searching for it. Someday I'll find it and open it just a crack, and then I'll run. Because if it ever opens, even a little, everything will come tumbling out and you won't be able to stop any of it. How you'll bleed then, bleed and bleed, and cry and moan. I couldn't stand that. And I can't stand for it not to be so."

Crane put his head down in his hands and rubbed his eyes hard. Without affect: that was the term that she used. Modern man without affect. Schizoid personality. But he also had a nearly split personality. The doctor had told him so. In the six sessions that he had gone to he had learned much of the jargon, and then he had broken it off. Split personality. Schizoid tendencies. Without affect. All to keep himself safe. It seemed to him to be real madness to take away any of the safeties he had painstakingly built, and he had quit the sessions.

And now this strange woman that he was locked up with was warning him not to open the door a crack. He rubbed his eyes harder until there was solid pain there. He had to touch her. The ticket agent had seen her, too, though. He had been concerned about leaving her alone with a strange man all night. So transparently worried about her, worried about Crane. Fishing for his name. He could have told the fool anything. He couldn't remember his face at all, only his clothes.

All right, the woman was real, but strange. She had an uncanny way of anticipating what he was thinking, what he was going to say, what he feared. Maybe these were her fears too.

She came back into the waiting room. She was wearing her black coat buttoned to her neck, her hands in the pockets. She didn't mention the cold.

Soon he would have to get more snow, trick the fool thermostat into turning on the furnace. Soon. A maniac must have put it on that wall, the only warm wall in the building. A penny-pinching maniac.

"If you decide to try to get more snow, maybe I should hold the door while you scoop it up," she said, after a long silence. The cold had made her face look pinched, and Crane was shivering under his overcoat.

"Can you hold it?" he asked. "There's a lot of pressure behind that door."

She nodded.

"Okay. I'll take the wastecan and get as much as I can. It'll keep in the men's room. There's no heat in there."

She held the doorknob until he was ready, and when he nodded, she turned it and, bracing the door with her shoulder, let it open several inches. The wind pushed, and the snow spilled through. It was over their heads now, and it came in the entire height of the door. She gave ground and the door was open five or six inches. Crane pulled the snow inside, using both hands, clawing at it. The Augean stable, he thought bitterly, and then joined her behind the door, trying to push it closed again. At least no blast of air had come inside this time. The door was packing the snow, and the inner surface of it was thawing slightly, only to refreeze under the pressure and the cold from the other side. Push, Crane thought at her. Push, you devil. You witch.

Slowly it began to move, scrunching snow. They weren't going to get it closed all the way. They stopped pushing to rest. He was panting hard, and she put her head against the door. After a moment he said, "Do you think you could move one of the benches over here?"

She nodded. He braced himself against the door and was surprised at the increase in the pressure when she left. He heard her wrestling with the bench, but he couldn't turn to see. The snow was gaining again. His feet were slipping on the floor, wet now where some of the snow had melted and was running across the room. He saw the bench from the corner of his eye, and he turned to watch her progress with it. She was pushing it toward him, the back to the wall; the back was too high. It would have to be tilted to go under the doorknob. It was a heavy oak bench. If they could maneuver it in place, it would hold.

For fifteen minutes they worked, grunting, saying nothing, trying to hold the door closed and get the bench under the knob without losing any more ground. Finally it was done. The door was open six inches, white packed snow the entire height of it.

Crane fell onto a bench and stared at the open door, not able to say anything. The woman seemed equally exhausted. At the top of the door, the snow suddenly fell forward, into the station, sifting at first, then falling in a stream. Icy wind followed the snow into the room, and now that the top of the column of snow had been lost, the wind continued to pour into the station, whistling shrilly.

"Well, we know now that the drift isn't really to the top of the building," the woman said wearily. She was staring at the opening.

"My words, almost exactly," Crane said. She always said what he planned to say. He waited.

"We'll have to close it at the top somehow."

He nodded. "In a minute. In a minute."

The cold increased and he knew that he should get busy and try to close the opening, but he felt too numb to cope with it. The furnace couldn't keep up with the draft of below-zero air. His hands were aching with cold, and his toes hurt with a stabbing intensity. Only his mind felt pleasantly numb and he didn't want to think about the problem of closing up the hole.

"You're not falling asleep, are you?"

"For God's sake!" He jerked straight up on the bench and gave her a mean look, a guilty look. "Just shut up and let me try to think, will you?"

"Sorry." She got up and began to pace briskly, hugging her hands to her body. "I'll look around, see if I can find anything that would fit. I simply can't sit still, I'm so cold."

He stared at the hole. There had to be something that would fit over it, stay in place, keep out the wind. He narrowed his eyes, staring, and he saw the wind-driven snow as a liquid running into the station from above, swirling about, only fractionally heavier than the medium that it met on the inside. One continuum, starting in the farthest blackest vacuum of space, taking on form as it reached the highest atmospheric molecules, becoming denser as it neared Earth, almost solid here, but not yet. Not yet. The hole extended to that unimaginable distance where it all began, and the chill spilled down, down, searching for him, wafting about here, searching for him, wanting only to find him, willing then to stop the ceaseless whirl. Coat him, claim him. The woman belonged to the coldness that came from the black of space. He remembered her now.

Korea. The woman. The village. Waiting for the signal. Colder than the station even, snow, flintlike ground, striking sparks from nails in boots, sparks without warmth. If they could fire the village, they would get warm, have food, sleep that night. Harrison, wounded, frozen where he fell. Lorenz, frostbitten; Jakobs, snowblind. Crane, too tired to think, too hungry to think, too cold to think. "Fire the village." The woman, out of nowhere, urging him back, back up the mountain to the bunkers that were half filled with ice, mines laid now between the bunkers and the valley. Ordering the woman into the village at gunpoint. Spark from his muzzle. Blessed fire and warmth. But a touch of ice behind the eyes, ice that didn't let him weep when Lorenz died, or when Jakobs, blinded, wandered out and twitched and jerked and pitched over a cliff under a fusillade of bullets. The snow queen, he thought. She's the snow queen, and she touched my eyes with ice.

"Mr. Crane, please wake up. Please!"

He jumped to his feet reaching for his carbine, and only when his hands closed on air did he remember where he was.

"Mr. Crane, I think I know what we can use to close up the hole. Let me show you."

She pulled at his arm and he followed her. She led him into the ladies' room. At the door he tried to pull back, but she tugged. "Look, stacks of paper towels, all folded together. They would be about the right size, wouldn't they? If we wet them, a block of them, and if we can get them up to the hole, they would freeze in place, and the drift could pile up against them and stop blowing into the station. Wouldn't it work?"

She was separating the opened package into thirds, her hands busy, her eyes downcast, not seeing him at all. Crane, slightly to one side of her, a step behind, stared at the double image in the mirror. He continued to watch the mirror as his hands reached out for her and closed about her throat. There was no struggle. She simply closed her eyes and became very limp, and he let her fall. Then he took the wad of towels and held it under the water for a few moments and returned to the waiting room with it. He had to clear snow from the approach to the door, and then he had to move the bench that was holding the door, carefully, not letting it become dislodged. He dragged a second bench to the door and climbed on it and pushed the wet wad of towels into the opening. He held it several minutes, until he could feel the freezing paper start to stiffen beneath his fingers. He climbed down.

"That should do it," the woman said.

"But you're dead."

Mary Louise threw the sugar bowl at him, trailing a line of sugar across the room.

He smiled. "Wishful thinking," he/she said.

"You're dead inside. You're shriveled up and dried up and rotting inside. When did you last feel anything? My God! You can't create anything, you are afraid of creating anything, even our child!"

"I don't believe it was our child."

"You don't dare believe it. Or admit that you know it was."

He slapped her. The only time that he ever hit her. And her so pale from the operation, so weak from the loss of blood. The slap meant nothing to him, his hand meeting her cheek, leaving a red print there.

"Murderer!"

"You crazy bitch! You're the one who had the abortion! You wanted it!"

"I didn't. I didn't know what I wanted. I was terrified. You made the arrangements, got the doctor, took me, arranged everything, waited in the other room writing policies. Murderer."

"Murderer," the woman said.

He shook his head. "You'd better go back to the ladies' room and stay there. I don't want to hurt you."

"Murderer."

He took a step toward her. He swung around abruptly and almost ran to the far side of the station, pressing his forehead hard on the window.

"We can't stop it now," the woman said, following him. "You can't close the door again now. I'm here. You finally saw me. Really saw me. I'm real now. I won't be banished again. I'm stronger than you are. You've killed off bits and pieces of yourself until there's nothing left to fight with. You can't send me away again."

Crane pushed himself away from the glass and made a half-hearted attempt to hit her with his fist. He missed and fell against the bench holding the door. He heard the woman's low laugh. All for nothing. All for nothing. The bench slid out from under his hand, and the drift pushed into the room like an avalanche. He pulled himself free and tried to brush the snow off his clothes.

"We'll both freeze now," he said, not caring any longer.

The woman came to his side and touched his cheek with her fingers; they were strangely warm. "Relax now, Crane. Just relax."

She led him to a bench, where he sat down resignedly. "Will you at least tell me who you are?" he said.

"You know. You've always known."

He shook his head. One last attempt, he thought. He had to make that one last effort to get rid of her, the woman whose face was so like his own. "You don't even exist," he said harshly, not opening his eyes. "I imagined you here because I was afraid of being alone all night. I created you. *I created you.*"

He stood up. "You hear that, Mary Louise! Did you hear that? I created something. Something so real that it wants to kill me."

"Look at me, Crane. Look at me. Turn your head and look. Look with me, Crane. Let me show you. Let me show you what I see. . . ."

He was shaking again, chilled through, shaking so hard that his muscles were sore. Slowly, inevitably he turned his head and saw the man half-standing, half-crouching, holding the bench with both hands. The man had gray skin, and his eyes were mad with terror.

"Let go, Crane. Look at him and let go. He doesn't deserve anything from us ever again." Crane watched the man clutch his chest, heard him moaning for Mary Louise to come help him, watched him fall to the floor.

She heard the men working at the drift, and she opened the office door to wait for them. They finally got through and the ticket agent squirmed through the opening they had made.

"Miss! Miss? Are you all right?"

"Yes. I broke into the office, though."

"My God, I thought . . . When we saw that the door had given under the drift, and you in here . . . alo—" The ticket agent blinked rapidly several times.

"I was perfectly all right. When I saw that the door wasn't going to hold, I broke open the inner office and came in here with my sketch book and pencils. I've had a very productive night, really. But I could use some coffee now."

They took her to the diner in a police car, and while she waited for her breakfast order, she went to the rest room and washed her face and combed her hair. She stared at herself in the mirror appraisingly. "Happy birthday," she said softly then.

"Your birthday?" asked the girl who had chosen to wait the night out in the diner. "You were awfully brave to stay alone in the station. I couldn't have done that. You really an artist?"

"Yes, really. And last night I had a lot of work to get done. A lot of work and not much time."

R. A. LAFFERTY

Sky

RAPHAEL ALOYSIUS LAFFERTY was born November 7, 1914, at Neola, Iowa, of Irish parents. Self-educated, he became an electrical engineer by way of a correspondence course and then worked for thirty-five years for electrical wholesalers before retiring to devote his time to writing.

He first tried to write when he was nineteen, and an editor scribbled on his rejected manuscript, "Hopeless, you don't know what life is. Live it for twenty-five years and try again." He forgot that advice until long afterward and then discovered that he had followed it almost exactly. He has six published science fiction novels: *Past Master, The Reefs of Earth, Space Chantey, Fourth Mansions, The Devil Is Dead* and *Arrive at Easterwine;* and two historical fantasies: *The Flame Is Green* and *The Fall of Rome.* There are two published collections of his science fiction stories: *Nine Hundred Grandmothers* and *Strange Doings.* He has had more than eighty stories published in magazines or original collections, and half of them have been anthologized.

His hobbies are geology, art, languages and history. He modestly disclaims any sort of competence despite the fact that he has a reading knowledge of all the languages of the Latin, German and Slavic families, as well as Gaelic and Greek, and during his military service in World

War II he learned to speak Pasar Malay and Tagalog.

Three of his novels, *Past Master, Fourth Mansions* and *The Devil Is Dead,* have been Nebula Award finalists, as was his novelette "Continued on the Next Rock." A Lafferty extravaganza views the universe madly, as with a distorting mirror, but the piercing sanity of the result reminds one that chaos, distorted, can be disconcertingly real.

The Sky-Seller was Mr. Furtive himself, fox-muzzled, ferret-eyed, slithering along like a snake, and living under the Rocks. The Rocks had not been a grand place for a long time. It had been built in the grand style on a mephitic plot of earth (to transform it), but the mephitic earth had won out. The apartments of the Rocks had lost their sparkle as they had been divided again and again, and now they were shoddy. The Rocks had weathered. Its once pastel hues were now dull grays and browns.

The five underground levels had been parking places for motor vehicles when those were still common, but now these depths were turned into warrens and hovels. The Sky-Seller lurked and lived in the lowest and smallest and meanest of them all.

He came out only at night. Daylight would have killed him: he knew that. He sold out of the darkest shadows of the night. He had only a few (though oddly select) clients, and nobody knew who his supplier was. He said that he had no supplier, that he gathered and made the stuff himself.

Welkin Alauda, a full-bodied but light-moving girl (it was said that her bones here hollow and filled with air), came to the Sky-Seller just before first light, just when he had become highly nervous but had not yet bolted to his underground.

"A sack of Sky from the nervous mouse. Jump, or the sun will gobble your house!" Welkin sang-song, and she was already higher than most skies.

"Hurry, hurry!" the Sky-Seller begged, thrusting the sack to her while his black eyes trembled and glittered (if real light should ever reflect into them he'd go blind).

Welkin took the sack of Sky, and scrambled money notes into his hands, which had furred palms. (Really? Yes, really.)

"World be flat and the Air be round, wherever the Sky grows underground," Welkin intoned, taking the sack of Sky and soaring along with a light scamper of feet (she hadn't much weight, her bones were hollow). And the Sky-Seller darted headfirst down a black well-shaft thing to his depths.

Four of them went Sky-Diving that morning, Welkin herself, Karl Vlieger, Icarus Riley, Joseph Alzarsi; and the pilot was—(no, not who you think, he had already threatened to turn them all in; they'd use that pilot no more)—the pilot was Ronald Kolibri in his little crop-dusting plane.

But a crop-duster will not go up to the frosty heights they liked to take off from. Yes it will—if everybody is on Sky. But it isn't pressurized, and it doesn't carry oxygen. That doesn't matter, not if everybody is on Sky, not if the plane is on Sky too.

Welkin took Sky with Mountain Whizz, a carbonated drink. Karl stuffed it into his lip like snuff. Icarus Riley rolled it and smoked it. Joseph Alzarsi needled it, mixed with drinking alcohol, into his main vein. The pilot Ronny tongued and chewed it like sugar dust. The plane named Shrike took it through the manifold.

Fifty thousand feet—You can't go that high in a crop-duster. Thirty below zero—Ah, that isn't cold! Air too thin to breathe at all—with Sky, who needs such included things as air?

Welkin stepped out, and went up, not down. It was a trick she often pulled. She hadn't much weight; she could always get higher than the rest of them. She went up and up until she disappeared. Then she drifted down again, completely enclosed in a sphere of ice crystal, sparkling inside it and making monkey faces at them.

The wind yelled and barked, and the divers took off. They all went down, soaring and gliding and tumbling; standing still sometimes, it seemed; even rising again a little. They went down to clouds and spread out on them: black-white clouds with the sun inside them and suffusing them both from above and below. They cracked Welkin's ice-crystal sphere and she stepped out of it. They ate the thin pieces of it, very cold and brittle and with a tang of ozone. Alzarsi took off his shirt and sunned himself on a cloud.

"You will burn," Welkin told him. "Nobody burns so as when sunning himself on a cloud." That was true.

They sank through the black-whiteness of these clouds and came into the limitless blue concourse with clouds above and below them. It was in this same concourse that Hippodameia used to race her horses, there not being room for such coursers to run on earth. The clouds below folded up and the clouds above folded down, forming a discrete space.

"We have our own rotundity and sphere here," said Icarus Riley (these are their Sky-Diver names, not their legal names), "and it is apart from all worlds and bodies. The worlds and the bodies do not exist for as long a time as we say that they do not exist. The axis of our present space is its own concord. Therefore, it being in perfect concord, Time stops."

All their watches had stopped, at least.

"But there *is* a world below," said Karl. "It is an abject world, and we can keep it abject forever if we wish. But it has at least a shadowy existence, and later we will let it fill out again in our compassion for lowly things. It is flat, though, and we must insist that it remain flat."

"This is important," Joseph said with a deep importance of one on Sky. "So long as our own space is bowed and globed, the world must remain flat or depressed. But the world must not be allowed to bow its back again. We are in danger if it ever does. So long as it is truly flat and abject it cannot crash ourselves to it."

"How long could we fall," Welkin asked, "if we had not stopped time, if we let it flow at its own pace, or at ours? How long could we fall?"

"Hephaestus once tumbled through space all day long," Icarus Riley said, "and the days were longer then."

Karl Vlieger had gone wall-eyed from an interior-turned sexual passion that he often experienced in diving. Icarus Riley seemed to be on laughing gas suddenly; this is a sign that Sky is not having perfect effect. Joseph Alzarsi felt a cold wind down his spine and a series of jerky little premonitions.

"We are not perfect," Joseph said. "Tomorrow or the next day we may be, for we *do* approach perfection. We win a round. And we win another. Let us not throw away our victory today through carelessness. The earth has bowed his old back a little bit, and we make ready for him! Now, guys, now!"

Four of them (or maybe only three of them) pulled the rings. The chutes unpeeled, flowered and jerked. They had been together like a sheaf in close conversation. But suddenly, on coming to earth, they were spread out over five hundred yards.

They assembled. They packed their chutes. That would be all the diving for that day.

"Welkin, how did you pack your chute so quickly?" Icarus asked her suspiciously.

"I don't know."

"You are always the slowest one of us, and the sloppiest. Someone always has to reroll your chute for you before it is used again. And you were the last one to land just now. How were you the first one to be packed? How did you roll it so well? It has the earmarks of my own rolling, just as I rolled it for you before we took off this morning."

"I don't know, Icarus. Oh, I think I'll go up again, straight up."

"No, you've sailed and dived enough for one morning. Welkin, did you even open your chute?"

"I don't know."

High on Sky, they went up again the next morning. The little plane named Shrike flew up as no plane had ever flown before, up through Storm. The storm-shrouded earth shrank to the size of a pea-doogie.

"We will play a trick on it," said Welkin. "When you're on Sky you can play a trick on anything and make it abide by it. I will say that the pea-doogie that was the world is nothing. See, it is gone.

Then I will select another pea-doogie, that one there, and I will call it the world. And that *is* the world that we will come down to in a little while. I've switched worlds on the world, and it doesn't know what happened to it."

"It's uneasy, though." Joseph Alzarsi spoke through flared nostrils. "You shook it. No wonder the world has its moments of self-doubt."

They were one million feet high. The altimeter didn't go that high, but Ronald Kolibri the pilot wrote out the extended figure in chalk to make it correct. Welkin stepped out. Karl and Icarus and Joseph stepped out. Ronald Kolibri stepped out, but only for a while. Then he remembered that he was the pilot and got back in the plane. They were so high that the air was black and star-filled instead of blue. It was so cold that the empty space was full of cracks and potholes. They dived half a million feet in no time at all. They pulled up laughing.

It was invigorating, it was vivifying. They stamped on the clouds, and the clouds rang like frosty ground. This was the ancestral country of all hoarfrost, of all grained-snow and glare-ice. Here was weather-maker, here was wind-son. They came into caves of ice mixed with moraine; they found antler hatchets and Hemicyon bones; they found coals still glowing. The winds bayed and hunted in packs through the chasms. These were the cold Fortean clouds, and their location is commonly quite high.

They came down below Storm, finding new sun and new air. It was pumpkin-summer, it was deep autumn in the sky.

They dropped again, miles and millennia, to full Sky-summer: the air so blue that it grew a violet patina on it to save the surface. Their own space formed about them again, as it did every day, and time stopped.

But not motion! Motion never stopped with them. Do you not realize that nothingness in a void can still be in motion? And how much more they of the great centrality! There was Dynamic; there was sustaining vortex; there was the high serenity of fevered motion.

But is not motion merely a relationship of space to time? No. That is an idea that is common to people who live on worlds, but it is a subjective idea. Here, beyond the possible influence of any worlds, there was living motion without reference.

"Welkin, you look quite different today," Joseph Alzarsi spoke in wonder. "What is it?"

"I don't know. It's wonderful to be different and I'm wonderful."

"It is something missing from you," said Icarus. "I believe it is a defect missing."

"But I hadn't any, Icarus."

They were in central and eternal moment, and it did not end, it could not end, it goes on yet. Whatever else seems to happen, it is merely in parentheses to that moment.

"It is time to consider again," Icarus mused after a while. There is no time or while in the Moment, but there is in the parentheses. "I hope it is the last time we will ever have to consider. We, of course, are in our own space and beyond time or tangent. But the earth, such as it is, is approaching with great presumption and speed."

"But it's *nothing* to us!" Karl Vlieger suddenly raged out in a chthonic and phallic passion. "We can shatter it! We can shoot it to pieces like a clay pigeon! It cannot rush onto us like a slashing dog. Get down, world! Heel, you cur! Heel, I say!"

"We say to one world 'rise' and it rises, and to another one 'heel' and it heels," Icarus sky-spoke in his dynamic serenity.

"Not yet," Joseph Alzarsi warned. "Tomorrow we will be total. Today we are not yet. Possibly we *could* shatter the world like a clay pigeon if we wished, but we would not be lords of it if we had to shatter it."

"We could always make another world," said Welkin reasonably.

"Certainly, but this one is our testing. We will go to it when it is crouched down. We cannot allow it to come ravening to us. Hold! Hold there, we order you!"

And the uprushing world halted, cowed.

"We go down," said Joseph. "We will let it come up only when it is properly broken."

("And they inclined the heavens and came down.")

Once more, three of them pulled the rings. And the chutes unpeeled, flowered and jerked. They had been like a sheaf together in their moment; but now, coming to earth, they were suddenly scattered out over five hundred yards.

"Welkin, you didn't have your chute at all today!" Icarus gaped with some awe when they had assembled again. "That is what was different about you."

"No, I guess I didn't have it. There was no reason to have it if I didn't need it. Really, there was never any reason for me to have used one at all ever."

"Ah, we *were* total today and didn't know it," Joseph ventured. "Tomorrow none of us will wear chutes. This is easier than I had believed."

Welkin went to the Sky-Seller to buy new Sky that night. Not finding him in the nearer shadows of the Rocks, she went down and down, drawn by the fungoid odor and the echoing dampness of the underground. She went through passages that were man-made, through passages that were natural, through passages that were unnatural. Some of these corridors, it is true, had once been built by men, but now they had reverted and become most unnatural deep-earth caverns. Welkin went down into the total blackness where there were certain small things that still mumbled out a faint white color; but it was the wrong color white, and the things were all of a wrong shape.

There was the dead white shape of Mycelium masses, the grotesqueness of Agaricus, the deformity of Deadly Amanita and of Morel. The gray-milky Lactarius glowed like lightless lanterns in the dark; there was the blue-white of the Deceiving Clitocybe and the yellow-white of the Caesar Agaric. There was the insane ghost-white of the deadliest and queerest of them all, the Fly Amanita, and a mole was gathering this.

"Mole, bring Sky for the Thing Serene, for the Minions tall and the Airy Queen," Welkin jangled. She was still high on Sky, but it had begun to leave her a little and she had the veriest touch of the desolate sickness.

"Sky for the Queen of the buzzing drones, with her hollow heart and her hollow bones," the Sky-Seller intoned hollowly.

"And fresh, Oh I want it fresh, fresh Sky!" Welkin cried.

"With these creatures there is no such thing as fresh," the Sky-Seller told her. "You want it stale, Oh so stale! Ingrown and aged and with its own mold grown moldy."

"Which is it?" Welkin demanded. "What is the name of the one you gather it from?"

"The Fly Amanita."

"But isn't that simply a poisonous mushroom?"

"It has passed beyond that. It has sublimated. Its simple poison has had its second fermenting into narcotic."

"But it sounds so cheap that it be merely narcotic."

"Not merely narcotic. It is something very special in narcotic."

"No, no, not narcotic at all!" Welkin protested. "It is liberating, it is world-shattering. It is Height Absolute. It is motion and detachment itself. It is the ultimate. It is mastery."

"Why, then it is mastery, lady. It is the highest and lowest of all created things."

"No, no," Welkin protested again, "not created. It is not born, it is not made. I couldn't stand that. It is the highest of all uncreated things."

"Take it, take it," the Sky-Seller growled, "and be gone. Something begins to curl up inside me."

"I go!" Welkin said, "and I will be back many times for more."

"No, you will not be. Nobody ever comes back many times for Sky. You will be back never. Or one time. I think that you will be back one time."

They went up again the next morning, the last morning. But why should we say that it was the last morning? Because there would no longer be divisions or days for them. It would be one last eternal day for them now, and nothing could break it.

They went up in the plane that had once been named Shrike and was now named Eternal Eagle. The plane had repainted itself during the night with new name and new symbols, some of them not immediately understandable. The plane snuffled Sky into its manifolds, and grinned and roared. And the plane went up.

Oh! Jerusalem in the Sky! How it went up!

They were all certainly perfect now and would never need Sky again. *They were Sky.*

"How little the world is!" Welkin rang out. "The towns are like fly specks and the cities are like flies."

"It is wrong that so ignoble a creature as the Fly should have the exalted name," Icarus complained.

"I'll fix that," Welkin sang. "I give edict: That all the flies on earth be dead!" And all the flies on earth died in that instant.

"I wasn't sure you could do that," said Joseph Alzarsi. "The wrong is righted. Now we ourselves assume the noble name of Flies. There are no Flies but us!"

The five of them, including the pilot Ronald Kolibri, stepped chuteless out of the Eternal Eagle.

"Will you be all right?" Ronald asked the rollicking plane.

"Certainly," the plane said. "I believe I know where there are other Eternal Eagles. I will mate."

It was cloudless, or else they had developed the facility of seeing through clouds. Or perhaps it was that, the earth having become as small as a marble, the clouds around it were insignificant.

Pure light that had an everywhere source! (The sun also had become insignificant and didn't contribute much to the light.) Pure and intense motion that had no location reference. They weren't going anywhere with their intense motion (they already *were* everywhere, or at the super-charged center of everything).

Pure cold fever. Pure serenity. Impure hyper-space passion of Karl Vlieger, and then of all of them; but it was purely rampant at least. Stunning beauty in all things along with a towering cragginess that was just ugly enough to create an ecstasy.

Welkin Alauda was mythic with nenuphars in her hair. And it shall not be told what Joseph Alzarsi wore in his own hair. An always-instant, a million or a billion years!

Not monotony, no! Presentation! Living sets! Scenery! The scenes were formed for the splinter of a moment; or they were formed forever. Whole worlds formed in a pregnant void: not spherical worlds merely, but dodecaspherical, and those much more intricate than that. Not merely seven colors to play with, but seven to the seventh and to the seventh again.

Stars vivid in the bright light. You who have seen stars only in darkness be silent! Asteroids that they ate like peanuts, for now they were all metamorphic giants. Galaxies like herds of rampaging elephants. Bridges so long that both ends of them receded over the light-speed edges. Waterfalls, of a finer water, that bounced off galaxy clusters as if they were boulders.

Through a certain ineptitude of handling, Welkin extinguished the old sun with one such leaping torrent.

"It does not matter," Icarus told her. "Either a million or a billion years had passed according to the time-scale of the bodies, and surely the sun had already come onto dim days. You can always make other suns."

Karl Vlieger was casting lightning bolts millions of parsecs long and making looping contact with clustered galaxies with them.

"Are you sure that we are not using up any time?" Welkin asked them with some apprehension.

"Oh, time still uses itself up, but we are safely out of the reach of it all," Joseph explained. "Time is only one very inefficient method of counting numbers. It is inefficient because it is limited in its numbers, and because the counter by such a system must die when he has come to the end of his series. That alone should weigh against it as a mathematical system; it really shouldn't be taught."

"Then nothing can hurt us ever?" Welkin wanted to be reassured.

"No, nothing can come at us except inside time and we are outside it. Nothing can collide with us except in space and we disdain space. Stop it, Karl! As you do it that's buggery."

"I have a worm in my own tract and it gnaws at me a little," the pilot Ronald Kolibri said. "It's in my internal space and it's crunching along at a pretty good rate."

"No, no, that's impossible. Nothing can reach or hurt us," Joseph insisted.

"I have a worm of my own in a still more interior tract," said Icarus, "the tract that they never quite located in the head or the heart or the bowels. Maybe this tract always was outside space. Oh, my worm doesn't gnaw, but it stirs. Maybe I'm tired of being out of reach of everything."

"Where do these doubts rise from?" Joseph sounded querulous. "You hadn't them an instant ago, you hadn't them as recently as ten million years ago. How can you have them now when there isn't any now?"

"Well, as to that—" Icarus began—(and a million years went by) —"as to that I have a sort of cosmic curiosity about an object in my own past—"—(another million years went by)—"an object called world."

"Well, satisfy your curiosity then," Karl Vlieger snapped. "Don't you even know how to make a world?"

"Certainly I know how, but will it be the same?"

"Yes, if you're good enough. It will be the same if you make it the same."

Icarus Riley made a world. He wasn't very good at it and it wasn't quite the same, but it did resemble the old world a little.

"I want to see if some things are still there," Welkin clamored. "Bring it closer."

"It's unlikely your things are still there," Joseph said. "Remember that billions of years may have passed."

"The things will be there if I put them there," Icarus insisted.

"And you cannot bring it closer since all distance is now infinite," Karl maintained.

"At least I can focus it better," Icarus insisted, and he did. The world appeared quite near.

"It remembers us like a puppy would," Welkin said. "See, it jumps up at us."

"It's more like a lion leaping for a treed hunter just out of reach," Icarus grudged. "But we are *not* treed."

"It can't ever reach us, and it wants to," Welkin piqued. "Let's reach down to it."

("And they inclined the heavens and went down.")

A most peculiar thing happened to Ronald Kolibri as he touched earth. He seemed to have a seizure. He went slack-faced, almost horror-faced, and he would not answer the others.

"What is it, Ronald?" Welkin begged in kindred anguish. "Oh, what is it? Somebody help him!"

Then Ronald Kolibri did an even more peculiar thing. He began to fold up and break up from the bottom. Bones slowly splintered and pierced out of him and his entrails gushed out. He compressed. He shattered. He splashed. Can a man splash?

The same sort of seizure overtook Karl Vlieger: the identical slack-face horror-face, the same folding up and breaking up from the bottom, the same hideous sequence.

And Joseph Alzarsi went into the same sundering state, baffled and breaking up.

"Icarus, what's happened to them?" Welkin screamed. "What is that slow loud booming?"

"They're dead. How could that be?" Icarus puzzled, trembling. "Death is in time, and we are not."

Icarus himself passed through time as he crashed earth, breaking up, spilling out more odiously than any of them.

And Welkin touched earth, crashed, then what? She heard her own slow loud booming as she hit.

(Another million years went by, or some weeks.)

A shaky old woman on crutches was going down the middle-of-the-night passages that are under the Rocks. She was too old a woman to be Welkin Alauda, but not too old for a Welkin who had lived millions of years outside of time.

She had not died. She was lighter than the others, and besides she had done it twice before unscathed. But that was before she had known fear.

Naturally they had told her that she would never walk again; and now most unnaturally she was walking with crutches. Drawn by the fungoid odor and the echoing dampness she went down in the total dark to where small things were glowing with the wrong color white and were all of the wrong shape. She wanted one thing only, and she would die without it.

"Sky for salving the broken Crone! Sky for the weal of my hollow bone!" she crackled in an old-woman voice. But it was only her own voice that echoed back to her.

Should a Sky-Seller live forever?

EDGAR PANGBORN

Mount Charity

EDGAR PANGBORN was born in New York City in 1909. His formal education consisted, he observes, of being moderately exposed to Harvard. He studied piano and composition at the New England Conservatory of Music and for a time planned a musical career before he turned to writing. Except for military service in New Guinea and the Philippines during World War II, he has worked as a free-lance writer and painter.

In 1951 he received a Special Award of Merit from *Ellery Queen's Mystery Magazine*. His published novels are *West of the Sun*, science fiction (1953); *A Mirror for Observers*, science fiction (1954), which won Pangborn the International Fantasy Award; *Wilderness of Spring*, a historical novel (1958); *The Trial of Callista Blake*, a novel concerned with capital punishment (1962); *Davy*, a novel of the future (1964); and *The Judgment of Eve*, a novel of the future (1966). *Good Neighbors and Other Strangers* (1972) is a collection of short stories.

To his list of admirable science fiction stories he has now added "Mount Charity," which was a finalist in the 1971 Nebula Awards balloting.

My name is Peregrine; I have two friends.

Do not touch me. Feel the air stir as I move it with my wing, and understand: I am flesh.

One of my friends is hiding yonder at the edge of the pines. He is Lykos. Think of a European wolf, larger and shaggier than your American timber wolves. Three thousand years ago his pelt was rich black; like my plumage it has whitened. My other friend carries on his work far from here, in a cave on one of the lower peaks of the Cascade Range. The distant ancestors of the Blackfoot Indians called that peak Mount Charity because of its good shelters, springs, areas of sweet grass, tempered winds. If you see him you will think of a tailless monkey, a Barbary ape. For his amusement and ours, after we discovered India, we named him Hanuman. He too has gone white. He was the first of us to understand that we do grow old. We already knew we could die. Once we were four.

I will not stand on your wrist. You would find our flesh cold. I like this arm of your chair. I like to watch the late sun on your face, Doctor, though I notice you need to turn away from it as I never do.

Speech is hard for me. I know your language well, but my throat labors over human sounds. Be patient with me.

We have watched you five summers. We like these hills you call Vermont. We like the young people who come in summer with their tents; and you exploit your version of Socratic method to stir their minds. A Socratic school, isn't it?

In a way. I chase them with logic. I want them to know fantasy and objective truth, to value both, and understand the differences. You call me Doctor, but it's fifteen years since I retired from practice. It will be hard, Peregrine, to convince me that you are not the dream of an old man fallen asleep in the sun.

You may feel more certain when Lykos comes to lie at your feet, and speak in a better voice than mine.

We cannot know our origin. While your science was growing

articulate we listened, in our fashion. You could explore—your miscroscopes, telescopes, mathematics, subtle method—as we never could. What we believe about our beginning is an imitation of your sort of speculation. Since nothing like us exists, so far as we know, anywhere on Earth except in our three bodies, and since our flesh can have very little in common with that of any Earth-born being, we think we may have originated from . . . let us imagine spores brought by a meteorite that fell on the Iberian Peninsula three thousand years ago. This unknown living dust was capable (we imagine) of entering a terrestrial host and growing until every part, while retaining the original design, became trans-muted into our substance, whatever it is, with its unearthly long life and tenacious memory, its partly humanlike powers of reason, imagination, affection. (Sometimes, it's true, we think in ways I cannot explain to you.) And we suppose that dust did enter the grown bodies of a peregrine hawk, a wolf, a monkey, a snake. We take this hypothesis because we have none better. Maybe when we die and your experts examine us they will provide an al-together different explanation. But we hope to live for some brief time yet. And it seems to us that your wise men, confronted by their own runaway technology, by the decay of political and social responsibility, above all by the horrors of human overbreeding, have enough to engage their energies for a long time—if a long time is still possible for any being on this planet—without bother-ing about three aliens, "impossible" creatures, who can only watch, reflect and finish (if we have time) a certain task.

We're not even sure it would be safe for your kind to handle us. This is a new concern, taught us by your science. We have never had much physical contact with the animal life of Earth—it dis-turbs us; our senses shrink. We can love you, but not by touch. (If you don't understand this, let it pass: it affects us more than you.) The leaves of a few plants are the only food that sustains us. Such contact as we have made with animal life, most of it accidental, has done no harm that we know of to either side, but we never know enough. I prefer that you do not put out your hand to me. Needless precaution, very likely, but sooner that than harm you.

The fourth of our number was killed by terrified peasants—smashed with stones and sticks. They may have felt pious anger at her serpentine shape as well as fear. It happened in the twelfth century of your Christian calendar. However, we have seen men of the present day provoked to the same idiotic destructiveness, by forms they find too remote from the little human pattern and therefore to be hated.

Ophis had stored her memory with knowledge of the great world below the tops of the grass. For centuries she had also been listening to the human things—under floors, behind walls, in garden hedges, beyond campfires. As much as she passed on to us is safe in Hanuman's faultless memory and in the written record that he labors over at Mount Charity. But Ophis died before we had begun that record, and so the rest of what she knew is beyond recovery.

If you have any wish to convince others of our existence, even those goodhearted scholars of yours who themselves would never hurt us, I beg you dismiss it. We dare not show ourselves. I came to you frightened, and am still frightened in spite of what we know about you. We are too familiar—forgive me—with the human habit of shooting first and then looking to see what the bullet struck.

We have searched your people in every generation for those few we might dare to approach, in need. It is long since we have spoken. Lykos, three hundred and fifty years ago, wished to save a woman he found lost in the woods, and could not quiet her fear of him except by using his mild human voice. Alas, his kindness! The poor soul reeled home dazed by the holy marvel, believing it a pure experience of the presence of God; and she chattered to the wrong ears, and so was burnt for a witch on the urgent recommendation of the then Archbishop of Cologne. More than once I have seen human kindness reach out to save a moth from the flame, and the hand frightens the silly beautiful thing directly into death.

We come to you now because we are truly in great need of help.

What threatens us would seem trivial to most others of your breed, supposing they could first accept the fact of our existence. We know you will not think in those terms, but you might well hesitate from other reasons. You have a right to know more about us who come begging. Let me talk on about us for a while.

In our time we have examined all the regions between the poles, except the seas. I have flown to the farthest islands. I know the upper air (how clean it once was!); Lykos and Hanuman for centuries searched the jungles, the prairies, steppes, tundra, and fields and pastures governed by men. They traveled everywhere with Ophis, while she lived. We have found no others of our kind. In the sea?—it's possible; there we can't go. Some of the dust that (may have) made us could have fallen there. I came to consciousness on a patch of ground near the mouth of what is called today the Guadalquivir, and the first beauty I saw and marveled at was the play of afternoon sunlight on the waters of the Atlantic; the first music I knew was counterpoint of wind and ocean. I think it was after my—should I say birth?—that a city grew up south of there; the Romans knew it as Gades, now Cádiz. Yes, there might be a few of us in the sea. I think they could hardly have discovered communication as we did; to them humanity might be no more than a fraction of the rain of death that falls slowly through the green spaces to the ooze. If the corruption of the sea by your breed threatens to destroy them, they will have no defense and no escape.

However, we have found no others. The hope of doing so has not quite gone, but it is faint. Yours is a huge world. Only men stultified by impatience or indifference believe it to be small. Only the pitiably ignorant believe it has been explored.

I'll tell you more of that first awareness. I came to it as mind without speech or knowledge or memory, in possession of an airy body that could fly without learning the art, see and hear keenly, discover the racing pleasures of the wind. With smell, hunger woke (nothing like a hawk's) and I pecked at leaves, drawn by this or that pungent scent, until I learned how hunger could be qui-

eted. But though my mind was empty and waiting, it was charged
by a flame of curiosity like that of no other animal, I now understand, except man. With no language, tradition or guide, no concept of communication, I watched the continuous wonderful flow
of life about me, and I was able to make comparisons, elementary
deductions; to move from small observations to large, combine
them, and forget nothing. I don't know how long I lived in this
beginning way. Only a few years, I think. I was teaching my mind
to do what my body could do without teaching: to fly.

Though I saw the roundness of the world and the invitation of
distances, I did not, during this time, fly beyond the Pyrenees, nor
very far out over the oceans. Short distances above northern
Africa, yes—how green it was then!—but I always returned. I think
I knew I would move on, but first I needed to understand more
of this region where my conscious existence began.

I witnessed endless killing of life by life. It made me timid,
showing me an image of death as motion-all-gone, followed usually
by engulfment in some hungry mouth, or decay. I found that most
creatures of my own size or smaller sheered away from me, the
hawks as scared as any of the others. My scent, I suppose, or else
something they feel by perceptions that have eluded your studies
so far, Doctor. Does my scent offend you?

No. Musky and strange. But to me, pleasant.

Good. Mosquitoes were bothering you a while ago. You won't
notice any while I stay here.

One day—I was still very young, if that is the right word—I was
flying above those nothern hills, and I saw Lykos crossing a ridge
where the snow was lying thinly. Beside him walked Hanuman.
This I knew to be altogether out of the pattern. Wolves I had
watched, fierce predators; monkeys were animals of the warm
southern part, never in these hills and certainly never in the company of a great black wolf. As I slid by and returned in wonder,
Lykos' golden eyes were moving to follow my flight, and with a
loving arm over his back crouched Hanuman. Then the monkey
stood up, swinging an arm out and in as I had seen human beings

do to summon others. I swooped lower still, overcoming fright. No wolf or monkey smell, but my own!—the leaf-mold smell that I encountered when I cleaned my feathers or slipped my head under my wing. I lit beside them unafraid, and little Ophis slid down from her easy riding-place in the deep fur of Lykos' neck. We were four.

The three were already well advanced in a private language that we still speak among ourselves. We acquired human languages later on, as we needed them. (The story of their growth from what they were three thousand years ago is one of the treasures already saved for you in that record of Hanuman's.) I picked up this one of ours in a few days, having already learned love at the moment when Hanuman touched me.

We have no sex. The bodies of Lykos and Hanuman are in the male design but without sexual desire, which we can understand only as observers; Ophis was in the female pattern. A matter of chance: we suppose the drifting dust entered whatever nearby host would admit it. I don't know which sex my body was before it was changed, and it's no matter. If we reproduce by spores, possibly (I am now only dreaming aloud)—possibly if we can die of old age, our bodies may dry and scatter the germs of our substance on the air? Does the thought frighten you?

No, Peregrine.

We know love in terms of devotion, or shared experience and compassion (in this sense we can love your breed, and we do) and of pleasure in nearness, of the sometimes wordless touching of self by self. Our bodies to you would seem cold; we are warm to one another. . . . Can you imagine a human being standing in the room where my body was becoming a living dust?

I can imagine it without distress.

Can you image yourself standing there?

That is harder.

I myself would not wish it. Human beings should live. I think my natural time of dying is still far off. When it comes, perhaps some human invalid, someone who would otherwise die—but it hardly matters. If our substance entered, only the frame, the outward image, would remain human. Human beings must live as human beings.

It is your world. You cannot be as we are, nor we as varied and adaptable and adventurous, beautiful, even happy, as your people might become if you will learn how to live; if you will start thinking of fewer and better, not of more and greedier. I think we ought to live too, a few of us, if it is possible, if we are certain our substance can be kept harmless to the natural life of Earth. But as we do not have your potential for evil, neither have we, to the full, your potential for good. It is you who must become the Earth-people if you can—the good husbandmen, the music makers and keepers of the vineyard.

Our great journeys began soon after that meeting on the mountainside. We crossed the Pyrenees, in the spring of a year in what you call the ninth century B.C. We traveled as we pleased through the forests that were later Gaul, along the northern coast of Europe, the shores of the Baltic, into the vast body of Asia. Years, and we reached the Pacific. I flew far up and down the coasts, seeing the roofs, smoke, fields of a civilization already stupendous. At that time we did not pause to learn much of it, because we wanted to know the world as a single vision. I found that region of fog where the greatest of oceans narrows to a strait dividing the continents, and I led my friends the long way there. Hanuman, with the aid of Lykos, contrived a raft. We waited till winter narrowed the strait to fewer miles, and crossed, aided as well as threatened by the fierce current and the pack ice. Part of the time Lykos swam, pulling the raft.

He was in no danger of sinking. We can endure a degree of cold that would be lethal to you, and our flesh is much more light and buoyant than yours. But we do fear the ocean, having had no way to learn enough about it. That day it seemed all menace and obscurity. I hoped as I flew that I could warn them of an ugly fin approaching, or shape rising out of the gray confusion—but that fog, that everlasting fog! Concealing us helpfully, yes, but making my sharp eyes useless. Well, we came through, and later returned safely. As a company we made that journey only one more time. To me, of course, ocean barriers are less than the divisions of a chessboard.

On that journey—already into the eighth century B.C. in your terms—we explored the entire coast of North America, across the north to Newfoundland, south to what you have made the Canal Zone, down to the Horn with many years of learning a new jungle, northward over the Andes, again Alaska. Decades later, back near our place of origin.

We studied most of the human settlements and cultures that we found, avoiding contact because we knew the dangers. In those centuries of our exploration we never appeared as more than a quick shadow at the corner of a human eye, a dot of wings circling in and out of the clouds.

Remember, Doctor: three thousand years is no great age. Before our minds awoke, Mohenjo-Daro had been buried and forgotten under a welter of later building. Great Agade of Babylonia was founded more than a thousand years before our waking—but we knew that city, in our time. Ophis in its cellars, Hanuman a fleeting shadow on midnight roofs. Lykos strolled its stinking alleys in the dark, listening to human voices, and the dogs cringed away unharmed.

Greece we knew, her few enlightened centuries. I have flown over Crete, over all the Grecian islands. We can say to you, Helen was indeed beautiful; the heart of Achilles did break at the death of his friend. I saw the burning of Troy town black on the sky— only one of the thousand wars we witnessed, all of them foul, vain and unnecessary. That one matters only because a poet made music. Yes, Odysseus of the many devices did set out from there on his homeward journey—but of that I know, as you do, only what is told by a better voice.

In a much later journey we passed by Antioch and Tyre, then on as far as a massive human disturbance—Alexandria, where we heard familiar Greek and Roman dialects. We followed the coast westward and came upon the legions before Carthage. By your calendar, that was 146 B.C.

That night Lykos and Hanuman prowled outside the camps and heard the cursing, complaining, occasionally thoughtful talk of soldiers, chatter of camp-followers and slaves, grunt of dice-players, squeak of wheels, spitting, snorting, belching, whine of whips —night sounds not greatly different from what we heard again in 1346 at the siege of Calais. Not deeply different, old man, from night as we heard it in the summer of 1863 outside Vicksburg. If we had been present I think we would have heard the same blending of black mirth, innocent obscenities, patience, aimless despair and fatigue, in the trenches of Verdun, or before the fighting began at Monte Cassino. We would hear it, possibly more hysterical, wherever soldiers talk to each other in the poisonous war your government carries on so blindly and endlessly in Vietnam.

We try to understand it.

I flew above Carthage. We had grown rather sophisticated then about the human thing. I knew what would happen. We guessed the dominance of Rome was inevitable, if only because of that beefy Roman stubbornness, and this city was the enemy's heart. We had heard gossip and truth about bilious Cato in his eighties. The old hater was dead then—he hated the Greeks too—but his hate still sputtered where the legions could hear it. In six days Carthage was smoke. Before I sought cleaner air I heard the screaming, glimpsed the usual human entertainments. Yet it was said there was not much laughter among the Roman officers—and yes, if you're curious, it's probably true that Scipio Aemilianus did weep, for the record, at this product of his good generalship.

Sickened of men, above all sickened of their self-delusions, we wandered down into jungle Africa—our third long journey there —and watched again your groping human pattern in the life of savage tribes. Those were rough jungles, as some of them are today. Once Lykos (he is coming to you now from the pines) fell into a pygmies' pit trap and we could not finish digging him out before they came. I darted among them and tore at their faces until they fled, gibbering of witchcraft.

I can't recall you ever looked handsomer, Peregrine.

Let me tend that leg, Lykos!

I *can* walk on three, Doctor. Our wounds heal; our green-blooded flesh has never taken any infection. But it's true we heal much more slowly than when we were young, the bullet does give me pain, and there at the joint I suppose it might interfere with the setting of the bone. However, sir—contact with our flesh—

Oh, you don't believe that yourself, do you? After all your time on Earth, and no harm done? Let me at least extract the bullet, and splint it. It would be simple, for me.

But about contact—some caution, Doctor—

After three thousand years and no harm done? Let me follow my own common sense. Besides, I'm—quite old. It makes no real difference. Rest here. I'll get what I need. . . .

He wouldn't call others with a telephone?

No, Lykos. I am sure. He's honest.

You have not made the request?

No, but I told him we came to make one.

Still time to retreat, Peregrine. We could let him think this surgery was what we came to ask.

Too timid, Lykos. We must make the request.

Something in his face—I think he has a cancer.

It's possible . . . Quiet. Do whatever he asks. . . .

Was that too much?

No, you're very quick and good. But Doctor, I do suggest avoiding contact with the green blood that's oozing where the bullet was. Let it drain. It clots quickly. Try not to touch it when you put on the splints.

This thing is a nasty little .22. What happened?

Some hunter. I was certain I was hidden but must have been careless. I ran off. I don't know what he thinks I was.

If he thinks. Splints now. This will be bad, you know. . . .

I've felt worse. . . . Now it will heal. Your kindness is spring in winter. Peregrine, go on with what you were telling him. Mm, those pygmies! I did get rather cross.

Yes, you expressed your thoughts with some freedom. Well, Doctor, it was after we had witnessed the decay and near-death of learning in what you call the early Middle Ages that Hanuman began work on his record. That dreary collapse, from the fourth century on, that blackout of Western culture for something like a thousand years, made clear to us how easy it is for a society as imperfectly developed, as precariously balanced in nature as yours, to let its light go out. Maybe there is a recurrent mental fatigue in human cultures, induced by the short periods of enterprise. You push on with your grand vigor for a while, and then— slump; abdication of intelligence as the governing force, and of course if that's complete enough it drags down virtually everything in a long ruin.

It seemed to us that in our limited way we might function as preservers of history. We thought that a detailed, scrupulously truthful record of all we knew, all we had observed from our detachment, might someday be a thing of value to you, even a source of guidance. Surely it's true, if a culture that forgets history is condemned to repeat it, the complement of the proposition *ought* to be true.

Qualify it, Peregrine—I imagine the Doctor will agree. No culture as yet has actually forgotten history because no culture has really possessed more than fragments of it. With that allowed for I guess the old saying may be true enough. I suppose a knowledge of history adequate for a trustworthy guide has never been possessed by more than a handful of scholars. Some have done their best to transmit it, but who reads? Men at large simply don't know their own past. Snippets hastily gulped in school—by those who have schools; simple and popular generalizations, mostly false and harmful.

I am forced to agree, Lykos.

Lykos is more a pessimist than I, maybe for the very reason that his affection for humanity is deeper.

Maybe. Never think I doubt the value of our record. I only wonder whether these volatile short-lived beings will ever find the wit to use it.

He and I speak alike, Doctor; think very much alike. But Lykos thinks in privacy, like all sentient beings. You might have to know us a hundred years or so to discover in how many ways we are— persons. Ophis was our humorist. Had a sweet small thorn in her speech that could make even Hanuman smile. He's all meditative thought, logic, philosophy—and compassion. His hands have changed visibly with that endless writing; both somewhat enlarged—he writes with either hand—and deep black grooves in thumbs and middle fingers.

We began our record in your ninth century A.D. We had hoped to give it to you in a time when you had begun to show, as a society of intelligent beings, more signs of intelligent behavior. Under present conditions we can hardly wait any longer for that. We may have waited too long already, counted too much on the power of your often brilliant individuals and minorities. The record is not finished. Hanuman has been able to bring it only a short way into your twentieth century. . . . Lykos, my throat is tired.

I'll go on, in my grumbling way. Are you sure, Doctor, that we're safe from interruption? I'm not prepared to meet anyone but you. *The kids all took off to a movie in the village and won't be back till after dark—you'll hear the two cars. No one else comes to see me here, or if anyone does, that door has a loose latch I didn't shut. You could push it open and then get into a closet or under my bed.*

I'm housebroken, too. (Peregrine, I don't feel that shrinking, when he strokes my head.)

(Good. You were always a sentimental pup.)

That was your private language, wasn't it?

Yes, I was telling old Featherpuff I like your touch. We conceived the idea of that record suddenly, but it took years to find a place to work on it and keep it safe. At length we chose a cave in the foothills of the Dinaric Alps. The entrance was larger than we liked; we did what we could with brush barricades. It seemed remote enough. Swarming Italy lay more than a hundred miles away across the Adriatic. Around our cave, gaunt wilderness, here and there goat trails, six miles away a mountain track that was used, but very little, by carts and horsemen. From our cliff we looked down on the distant roofs of a peasant village, but we were sheltered from it not only by our height, but by ugly gorges, dense woods, tumbled rocks. Bears, the beasts in my shape, and that was also a country thick with belief in vampires, witches, all manner of spooks. No man ventured far alone, even by day, and two or more men together are sure to make a noise. Our secret trail was easy for Hanuman. I had enough trouble with parts of the climb so that I was sure no other wolf would try it, and men would be deterred unless they had some compelling motive. Ophis knew many little approaches but preferred to ride my neck—that trifling weight. . . .

Come back to the story, Lykos.

Yes. That cave served us five hundred years. Hanuman developed the full plan of his work. No feeling of immediate urgency was pushing us in those centuries, only the larger sense of it, awareness of the insecurity of all things living. We could not be certain the civilization of Europe would recover any force and virtue, but by that time we had our own perspective. We were in touch with the rest of the world, with men's continual failures, recoveries, groping advances.

Peregrine of course was Hanuman's best reporter, traveling wherever wings can go. We knew of the Aztecs, Mayas, Incas, the primitive peoples, the tribal groups and young civilizations in this northern continent. China, the Mongols, India, the shut-away people of Australia, the human experience in jungle, veldt, seacoast of Africa. In our record is more than you can ever learn elsewhere of the wonderful voyages that carried men to the islands of the Pacific. There's no settled place in the world from the Arctic to Patagonia where Peregrine has not listened in the dark to the talk of men. I myself made many journeys, with Ophis and then alone.

Often Hanuman left his work to come with me, because he was

our best thief. In those centuries the monasteries were almost our only source of parchment, vellum, other writing fabrics. Hanuman made ink from gum and soot, and slotted bamboo pens long before Europe had anything better than the quill; papers we had to steal. Robbing the poor monks' scriptoria was often easier than getting what we needed from cellars or other storage places, and it was always more fun. In the monastic records of eastern Europe from the ninth into the fourteenth century, there may well be here and there an embarrassed mention of the theft of writing materials by the Devil; if so, Devil is to be taken in the Pickwickian sense. Then we'd have the stiff task of conveying our loot by secret ways to the cave. Hanuman was writing at that time in the compact, rather inflexible Latin of the Augustan age, and he wrote with almost no margins in a script hardly thicker than the legs of a millipede; nevertheless our greed for the precious material was insatiable. For Hanuman—always the master intelligence of our company, before whom we others are only loving fools—would not leave out one fact that might be of importance to men, and he was bound to have it all in such perfect order that the record could be used by any human scholar with ability to read and courage to endure the truth.

Our plunder had to travel mostly on my back. I had narrow escapes. Sometimes I had sore feet. But it was worth any effort. And that part of it, that product of five hundred years of toil, was all destroyed.

The year was 1348, the month of May. Ophis had died two hundred years before. I was traveling southward through France, where the Hundred Years' War had already built up the true monument to princely quarrels—ruin and desolation. And as I started down the Rhone valley I began to overhear men talk of that other plague, the Black Death, for it was then, as we knew, in full fury at Avignon. My mind was drenched with the presence of death, when Peregrine found me with the news of our own disaster.

A young man out hunting very bravely alone had taken a fall

into a spot from which he could see our cave entrance. Intent at his work, Hanuman had not been aware of him until he tumbled and cursed in pain. Then from behind the brush barricade Hanuman watched him, not too badly hurt, limping and scrambling nearer. He had saved his bow and hunting knife in the fall, but lost his arrows; he was bleeding, lamed, scared, and wanted shelter because the sky was churning with the threat of storm. Hanuman stayed motionless in the barricade until the young man pushed aside part of it and entered the cave. Then he moved to better concealment and called in a human voice: "Go away! Go away!" He had a desperate hope that if the boy could be frightened off there might be a chance to get the record out of danger before others were brought to look at the place.

The young hunter was properly frightened, and plunged out of the cave—with Hanuman's pen and the strip of parchment he had been busied with—and he searched for the source of the call. Then his keen eyes found Hanuman's face as the gusty wind shoved bushes aside. He yelled and fled, tumbling and struggling down the incline mad with terror. And while Hanuman listened to the diminishing uproar of his retreat, the wind fetched in a stupendous rain, a battering downpour that was to last all night and on into the morning. Yet even if he had had a dry place to take it, Hanuman thinks, he could never have got the record safe—it was too big, and those people were braver than he supposed.

They came in the morning even before the rain had ceased. They brought a priest, and oil, and torches, a dozen men with spears and arrows and axes. Fifty yards off in dense growth on the higher ground, Hanuman listened to a great droning of dog-Latin exorcism, prayers in the dialect, howling and pounding of metal to drive away Satan. He heard himself described two or three times by the scared (and very proud) young man, as twice the height of two tall men, with flaming nostrils that poured forth the stench of Hell, and a voice that turned a man's blood to milk.

Then there was real fire, and heaving smoke, and black scraps of priceless parchment floating out and down the hillside on the damp wind.

Hanuman came away to a clearing where he was accustomed to meet Peregrine and me, and Peregrine found him there and brought me word. When we were all three together—

We do not weep, Doctor. We come together, and—rest. As we had done after Ophis died, we went into thick woods, and I lay where Hanuman could lean against me with Peregrine in his arms. We rest. We abandon thought, memory, sorrow, everything except our trusting and healing nearness to each other; for this, together with our imperfect but perfectible knowledge of natural law, is the only aspect of life that will never deceive or betray us. After that time of retreat, we at length roused ourselves, to consider how to take up our task of recordmaking once more, from the beginning.

We returned to this continent. Another raft of vines and branches securely woven by Hanuman with what clumsy help I could provide; another crossing of that fogbound channel, our last. I don't think I could swim it now, pulling a raft. Before we crossed, Peregrine had surveyed the ranges from Alaska to the southern Sierras. Of many good places, Mount Charity seemed the best for our needs.

Standing on its flat summit you are in the center of a vast bowl, and the bottom of the bowl is the green jade of treetops. They clothe a valley so many-angled, so tumbled and broken up with lesser elevations and spurs of the greater peaks, that it should hardly be called a valley at all. There are small lakes, and streams. A river flows off underground, and where it emerges, if it does, even I have never been sure. And all around the summit, where the winds are never violent, stand the snow-topped giants. They look as though a shout might reach them, though the nearest one, says Peregrine, is twenty-four miles away. For the last ten or fifteen years, of course, the air has not been that clear, but we remember.

We knew men would never come there for grazing livestock, let alone clearing and farming: little enough for even goats to find. But for us there has been rich plenty. The needles of western pine and larch for us are sustaining food. We brought with us the seeds

of European herbs we have grown used to, and they have naturalized well. Myrtle also grows there, which we enjoy, in patches of
open ground near our cave. There is in particular one little
meadow directly below us. It is really a large outcropping of rock,
slightly tilted, so that over the centuries enough soil has built up
there to support small plants, wild grasses, though not trees. To us
this is the loveliest of all the world's meadows. We have thought
of it and tended it as our garden since 1377. You probably remember that Edward III of England died that year, one of the great
princes whose masterpiece was the Hundred Years' War. And a
man who served him as soldier, valet, envoy, political handyman,
and compared to whom (in my view) Edward and nearly all the
other monarchs of European history were not much more than
hoptoads in fancy clothes, was then getting on for forty—a friend
of yours, I believe, Geoffrey Chaucer. (I hope you'll excuse my
slipping in to look at your books a couple of months ago, when
nobody was around and you left the door on that loose latch.) Yes,
that little meadow has been our garden for very nearly six hundred years.

Indians traveled by once in a great while, making use of an open
space farther down the mountainside for their overnight camps on
journeys across the range. Those had to be important journeys, for
they disliked and dreaded the dark forest of the lower ground, and
the cruel passes through the heights. We learned from their talk
that when they reached this place they called Mount Charity they
felt safe. "Charity" is the nearest English translation we can find,
but in the original there was some overtone of the supernatural,
for they imagined themselves in the presence of a friendly spirit
who would grant travelers protection so long as they were careful
not to outstay their welcome. Later, I regret to say, this benign
legend may have taken on an odd flavor of Wolf Spirit. If we have
the future hours together that I hope we may, Doctor, you might
ask me about that sometime.

Our cave entrance is obscure: we helped nature. The cave itself
is an immense fissure directly underlying the mountain's summit.

A main gallery runs inward a hundred yards. There are side galler-ies; at the end of one is a pool that receives sweet water from every rain and has nourished our contemplation for the centuries. In another, daylight enters from a crack in the western face of the cliff thirty feet above the cave floor: there is our library, and our record; there Hanuman works, reached by the sun for a little while in the evenings, and in the dark he has the candles he himself makes from bayberry and other sources. At certain seasons the moon is with him.

A rock fall—we think at least a thousand years ago—closed up the lower part of the cave entrance. The upper part can be shut, if we choose, with an artificial rock we made, convincing to look at, if you have the enterprise to scramble up a steep-slanted boul-der under the cliff's overhang and peer in at it, but not very strong. So far as we know, the Indians never came up to look at it. Maybe they would have felt it a trespass on the spirit's dwelling place. A good spelunker would catch on to it in no time, or for that matter an enterprising Boy Scout.

Paper was again a problem. It cost us a few years of experiment and trouble to work out a method of manufacturing it ourselves from oat grass. In the fourteenth century we could still feel we might have plenty of time. To this day, on Mount Charity, you can find small clearings where an odd type of oat grass still seeds itself in yearly. We have helped it a little, to be sure, for sentimental reasons. Naturally as soon as the Spanish settlements in California were stable enough to provide us with paper, we were ready with Hanuman's light fingers and my quiet feet, and we enjoyed the game almost as much as in old times. But your antiquarians and possibly your chemists may someday be interested in studying the paper we made: it is flexible even now, safe to handle with care, and most of Hanuman's ink shows up as sharply as yesterday.

There is great plenty of it, for Hanuman was determined to bring back from his memory every page of the lost account, while also dealing with the constant flow of new events, as Peregrine brought word from other continents and I came in with more about the Indian world of North and South America. You see the importance of that, Doctor, considering what slight concern the white pioneers had for the history of any people but themselves.

The nineteenth and twentieth centuries are enormously documented, and I daresay all the important facts can be found in the human records. Nevertheless Hanuman wishes to bring his account to the present time, if only because (we hope) there is a value in the viewpoint of three thousand years.

Doctor, I think we are tiring you excessively. You look—
Please, go on!

I'll take it up again, Lykos. We weren't too worried, Doctor, when the Union Pacific came into Portland—it was far away. The road linking Eugene with Boise did frighten us, but—
They're after Mount Charity.

Yes, Doctor. We ought to have been making ready for flight seventy-odd years ago, when the horseless carriage started driving the stables out of business. But our foresight is only a little better than human. And like you we have that way, that human way, of imagining the cup may pass.

Several years ago a trail across the southern part of our bowl in the hills was widened and blacktopped. Now a spur, a scenic highway, is to be driven all the way to the flat summit of Mount Charity. The summit will be *developed,* as they call it, into a parking lot for an estimated eight hundred cars. There is to be a hotel in our garden, which the developers have already named, in their blueprints, Overlook Inn—The Home of Creative Viewing.

Christ! Let me think—I have some money—

Not enough for what you're thinking, Doctor. Sit quiet, please. Rest. Peace. Let me tell you what our hope is, much more modest. Work won't start on this obscenity until next summer, maybe not then. Some environmentalists are already fighting it. They can't win—too many more urgent things demand their effort and funds, and the money back of the hotel thing is big—but they will delay

it, and that wins us time. Could you remodel this house a little?—
maybe a bigger cellar, some other things—to give us a hiding place
and storage for our records, for ten or fifteen years—

*Yes. Yes, anything, whatever I have. My God, I must write a will,
so that the kids will have the place. Stupid of me to neglect it so
long, but I get tired easily—discouraged—*

Please rest yourself while I finish, Doctor. We must have the
young people in it, yes. We'll need their help. But . . . you understand, don't you? If the secret of our existence is known too soon,
Hanuman's effort to complete the story is done for. Even supposing the best, supposing there were no immediate wish to destroy
us, to be smothered in your people's good intentions would be as
lethal as—as the Pentagon trying to make me tell them all the
good news of Russian and Chinese military—

Stop a moment, Peregrine. That sickens me too much.

I'm sorry, Doctor. It was a foolish example. . . . May I go on?

Yes.

We came to you first, and you only, because we have no one else.
You understand, your students—some changes in the group each
summer, and we can't follow them, study them. I told you, we
studied you a long while before we dared approach. So, now, will
you tell us which of these young people we can trust for secrecy?
You know them. We don't.

Trust them all.

But—

*This is my one piece of human knowledge you must accept.
Trust them all, Peregrine. Oh—wonderful—even if I only dream
it! To know the past, make it a truer guide! Something I can do—
not just preach while the time runs out—*

Peregrine—

He's dead. His heart couldn't bear joy.

Yes, that was joy. . . . I hear the cars.

He wrote no will, Lykos. They won't have this place.

They'll find some way to help us.

But—what if—

Then it happens. But Peregrine, we must stop waiting for perfection. And I think this generation is something new on Earth. They are the first to understand they could lose their world—*their* world, Peregrine—and my heart tells me they are too good to let it go. Come with me. We're going to them now, and we will trust them all.

ROBERT SILVERBERG

Good News from the Vatican

ROBERT SILVERBERG is a native of New York City who has been a professional writer all of his working life. He began selling stories in 1954, while an undergraduate at Columbia College. He graduated with an A.B. degree, married Barbara H. Brown, an electronics engineer, and received his first Hugo Award—in a special category as science fiction's most promising new author—all in the year 1956. Until they moved to California in 1972, the Silverbergs made their home in the Riverdale section of New York City, in a venerable mansion that was formerly owned by Fiorello La Guardia.

The only reason that Silverberg does not challenge Poul Anderson's status as science fiction's most prolific writer is because so much of Silverberg's output has been in other arenas—he has written voluminously in the fields of popular science, history and biography, and has produced a series of distinguished books about archaeology. Under his own name and such pseudonyms as Walter Drummond, Iver Jorgenson, Calvin M. Knox, David Osborne and (with Randall Garrett) Robert Randall, he has had so many books and stories published that he himself has lost track of the totals.

As evidence that the awesome quantity of Silverberg's production has not affected his status as an admirable literary craftsman, he has been

127

a Hugo and Nebula Awards finalist some twenty times—more than any other writer. Among his more recent books are *Thorns* (1967—Hugo and Nebula Awards finalist); *Tower of Glass* (1970—Nebula Award finalist); *The Masks of Time* (1968—Nebula Award finalist); *Up the Line* (1969—Hugo and Nebula Awards finalist); *To Live Again* (1969); *Downward to Earth* (1970); *Son of Man* (1971). His novella "Nightwings" won a Hugo Award in 1968. His short story "Passengers" won a Nebula Award in 1969.

Despite his massive literary output, Silverberg has found time to perform diverse duties for Science Fiction Writers of America, of which he is a past president. He originated the organization's *Hall of Fame* anthologies, and edited the first volume in the series.

With the 1971 balloting, Silverberg has added two more Nebula Awards to his total—for his novel *A Time of Changes* and for his short story "Good News from the Vatican." He thus ties Samuel R. Delany for the position of author with the most Nebula Awards (three), and he adds his name to the select group of authors—including only Delany and Roger Zelazny—who have won two Nebula Awards in one year.

This is the morning everyone has waited for, when at last the robot cardinal is to be elected pope. There can no longer be any doubt of the outcome. The conclave has been deadlocked for many days between the obstinate advocates of Cardinal Asciuga of Milan and Cardinal Carciofo of Genoa, and word has gone out that a compromise is in the making. All factions now are agreed on the selection of the robot. This morning I read in *Osservatore Romano* that the Vatican computer itself has taken a hand in the deliberations. The computer has been strongly urging the candidacy of the robot. I suppose we should not be surprised by this loyalty among machines. Nor should we let it distress us. We *absolutely must not* let it distress us.

"Every era gets the pope it deserves," Bishop FitzPatrick observed somewhat gloomily today at breakfast. "The proper pope for our times is a robot, certainly. At some future date it may be desirable for the pope to be a whale, an automobile, a cat, a mountain." Bishop FitzPatrick stands well over two meters in height and his normal facial expression is a morbid, mournful one. Thus it is impossible for us to determine whether any particular pronouncement of his reflects existential despair or placid acceptance. Many years ago he was a star player for the Holy Cross championship basketball team. He has come to Rome to do research for a biography of St. Marcellus the Righteous.

We have been watching the unfolding drama of the papal election from an outdoor café several blocks from the Square of St. Peter's. For all of us, this has been an unexpected dividend of our holiday in Rome; the previous pope was reputed to be in good health and there was no reason to suspect that a successor would have to be chosen for him this summer.

Each morning we drive across by taxi from our hotel near the Via Veneto and take up our regular positions around "our" table. From where we sit, we all have a clear view of the Vatican chimney through which the smoke of the burning ballots rises: black smoke if no pope has been elected, white if the conclave has been successful. Luigi, the owner and headwaiter, automatically brings us our preferred beverages: Fernet-Branca for Bishop FitzPatrick, Campari and soda for Rabbi Mueller, Turkish coffee for Miss Harshaw, lemon squash for Kenneth and Beverly, and Pernod on the rocks for me. We take turns paying the check, although Kenneth has not paid it even once since our vigil began. Yesterday, when Miss Harshaw paid, she emptied her purse and found herself 350 lire short; she had nothing else except hundred-dollar travelers' checks. The rest of us looked pointedly at Kenneth but he went on calmly sipping his lemon squash. After a brief period of tension Rabbi Mueller produced a 500-lire coin and rather irascibly slapped the heavy silver piece against the table. The rabbi is known for his short temper and vehement style. He is twenty-eight years old, customarily dresses in a fashionable plaid cassock and silvered sunglasses, and frequently boasts that he has never performed a bar mitzvah ceremony for his congregation, which is in Wicomico County, Maryland. He believes that the rite is vulgar and obsolete, and invariably farms out all his bar mitzvahs to a franchised organization of itinerant clergymen who handle such affairs on a commission basis. Rabbi Mueller is an authority on angels.

Our group is divided over the merits of electing a robot as the new pope. Bishop FitzPatrick, Rabbi Mueller and I are in favor of the idea. Miss Harshaw, Kenneth and Beverly are opposed. It is interesting to note that both of our gentlemen of the cloth, one quite elderly and one fairly young, support this remarkable departure from tradition. Yet the three "swingers" among us do not.

I am not sure why I align myself with the progressives. I am a man of mature years and fairly sedate ways. Nor have I ever concerned myself with the doings of the Church of Rome. I am unfamiliar with Catholic dogma and unaware of recent currents of thought within the Church. Still, I have been hoping for the election of the robot since the start of the conclave.

Why? I wonder. Is it because the image of a metal creature upon the Throne of St. Peter's stimulates my imagination and tickles my sense of the incongruous? That is, is my support of the robot purely an aesthetic matter? Or is it, rather, a function of my moral cowardice? Do I secretly think that this gesture will buy the robots off ? Am I privately saying, Give them the papacy and maybe they won't want other things for a while? No. I can't believe anything so unworthy of myself. Possibly I am for the robot because I am a person of unusual sensitivity to the needs of others.

"If he's elected," says Rabbi Mueller, "he plans an immediate time-sharing agreement with the Dalai Lama and a reciprocal plug-in with the head programmer of the Greek Orthodox Church, just for starters. I'm told he'll make ecumenical overtures to the rabbinate as well, which is certainly something for all of us to look forward to."

"I don't doubt that there'll be many corrections in the customs and practices of the hierarchy," Bishop FitzPatrick declares. "For example, we can look forward to superior information-gathering techniques as the Vatican computer is given a greater role in the operations of the Curia. Let me illustrate by—"

"What an utterly ghastly notion," Kenneth says. He is a gaudy young man with white hair and pink eyes. Beverly is either his wife or his sister. She rarely speaks. Kenneth makes the sign of the Cross with offensive brusqueness and murmurs, "In the name of the Father, the Son and the Holy Automaton." Miss Harshaw giggles but chokes the giggle off when she sees my disapproving face.

Dejectedly, but not responding at all to the interruption, Bishop FitzPatrick continues, "Let me illustrate by giving you some figures I obtained yesterday afternoon. I read in the newspaper *Oggi* that during the last five years, according to a spokesman for the *Missiones Catholicae*, the Church has increased its membership in Yugoslavia from 19,381,403 to 23,501,062. But the government census taken last year gives the total population of Yugoslavia at 23,575,194. That leaves only 74,132 for the other religious and irreligious bodies. Aware of the large Moslem population of Yugoslavia, I suspected an inaccuracy in the published statistics and consulted the computer in St. Peter's, which informed me"— the bishop, pausing, produces a lengthy printout and unfolds it across much of the table—"that the last count of the Faithful in Yugoslavia, made a year and a half ago, places our numbers at 14,206,198. Therefore an overstatement of 9,294,864 has been made. Which is absurd. And perpetuated. Which is damnable."

"What does he look like?" Miss Harshaw asks. "Does anyone have any idea?"

"He's like all the rest," says Kenneth. "A shiny metal box with wheels below and eyes on top."

"You haven't seen him," Bishop FitzPatrick interjects. "I don't think it's proper for you to assume that—"

"They're all alike," Kenneth says. "Once you've seen one, you've seen all of them. Shiny boxes. Wheels. Eyes. And voices coming out of their bellies like mechanized belches. Inside, they're all cogs and gears." Kenneth shudders delicately. "It's too much for me to accept. Let's have another round of drinks, shall we?"

Rabbi Mueller says, "It so happens that I've seen him with my own eyes."

"You *have?*" Beverly exclaims.

Kenneth scowls at her. Luigi, approaching, brings a tray of new drinks for everyone. I hand him a 5000-lire note. Rabbi Mueller removes his sunglasses and breathes on their brilliantly reflective surfaces. He has small, watery gray eyes and a bad squint. He says, "The cardinal was the keynote speaker at the Congress of World Jewry that was held last fall in Beirut. His theme was 'Cybernetic Ecumenicism for Contemporary Man.' I was there. I can tell you that His Eminence is tall and distinguished, with a fine voice and a gentle smile. There's something inherently melancholy about his manner that reminds me greatly of our friend the bishop, here. His movements are graceful and his wit is keen."

"But he's mounted on wheels, isn't he?" Kenneth persists.

"On treads," replies the rabbi, giving Kenneth a fiery, devastating look and resuming his sunglasses. "Treads, like a tractor has. But I don't think that treads are spiritually inferior to feet, or, for that matter, to wheels. If I were a Catholic I'd be proud to have a man like that as my pope."

"Not a man," Miss Harshaw puts in. A giddy edge enters her voice whenever she addresses Rabbi Mueller. "A robot," she says. "He's not a man, remember?"

"A *robot* like that as my pope, then," Rabbi Mueller says, shrugging at the correction. He raises his glass. "To the new pope!"

"To the new pope!" cries Bishop FitzPatrick.

Luigi comes rushing from his café. Kenneth waves him away. "Wait a second," Kenneth says. "The election isn't over yet. How can you be so sure?"

"The *Osservatore Romano,*" I say, "indicates in this morning's edition that everything will be decided today. Cardinal Carciofo has agreed to withdraw in his favor, in return for a larger real-time allotment when the new computer hours are decreed at next year's consistory."

"In other words, the fix is in," Kenneth says.

Bishop FitzPatrick sadly shakes his head. "You state things much too harshly, my son. For three weeks now we have been without a Holy Father. It is God's Will that we shall have a pope; the conclave, unable to choose between the candidacies of Cardinal Carciofo and Cardinal Asciuga, thwarts that Will; if necessary, therefore, we must make certain accommodations with the realities of the times so that His Will shall not be further frustrated. Prolonged politicking within the conclave now becomes sinful. Cardinal Carciofo's sacrifice of his personal ambitions is not as self-seeking an act as you would claim."

Kenneth continues to attack poor Carciofo's motives for withdrawing. Beverly occasionally applauds his cruel sallies. Miss Harshaw several times declares her unwillingness to remain a communicant of a church whose leader is a machine. I find this dispute distasteful and swing my chair away from the table to have a better view of the Vatican. At this moment the cardinals are meeting in the Sistine Chapel. How I wish I were there! What splendid mysteries are being enacted in that gloomy, magnificent room! Each prince of the Church now sits on a small throne surmounted by a violet-hued canopy. Fat wax tapers glimmer on the desk before each throne. Masters of ceremonies move solemnly through the vast chamber, carrying the silver basins in which the blank ballots repose. These basins are placed on the table before the altar. One by one the cardinals advance to the table, take ballots, return to their desks. Now, lifting their quill pens, they begin to write. "I, Cardinal ———, elect to the Supreme Pontificate the Most Reverend Lord my Lord Cardinal ———." What name do they fill in? Is it Carciofo? Is it Asciuga? Is it the name of some obscure and shriveled prelate from Madrid or Heidelberg, some last-minute choice of the anti-robot faction in its desperation? Or are they writing *his* name? The sound of scratching pens is loud in the chapel. The cardinals are completing their ballots, sealing them at the ends, folding them, folding them again and again, carrying them to the altar, dropping them into the great gold chalice. So have they done every morning and every afternoon for days, as the deadlock has prevailed.

"I read in the *Herald Tribune* a couple of days ago," says Miss Harshaw, "that a delegation of two hundred and fifty young Catholic robots from Iowa is waiting at the Des Moines airport for news of the election. If their man gets in, they've got a chartered flight ready to leave, and they intend to request that they be granted the Holy Father's first public audience."

"There can be no doubt," Bishop FitzPatrick agrees, "that his election will bring a great many people of synthetic origin into the fold of the Church."

"While driving out plenty of flesh-and-blood people!" Miss Harshaw says shrilly.

"I doubt that," says the bishop. "Certainly there will be some feelings of shock, of dismay, of injury, of loss, for some of us at first. But these will pass. The inherent goodness of the new pope, to which Rabbi Mueller alluded, will prevail. Also I believe that technologically-minded young folk everywhere will be encouraged to join the Church. Irresistible religious impulses will be awakened throughout the world."

"Can you imagine two hundred and fifty robots clanking into St. Peter's?" Miss Harshaw demands.

I contemplate the distant Vatican. The morning sunlight is brilliant and dazzling, but the assembled cardinals, walled away from the world, cannot enjoy its gay sparkle. They all have voted, now. The three cardinals who were chosen by lot as this morning's scrutators of the vote have risen. One of them lifts the chalice and shakes it, mixing the ballots. Then he places it on the table before the altar; a second scrutator removes the ballots and counts them. He ascertains that the number of ballots is identical to the number of cardinals present. The ballots now have been transferred to a ciborium, which is a goblet ordinarily used to hold the consecrated bread of the Mass. The first scrutator withdraws a ballot, unfolds it, reads its inscription; passes it to the second scrutator, who reads it also; then it is given to the third scrutator, who reads the name aloud. Asciuga? Carciofo? Some other? *His?*

Rabbi Mueller is discussing angels. "Then we have the Angels of the Throne, known in Hebrew as *arelim* or *ophanim*. There are seventy of them, noted primarily for their steadfastness. Among them are the angels Orifiel, Ophaniel, Zabkiel, Jophiel, Ambriel, Tychagar, Barael, Quelamia, Paschar, Boel and Raum. Some of these are no longer found in Heaven and are numbered among the fallen angels in Hell."

"So much for their steadfastness," says Kenneth.

"Then, too," the rabbi goes on, "there are the Angels of the Presence, who apparently were circumcised at the moment of their creation. These are Michael, Metatron, Suriel, Sandalphon, Uriel, Saraqael, Astanphaeus, Phanuel, Jehoel, Zagzagael, Yefefiah and Akatriel. But I think my favorite of the whole group is the Angel of Lust, who is mentioned in Talmud *Bereshith Rabba* Eighty-five as follows, that when Judah was about to pass by—"

They have finished counting the votes by this time, surely. An immense throng has assembled in the Square of St. Peter's. The sunlight gleams off hundreds if not thousands of steel-jacketed crania. This must be a wonderful day for the robot population of Rome. But most of those in the piazza are creatures of flesh and blood: old women in black, gaunt young pickpockets, boys with puppies, plump vendors of sausages, and an assortment of poets, philosophers, generals, legislators, tourists and fishermen. How has the tally gone? We will have our answer shortly. If no candidate has had a majority, they will mix the ballots with wet straws before casting them into the chapel stove, and black smoke will billow from the chimney. But if a pope has been elected, the straw will be dry, the smoke will be white.

The system has agreeable resonances. I like it. It gives me the satisfaction one normally derives from a flawless work of art: the *Tristan* chord, let us say, or the teeth of the frog in Bosch's *Temptation of St. Anthony*. I await the outcome with fierce concentration. I am certain of the result; I can already feel the irresistible religious impulses awakening in me. Although I feel, also, an odd nostalgia for the days of flesh-and-blood popes. Tomorrow's newspapers will have no interviews with the Holy Father's aged mother in Sicily, nor with his proud younger brother in San Francisco. And will this grand ceremony of election ever be held again? Will we need another pope, when this one whom we will soon have can be repaired so easily?

Ah. The white smoke! The moment of revelation comes!

A figure emerges on the central balcony of the facade of St. Peter's, spreads a web of cloth of gold and disappears. The blaze of light against that fabric stuns the eye. It reminds me perhaps of moonlight coldly kissing the sea at Castellammare or, perhaps even more, of the noonday glare rebounding from the breast of the Caribbean off the coast of St. John. A second figure, clad in ermine and vermilion, has appeared on the balcony. "The cardinal archdeacon," Bishop FitzPatrick whispers. People have started to faint. Luigi stands beside me, listening to the proceedings on a tiny radio. Kenneth says, "It's all been fixed." Rabbi Mueller hisses at him to be still. Miss Harshaw begins to sob. Beverly softly recites the Pledge of Allegiance, crossing herself throughout. This is a wonderful moment for me. I think it is the most truly contemporary moment I have ever experienced.

The amplified voice of the cardinal archdeacon cries, "I announce to you great joy. We have a pope."

Cheering commences, and grows in intensity as the cardinal archdeacon tells the world that the newly chosen pontiff is indeed *that* cardinal, that noble and distinguished person, that melancholy and austere individual, whose elevation to the Holy See we have all awaited so intensely for so long. "He has imposed upon himself," says the cardinal archdeacon, "the name of—"

Lost in the cheering. I turn to Luigi. "Who? What name?"

"Sisto Settimo," Luigi tells me.

Yes, and there he is, Pope Sixtus the Seventh, as we now must call him. A tiny figure clad in the silver and gold papal robes, arms outstretched to the multitude, and, yes! the sunlight glints on his cheeks, his lofty forehead, there is the brightness of polished steel. Luigi is already on his knees. I kneel beside him. Miss Harshaw, Beverly, Kenneth, even the rabbi all kneel, for beyond doubt this is a miraculous event. The pope comes forward on his balcony. Now he will deliver the traditional apostolic benediction to the city and to the world. "Our help is in the Name of the Lord," he declares gravely. He activates the levitator jets beneath his arms; even at this distance I can see the two small puffs of smoke. White smoke, again. He begins to rise into the air. "Who hath made heaven and earth," he says. "May Almighty God, Father, Son and Holy Ghost, bless you." His voice rolls majestically toward us. His shadow extends across the whole piazza. Higher and higher he goes, until he is lost to sight. Kenneth taps Luigi. "Another round of drinks," he says, and presses a bill of high denomination into the innkeeper's fleshy palm. Bishop FitzPatrick weeps. Rabbi Mueller embraces Miss Harshaw. The new pontiff, I think, has begun his reign in an auspicious way.

GARDNER R. DOZOIS

Horse of Air

GARDNER R. DOZOIS was born July 23, 1947, in Salem, Massachusetts, his ancestry conveniently half Irish and the remainder an amalgamation of French, Scottish, Dutch and American Indian. He spent three years of army service as a military journalist in Nuremberg, Germany, and since then he has worked as journalist, radio and TV broadcaster, busboy, IBM card filer, and editorial reader for Dell and Award Books and UPD Magazines. Along the way he took part in amateur theatrics and dabbled in photography, anthropology, sociology, natural history and history, exercising his body in bicycling and swimming and his mind in worrying, and he began to write.

His first story was sold in 1966, and the total now exceeds a baker's dozen. In addition to the science fiction magazines, he has contributed stories to several volumes of the *Orbit* series, *Quark 1,* *New Dimensions I* and *II,* and *Universe II.* His short story "A Dream at Noonday," was a finalist in the 1970 Nebula Award balloting. Dozois is the editor of a collection of stories, *A Day in the Life* (1972). He is a member of Science Fiction Writers of America and the SFWA Speakers' Bureau, and he has been a guest instructor at the Clarion Writers' Workshop.

In the 1971 Nebula Award balloting his name appeared on the final

138

ballot twice: with his novelette "A Special Kind of Morning" and with his short story "Horse of Air."

Sometimes when the weather is good I sit and look out over the city, fingers hooked through the mesh.

—The mesh is weather-stained, beginning to rust. As his fingers scrabble at it, chips of rust flake off, staining his hands the color of crusted blood. The heavy wire is hot and smooth under his fingers, turning rougher and drier at a rust spot. If he presses his tongue against the wire, it tastes slightly of lemons. He doesn't do that very often—

The city is quieter now. You seldom see motion, mostly birds if you do. As I watch, two pigeons strut along the roof ledge of the low building several stories below my balcony, stopping every now and then to pick at each other's feathers. They look fatter than ever. I wonder what they eat these days. Probably it is better not to know. They have learned to keep away from me anyway, although the mesh that encloses my small balcony floor to ceiling makes it difficult to get at them if they do land nearby. I'm not really hungry, of course, but they are noisy and leave droppings. I don't really bear any malice toward them. It's not a personal thing; I do it for the upkeep of the place.

(I hate birds. I will kill any of them I can reach. I do it with my belt buckle, snapping it between the hoops of wire.)

—He hates birds because they have freedom of movement, because they can fly, because they can shift their viewpoint from spot to spot in linear space, while he can do so only in time and memory, and that imperfectly. They can fly here and look at him and then fly away, while he has no volition: if he wants to look at them, he must wait until they decide to come to him. He flicks a piece of plaster at them, between the hoops—

Startled by something, the pigeons explode upward with a whir of feathers. I watch them fly away: skimming along the side of a building, dipping with an air current. They are soon lost in the maze of low roofs that thrust up below at all angles and heights, staggering toward the Apartment Towers in the middle distance. The Towers stand untouched by the sea of brownstones that break around their flanks, like aloof monoliths wading in a surf of scummy brown brick. Other towers march off in curving lines toward the horizon, becoming progressively smaller until they vanish at the place where a misty sky merges with a line of low hills. If I press myself against the mesh at the far right side of the balcony, I can see the nearest Tower to my own, perhaps six hundred yards away, all of steel and concrete with a vertical line of windows running down the middle and rows of identical balconies on either side.

Nearest to me on the left is a building that rises about a quarter of the way up my Tower's flank: patterns of dark-brown and light-red bricks, interlaced with fingers of mortar, weathered gray roof shingles, a few missing here and there in a manner reminiscent of broken teeth; a web of black chimney and sewage pipes crawling up and across the walls like metallic creepers. All covered with the pale splotches of bird droppings. The Towers are much cleaner; not so many horizontal surfaces. Windows are broken in the disintegrating buildings down there; the dying sunlight glints from fangs of shattered glass. Curtains hang in limp shreds that snap and drum when a wind comes up. If you squint, you can see that the wind has scattered broken twigs and rubbish all over the floors inside. No, I am much happier in one of the towers.

(I hate the Towers. I would rather live anywhere than here.)

—He hates the Towers. As the sun starts to dip below the horizon, settling down into the concrete labyrinth like a hog into a wallow, he shakes his head blindly and makes a low noise at the back of his throat. The shadows of buildings are longer now, stretching in toward him from the horizon like accusing fingers. A deep gray gloom is gathering in the corners and angles of walls, shot with crimson sparks from the foundering sun, now dragged under and wrapped in chill masonry. His hands go up and out, curling again around the hoops of the mesh. He shakes the mesh

violently, throwing his weight against it. The mesh groans in metallic agony but remains solid. A few chips of concrete puff from
the places where the ends of the mesh are anchored to the walls.
He continues to tear at the mesh until his hands bleed, half-healed
scabs torn open again. Tiny blood droplets spatter the heavy wire.
The blood holds the deeper color of rust—

If you have enough maturity to keep emotionalism out of it, the
view from here can even be fascinating. The sky is clear now, an
electric, saturated blue, and the air is as sharp as a jeweler's glass.
Not like the old days. Without factories and cars to keep it fed,
even the eternal smog has dissipated. The sky reminds me now of
an expensive aquarium filled with crystal tropical water, me at the
bottom: I almost expect to see huge eyes peering in from the
horizon, maybe a monstrous nose pressed against the glass. On a
sunny day you can see for miles.

But it is even more beautiful when it rains. The rain invests the
still landscape with an element of motion: long fingers of it brushing across the rooftops or marching down in zigzag sheets, the
droplets stirring and rippling the puddles that form in depressions,
drumming against the flat concrete surfaces, running down along
the edges of the shingles, foaming and sputtering from down-
spouts. The Towers stand like lords, swirling rain mists around
them as a fine gentleman swirls his jeweled cloak. Pregnant gray
clouds scurry by behind the Towers, lashed by wind. The constant
stream of horizontals past the fixed vertical fingers of the Towers
creates contrast, gives the eye something to follow, increases the
relief of motion. Motion is heresy when the world has become a
still life. But it soothes, the old-time religion. There are no atheists
in foxholes, nor abstainers when the world begins to flow. But does
that prove the desirability of God or the weakness of men? I drink
when the world flows, but unwillingly, because I know the price.
I have to drink, but I also have to pay. I will pay later when the
motion stops and the world returns to lethargy, the doldrums
made more unbearable by the contrast known a moment before.
That is another cross that I am forced to bear.

But it is beautiful, and fresh-washed after. And sometimes there is a rainbow. Rain is the only aesthetic pleasure I have left, and I savor it with the unhurried leisure of the aristocracy.

—When the rain comes, he flattens himself against the mesh, arms spread wide as if crucified there, letting the rain hammer against his face. The rain rolls in runnels down his skin, mixing with sweat, counterfeiting tears. Eyes closed, he bruises his open mouth against the mesh, trying to drink the rain. His tongue dabs at the drops that trickle by his mouth, licks out for the moisture oozing down along the links of wire. After the storm, he sometimes drinks the small puddles that gather on the balcony ledge, lapping them noisily and greedily, although the tap in the kitchen works, and he is never thirsty—

Always something to look at from here. Directly below are a number of weed-overgrown yards, chopped up unequally by low brick walls, nestled in a hollow square formed by the surrounding brownstones. There is even a tree in one corner, though it is dead and its limbs are gnarled and splintered. The yards were never neatly kept by the rabble that lived there, even in the old days: they are scattered with trash and rubbish, middens of worn-out household items and broken plastic toys, though the weeds have covered much. There was a neat, bright flower bed in one of the further yards, tended by a bent and leather-skinned foreign crone of impossible age, but the weeds have overgrown that as well, drowning the rarer blossoms. This season there were more weeds, fewer flowers—they seem to survive better, though God knows they have little else to recommend them, being coarse and ill-smelling.

In the closest yard an old and ornate wicker-back chair is still standing upright; if I remember correctly, a pensioner bought it at a rummage sale and used it to take the sun, being a parasite good for nothing else. Weeds are twining up around the chair; it is half hidden already. Beyond is a small concrete court where hordes of ragged children used to play ball. Its geometrical white lines are nearly obliterated now by rain and wind-drifted gravel. If you look

sharp at this clearing, sometimes you can see the sudden flurry of
a small darting body through the weeds; a rat or a cat, hard to tell
at this distance.

Once, months ago, I saw a man and a woman there, my first
clear indication that there are still people alive and about. They
entered the court like thieves, crawling through a low window,
the man lowering the girl and then jumping down after. They
were dressed in rags, and the man carried a rifle and a bandolier.
After reconnoitering, the man forced one of the rickety doors into
a brownstone, disappearing inside. After a while he came out
dragging a mattress—filthy, springs jutting through fabric—and
carried it into the ball court. They had intercourse there for the
better part of the afternoon, stopping occasionally while the man
prowled about with the rifle. I remember thinking that it was too
bad the gift of motion had been wasted on such as these. They left
at dusk. I had not tried to signal them, leaving them undisturbed
to their rut, although I was somewhat sickened by the coarse
brutality of the act. There *is* such a thing as *noblesse oblige.*

(I hate them. If I had a gun I would kill them. At first I watch
greedily as they make love, excited, afraid of scaring them away
if they should become aware of me watching. But as the afternoon
wears on, I grow drained, and then angry, and begin to shout at
them, telling them to get out, get the hell out. They ignore me.
Their tanned skin is vivid against asphalt as they strain together.
Sweat makes their locked limbs glisten in the thick sunlight. The
rhythmic rise and fall of their bodies describes parabolic lines
through the crusted air. I scream at them and tear at the mesh,
voice thin and impotent. Later they make love again, rolling from
the mattress in their urgency, sprawling among the lush weeds,
coupling like leopards. I try to throw plaster at them, but the angle
is wrong. As they leave the square, the man gives me the finger.)

Thinking of those two makes me think of the other animals that
howl through the world, masquerading as men. On the far left,
hidden by the nearest brownstones but winding into sight further
on, is a highway. Once it was a major artery of the city, choked

with a chrome flood of traffic. Now it is empty. Once or twice at the beginning I would see an ambulance or a fire engine, once a tank. A few weeks ago I saw a jeep go by, driving square in the middle of the highway, ridden by armed men. Occasionally I have seen men and women trudge past, dragging their possessions behind them on a sledge. Perhaps the wheel is on the way out.

Against one curb is the overturned, burned-out hulk of a bus: small animals use it for a cave now, and weeds are beginning to lace through it. I saw it burning, a week after the Building Committee came. I sat on the balcony and watched its flames eat up at the sky, although it was too dark to make out what was happening around it; the street lights had been the first things to go. There were other blazes in the distance, glowing like campfires, like blurred stars. I remember wondering that night what was happening, what the devil was going on. But I've figured it out now.

It was the niggers. I hate to say it. I've been a liberal man all my life. But you can't deny the truth. They are responsible for the destruction, for the present degeneration of the world. It makes me sad to have to say this. I had always been on their side in spirit, I was more than willing to stretch out a helping hand to those less fortunate than myself. I always said so; I always said that. I had high hopes for them all. But they got greedy, and brought us to this. We should have known better, we should have listened to the so-called racists, we should have realized that idealism is a wasting disease, a cancer. We should have remembered that blood will tell. A hard truth: it was the niggers. I have no prejudice; I speak the cold facts. I had always wished them well.

(I hate niggers. They are animals. Touching one would make me vomit.)

—He hates niggers. He has seen them on the street corners with their women, he has seen them in their jukeboxed caves with their feet in sawdust, he has heard them speaking in a private language half devised of finger snaps and motions of liquid hips, he has felt the inquiry of their eyes, he has seen them dance. He envies them for having a culture separate from the bland familiarity of his own, he envies their tang of the exotic. He envies their easy sexuality. He fears their potency. He fears that in climbing up they will shake him down. He fears generations of stored-up hate. He hates them because their very existence makes him uncomfortable. He hates them because sometimes they have seemed to be happy on their tenement street corners, while he rides by in an air-conditioned car and is not. He hates them because they are not part of the mechanism and yet still have the audacity to exist. He hates them because they have escaped—

Dusk has come, hiding a world returned to shame and barbarism. It occurs to me that I may be one of the few members of the upper class left. The rabble were always quick to blame their betters for their own inherent inferiority and quick to vent their resentment in violence when the opportunity arose. The other Apartment Towers are still occupied, I think; I can see the lights at night, as they can see mine, if there is anyone left there to see. So perhaps there are still a few of us left. Perhaps there is still some hope for the world after all.

Although what avail to society is their survival if they are as helpless as I? We may be the last hope of restoring order to a land raped by Chaos, and we are being wasted. We are born to govern, to regulate, prepared for it by station, tradition and long experience: leadership comes as naturally to us as drinking and fornication come to the masses of the Great Unwashed. We are being wasted, our experience and foresight pissed away by fools who will not listen.

And we dwindle. I speak of us as a class, as a corporate "we." But there are fewer lights in the other Towers every month. Last night I counted less than half the number I could see a year ago. On evenings when the wind grows bitter with autumn cold, I fear that I will soon be the only one left with the courage to hold out. It would be so easy to give in to despair; the quietus of hopelessness is tempting. But it is a siren goddess, made of tin. Can't the others see that? To give up is to betray their blood. But still the lights dwindle. At times I have the dreadful fancy that I will sit here one

night and watch the last light flicker out in the last Tower, leaving
me alone in darkness, the only survivor of a noble breed. Will some
improbably alien archaeologist come and hang a sign on my cage:
The Last of the Aristocracy?

Deep darkness now. The lights begin to come on across the gulfs
of shadow, but I am afraid to count them. Thinking of these things
has chilled me, and I shudder. The wind is cold, filled with dampness. There will be a storm later. Distant lightning flickers behind
the Towers, each flash sending jagged shadows leaping toward me,
striking blue highlights from every reflecting surface. Each lightning stroke seems to momentarily reverse the order of things,
etching the Towers in black relief against the blue-white dazzle of
the sky, then the brilliance draining, leaving the Towers as before:
islands of light against an inky background of black. The cycle is
repeated, shadows lunging in at me, in at me, thrusting swords of
nigger blackness. It was on a hellish night like this that the Building Committee came.

It was a mistake to give them so much power. I admit it. I'm not
too proud to own up to my own mistakes. But we were tired of
struggling with an uncooperative and unappreciative society. We
were beaten into weariness by a horde of supercilious bastards,
petty and envious little men hanging on our coattails and trying
to chivy us down. We were sick of people with no respect, no
traditions, no heritage, no proper ambitions. We were disgusted
by a world degenerating at every seam, in every aspect. We had
finally realized the futility of issuing warnings no one would listen
to. Even then the brakes could have been applied to our skidding
society if someone had bothered to listen, if anyone had had the
guts and foresight to take the necessary measures. But we were
tired, and we were no longer young.

So we traded our power for security. We built the Towers; we
formed a company, turned our affairs over to them, and retired
from the world into our own tight-knit society. Let the company
have the responsibility and the problems, let them deal with the
pressures and the decisions, let them handle whatever comes; we

will be safe and comfortable regardless. They are the bright, ambitious technicians; let them cope. They are the expendable soldiers; let them fight and be expended as they are paid for doing; we shall be safe behind the lines. Let them have the mime show of power; we are civilized enough to enjoy the best things of life without it. We renounce the painted dreams; they are hollow.

It was a mistake.

It was a mistake to give them the voting proxies; Anderson was a fool, senile before his time. It was all a horrible mistake. I admit it. But we were no longer young.

And the world worsened, and one day the Building Committee came.

It was crisis, they said, and Fear was walking in the land. And the Charter specified that we were to be protected, that we must not be disturbed. So they came with the work crews and meshed over my balcony. And welded a slab of steel over my door as they left. They would not listen to my protest, wrapped in legalities, invulnerable in armor of technical gobbledygook. Protection was a specific of the Charter, they said, and with the crisis this was the only way they could ensure our protection should the outer defenses go down; it was a temporary measure.

And the work crews went about their business with slapdash efficiency, and the balding, spectacled foreman told me he only worked here. So I stood quietly and watched them seal me in, although I was trembling with rage. I am no longer young. And I would not lose control before these vermin. Every one of them was waiting for it, hoping for it in their petty, resentful souls, and I would let myself be flayed alive before I would give them the satisfaction. It is a small comfort to me that I showed them the style with which a gentleman can take misfortune.

(When I finally realize what they are doing, I rage and bluster. The foreman pushed me away. "It's for your own good," he says, mouthing the cliché halfheartedly, not really interested. I beat at him with ineffectual fists. Annoyed, he shrugs me off and ducks through the door. I try to run after him. One of the guards hits me in the face with his rifle butt. Pain and shock and a brief darkness. And then I realize that I am lying on the floor. There is blood on my forehead and on my mouth. They have almost finished maneuvering the steel slab into place, only a man-sized crack left open. The guard is the only one left in the room, a goggled technician just squeezing out through the crack. The guard turns toward the door. I hump myself across the room on my knees, crawling after him, crying and begging. He plants his boot on my shoulder and pushes me disgustedly away. The room tumbles, I roll over twice, stop, come up on my elbows and start to crawl after him again. He says, "Fuck off, dad," and slaps his rifle, jangling the magazine in the breech. I stop moving. He glares at me, then leaves the room. They push the slab all the way closed. It makes a grinding, rumbling sound, like a subway train. Still on my knees, I throw myself against it, but it is solid. Outside there are welding noises. I scream.)

There is a distant rumbling now. Thunder: the storm is getting nearer. The lightning flashes are more intense, and closer together. They are too bright, too fast, blending into one another, changing the dimensions of the world too rapidly. With the alternating of glare and thrusting shadow there is too much motion, nothing ever still for a second, nothing you can let your eye rest on. Watching it strains your vision. My eyes ache with the motion.

I close them, but there are squiggly white afterimages imprinted on the insides of my eyelids. A man of breeding should know how to control his emotions. I do; in the old circles, the ones that mattered, I was known for my self-discipline and refinement. But this is an unseasonable night, and I am suddenly afraid. It feels like the bones are rattled in the body of the earth, it feels like maybe it will come now.

But that is an illusion. It is not the Time; It will not come yet. Only I know when the Time is, only I can say when It will come. And It will not come until I call for It, that is part of the bargain. I studied military science at Annapolis. I shall recognize the most strategic moment, I shall know when the Time is at hand for vengeance and retribution. I shall know. And the Time is not now. It will not come tonight. This is only an autumn storm.

I open my eyes. And find my stare returned. Windows ring me on all sides like walls of accusing, lidless eyes. Lightning oozes across the horizon: miniature reflections of the electric arc etched in cold echoes across a thousand panes of glass, a thousand matches struck simultaneously in a thousand dusty rooms.

A sequence of flares. The sky alternates too quickly to follow. Blue-white, black. Blue-white. Black again. The roofs flicker with invested motion, brick dancing in a jerky, silent-movie fashion.

Oh, God, the chimneys, humped against dazzle, looming in shadow. Marching rows of smoky brick gargoyles, ash-cold now with not an ember left alive. The rows sway closer with every flash. I can hear the rutch of mortar-footed brick against tile, see the waddling, relentless rolling of their gait. They are people actually, the poor bastard refugees of the rabble frozen into brick, struck dumb with mortar. I saw it happen on the night of the Building Committee, thousands of people swarming like rats over the roofs to escape the burning world, caught by a clear voice of crystal that metamorphosed them with a single word, fixing them solid to the roofs, their hands growing into their knees, their heels into their buttocks, their heads thrown back with mouths gaped in a scream, flesh swapped for brick, blood for mortar. They hump toward me on their blunt knees in ponderously bobbing lines. With a sound like fusing steel, nigger-black shadows humping *in* at me. Christ hands sealing my eyes with clay stuffing down my mouth my throat filling Oh God oh christ christ *christ*

It is raining now. I will surely catch a chill standing here; there are vapors in the night air. Perhaps it would be advisable to go inside. Yes, I do think that would be best. Sometimes it is better to forget external things.

—He crawls away from the mesh on his hands and knees, although he is healthy and perfectly able to stand. He often crawls from place to place in the apartment; he thinks it gives him a better perspective. Rain patters on the balcony behind, drums against the glass of the French windows that open into the apartment. He claws at the framework of the windows, drags himself to his feet. He stands there for a moment, face pressed flat against the glass, trembling violently. His cheeks are wet. Perhaps he has been crying. Or perhaps it was the rain—

I turn on the light and go inside, closing the French windows firmly behind me. It is the very devil of a night outside. In here it is safe, even comfortable. This place is only a quarter of my actual apartment, of course. The Building Committee sealed me in here, cut me off from the rest of my old place, which occupied most of this floor. Easier to defend me this way, the bastards said. So this apartment is smaller than what I'm used to living in, God knows. But in a strange way the smallness makes the place more cozy somehow, especially on a piggish night like this when fiends claw the windowpane.

I cross to the kitchen cubicle, rummage through the jars and cans; there's some coffee left from this week's shipment, I think. Yes, a little coffee left in one of the jars: instant; coarse, murky stuff. I had been used to better; once we drank nothing but fine-ground Colombian, and I would have spat in the face of any waiter who dared to serve me unpercolated coffee. This is one of the innumerable little ways in which we pay for our folly. A thousand little things, but together they add up into an almost unbearable burden, a leering Old Man of the Sea wrapped leech-fashion around my shoulders and growing heavier by the day. But this is defeatist talk. I am more tired than I would allow myself to admit. Here the coffee will help; even this bitter liquid retains that basic virtue in kind with the more palatable stuff. I heat some water, slosh it over the obscene granules into a cup. The cup is cracked, no replacement for it: another little thing. A gust of wind rattles the glass in the French windows. I will not listen to it.

Weary, I carry the steaming cup into the living room, sit down in the easy chair with my back to the balcony. I try to balance the cup on my knee, but the damn thing is too hot; I finally rest it on the chair arm, leaving a moist ring on the fabric, but that hardly matters now. Can my will be weakening? Once I would have considered it sacrilege to sully fine furniture and would have gone to any length to avoid doing so. Now I am too wrapped in lassitude to get up and go into the kitchen for a coaster. Coffee seeps slowly into fabric, a widening brownish stain, like blood. I am almost too tired to lift the cup to my lips.

Degeneration starts very slowly, so deviously, so patiently that it almost seems to be a living thing; embodied it would be a weasel-like animal armed with sly cunning and gnawing needle teeth. It never goes for your throat like a decent monster, so that you might have a chance of beating it down: it lurks in darkness, it gnaws furtively at the base of your spine, it burrows into your liver while you sleep. Like the succubi I try to guard against at night, it saps your strength, it sucks your breath in slumber, it etches away the marrow of your bones.

There is enough water in the tank for one more bath this week; I should wash, but I fear I'm too tired to manage it. Another example? It takes such a lot of *effort* to remain civilized. How tempting to say, "It no longer matters." It does matter. I say it does. I will make it matter. I cannot afford the seductive surrender of my unfortunate brethren; I have a responsibility they don't have. Perhaps I am luckier to have it, in a way. It is an awesome responsibility, but carrying it summons up a corresponding strength, it gives me a reason for living, a goal outside myself. Perhaps my responsibility is what enables me to hang on, the knowledge of what is to come just enough to balance out the other pressures. The game has not yet been played to an end. Not while I still hold my special card.

Thinking of the secret, I look at the television set, but the atmospherics are wrong tonight for messages, and it's probably too late for the haphazard programming they put out now. Some nights I leave the test pattern on, enjoying the flickering highlights it sends across the walls and ceilings, but tonight I think it will be more comfortable with just the pool of yellow glow cast by the lamp next to my chair, a barrier against the tangible darkness.

Looking at the television always reawakens my curiosity about the outside world. What is the state of society? The city I can see from my balcony seems to have degenerated into savagery, civilization seems to have been destroyed, but there are contradictions, there are ambiguities. Obviously the Building Committee must still be in existence somewhere. The electric lights and the plumbing still work in the Towers, a shipment of food supplies rattles up the pneumatic dumbwaiter into the kitchen cubicle twice a week, there are old movies and cartoons on television, running continuously with no commercials or live programming, never a hint of news. Who else could it be for but us? Who else could be responsible for it but the Building Committee? I've seen the city; it is dark, broken, inhabited by no one but a few human jackals who eke out a brute existence and hunt each other through the ruins. These facilities are certainly not operated for them—the other towers are the only lighted buildings visible in the entire wide section of city visible from here.

No, it is the Building Committee. It must be. They are the only ones with the proper resources to hold a circle of order against a widening chaos. Those resources were vast. I know: we built them, we worked to make them flexible, we sweated to make them inexhaustible. We let their control pass out of our hands. One never finishes paying for past sins.

What a tremendous amount of trouble they've gone to, continuing to operate the towers, even running a small television station somewhere to force-feed us the "entertainment" specified in the Charter. And never a word, never a glimpse of them, even for a second. Why? Why do they bother to keep up the pretense, the mocking hypocrisy of obeying the Charter? The real power is theirs now, why do they bother to continue the sham and lip service? Why don't they just shut down the towers and leave us to starve in our plush cells? Is it the product of some monstrous, sadistic sense of humor? Or is it the result of a methodical, fussily prim sense of order that refuses to deny a legal technicality even when the laws themselves have died? Do they laugh their young men's laughter when they think of the once formidable old beasts they have caged?

I feel a surge of anger. I put the half-emptied cup carefully down on the rug. My hand is trembling. The Time is coming. It will be soon now. Soon they will heap some further indignity on me and force my hand. I will not have them laughing at me, those little men with maggots for eyes. Not when I still have it in my power to change it all. Not while I still am who I am. But not just yet. Let them have their victory, their smug laughter. An old tiger's fangs may be blunt and yellowing, but they can still bite. And even an old beast can still rise for one more kill.

I force myself to my feet. I have the inner strength, the discipline. They have nothing, they are the rabble, they are children trying out as men and parading in adult clothing. It was we who taught them the game, and we still know how to play it best. I force myself to wash, to fold the bed out from the wall, to lie still, fighting for calm. I run my eyes around the familiar dimensions of the apartment, cataloguing: pale blue walls, red draw curtains for the French windows, bookshelves next to the curtains, a black cushioned stool, the rug in patterns of orange and green against brown, a red shaggy chair and matching couch, the archways to the kitchen and bath cubicles. Nothing alien. Nothing hostile. I begin to relax. Thank God for familiarity. There is a certain pleasure in looking at well-known, well-loved things, a certain unshakable sense of reality. I often fall asleep counting my things.

(I hate this apartment. I hate everything in this apartment. I cannot stand to live here any longer. Someday I will chop everything to unrecognizable fragments and pile it in the middle of the floor and burn it, and I will laugh while it burns.)

—He is wakened by a shaft of sunlight that falls through the uncurtained French windows. He groans, stirs, draws one foot up, heel against buttock, knee toward the ceiling. His hand clenches in the bedclothes. The sound of birds reaches him through the insulating glass. For a moment, waking, he thinks that he is elsewhere, another place, another time. He mutters a woman's name and his hand goes out to grope across the untouched, empty space beside him in the double bed. His hand encounters only the cool of sheets, no answering warmth of flesh. He grimaces, his bent leg snaps out to full length again, his suddenly desperate hand rips the sheet free of the mattress, finding nothing. He wrenches to his feet, neck corded, staggering. By the time his eyes slide open he has begun to scream—

. . . ow it. I will not allow it. Do you hear me, bastards? *I will not allow it.* I will not stand for it. You've gone too far, I warn you, too far, I'll kill you. D'you hear? Niggers and thieves. The past is all I have. I will not have you touching it, I will not have you sliming and defiling it with your shitty hands. You leave her out of it, you leave her alone. What kind of men are you, using her against me? *What kind of men are you?* Rabble not worth breath. Defiling everything you touch, everything better than you, finer than you. I will not allow it.

It is time. It is *Time.*

The decision brings a measure of calm. I am committed now. They have finally driven me too far. It is time for me to play the final card. I will not let them remain unpunished for this another second, another breath. I will call for It, and It will come. I must keep control, there must be no mistakes. This is retribution. This is the moment I have waited for all these agonizing months. I must keep control, there must be no mistakes. It must be executed with dispatch, with precision. I breathe deeply to calm myself. There will be no mistakes, no hesitations.

Three steps take me to the television. I flick it on, waiting for it to warm. Impatience drums within me, tightly reined as a rearing Arabian stallion. So long, so long.

A picture appears on the screen: another imbecilic movie. I think of the Building Committee, unaware, living in the illusion of victory. Expertly I remove the back of the television, my skilled fingers probing deep into the maze of wires and tubes. I work with the familiarity of long practice. How many hours did I crouch like this, experimenting, before I found the proper frequency of the

Others by trial and error? Patience was never a trait of the rabble; it is a talent reserved for the aristocracy. They didn't count on my patience. Mayflies themselves, they cannot understand dedication of purpose. They didn't count on my scientific knowledge, on my technical training at Annapolis. They didn't count on the resources and ingenuity of a superior man.

I tap two wires together, creating sparks, sending messages into ether. I am sending on the frequency of the Others, a prearranged signal in code: The Time is now. Let It come. Sweat in my eyes, fingers cramping, but I continue to broadcast. The Time is now. Let It come. At last a response, the Others acknowledging that they've received my order.

It is over.

Now It will come.

Now they will pay for their sins.

I sit back on my heels, drained. I have done my part. I have launched It on Its way, given birth to retribution, sowed the world with dragon's teeth. And they laughed. Now It is irreversible. Nothing can stop It. An end to all thieves and niggers, to all little men, to all the rabble that grow over the framework like weeds and ruin the order of the world. I stagger to the French windows, throw them open. Glass shatters in one frame, bright fragments against the weave of the rug. Onto the balcony where buildings press in at me unaware of Ragnarok. I collapse against the mesh, fingers spread, letting it take my weight. No motion in the world, but soon there will be enough. Far north, away from the sight of the city, the spaceships of the Others are busy according to plan, planting the thermal charges that will melt the icecap, shattering the earth-old ice, liberating the ancient waters, forming a Wave to thunder south and drown the world. I think of the Building Committee, of the vermin in the ruins of the city, even of my fellows in the other towers. I am not sorry for them. I am no longer young, but I will take them with me into darkness. There will be no other eyes to watch a sun I can no longer see. I have no regrets. I've always hated them. I hate them all.

(I hate them all.)

—He hates them all—

A moaning in the earth, a trembling, a drumming as of a billion billion hoofs. The tower sways queasily. A swelling, ragged shriek of sound.

The Wave comes.

Over the horizon, climbing, growing larger, stretching higher, filling up the sky, cutting off the sunlight, water in a green wall like glass hundreds of feet high, topped with fangs of foam, the Wave beginning to topple in like the closing fist of God. Its shadow over everything, night at noon as it sweeps in, closes down. The Towers etched like thin lines against its bulk. It is curling overhead is the sky now there is no sky now but the underbelly of the Wave coming down. I have time to see the Towers snapped like matchsticks broken stumps of fangs before it hits with the scream of grating steel and blackness clogs my throat to

(I have destroyed the world.)

—The shadow of the mesh on his face—

Sometimes you can see other people in the other tower apartments, looking out from their own balconies. I wonder how they destroy the world.

—He turns away, dimly remembering a business appointment. Outside the lazy hooting of rush-hour traffic. There is a cartoon carnival on Channel Five—

GEORGE ZEBROWSKI

Heathen God

George Zebrowski was born December 28, 1945, in Villach, Austria, of Polish parents. He grew up in England, Manhattan, the Bronx and Miami, and he is one of an extremely small group of authors who have achieved literary success in a second language. He attended Harpur College and the State University of New York at Binghamton, majoring in philosophy, and he brings his interest in this field to his writing—several of his science fiction stories utilize philosophical concepts.

He is a member of the World Future Society, Science Fiction Writers of America, and the SFWA Speakers' Bureau. He has reviewed books for *Crawdaddy, Science Fiction Review* and *Riverside Quarterly;* has been a reader for Dell Books; has sold fiction to *The Magazine of Fantasy and Science Fiction, If, Infinity* and to several forthcoming collections of original stories. Currently he lectures in science fiction at SUNY-Binghamton, edits the *SFWA Bulletin* and writes. His two forthcoming novels are *The Omega Point* and *Macrolife.*

The story "Heathen God" was a 1971 Nebula Award finalist.

*". . . every heathen deity has its
place in the flow of existence."*

The isolation station and preserve for alien flora and fauna on
Antares IV had only one prisoner, a three-foot-tall gnomelike
biped with skin like creased leather and eyes like great glass
globes. His hair was silky white and reached down to his shoulders,
and he usually went about the great natural park naked. He lived
in a small white cell located in one of the huge blocklike administration modules. There was a small bed in the cell, and a small
doorway which led out to the park. A hundred feet away from the
door there was a small pool, one of many scattered throughout the
park. It reflected the deep-blue color of the sky.

The gnome was very old, but no one had yet determined quite
how old. And there seemed to be no way to find out. The gnome
himself had never volunteered any information about his past. In
the one hundred years of his imprisonment he had never asked
the caretaker for anything. It was rumored among the small staff
of Earthmen and humanoids that the gnome was mad. Generally
they avoided him. Sometimes they would watch his small figure
standing under the deep-blue sky, looking up at the giant disk of
Antares hanging blood red on the horizon, just above the well-
pruned trees of the park, and they would wonder what he might
be thinking.

The majority of Earthmen spread over twelve star systems did
not even know of the gnome's existence, much less his importance. A few knew, but they were mostly scholarly and political
figures, and a few theologians. The most important fact about the
alien was that sometime in the remote past he had been responsible for the construction of the solar system and the emergence of
intelligent life on Earth.

The secret had been well kept for over a century.

In the one hundred and fourth year of the alien's captivity two
men set out for Antares to visit him. The first man's motives were
practical: the toppling of an old regime; the other man's goal was

to ask questions. The first man's political enemies had helped him undertake this journey, seeing that it would give them the chance to destroy him. The importance of gaining definitive information about the alien was in itself enough reason to send a mission, but combined with what they knew about the motives of the man they feared, this mission would provide for them the perfect occasion to resolve both matters at the same time. In any case, the second man would bring back anything of value that they might learn about the gnome.

Everything had been planned down to the last detail. The first ship carrying the two unsuspecting men was almost ready to come out of hyperspace near Antares. Two hours behind it in the warp was a military vessel—a small troop ship. As the first vessel came out of nothingness into the brilliance of the great star, the commander of the small force ship opened his sealed orders.

As he came down the shuttle ramp with his two companions, Father Louis Chavez tried to mentally prepare himself for what he would find here. It was still difficult to believe what his superiors had told him about the alien who was a prisoner here. The morning air of Antares IV was fresh, and the immediate impression was one of stepping out into a warm botanical garden. At his left Sister Guinivere carried his small attaché case. On his right walked Benedict Compton, linguist, cultural anthropologist, and as everyone took for granted, eventual candidate for first secretary of Earth's Northern Hemisphere. Compton was potentially a religious man, but the kind who always demanded an advance guarantee before committing himself to anything. Chavez felt suspicious of him; in fact he felt wary about this entire visit to Antares IV.

On Earth the religio-philosophic system was a blend of evolutionary Chardinism and Christianity, an imposing intellectual structure that had been dominant for some two hundred years now. The political structure based its legitimacy and continuing policies on it. Compton, from what he had learned, had frightened some high authorities with the claim that the gnome creature here on Antares IV was a potential threat to the beliefs of mankind. This, combined with what was already known about the alien's past, was seemingly enough to send this fact-finding mission. Only a few men knew about it, and Chavez remembered the fear he had sensed in them when he had been briefed. Their greatest fear was that somehow the gnome's history would become public knowledge. Compton, despite his motives, had found a few more political friends. But Chavez suspected that Compton wanted power not for himself, but to do something about the quality of life on Earth. He was sure the man was sincere. How little of the thought in our official faith filters out into actual policy, Chavez thought. And what would the government do if an unorganized faith—a heresy in the old sense—were to result from this meeting between Compton and the alien? Then he remembered how Compton had rushed this whole visit. He wondered just how far a man like Compton would go to have his way in the world.

Antares was huge on the horizon, a massive red disk against a deep-blue sky. A slight breeze waved the trees around the landing square. The pathway which started at the north corner led to three blocklike administration buildings set on a neat lawn and surrounded by flowering shrubs and fruit-bearing trees. The buildings were a bright white color. The walk was pleasant.

Rufus Kade, the caretaker, met them at the front entrance to the main building. He showed them into the comfortable reception room. He was a tall, thin botanist, who had taken the administrative post because it gave him the opportunity to be near exotic plants. Some of the flora came from worlds as much as one hundred light-years away from Antares. After the introductions were over, Kade took the party to the enclosed garden which had a pool in its center, and where the gnome spent most of his time.

"Do you ever talk with him, Mr. Kade?" Father Chavez asked. The caretaker shook his head. "No," he said. "And now I hope you will all excuse me, I have work to do." He left them at the entrance to the garden path.

Compton turned to Father Chavez and said, "You are lucky; you're the only representative of any church ever to get a chance to meet what might be the central deity of that church." He smiled. "But I feel sorry for you—for whatever he is, he will not be what you expect, and most certainly he will not be what you want him to be."

"Let's wait and see," Chavez said. "I'm not a credulous man."

"You know, Chavez," Compton said in a more serious mood, "they let me come here too easily. What I mean is they took my word for the danger involved with little or no question."

"Should they have not taken your word? You are an important man. You sound as if you didn't quite tell them everything."

They walked into the garden. On either side of them the plants were luxurious, with huge green leaves and strange varicolored flowers. The air was filled with rich scents, and the earth gave the sensation of being very moist and loosely packed. They came into the open area surrounding the pool. Sister Guinivere stood between the two men as they looked at the scene. The water was still, and the disk of Antares was high enough now in the morning sky to be reflected in it.

The gnome stood on the far side, watching them as they approached, as if he expected them at any moment to break into some words of greeting. Father Chavez knew that they would appear as giants next to the small figure. It would be awkward standing before a member of a race a million years older than mankind and towering over him. It would be aesthetically banal, Chavez thought.

As they came to the other side of the pool Compton said, "Let me start the conversation, Father."

"If you wish," Chavez said. *Why am I afraid, and what does it matter who starts the conversation*, he thought.

Compton walked up to the standing gnome and sat down cross-legged in front of him. It was a diplomatic gesture. Father Chavez felt relieved and followed the example, motioning Sister Guinivere to do the same. They all looked at the small alien.

His eyes were deep-set and large; his hair was white, thin and reached down to his shoulders. He had held his hands behind his back when they had approached, but now they were together in front of him. His shoulders were narrow and his arms were thin. He wore a one-piece coverall with short sleeves.

Chavez hoped they would be able to talk to him easily. The gnome looked at each of them in turn. After a few minutes of silence it became obvious that he expected them to start the conversation.

"My name is Benedict Compton," Compton said, "and this is Father Chavez and Sister Guinivere, his secretary. We came here to ask you about your past, because it concerns us."

Slowly the gnome nodded his head, but he did not sit with them. There was more silence. Compton gave Chavez a questioning look.

"Could you tell us who you are?" Chavez asked. The gnome moved his head sharply to look at him. It's almost as if I interrupted him at something, Chavez thought. There was a sad look on the face now, as if in that one moment he had understood everything—why they were here and the part he would have to play.

Chavez felt his stomach grow tense. He felt as if he were being carefully examined. Next to him Compton was playing with a blade of grass. Sister Guinivere sat with her hands folded in her lap. Briefly he recalled the facts he knew about the alien—facts which only a few Earthmen had been given access to over the last century. Facts which demanded that some sort of official attitude be taken.

The best-kept secret of the past century was the fact that this small creature had initiated the events which led to the emergence of intelligent life on Earth. In the far past he had harnessed his powers of imagination to a vast machine, which had been built for another purpose, and had used it to create most of the life on Earth. He had been caught at his experiments in cosmology, and exiled. Long before men had gone out to the stars he had been a wanderer in the galaxy, but in recent years he had been handed over to Earth authorities to keep at this extraterrestrial preserve. Apparently his people still feared his madness. This was all they had ever revealed to the few Earthmen who took charge of the matter.

It was conjectured that the gnome's race was highly isolationist; the gnome was the only member of it that had ever been seen by Earthmen. The opinion was also held that his culture feared contact with other intelligent life, and especially with this illegitimate creation. Of the few who knew about the case, only one or two had ever expressed any disbelief. It was after all, Chavez thought, enough to make any man uneasy. It seemed safer to ignore the matter most of the time.

Since that one contact with Earth, the gnome's race had never come back for him and had never offered further explanations. A century ago they had simply left him in Earth orbit, in a small vessel of undeniably superior workmanship. A recorded message gave all the information they had wanted to reveal. Their home world had never been found, and the gnome had remained silent. Benedict Compton had set up this meeting, and Chavez had been briefed by his superiors and instructed to go along as an observer.

Chavez remembered how the information had at first shaken and then puzzled him. The tension in his stomach grew worse. He wondered about Compton's motives; but he had not dared to question them openly. On Earth many scientists prized the alien as the only contact with a truly advanced culture, and he knew that more than one young student would do anything to unlock the secrets that must surely exist in the brain of the small being now standing in front of him. He felt sure that Compton was hoping for some such thing.

Suddenly the small figure took a step back from them. A small breeze waved his long white hair. He stopped and his small, gnarly body took on a strange stature; his face was grief-stricken and his low voice was sad. It wavered as he spoke to them. "I made you to love each other, and through yourselves, me. I needed that love.

No one can know how much I needed it, but it had to be freely given, so I had to permit the possibility of it being withheld. There was no other way, and there still is not."

Chavez looked at Compton for a reaction. The big man sat very still. Sister Guinivere was looking down at the grass in front of her feet. Chavez felt a stirring of fear and panic in his insides. It felt as if the alien was speaking only to him—as if *he* could relieve the thirst that lived behind those deep-set eyes in that small head.

He felt the other's need. He felt the deprivation that was visible on that face, and he felt that at any moment he would feel the awesome rage that would spill out onto them. This then, he thought, is the madness that his race had spoken about. All the power had been stripped from this being, and now he is a beggar.

Instead of rage there was sadness. It was oppressive. It hung in the air around them. What was Compton trying to uncover here? How could all this benefit anyone? Chavez noticed that his left hand was shaking, and he gripped it with the other hand.

The gnome raised his right hand and spoke again. *Dear God, help me,* Chavez prayed. *Help me to see this clearly.* "I fled from the hive mind which my race was working toward," the gnome said in a louder voice than before. "They have achieved it. They are one entity now. What you see in this dwarfed body are only the essentials of myself—the feelings mostly. They wait for the day when the love in my children comes to fruition and they will unite, thus recreating my former self—which is now in them. Then I will leave my prison and return to them to become the completion of myself. This body will die then. My longing for that time is without limit, and I will make another history like this one and see it through. Each time I will be the completion of a species and its moving spirit. And again they will give birth to me. Without this I am nothing."

There was a loud thunderclap overhead, the unmistakable sound of a shuttle coming through the atmosphere. But it was too early for the starship shuttle to be coming back for them, Chavez thought. Compton jumped up and turned to look toward the ad-

ministration buildings. Chavez noticed that the gnome was looking at him. *Do your people worship a supreme being?* Chavez
thought the question. *Do they have the idea of such a being?*
Surely you know the meaning of such a being.

I don't know any such thing, the thought spoke clearly in his
head. *Do you know him?*

"It's a shuttle craft," Compton said. "Someone's coming to join
us."

Chavez got to his feet and went over to Compton. Sister Guinivere struggled to her feet and joined them. "What is it?" she asked.

"I—I don't know who it could be," Compton said. Chavez noticed the lack of confidence in the other's voice. Behind them the
gnome stood perfectly still, unaffected by the interruption.

"They've landed by now," Compton said. "It could only be one
thing, Father—they've found out my plans for the gnome." Compton came up to him and spoke in a low voice. "Father, this is the
only way to get a change on Earth—yes, it's what you think, a cult,
with me as its head, but the cause is just. Join me now, Father!"

Then it's true, Chavez thought. He's planning to bypass the
lawful candidacy. Then why did they let him come here?

There was a rustling sound in the trees and shrubs around the
pool area. Suddenly they were surrounded by armed men. Twenty
figures in full battle gear had stepped out from the trees and
garden shrubs. They stood perfectly still, waiting.

Antares was directly overhead now, a dark-red circle of light
covering twenty percent of the blue dome that was the sky. Noon-
time.

Compton's voice shook as he shouted, "What is *this?* Who the
devil are you?"

A tall man immediately on the other side of the pool from them
appeared to be the commanding officer. He wore no gear and
there were no weapons in his hands. Instead he held a small piece
of paper which he had just taken out of a sealed envelope.

"Stand away, Father, and you too, Sister!" the officer shouted.
"This does not concern you." Then he looked down at the paper

in his hand and read: "Benedict Compton, you have been charged with conspiracy to overthrow the government of the Northern Hemisphere on Earth by unlawful means, and you have been tried and convicted by the high court of North America for this crime. The crime involves the use of an alien being as your co-conspirator to initiate a religious controversy through a personally financed campaign which would result in your becoming the leader of a subversive cult, whose aim would be to seize power through a carefully prepared *hoax*. You and your co-conspirator are being eliminated because you are both enemies of the state." The officer folded the paper and put it back in its envelope and placed it in his tunic.

Chavez noticed that Sister Guinivere was at his side, and he could tell that she was afraid. Compton turned to Chavez.

"Father, protect the gnome, whatever he is. Use what authority you have. They won't touch you."

"The execution order is signed by Secretary Alcibiad herself!" the tall officer shouted.

Chavez was silent.

"Father, please!" Compton pleaded. "You can't let this happen." Chavez heard the words, but he was numb with surprise. The words had transfixed him as effectively as any spear. He couldn't move, he couldn't think. Sister Guinivere held his arm.

Suddenly Compton was moving toward the gnome.

"Shoot!"

The lasers reached out like tongues.

The little figure fell. And the thought went out from him in one last effort, reaching light-years into space. *I loved you. You did not love me, or each other.* They all heard the thought, and it stopped them momentarily. Compton was still standing, but his right arm was gone, and he was bleeding noisily onto the grass.

"Shoot!" The order went out again.

Again the lasers lashed out. Compton fell on his back, a few yards from the gnome. Sister Guinivere fell to the grass on her knees, sobbing. She began to wail. The soldiers began to retreat back to their shuttle craft. Father Chavez sat down on the ground. He didn't know what to do. He looked at the two bodies. There was smoke coming from Compton's clothing. The gnome's hair was aflame.

The tall officer now stood alone on the other side of the pool. Chavez knew that his orders had probably been sealed, and he only now felt their full force. After a few moments the tall officer turned and went after his men.

The alien knew this would happen, Chavez thought. He knew, and that was why he told us everything.

When the great disk of Antares was forty-five degrees above the horizon, Rufus Kade came out to them. He put the two bodies in plastic specimen bags. Sister Guinivere was calm now and was holding Father Chavez's hand. They both stood up when Kade was finished with the bodies.

"They had an official pass from way up," Kade said. "I even checked back on it."

He walked slowly with them to the administration building. The shuttle to the starship was ready.

Thirty hours out from Antares, Father Chavez sat alone in his small cabin looking at the small monitor which showed him where he had been. Soon now the brilliance of the stars would be replaced by the dull emptiness of hyperspace. Antares was a small red disk on the screen.

Momentarily Chavez resented the fact that he had been a creation to the gnome. In any case the alien had not been God. His future importance would be no greater than that of Christ—probably less. He had been only an architect, a mere shaper of materials which had existed long before even his great race had come into being. But still—was he not closer to God than any *man* had ever been? Or would be?

The completion for which the gnome had made man would never take place now. The point of mankind's existence as he had made it was gone. And the alien had not known God. If there was such a being, a greatest possible being, he now seemed hopelessly remote . . .

O Lord, I pray for a sign! Chavez thought.

But he heard only his thoughts and nothing from the being who would surely have answered in a case like this. And he had stood by while they killed the gnome there in the garden by the poolside, on that planet circling the red star whose diameter was greater than the orbit of Mars. Despite all his reasoning now, Chavez knew that he had stood back while they killed that part of the small creature which had loved humanity.

But what had he said? The *rest* of the gnome's being *was* humanity, and it still existed; except that now it would never be reunited with him. *"Do not fear,"* the holy Antony had said three thousand years ago, *"this goodness as a thing impossible, nor its pursuit as something alien, set a great way off: it hangeth on our own arbitrament. For the sake of the Greek learning men go overseas . . . but the city of God is everywhere . . . the kingdom of God is within. The goodness that is in us only asks the human mind."* What we can do for ourselves, Chavez thought, that's all that is ours now: goals.

He took a deep breath as the starship slipped into the nothingness of hyperspace. He felt the burden of the political power which he now carried as a witness to the alien's murder, and he knew that Compton's life had not been for nothing. He would have to hide his intentions carefully, but he knew what he would have to do.

In time, he hoped anew, we may still give birth to the semblance of godhood that lives on in mankind, on that small world which circles a yellow sun.

JOANNA RUSS

Poor Man,
Beggar Man

JOANNA RUSS was born February 22, 1937, in the Bronx, New York. Her parents are schoolteachers, and science, literature and books were part of her early environment. She was a Westinghouse STS scholar in 1954. She received her B.A. degree in English from Cornell University in 1957 and her M.F.A. degree in playwriting from the Yale Drama School in 1960. She has acted in community theater (the Brooklyn Heights Players) and semiprofessional groups (the West Broadway Workshop).

She began writing at the age of thirteen, and her more than thirty published stories have appeared in science fiction publications such as *The Magazine of Fantasy and Science Fiction* and the *Orbit* series, and also in such general publications as *Manhattan Review, Epoch, Cimarron Review, The Little Magazine, South, Red Clay Reader* and *William and Mary Review.*

At present she is assistant professor of English at Cornell University, teaching creative writing and even, on occasion, science fiction reading. She also reviews books for *The Magazine of Fantasy and Science Fiction* and *College English,* contributes an occasional article to scholarly publications, belongs to Science Fiction Writers of America and the Modern Language Association, and reports that the only hobby she has time for is eating. She offers as her personal philosophy: "Women ought to run things, as we are friendlier than men, but alas, that is only because we are not allowed to run things."

Her two novels, *Picnic on Paradise* and *And Chaos Died,* were both Nebula Award finalists, as was her novelette "The Second Inquisition." In the 1971 Nebula Award balloting her novelette "Poor Man, Beggar Man" appeared on the final ballot.

A strange man, with a black cloak wrapped about him and a fold of it drawn over his head to hide his face, with the easy, gliding step of one who no longer cares if his feet go over rough or smooth, a man who smelled the smell of cooking at a turn in the narrow, rocky path, but to whom it meant nothing but a signal about what somebody else was doing, nothing more, this fellow—who was of a fairly ordinary and nonformidable appearance (though perhaps a bit mysterious)—slipped along the winding path outside Alexander's camp near the Indus River as if he knew where he was going. But he had no business being there, certainly not in the heat of the afternoon, though the vegetation around him cast the path into a certain tenebrous gloom. Light and shade spotted him. It was early in the Indian summer and petals and yellow dust dropped on the path and on the leaf mold to either side. He shook himself free. He reached an open place and continued, not looking round.

A quarter of a mile from the general's tent the path ascended, became rockier and more open; a guard lounged on a rock, absorbed in a bluebottle he held between thumb and forefinger. He did not see the stranger as he passed, nor did he return his salute. Muffled to the chin, the stranger passed servants clearing dishes from a board table set up in the open sunlight (for the general's tent commanded a view of the valley from an uninterrupted but therefore somewhat inhospitable height). He stepped inside the tent, bending under the canvas flap, his black cloak trailing. He found his man seated at a low table, calling for a map; he put one hand on his shoulder and then he said quite diffidently—

"Come, I'm still a civilized fellow."

"Apollo guard us!" choked the conqueror, turning pale. The
stranger laughed and shook his head, still with the inoffensive and
friendly manner that had made him so popular, and that had
occasioned such grief when Alexander had murdered him at the
age of twenty-eight.

"Your teacher, Aristotle, wouldn't like that," he said, shaking his
head humorously, and he sat down on the edge of the table, closing
his hand around a wine cup.

"Take your hands off that!" said Alexander automatically, and
then he said, his color coming back, "Take it."

"Oh no, thank you," said his dead friend, smiling apologetically,
"I couldn't, now. You have no idea what an inconvenience it is, to
be dead—"

"Take it!" said the conqueror.

"Ah, but—" and his murdered friend put the wine cup down.

"Well?" said Alexander. The dead man smiled, the mild smile
of those who provoke and endure insult; he smiled, backing away.
"I thought," he said, "that the novelty of my appearance—"

"Doesn't last."

"Ah, but you owe me—"

"What?"

The ghost wandered away a few steps, past the ray of brilliant
sunlight that entered the tent through the front flap, brushing the
canvas wall with his shoulder and causing not a ripple. "I remember," he said, "I remember." Alexander watched him intently in
the half light, the light that made of the conqueror, of his handsome face and bronze figure, a statue.

"Ah, what I remember!" broke out the ghost, with a genuine
laugh. "I remember your amazing forcefulness when you got
drunk." The man at the table watched him. "And I remember,"
added the ghost, padding round the room, "sitting with my feet
up and my knees under my chin on some kind of marble shelf, like
a schoolboy, and watching you rant—"

"I never rant."

"Rave, then. But you mustn't split hairs. My word, they tried to

hold you back, didn't they? And my sister was your old nurse—
what a scandal! I hear you shut yourself up for three days." Here
he paused in the darkest corner of the tent. "You know," he said,
coming out into the light, dragging his cloak carelessly off one
shoulder, "you know," he said, his whole face becoming clearer,
his brow rising, his eyes opening as they do in strong feeling when
the face is about to become a mask, "you know" (with an expression almost of amazement) "I do remember it quite well. I have
analyzed it a hundred times. I had no idea what hit me. I thought
the room had turned round and the floor had come up and thrown
itself against me. And then something hit me in the chest and I bit
my tongue, do you know, and I saw your face—"

Here Alexander broke into a roar of laughter that might have
been heard even outside the tent, but the tent flaps did not move;
they hung quite still.

"My dear friend," he said affectionately, "really I am very sorry,
but you know you might have come back four years ago. I feel for
you, I do, but I'm afraid time has rather worn the whole affair
away. You see—" and he pointed to the litter of papers on his desk.

"Ah," said the ghost wisely, "but *I* don't age, you see."

"That's too bad," said the emperor, putting his elbows on the
table and his chin in his hands, "and now—"

"Now?" said the ghost expectantly.

"Now be a good fellow and go away."

"No."

"Then *I* shall," but when the emperor pushed back his chair and
got up, he saw that the friend he had killed was somehow sitting
in it and fingering his papers and that he did not like.

"My, look at this," said his friend.

"Let that be!"

"You're going to India; how nice."

"Will you—!" and he snatched the stranger's hand, but the shock
of finding it flesh and blood was too much for him and he started
back, shouting, "Guards!" No one came.

"Ah, nonsense," said his friend quietly. He sat at the table as a

secretary or accompanying philosopher sits and writes down a
great man's words; his black cloak had slipped off his shoulders and
lay half on the seat and half on the dirt floor, like a pool of ink. He
picked up one document after another, carefully and respectfully.
It had always been remarkable how this man could pick things up;
his hand closed around a cup, a vase, a woman's hand, with such
gentleness and such attentive curiosity that one might almost
imagine inanimate objects feeling actual pleasure at his touch.
Women had liked him and he had evaded them.

"You're going to India," he said. He was looking at marks on a
map. Alexander strode matter-of-factly to the tent flap to get
friends or attendants who would rid him of this annoyance, but the
tent flap hung straight as stone. He could not move it.

"What do you want from me?" he said between his teeth.

"We-ell," drawled the stranger.

"*What?*" shouted the king, losing his patience.

"You're growing afraid."

"Not I!"

"Yes you are, and you'll do it."

"Do *what!*"

"Quietly." He studied the map. "Look at this," he said. "You're
going to cross the Indus, you'll be another seven years away from
home, your army will mutiny and by the time you establish another Alexandria—how many Alexandrias are there by this time?
—at the eastern edge of the world, your government in the west
will have collapsed and you'll have to begin all over again. Good
Lord, what an agenda!"

"Stop playing with me," said the king, and he sat, with considerable dignity, on a low bench near the opening of the tent.

"Why not? You used to play with me," said the ghost reasonably.

"I used to."

"Precisely. You used to."

"Death hasn't steadied your character," said Alexander.

"Or sweetened yours!"

"Those who want to get kicked will get kicked," said the king.

"Yes, precisely," said his friend, blinking. "Well, what I want is this. I want you to turn back, go spend the next winter in Heliopolis, renamed from Babylon (what a change!), and withdraw your borders to the edge of Persia. You're a fool. You can't keep what you've got. As it is, the empire will fall apart three days after your death. You think you can put up a few carved pillars, appoint a satrap and a place is yours. Nonsense."

"And—" said Alexander.

"And," repeated the ghost, looking a little bewildered, "and— well—there you are." Alexander rose to his feet. "I'm not done—" But a sudden breeze blasted the tent flap into the air as if someone's violent enthusiasm had flung it skyward. Grinning cheerfully, though perhaps with a certain awkwardness, Alexander walked to his friend and embraced him.

"Would you believe me," he said, "if I told you that I had repented? Sincerely repented? Why, man, I saw no one for three days; they thought I would abandon them in the middle of the desert. So much grief! But you should have known enough to keep away from me." He patted, without shrinking, his friend's unnaturally solid back. "And the story about your sister was true," he said, "though embroidered a little, I'll admit. I was truly fond of her and hated to cause her pain. And you—" His voice thickened. "Well, you know—"

"Ah," said the ghost, helplessly blinking.

"*You* know," said Alexander tenderly. "*You* know." And then, without another word, only looking back with smiling and compassionate regret, he walked out of the tent.

Left alone, the stranger gazed thoughtfully after him for the space of a minute. Then, with extraordinary rapidity, he whipped his cloak from the chair near the low table, wrapped it into a small package, and flung it into the air. Watching it as it hung suspended between the roof and the floor, he laughed to himself, a noiseless fit that doubled him up. As soon as he took his gaze off the cloak, it fell like any other object, gracelessly unfolding itself in a scattered bundle like a wounded goose. He picked it up and put it on.

Now for the other one, he thought, and he sat down on the bench near the canvas wall, quite composed. His name was Cleitus. He had been known in life as Cleitus the Black.

In Persia, in order to secure his political position, Alexander had married (and caused two hundred of his nobles to do likewise, although their sentiments on the matter had not been ascertained at the time) a Persian lady of aristocratic birth. Roxane, as his wife was called, had spent most of her childhood in a courtyard with a mosaic marble floor, either learning to read and write (which she despised) or chasing a striped ball with several other girls who kissed her hand in the morning and in the evening and said "my lady." When she was seventeen she was surprisingly and suddenly married to a man famous, handsome, young and formidable. Three weeks' absence from home made her desperately sick for her courtyard, which she had always considered a prison before, and in which she had longed to stand on a chair piled on another chair piled on a table so that she could see out of it and view the great world.

She came into the tent five minutes after Alexander had left it and two minutes after the stranger had seated himself on a bench.

"Eh!" she said, startled. He was down on his knees, bowing, before she could take fright and run. Then he kissed her hand, which comforted her because that was so familiar.

"Who are you?" said she, sensibly. He only smiled at her, as vaguely and disarmingly as a man who has never been anything else but a woman's bumbling pet, and he kissed her hand again. "I, madam," he said, "am called Theophrastus."

"What a foolish name!" said Roxane, giggling, for she had never learned to lie or be polite either.

"My lady," he said, suddenly affecting to look alarmed, "should you be here alone with me? That is—I mean—I believe—" Roxane tossed her head.

"Nobody follows me around," she said, *"here.* Nobody would dare hurt me," she added, "I suppose."

"Nobody with any heart would," said he. She colored.

"Madam," he said quickly, "I must find the emperor."

"I don't know where he is," said she, sitting plump on the bench. She looked interested and expectant. The ghost began to walk up and down like a man tormented in his mind by the urgency of something. He said "Ah, but madam!" and then he shook his head to himself a few times and said, "Madam—"

"Why, what's the matter?" cried Roxane, who was entirely ignorant and hence unafraid. The ghost came and sat down beside her with his black cloak (looking rather foolish) dragging behind him.

"You know, madam," he said earnestly, "that your husband, his Imperial Majesty, *pai dios—*"

"Yes, yes," said Roxane impatiently, clasping her hands.

"Your husband," said the ghost, looking round as if afraid they might be overheard, "has no doubt told you, madam, that he intends to cross the river in a few days' time and for this he will need native scouts, guides, madam, to acquaint him with the towns and villages that may lie beyond." Roxane nodded, perfectly attentive. "Well now," continued the ghost, "and, madam, I tell you—I tell you, I am nearly out of my senses—these guides whom your husband has engaged now refuse to go anywhere. They have scattered to the four winds, madam." He looked at her apologetically, as if what he was about to say was too foolish to be believed and in any case utterly beyond her notice, and then he said, "They are afraid, madam, of the ghosts."

"Ghosts!" shouted Roxane, sitting bolt upright.

"Oh yes, but it's nothing, some native foolishness, people walking about with their feet on backward—"

Roxane sprang to her feet and began walking nervously around the tent.

"If there are ghosts out there," she said, "I won't let him go."

"But his Imperial Majesty—" said the ghost, coughing faintly.

"Never you mind about that," she said. "I know what's what and I know—" She turned to him suspiciously. "What kind of ghosts?"

"Kind?" said the ghost, puzzled.

"Yes," she said. "Are they—are they—" (she whispered this)— "bloodsuckers?"

"Uh—no," said the ghost, his wits scattered.

"Oh, then it's all right," she said, relieved. "You can keep away the other kinds, but *that* kind—" Suddenly she looked at him keenly. "You don't really know, do you?" she said.

"Of course I do," he said. She frowned. "No—you—don't," she said with emphasis. Her face darkened. "You're Greek!"

He admitted it.

"Ha!" she said. "You probably don't believe in them at all."

He protested that he did.

"No you don't," she said. "I can tell. You'll tell my husband it's a lot of nonsense. I know."

"Madam!" he protested. "On my honor—"

"Greek honor!" she cried. "You'll tell my husband it's some Asiatic foolishness." She darted to him, grabbing his shoulders and furiously shaking him. "Yes you will!" she shouted. "You'll tell him it's nonsense and then he'll go out there and then—" and she turned away and screwed up her face. She began to cry.

"Now, now, now," he said.

"He'll get killed!" wailed little Roxane. "He will! He will!"

"No, no, no," said the stranger, stroking her hair. She leaned against him, sobbing a little. Then she pulled away.

"I'm rather homesick," she said sharply, explaining her conduct.

"Of course, of course," said the ghost in the tone women used to love so when he was alive. "It's only natural, of course."

"You shouldn't pat my head," said Roxane, sniffling.

"Yes, of course," he said smoothly, "of course. But it calms you, doesn't it? and it does so distress me to see you upset."

"It makes my eyes red," said Roxane, blowing her nose in her long, Persian sleeve.

"It makes you unhappy," said he, "and I don't like to see people unhappy, you know, though I have so few feelings myself." He smiled. "I had a wife like you once; she was much cleverer than I and she hated the court: a real intellectual."

"I'm stupid," said Roxane spitefully. "I believe in ghosts."

"Ah, but," said the man, as if he had made an astonishing discovery, "so do I!"

"Really?" said she.

"Ah yes. I've seen too many not to believe in them. But the kind I believe in are not those Indians with their feet put on backward or your Persian demons and afreets that suck blood but a kind— well, a kind—"

"A Greek kind?" asked Roxane, fascinated.

"No, I think a universal kind," he said with a slight, guilty laugh, stroking her hair. "The kind, you see— You see, when a poor wretch dies, some unfortunate idiot, many times he dies with an unfulfilled passion, something that tormented him all his life but something he never mastered or settled with. And this poor fool, he finds after his death that he's not one of the blessed dead that lie in the ground or end up in the fire and are gone, that's it, the lucky ones. Most of these men—and women, too, you know—most of them are nothing much, no force of character, you might say, so they simply blow about with the wind like old rags, drifting from place to place."

"Ooooh—yes—yes—" whispered Roxane.

"Now for most of us," he went on, cupping her face in his hands, "that's it, you see, but for a few—" He smiled enchantingly. "A few have too much feeling to stand for that; they want too much, and these are the dead you hear about in songs and stories, who come back to pay off debts or wreak vengeance, you know, or take care of their children. And some— ah, some! they have a driving passion, a force that won't let them rest. They have hard bodies like you and me. You can see them, too. And you can find them—why, anywhere! In the marketplace at high noon, in temples, theaters—"

"They don't cast shadows!" Roxane broke in eagerly.

"Ah, but they do," he said, "indeed they do and sometimes" (with the same slight, guilty laugh, picking up his cloak and cradling it in his arms) "sometimes they even carry their shadows

around with them. They do all sorts of odd things. But they are
poor folk, after all, you know."

"Why?" she whispered.

"Why?" he said lightly. "Why, because they only live while their
passion is unsatisfied, you see. And as soon as they get what they
come back for, they die for good. But they *must* come back, you
know, they can't help themselves. They want it so much. You
know yourself" (here she shuddered) "what it feels like to go about
wanting something desperately, don't you?"

"Oh, I do!" sadly.

"Well, there you are." He stopped, looked tenderly at her, and
then, as if it were the natural sequence of his discourse, kissed her,
pulling her up to him by the shoulders.

"Ah, that's wrong!" cried she, bursting into tears because she
had a husband but nobody, really, and he—smiling—because she reminded him (perhaps) of three or four memories picked out of his
memories of women or perhaps all of them, because he had loved
and pitied everything living when he himself was alive.

"Little one wants to go home, doesn't she?" he whispered, holding her against him. "Little one's lonely? Eh?" kissing her hair.

"Yes, yes," she sobbed, pushing him away. As if she were coming
out of an enchantment, she looked at him doubtfully, ready to run
away.

"Madam," he said briskly, "if you would permit me—I mean to
utter no treason against his Imperial Majesty, but a man of affairs,
a man preoccupied with questions of state—a busy man, in short
—why, such a man may neglect those nearest and dearest to him
without the least design. He may not even realize that he is so
doing, his mind being preoccupied as it is."

"Ah?" said Roxane, bewildered but sure there was something
good coming.

"In such cases," said the stranger, with a bland smile, "a short
absence may be the best— ah, madam, forgive me offering you
advice, but as an old friend of the family, as it were, I feel—"

"Well—" said Roxane, trying to look like a *grande dame.*

"I feel," he continued, "that if your husband could be presented —though not in reality, of course—with the prospect of losing you —if he could be made to imagine it, so to speak, he would at once realize the void, the gap, if I may say it, the absence in his life and he would—with a rush of feeling, of repentance, as it were, though far be it from me—he would immediately regret that his business affairs had taken him so often and so far away from you."

"Well, ye-es," said Roxane.

"Many men," continued the stranger, with unction, "many men only realize their true feelings when those feelings are threatened, as it were. They—"

"Yes, but how?" Roxane broke in impatiently.

"How?" he said.

"How could I do it?"

He bowed (as best he could from a sitting position).

"How?" she repeated anxiously. "Come, tell me and do stop beating about it like that!"

"Madam has seized the thought at once," said the stranger admiringly.

"I always do," she said, "I'm very quick, but really, if you won't—"

"A minute, a minute." He cleared his throat. "Could you not—" he said, and then: "There is an Indian village a few miles from this camp."

"Yes indeed," said Roxane promptly.

"You have never been to this village," he said, "but you can go there easily enough. In daylight, of course. The path is wide and unmistakable. If you don't mind staying with one of the farmers —a comparatively rich and luxurious household, of course—"

"Pooh! I don't care," she said.

"Well then, that's that! Stay for a night and he'll go wild without you. And I wouldn't be surprised if he gives up this Indian project, too. You'll get a good deal more attention from him from now on." He spread his hands. "That's it."

"Oh!" exclaimed Roxane, then "Oh!" again in delight. She

sprang to her feet. "I shall," she said, "this very night. Thank you."
She started to run out of the tent, exclaiming "Yes—I must—" and
then she turned around abruptly, saying, "Don't tell!" He took her
hand and she cried "Really!" quite unaffectedly, snatching it away
with a disgusted expression. He bowed low—a real bow this time
—and the princess rushed out.

Left to himself, the dead man appropriated two items of his
former master's property: a pen and a piece of paper. With the
appropriately serious expression, he began to write a letter, a
letter such as those written to husbands by adventurous and fleeting wives who are only too delighted to be running away with
somebody interesting, but who write of the whole matter in terms
of the deepest and direst compulsion. He was laughing soundlessly
to himself by the time he had finished. Ah! that kiss had been
sweet! *but only for old times' sake,* he thought. The static qualities
of death oppressed him; he felt that mutability was mankind's only
hope, even though it took the flowers and pleasures of one's time.
Most terrible about the dead was the way in which they did not,
could not, could never, could never even hope to change. *Change,*
he thought, with unspeakable anguish. Outside the tent, as trans-
parent to his sight as the sky, the sun was beginning to set. Little
Roxane would be in her Indian village by evening, very curious,
very delighted to see how the peasants lived and playing alter-
nately the milkmaid and the great lady. He envied her. He envied
Alexander, he envied every common soldier, he envied every dog,
every rat, every louse on that inhospitable, rocky eminence. They
could be hungry. They could be in pain. They might not walk
through the worst of Alexander's battles no more in danger than
the rain that rotted the bodies of the dead. Did men want little—
or get much? He could not tell. With the mild, ingenuous face and
diffident manner that had made him so popular in Alexander's
court, he wandered about the tent with the letter in his hand.
Dinners were cooking all over the camp, three and a quarter miles
of dinners. The thought of so much human busy-ness caused him
considerable pain. He moved unsteadily and blindly against Alex-

ander's campaign table, and then as the innocent maps and memoranda stared up at him in the gloom, his brow cleared. He dropped the letter on the center of the heap. Alexander would look for his lady in the woods, not in the village, misled by the fanciful instructions of a dead man, and in the woods— his blind face stirred with a painful rage. *That damned fool!* The sentry who would find it would run to him—not a moment too soon; that would be seen to —and Alexander, who knew perfectly well that his wife detested writing and could not spell, would—! The ghost bent over in a silent fit of laughter. Oh, the emperor would call himself an idiot but he would go! He despised his wife, no doubt, but he would go! He would know it was a trap, but he would go! What had the Athenian philosopher said? Ghosts hate crowds? Ah yes, that was it. *In silence and in little company and most of all at night—* The fool! Men were easiest to manipulate alone, in silence, and in the dark; that was all. Even that great fool, that king of fools, that king of kings . . . Laughing still to himself, the emperor's friend walked toward the tent wall, his cloak folded over his arm. He could have gone out any way he chose, but he chose to melt through the wall like a mist, astonishing anyone who saw him. No one saw him.

When Alexander received his wife's letter he was lying on a divan after supper, hearing one of his tame philosophers read him a discourse on the immortality of the soul. It did not please him. He had drunk moderately at table. He received the letter curtly, read it abruptly and gave vent to his feelings with a roar of rage.

"My lord!" exclaimed the tame philosopher.

"Damn her!" cried the king.

"The immortality of the soul—" ventured the philosopher, trembling.

"Damn the immortality of the soul!" shouted the conqueror, his neck swelling. He began to put on his armor. He dashed to the wall, seized his shield and rushed out, looking in again only to snatch up his sword from where it stood by the entrance to the tent. His face was scarlet and distorted, like a djinn's.

"And damn *you!*" he shouted.

They searched the area north of the camp, taking no chances; they shouted to each other; someone found footprints but they were not the proper size. Soon, through his own impetuosity and his soldiers' fear of becoming separated, the emperor and one of his philosophers, a historian, one Aristophorus, found themselves ahead of the search party. They were in a little glade.

"Rest yourself, rest yourself," said Alexander, and the old man, tottering to a fallen log, said "Yes, my lord." He was carrying a torch. He took off his sandals and sat, his back hunched over, his beard pointing at his knees.

"Why don't they shout?" said Alexander suddenly. "I told them to shout."

"They will catch up with us, my lord," said the philosopher, rubbing his feet, "no doubt." Alexander repeated "No doubt" and wandered to the other side of the glade, into which a faint radiance had already begun to creep from the rising moon. He peered into the darkness.

"I can't see any lights," he said.

"According to Aristotle," said the philosopher contentedly, "the eye sends out rays which are reflected by objects in its path, thus producing sight. But when the rays are reflected strongly by any object—and those objects composed of the element of fire are most vigorous in the exercise of this property—then other objects appear but weak and faint in comparison."

"Put it out!" said the young man, and as the old one only stared at him uncomprehendingly, Alexander seized the torch himself and thrust it upside down against the earth. Immediately the darkness around them seemed to rush in as if the circle of light had been snapped like a hoop; Alexander leaned between two trees at the edge of the little clearing.

"I can't—" he said, and then, conscious that he had spoken more softly than before, "I can't see a thing."

"They will catch up with us, my lord," said the old man. With

the moon rising and the firelight gone, something very peculiar
was happening to the little glade; objects were melting and changing; they ran one into the other as if nothing in the universe were
stable. The clearing looked like the bottom of the sea. Alexander
walked rapidly back and forth for a few moments, then turned (as
if the place were affecting his nerves) and stared at the old man.

"I'm afraid to talk out loud," he said, as if stating a fact, and then
he said sharply "Who are you?"

"What, my lord?" said the old man, startled, but his imperial
master did not answer, only shook his head as a man does who has
found a mote in his eye. He walked about again and then stopped
as if the indistinct light and the masses of shade confused him; he
said, "I hear no one."

"Why no, my lord," said the old man placidly, stroking his
toes, "I daresay they have passed us by and we must wait until
morning."

"Fool!" said Alexander. He stopped in the middle of the glade
irresolutely. Then he said, "Get out of here, old man."

"My lord?" said the philosopher mildly.

"Get out of here!"

"But my lord—!"

"Get out! That's a command! You'll find the others soon
enough."

"Will you—" began the philosopher, but Alexander (who had
drawn his sword) waved him imperiously away.

"Get out!" he roared.

"But my dear lord—" (shocked,) and then the king urged him
with such fury that the old man flew out of the clearing with his
sandals still in his hands. He saw the lights of the soldiers' torches
at once, as Alexander had said he would, and they spent the rest
of the night looking for the emperor, but they did not find him.

Left alone, and doubly uncertain of himself, Alexander turned
back into the glade, only to see his friend lounging against a tree
in the moonlight at the opposite end. The moon had risen and it
bathed the little glade in livid quicksilver; the king felt his nerves

give way; he had an impulse either of love or of despair that made him want to bury his head in his friend's knees and beg . . .

"I like a light in which I can judge distances," he said grimly.

"There are no distances here," said the dead man. "Here things are very close together."

"My wife?" said the conqueror.

"Quite safe." They looked one another over for a few moments, the one erect and bristling like a dog, the other curved against his tree as he had curved against every surface, every command, every necessity in his short and easy life.

"Your fine world!" said Alexander contemptuously, indicating the clearing with a gesture that was almost—but not quite—a snap of the fingers.

"No," said the dead man, smiling urbanely, "yours. The real world. Like the bottom of the sea. As you look at my features they seem to swarm and melt. They could be anybody's."

"Imagination!" with scorn.

"Ah, the imagination . . . the imagination, which the philosophers say gives color to everything." The dead man detached himself from his tree and moved noiselessly into the clearing, over grass the color of mercury. "My dear friend," he said lightly, "my dear, dear friend, you must remember that I am dead and so I look at things from a very special point of view. I know, you see, the torments of desire after death, desire too late to satisfy desire, and I want you to avoid the same fate as myself. You must not spend eternity longing for your wife and your cook and your mattress-maker, for you neglect them; you know you do."

"Bah! Don't want them," said Alexander.

"No?" With the same fixed smile the dead man moved toward him, like a walking corpse or a man in a dream.

"Keep away!" cried the king in horror.

"Why?" said his friend gently. "Because I have a white face? Because I look like a leper? My face is white, my dear friend, through an excess of passion. My movements are slow because I am dead."

"Damn you, what do you want?" cried Alexander, breathing hard.

"Want? The man who killed me."

"I never—never—!" cried the king passionately.

"Never? Never?" Color came flooding into the dead man's face, making it look black under the moon. "Never intended? Never meant? Oh no, I daresay! No one ever intends to kill a pet! One wrings the poor bird's neck in a moment of sheer, unthinking irritation, isn't that right? One kicks the clown and behold! the poor fool falls downstairs and breaks his neck. Bah! One shatters a vase, merely." They looked at each other for the space of a minute and then—as if the outburst had broken his mood and reassured him—

"I never disliked you," said Alexander sullenly.

"Oh, no!" in a tone half between a laugh and a sob. "Oh, no!" more quietly.

"No, never," said the king stolidly, and he went and sat on the fallen log.

"I'm not through," said his friend mildly. "Do you know what you missed?" He leaned over the seated man. "For one, your wife's sweet little tongue that I tasted some four hours ago." Alexander said nothing. "Ah, you don't care? You have glory?"

"I do," said the monarch.

"Yes, like the sunset, I suppose. All the color and light that belong to nobody belongs to you. Names! What else do you have: love?"

"We don't deal in that commodity," said Alexander with a flash of teeth.

"Ah! there you speak like your father. Your father, whom your mother poisoned with the poison they use to drive rats mad, and who died blubbering over a servant girl who was the only one in the palace foolish and brave enough to give him a drink of water."

"One can avoid being poisoned," said Alexander, grinning again.

"Yes, one can," said his friend, "and I daresay if you avoid being

poisoned or assassinated or stabbed in a mutiny—and you have
been pretty successful so far—you will live to be an old man."

"You tire me out," said Alexander, rising.

"Ah! but wait—can you get by, do you think, at the end?"

"You've shot your bolt, man!"

"No, wait—listen—there's my wife. I think about her all the
time, about the colors of her face and hair and the remoteness she
had for me, and how I liked her the better for that, I think. Oh!
don't you wander about when you're dead, remembering things
like that!"

"I can remember what I've done," said Alexander, laughing,
"which is more than you can manage, I think. Now! Let me go. I
have no time for any more."

"No, no," said his friend softly.

"Ah, yes!" answered the king, as softly.

"Try," said the dead man. The king drew his sword. "Try." His
friend was smiling charmingly; he stretched forth his neck as if to
offer it to the knife. "I can keep you here," he said. "That's one
thing I can do."

"For what!" harshly.

"You'll see."

The king began to laugh. He walked about the clearing, roaring
with mirth. The moonlight struck sparks from his sword hilt and
a line of silver blazed along the blade; he whirled his sword above
his head like a boy going into battle for the first time; he struck the
trunks of trees with it and laughed.

"I have something to show you," said the dead man quietly.

"What?" gasped the king, "what?" half out of breath.

"Something, dear boy." Alexander could not stop laughing. He
sat on the log and roared, rocking back and forth. The moon must
have gone behind a cloud, for the little glade grew darker and
darker; in the gloom, in the midst of the indistinct mass of confused shadows, sat Alexander laughing. He looked up and found,
to his surprise, that his dead friend had come up behind him and
now held him by the shoulders in a grip so strong and yet so light

that he could not break it. He was forced to turn to one side; he tried to turn back and could not; he struggled impotently under the dead man's grip while his friend's face, so close to his own, moved not an inch, showed not by the slightest alteration in its expression that to control the warrior of the age was any effort for him, a soft and an always soft-living man.

"Look," he said, "look ahead," in a voice almost like love, and changing the position of his hands so that he held the king's face (that king whose arms now hung uselessly at his sides), forced him to turn his gaze.

Alexander gave a scream like the scream of the damned, like the yell of a hurt animal that has nothing to restrain it: no discretion, no prudence, no fear. He would have fallen to the ground if the dead man had not held him.

"There, there, there!" said the dead man in a soft, enthusiastic, urgent whisper, his eyes glittering. "There, look! look!" He grasped the king's shoulders with a vehemence that left marks; he shook him. "There's glory for you!" he whispered, and finally let-ting him go, retreated across the clearing, never taking his eyes off him, never moving his rigidly spread hands, blending into the stippled shadow and the uncertain light until one looking after him would never have known that there was any such person.

Alexander sat drooping on the fallen log as the old philosopher had before him. The moon was setting; morning was near. His soldiers, horribly frightened at losing him in the middle of the night, would find him at last, though he would not speak to them. He would raise his handsome face and say nothing. They would bring his wife to him (she had gotten worried and had sent a messenger back to the camp in the middle of the night) and he would look at her, say her name in a tone of surprise—and faint. Two days later the army, the Persian queen's handmaids, the king's philosophic retinue and the royal couple themselves would pack all their gear and start on the return march to Babylon, now called Heliopolis.

The rumors were started by an Egyptian professor whose

cataloguing system for the library at Egyptian Alexandria was summarily rejected by the emperor. Alexander, he said, was mad and had been shut up. He was drunk all day. He alternated wintry midnight swims with bouts of fever. His wife had left him. "No, no," said Aristophorus heatedly, "the truth is—" and hurried away to attend to something else.

Egyptian Alexandria, Babylonian Alexandria, Alexandretta . . . one room of the palace at Heliopolis had a replica (about seven feet high) of a monument Alexander had caused to be built to the memory of his dead friend as soon as he (Alexander) had returned to that city. The monument was a bronze tower, eighty feet high, with a platform at the top—"for jumping," Alexander had said disingenuously, watching Aristophorus twitch. He drank for hours at the foot of the replica, in a desultory way. He talked to it once in a while.

One afternoon in that part of late winter when a stone house— even in the Babylonian climate—becomes a place to freeze the living and preserve the dead, Aristophorus found his master asleep at the foot of the monument.

"You're drunk, my lord," said he sadly and disapprovingly.

"You're middle-class," said Alexander.

"That monument ought to be destroyed," said Aristophorus, weeping.

"It has charm," said Alexander.

"It's graceless!" weeping harder.

"It's necessary." Alexander rolled over and fetched himself up on a step, blinking like an owl. "We want to honor our dead friend, Aristophorus." He discovered a wineskin under a heap of outer garments on the step. "Bravo!"

"My lord, my lord!" wept the old philosopher.

"My lord, my lord!" mimicked Alexander. He lay in the heap of clothes, idly. "You think I'm drunk but I'm not." He sighed. "I haven't got properly drunk for years. I'm too used to it."

"Oh, my lord!"

"Bah! get out of my sight!" and when he was left alone, his face settled into an expression of perfect vacancy. The stone hall was covered with stately, patterned hangings that gave the walls a spurious, slightly ridiculous dignity. There was one uncovered window. Alexander ambled tiredly over to it. It gave on a small court and a garden; someone was hoeing. As the king watched he closed both hands unconsciously; the sight of anyone working always affected him. The slave outside bent himself double, clearing and pulling; then he straightened and rubbed his back. A faint, disorganized sound, of which he was not aware, came from the king's throat; he lifted the wineskin to drink and halted halfway. He remembered, with satisfaction, wresting a cup from the old philosopher when the man would drink from it in a dramatic, despairing show that he too would sink to the king's dreadful level. Alexander laughed. "I'm sick," he said. He leaned on the stone windowsill, watching the sky and shivering. He thought *The words they use for drunkenness. Smashed. Stoned. Blind. Hit yourself over the head with a rock.* Ah!—to fall— His shivering increased. He thought again, with pleasure, that he was sick. *Wipe it out,* he thought. He leaned his head in his hands. They worried him about his wife; who would protect her? they said. Yes, that was right. . . . Slipping to his knees, he leaned his back against the clammy stone wall with a kind of comfort. The dead man had said once— what had he said? "Comfort, above all." But that had been when he was alive.

"My dear lord," said someone. Alexander opened his eyes. "Go away," he said.

"My lord, my lord—" said the old philosopher.

When he opened his eyes again he saw that Aristophorus had gone. He knew that he was sick and it alarmed him. He dragged himself to his feet and started toward the monument. *"Oh my dear, my dear,"* he said passionately to nobody in particular. *"My dear, my dear, my dear . . ."*

The late afternoon sunlight, wintry and wan, came through the uncovered window and made a square on the floor. He lay on the floor. He opened his eyes for the third time (when the drowning man goes down) and saw the face he had expected to see.

"You're dying," said his friend, and there were tears in his eyes. Alexander said nothing, only lay on the stone floor with his mouth slightly open and his eyes vacant. His breathing was quick and shallow. "Clown," he managed to say. "Jackal. But I kept you around."

"I've kept *you* around. Doing nothing. For the last four years."

"Ah!—ah!" cried Alexander, for the floor was sinking and bellying under him. "Help!" he cried. Crouched over him, his nurse's son, his harpy, his old friend watched him intently. "Courage, man!" he cried, "courage! It only lasts a moment! Keep your head clear."

"Call my wife," said the king, with an effort. The dead man shook his head.

"Oh yes," said Alexander grimly. "Oh, yes."

"Never," said the other. "I don't share."

"Roxane!" cried Alexander, and then before his friend could stop him, "Roxane!" so that the walls re-echoed with it. There was the sound of light steps in the passageway. "You cruel fool!" whispered the dead man angrily, and he rose to his feet and darted to her, barring the way. She carried her eight months' pregnancy in front of her like a basket, hurrying along the hall with little breathless steps.

"My dear," he said, "my dear, it's nothing, nothing. Go back. Please go back."

"Good heavens, it's you," said she matter-of-factly.

"Yes, love, go back," he said, "go back. Go rest." He held out his hands, smiling tenderly.

"Oh, no," said the queen wisely, "there's something, *I* can tell," and she pushed past him. She began telling her husband that he really must go to bed; then she stopped, puzzled, and then a little intake of breath announced that she had seen the dying man's face. The dead man trembled; he stood at the window where the king had stood, but saw nothing. At his back the princess gave a little scream.

"My dear," said the dead man, turning round (she was kneeling at Alexander's side) "my dear, he'll be quite well, I promise you," (but she seemed not to hear him) "my dear, I promise you—" but she rushed out, crying different names out loud. She stopped at the doorway, looking right past the dead man as if she were looking through him. Her face expressed nothing but surprise, although she was wringing her hands.

"My dear," he said calmly, "what you see is a delusion. The man is not suffering A the end fever is not unpleasant, I assure you; the body sinks ʲ . the mind floats like a piece of ash, and you will only make your ʰ ʲand's last moments needlessly unhappy if you cry and wring your hands and behave in an unconsidered and haphazard way."

"Aristophorus!" screamed the princess, "Aristophorus!" and she rushed out of the room.

I am beginning to fade, the dead man thought, going back to Alexander. His attack of trembling hit him again and he knelt by the dying man, taking the unconscious face in his hands.

"King," he whispered urgently. "King." Alexander opened his eyes. "Listen to me."

"No," said the dying man. His friend, cradling the conqueror's head in his hands, smiled with a radiant and serene joy; "Live," he whispered. "Live. Live."

"Can't," said Alexander brusquely, trying to shrug. He closed his eyes. Gently the dead man let his friend's head down onto the floor; he stood up; he moved away. Roxane had come back in with friends, philosophers, doctors; they crowded round the emperor while his friend (whom nobody saw) wandered out of the room into a passageway and down that passageway into another. In the garden (he looked out of a window) the gardener still hoed and weeded last year's dried stalks. The dead man had carried Alexander's wineskin with him and a cup he found near it; he poured himself a drink and sat down on the floor by the window where the pale sunlight came in. Then he stood up. "You butcher!" he shouted, "you bully, you egoist, you killer in love with your own greatness!" and then he said "How I loved you, how I admired you!" raising the cup in one hand and his other empty hand to the ceiling in an attitude of extreme and theatrical grief. His arms sank; he sat again on the floor. *Now I die too,* he thought. He thought, with a certain amusement, of that night in the Indian forests near the river and what he had shown the great Alexander. Like the demons in the old stories he had shown him all the world; he had shown it filled with Alexandrias and Alexandrettas as numerous as the stars, with carved pillars set up in the East as far as the kingdoms of Ch'in and Ch'u, farther than Han, satraps ruling the undiscovered continents on the other side of the globe, tablets commemorating Alexander in the lands of the Finns and the Lapps, in the lands of the Alaskan Eskimos, empire up to the Arctic Circle and down into Africa, over the Cape and through the other side, Alexanders here, Alexanders there, a fulfilled empire, a safe empire, a satisfied dream. And then two words: *What then?*

Legend has it that great Alexander wept because there were no more worlds to conquer; in truth, he bellowed like a bull.

No one, thought the dead man, *feels more despair than a man who has been robbed of his profession. Luckily I never had one.* A sound from the room he had just quitted hit him and made him catch his breath. How terrible to die, he thought, how terrible! He took a drink from the wine cup and noted that his hand was shaking. From the next room came a sharp cry, little Roxane wailing for her man. The dead man, whose heart seemed to have stopped, sat motionless while his face became clear of all expression, taking on the beautiful, grave melancholy of all faces whose owners are absent, temporarily or otherwise. Gently and carefully he put the wine cup down on the damp, stone floor, with the concentrated gentleness of all the times he had picked things up only to put them down—cups, flowers, jewelry, paintings and women's hands. He thought of all the things he had touched and never owned, of all the women he had liked and avoided. The one man he had admired so passionately and so passionately envied was dead. Nothing was left. He thought, as if thinking of a picture,

of his wife—a dissatisfied Sappho who had written verses and left
the court to live with some businessman. He doubled over, not in
laughter this time, but as if Alexander's blade, that had long ago
stabbed through his vitals, once again tore him. The dead forget
nothing. The blade had ripped apart the intricate webs that kept
him alive, it had startled and hurt him, it had broken his heart.
Silently he bent over and fell to the floor. He stretched along it
with a kind of sigh, as if going to sleep, and the moment he closed
his eyes he disappeared. The wine cup stood alone on the floor. An
attendant who had heard the news of the king's death ran excit-
edly through the room and out into the garden.

"Something has happened!" he shouted to the gardener. The
gardener threw down his hoe and the two talked together in low
whispers.

"It'll be hard on us," the gardener said, shaking his head. The
attendant clapped him on the back. "Don't forget," he said, "we
stand together." He added generously "I don't forget my rela-
tives." The gardener nodded solemnly. He picked up his tools, the
attendant helping him. Together they disappeared into another
part of the court. The sun (for it was now late afternoon) moved
a little; the square of light on the floor altered its position somewhat and touched the standing wine cup with a spark of gold.
Nearby lay the wineskin, on its side but closed by some considerate
hand—or so it seemed, for the floor remained clean. Nothing
moved. Everything remained as it was. It was exactly as if nothing
had happened.

NOTE ON "POOR MAN, BEGGAR MAN": It is riddled with inaccuracies. Cleitus
the Black was one of Alexander's generals, whom Alexander actually did kill
in 328 B.C., as Cleitus became incensed at the *proskynesis* (Asiatic knee-crawl-
ing) Alexander demanded of his associates. Alexander was drunk at the time,
Cleitus' sister had indeed been his old nurse, and from that day on Alexander
exempted Macedonians from the Persian court etiquette of *proskynesis*.

However, Alexander did cross the Indus in 326 B.C. It was the Beas or
Hyphasis River that his army refused to cross; after three probably rather
unpleasant days, Alexander consented to return to a more westerly portion of
the world.

Even more at variance with my story, Alexander had not—in 326 B.C.—
married Roxane. She was a Sogdian, to be exact, and he married her in 324
at Susa, so that she could not possibly have been with him at the historically
crucial moment when he decided to penetrate no farther into India. In fact,
Alexander also married Darius' daughter Barsine in 324 B.C. In 324 he returned
to Babylon. He died of fever on June 13, 323. He was thirty-three years old.

In character he was far from the blunt-minded bully my story suggests; in
historical fact, my Alexander and my Cleitus put together would have made up
a much better facsimile of the historical Alexander.

Perhaps that is the whole point of the story.

J. R.

DORIS PITKIN BUCK

The Giberel

DORIS PITKIN BUCK was born in New York City on January 3, 1898. She remembers an incident of childhood as providing her first impulse toward creativity: ". . . someone showed me a piece of alabaster that let light through. I was fascinated. Later that same day I saw an old, old woman with the pale skin of extreme age. But she was beautiful. Like a glow of light. I stared a long time, gaping, before I told myself: *alabaster!*"

She received her A.B. degree from Bryn Mawr College in 1920, her M.A. degree from Columbia University in 1925. Her first professional writing, in the 1930s, consisted of newspaper articles on wine and wine etiquette, and these brought her, in the way of readers' response, an avalanche of such questions as: "What is the correct wine to accompany graham crackers and milk?" Much later she began writing science fiction, both poetry and short stories. Her first published fiction was a short story in a 1952 issue of *The Magazine of Fantasy and Science Fiction.* She attended the Milford Conferences and became a charter member of Science Fiction Writers of America.

Now three times a grandmother, she lives in North Carolina, practices hobbies ranging from little theater to gardening to cooking, pursues literary interests ". . . from Anatole France to Ellery Queen, from Beowulf and the Mabinogion to Steve Canyon—with special roses for Blake and Emily Dickinson," and continues to exercise her impeccable craftsmanship in adding to a modest literary corpus of powerful short stories such as "The Giberel," which envisions a future of man so remote that it seems to touch his past.

Aramere fell asleep, small flexible fingers closed about her new toy, the wheel. Wheels could spin. Usually when told to rest she lay in half dreams in her temple cubicle with all her fingers close together as if they were stiff and could hardly move. Now she used them recklessly. Her wheel spun.

She was so happy that the Star Priests' talk, drifting in fragmented, left her unworried, as a deep voice spoke, "I spit upon the Bomb."

One answered, "Why so? Perchance it made us evolve . . . something better than the forefathers of our forefathers."

"We do not know what men were like before. Even their bones have crumbled."

"Could be they had no thumbs in those days. No thumbs at all."

Aramere knew the routine that would follow. The nearly rigid first joints of the priests' fingers would stroke the hard spurs sticking out above their wrists. As she dozed, worn out from play, she touched her own, proudly. Her thumb was like everyone else's.

She laid the wheel against her cheek and told it maybe what the priests said had no meaning, even for them. Or maybe they had meaning for—she repeated to herself—for toadfolk. Somebody had told her such people were hardly human though they dared think *they* had forms and hands finer than anyone in all the rest of the world. Her breath came in a little gulp at the idea. For weren't they shorter, sometimes a whole head shorter, than her people, giberels? Didn't they work by *day*, those toadfolk?

Aramere's thoughts veered off. Tonight: her third birthday. She could almost see toys that would be hers in a new home, for the

temple foundling had been wooed by a foster mother as in some
lands maids are wooed to gain their consent to a marriage. Her
hand still clutched a cake. As she waited for her mother's return,
her mouth knew unfamiliar tastes, sweet and spicy.

She waked in the dark. She felt a hand over her mouth. She tried
to bite it.

The bite did her little good. Fists shoved at her jaw. Palms
pressed down against her head. She wanted to scratch, but her
nails were still soft, as they would be till she was seven.

Through the night's blackness she was half pushed, half carried
outside. Wind hit her face. Her body, sweaty from attempts to
twist and turn, chilled. Her mouth felt dry. Her jaws were held
firmly or her teeth would have chattered.

The strangers carried Aramere a long way, then set her down
in a field. She was too sick with fright to notice the planted rows
that stretched indistinct in the starlight, almost out of sight.

"The girl seems the right size for a giberel. She's like to us,"
several voices argued in her behalf.

They brought a stick, straight, smooth, polished, and held her
against it, so frightened she would have slumped in a heap on the
ground without support.

"Sixty measures."

"As giberels should be."

"She may be fit to adopt."

"But this foundling's a she-freak though she is not dwarfish. We
watched her in the House Where Stars Are Worshiped. Her
fingers on both hands move easily, as with toadfolk, when she
thinks no one watches."

Voices said together, "We could lose our own humanity if we
opened our clans to a neither-which-nor-t'other."

"Were she to marry some true giberel—who knows—the off-
spring might be like toadfolk working in the soil all day, as worms
do." They murmured, assenting.

"Were she dead, her life blood could water our depleted
earth—"

"Depleted for century on century." The giberels chanted it like a ritual.

"Her body could nourish plants which we and the mud-fingered toadfolk are forced to share."

"It would be better so," a chilly voice reasoned, "since she could never be certain of breeding true."

Aramere's large eyes opened wider. She caught a glimpse of a boy a year or two older on the fringes of the crowd. He tried to gesture reassurance, but he was too little to help.

They peered at her in the obscurity. "Who in all the centuries of humanity has had such eyes?" She felt hostility, like a fall into chilly water that would close over her head. She had fallen so once on a December day.

A softer voice: "When she closes her eyes, she has the giberel beauty. Perhaps she was a found child."

"No! Those hands betray her."

"Then why let the toadling live on? Why wait?" It was the chilly-water voice.

Aramere began to wriggle desperately. She pressed her toes into the soft earth of the field, trying to jump forward. Starlight helped her to see. Orange starlight. Gold starlight. Starlight like the reddest rose. The stars were friends, she was sure. She took a deep breath, ready to run if once the stiff hands that pressed so hard let her go, even a little.

"Why wait?" the chilly voice asked again.

Hands pressed her tighter yet.

"How shall we kill?" It was the cold voice.

"Break the neck and leave the body?"

"Bury. Then she will nourish what grows here." In a rush: "Bury her alive."

"Show hands. Show hands for the manner of this child's death. A broken neck?" Silence fell. In the stillness Aramere saw three hands go into a slow clench and lift over slim bodies. *Harm! Harm to you!* the fists screamed. She wanted to put her hands over her large eyes to shut out the screaming of the fists. She crouched frozen now with terror. She could have done nothing even if she were body-free.

"A live burial?" Fists shot up. Many. Many.

What was burial?

Hands still held her. But now some who surrounded her bent over, their spadelike hands scooping up earth and patting it into pellets. They placed these at the rim of a depression they made. The giberels hummed—a small sad music.

The cold voice said over it, "Much treachery lurks in mother love. A barren woman craved this death-morsel. Her craving drew her to the House Where Stars Are Worshiped."

Another added, "Malformed plasm, evilly begotten, is brought there. They hold it for adoption, for sacrifice, for whatever they sense to be the Will of the Stars. A barren giberel found this girl-child—"

A shriek tore the night. The pressure on Aramere's body loosened a little. Warm arms wrapped themselves about her—her new mother. Aramere began to sob. Hot tears came to wash all the coldness into the blackest part of the night.

"You cannot kill my foundling, true giberel or no." Then, almost taunting, "And what is a giberel? No one even knows the meaning of the word."

Someone shouted, "That's one of the many meanings lost when the Bomb fell." But most of them tried to hiss her into silence.

Aramere's mother cried over the noise, "I tell you all, she has value."

"What value, demented woman?" Once more the cold started to slap like water against Aramere.

Her mother's arms wrapped her more intensely. More warmly.

"She has crop-magic. The power of which we have legends. Take your hands off her. We shall yet eat our fill."

"How know you this, woman?"

"I watched her. I saw a marvel. Certainty is in me, as it was that you gathered to do her harm. I knew."

Several voices demanded, "So you came running?"

"So I came running."

"For nothing you winded yourself. We have passed a doom upon this child who, though she is tall and fair like a maple tree, is no purebred creature. She is a menace to be destroyed."

"It is so." The giberels began to hum again.

"This is no ritual. It is murder."

"Justice."

"You lie in your throat of ice, Cold Tone. Proceed with this and I shall have you arraigned."

"And I shall stop your proceedings, easily, as I have stopped this false adoption."

"You have not heard me out. Crop-magic lives in this child. My words are true. I have seen a marvel—as I said."

They stopped their humming to ask, "What marvel?"

"When she passes a food plant, it bends its head. Very little, for she is still young. But it bends."

"It does," Aramere piped.

"Throw her in the grave," Cold Tone ordered.

Many voices babbled, "We have our legends of miracles, of abundance long past or to come. If she has a body of magic, perhaps a new plant will grow from her grave. A plant with fruits twenty times larger than all the fruits we know."

Suddenly Aramere shrilled, still clinging to her new parent, "I know what I can do, though I have never done it all the way."

"Yes? Yes?" With a rising inflection: "What can you do?"

"I can look at the stars."

For a moment they were silent. Then: "She mocks us."

"No. She gives a message. Aramere, whisper it to me."

"When I watch stars, I draw their light into my reflecting eyes. Afterward, if I look at a plant it will grow. Grow taller than in the light of the one star that shines from daybreak till evening." They all heard.

"She mocks. Heap earth over her slowly."

"Slowly."

As in an antiphonal chant: "Slowly."

Aramere gulped, choked, "I have not done it yet. But I can."

Frigid laughter answered. Hands as cold started to push her toward the shallow pit.

She screamed, "I can. I can."

With all her strength she reached toward a bushy plant in the nearest row. She could almost touch it. She looked beyond it, and up. Stars were all the colors she had ever seen. Her eyes drank them as mouths drink water.

She was jostled this way and that, pulled from the plant in the row.

And suddenly the plant reached for her, long boughs creeping toward the brightness of her eyes like moths seeking flame.

"Fools!" Aramere's mother chided. "Every moonless night do we not stand in fields the toadfolk mess with by day? Do we not reach toward the night-heaven with our bodies, with our heron necks? And the shining particles in our giberel eyes catch and mirror the far turbulence of stars that in the old times, the wise times before the Bomb, were known to increase growth. We move blindly now, yet we understand that. Without the night-stars and the day-star there would be little new, by sowing, by harvest."

A second plant stretched toward Aramere.

In sudden revulsion the giberels cried, "We have been given our miracle. See one plant here. Another. And another. Forget her toadfolk hands with supple fingers. Forget. Remember only her potent eyes. Honor to Aramere!" They danced away under Aramere's stars into the night.

Aramere rested exhausted against her mother. She failed to understand murmured heresies. "Who knows what the stars hold in store for us? Change. Change. Mayhap they try to give back what the Bomb destroyed." Then the woman forgot stars and their mysteries as she kissed Aramere from silken hair to knees, from spurlike thumb to the quick-moving fingers no giberel had ever known.

Aramere's eyes focused starlight onto the crops that in endless rhythm toadfolk tended with their hands by day and giberels with their eyes by night. Each year as the harvest was gathered under sun or counted in moonlight, the yield was greater, though some said the earth never forgot, never forgave its old scars. Others whispered that if perhaps a savior arose— There for lack of imagination the whispers died.

To Aramere that was a vast indifference. She did her work. She was revered, almost a goddess to the peoples whose hunger she lessened. Even toadfolk made her a home with lintels carved and painted to resemble fruits and edible pods. They and the giberels roofed it with overlapping thatch, thickness on thickness. At the doorway her own spring gushed, surrrounded with a stone rim, green like early spring because she was a virgin.

She was accustomed to receive offerings and artifacts. But those who brought them stayed only to genuflect and lay out their gifts in patterns. They never waited like the giberel who stood before her now. He lingered to sing cadences repeating the sounds of her name. Recklessly he gathered peach branches that would fruit. He set these in bowls beside her door. Later he floated apple blossoms, each resting singly on clear water. She had been taught letters by her parent and spelled out *Aramere* between little gasps at anyone so rash as to pluck his apple blooms to make them say her name in color and perfume.

"How many nights of stars," at last he asked her, "until we lie in each other's arms? How many, Aramere? The sacred circle, the great woman symbol," he bowed at the word as all giberel lovers did, "should be formed to dance our marriage."

"I shall never marry," she told him at dawn, when giberels feel the coming of sleep. "Never marry," she said clearly at twilight, looking into the dusk.

At first he thought this the shyness of a maiden. At last the man required of her, but gently, "Give your reason for nay-saying."

She shook her head. "Dear love, leave me."

"When you call me your love?"

"Leave me."

"Never."

"Harm might come from my surrender."

"How so?"

"Dreads press me down like weights. I have felt them since I was a child and they took me out, ready to bury me. An old man said then I could never breed true and were better dead."

"From such desire as mine, only good can come. Our child will be truest giberel of them all. I will prove you can breed true."

"But if I should fail you?"

"If we laugh in the fullness of delight, you cannot fail."

She looked at him mutely, trembling.

"Did your courage fail when you were a child and they called you toadling, she-freak, death-morsel?"

"Then it was I alone. Never could I be brave for myself and for a child too." She wept in his arms. "This cannot be. Cannot. I—I—" But she clung tightly. "Comfort me," she cried.

"Who is true will breed true," he said, and worshiped her with his eyes. "And now," his voice grew in power, "now our minds chime, I shall go to bespeak our wedding circle."

Aramere turned her head toward the Easer of Labor, the deft-fingered toadwife, the one strange-race who ever touched a giberel and then only at childbirth. "He said that from happiness such as ours, only good could come. But I have given birth to a monster."

"Sleep. Sleep for now."

"Take away our son. Tell my husband when he comes back from hunting—" Aramere broke off.

"Nah. Nah. Tell your husband this son of his will shoot better arrows than the best hunter."

"He will hate his child. So sure he was it would be a wonder."

"Say then, with plenty of tears and some sobs, mind, how you were forced in the forest by a Thing come from the stars to look into your long, large eyes. Who knows those eyes of yours didn't call something?" She winked.

"A lie. I would have killed myself." Aramere pulled her babe's cover up to its chin and held it there.

"Rest. Every mother rests after a birthing."

"But his father . . ."

"Tish posh. Face that when he comes."

Aramere sat up straight in her bed, for all her weakness. "He will never believe in me again," she said in a voice of winter. Then words died in her throat.

The Easer pushed her back on the pillow. "Drink this. Brewed from the best."

Aramere turned her head away. "Nothing can ease me." She pulled the baby's sheet tighter round its chin. "Nothing." But the midwife forced some of the drink into her mouth.

After Aramere slept, the Easer turned the baby's sheet down. "Giberel," she muttered, "except the hand. Except the hand," she repeated several times. She squinted. The thumb was like nothing on any child she'd seen. It could twist around. The child flexed it. It met any finger neatly. It even doubled up in the palm.

"Could be no calamity at all," the woman told the baby. "With a thumb like yours, what couldn't I do?" She glanced at her own hand as her fingers patted the newly born.

Must everyone stay the same, she wondered, going against everything she'd ever heard. She pressed her lips so tight together her mouth was no more than a line across her face, for such a thought must stay unvoiced. She'd been in the world long enough to know when people stoned old women. "Firmest grip ever I met. Could hold the whole earth with that." But she did not say it aloud.

KATHERINE MACLEAN

The Missing Man

KATHERINE MACLEAN was born January 22, 1925, in Montclair, New Jersey. In high school she won a biology award but turned down the offer of a premed scholarship. She received her B.A. degree from Barnard College and has done graduate study at several universities, most of it in psychology. She has worked as laboratory technician in penicillin research, EKG technician, office manager and payroll bookkeeper, reporter, photographer, detective, editor, book reviewer, public relations and publicity writer, factory quality controller and assembly line worker. She lectures, she has taught creative and expository writing courses at the University of Connecticut, and currently she teaches writing, English and literature (including science fiction) at the University of Maine. She is a member of Science Fiction Writers of America and the S.F. Research Association.

She also writes too few science fiction stories, about "ideas and insights and new viewpoints and far-out logic trips and flashes of light in the mind . . . also good melodrama about people trying to avert world catastrophe, rescue their friends or avoid disaster. . . . I don't find it unreal, it's life. Security and boredom are the escape from life and are unreal, not adventure and hazard in a strange universe." Her stories have been widely anthologized and eight of them appeared in a collection, *The Diploids and Other Flights of Fancy* (1962).

A Katherine MacLean story is an event, and this year's event is "The Missing Man," the Nebula Award-winning novella for 1971.

YOU ARE NOT ALONE announced the sign, flashing neon red in the dark sky. People in the free mixed streets looked up and saw it as they walked back from work. It glowed red behind them in the sky as they entered the gates of their own Kingdoms; their own incorporated small countries and their own laws inside their gates. They changed into their own strange costumes, perhaps light armor, and tourneyed, tilting lances against each other, winning ladies. Or in another Kingdom, with a higher wall around its enclosed blocks of city, the strange lotteries and rites of the Aztec sadist cult, or the simple poverty and friendliness of the Brotherhood Love Communes. They were not alone.

Nonconformists who could not choose a suitable conformity lived in the mixed public areas, went to mixing parties, wondering and seeking. Seeking whom? To join with to do what? Returning from the parties late and alone, they passed the smaller signs flashing red in the store windows.

YOU ARE NOT ALONE
Find your own Kind, Find your own Hobby.
Find your own Mate, Find your own Kingdom.
Use "Harmony" Personality Diagnosis and Matching Service.

Carl Hodges was alone. He stood in a deserted and ruined section of the city and saw the red glow of the sign reflecting against the foggy air of the sky of New York, blinking on and off like the light of a flickering red flame. He knew what the glow said. *You are not alone.*

He shut his eyes, and tears trickled from under his closed eyelids. Damn the day he had learned to do time track. He could remember and return to Susanne, he could even see the moment of the surfboard and his girl traveling down the front slope of a slanted wave front, even see the nose of the board catch again under the ripple, the wave heaving the board up, up and over, and whipping down edge first like an ax. He knew how to return for pleasure to past events, but now he could not stop returning. It happened again before his eyes, over and over. *Think about something else!*

"Crying again, Pops?" said a young insolent voice. A hand pushed two tablets against his mouth. "Here, happy pills. Nothing to cry about. It's a good world."

Obediently Carl Hodges took the pills into his mouth and swallowed.

Soon memory and grief would stop hurting and go away. Think about something else. Work? No, he should be at work, on the job instead of vacationing, living with runaway children. Think about fun things.

It was possible that he was a prisoner, but he did not mind. Around him collecting in the dark, stood the crowd of runaway children and teen-agers in strange mixed costumes from many communes across the United States. They had told him that they had run away from the Kingdoms and odd customs of their parents, hating the Brotherhood, and conformity, and sameness of the adults they had been forced to live with by the law that let incorporated villages educate their own children within the walls.

The teeners had told him that all rules were evil, that all customs were neurotic repetition, that fear was a restriction, that practicality was a restriction, and mercy was a restriction.

He told himself they were children, in a passing phase of rebellion.

The pill effect began to swirl in a rosy fog of pleasure into his mind. He remembered fun. "Did I tell you," he muttered to the runaway teener gang that held him as a prisoner-guest, "about the last game of Futures I played with Ronny? It was ten-thirty, late work, so when we finished we disconnected the big computer from its remote controls and started to play City Chess. We had three minor maintenance errors as our only three moves. He wiped out my half of the city, by starting an earthquake from a refrigerator failure in a lunchroom. It wiped out all the power plant crew with food poisoning, and the Croton power plant blew up along a fault line. That was cheating because he couldn't prove the fault line. I wiped out his technocrats in Brooklyn Dome just by reversing the polarity on the air-conditioning machine. It's a good thing our games aren't real. Everyone is wiped out totally by the end of a good game."

A blond kid who seemed to be the leader stepped forward and took Carl Hodges' arm, leading him back toward his cellar room. "You started to tell me about it, but tell me again. I'm very interested. I'd like to study Maintenance Prediction as a career. What does reversing the leads on the air-conditioning machine do to destroy a place?"

"It changes the smell of the air," said Carl Hodges, the missing man who knew too much. "You wouldn't think that would make a lot of difference, would you?"

Since June 3, every detective the police could spare had been out looking for a missing computerman who had been last seen babbling about ways to destroy New York City.

Judd Oslow, Chief of Rescue Squad, sounded excited on the phone. "Your anti-chance score is out of sight, George. I want you to guess for us where Carl Hodges is and give us another hit like the first three. I'm not supposed to send my men after Carl Hodges, it's not my department, but that's my neck on the block, not yours. Brace yourself to memorize a description."

"Sure." George made ready to visualize a man.

"Carl Hodges, twenty-nine years old, a hundred and forty pounds, five feet nine inches tall, brown hair, hazel eyes."

George visualized someone shorter and thinner than himself. He remembered some short underweight men who were always ready to fight to prove they were bigger.

"His job is assistant coordinator of computer automation city services," read Judd Oslow.

"What's that?" George wanted to get the feel of Carl Hodges' job.

"Glorified maintenance man for the city, the brains for all the maintenance and repair teams. He uses the computer to predict wear and accidents and lightning strikes and floods that break down phone lines, power and water lines and he sends repair teams to strengthen the things before they are stressed so they don't break. He prevents trouble."

"Oh." George thought: Carl Hodges will be proud of his job. He won't want to be bigger. "How does he act with his friends? How does he feel?"

"Wait for the rest." Judd read, "Hobbies are chess, minimax and surfing. No commune. Few friends. One girl who met with a fatal accident when they were on a love trip last month. He's not happy. He was last seen at a Stranger's introduction party, Thirty-sixth Street and Eighth. He might have been spaced out on drugs, or he might have been psychotic, because he was reported as mumbling continuously on a dangerous subject he was usually careful to keep quiet about."

"What subject?"

"Secret."

"Why?"

"Panic."

"Oh." George restrained his natural anger at being confronted with a secret, and remembered an excuse for the authorities. Panic, or any other group stimulation that could send many people unexpectedly in the same direction, could cause destructive crowding and clogging in the walkways and transportation. People could get jammed in, pushed, trampled, suffocated. In a city of tremendous population and close and immediate access to everything, safety from crowding was based on a good scatter of differences, with some people wanting to be in one place and others in another, keeping them thinly spread. Sometimes the authorities kept secrets, or managed the news to prevent interesting things from pulling dangerous jammed crowds into one place.

The Chief of Rescue Squad got the TV connection to the public phone turned on, and let George look at a photograph of the missing man. A wiry undersized scholar with a compressed mouth and expressionless eyes. George tried to tune in by pretending it was his own face in the mirror. Staring into its eyes, he felt lonely.

He started by going to the Stranger's introduction party. He followed his impulses, pretending to be Carl Hodges. He wandered the city closely on the trail of Carl Hodges, but he did not feel it with any confidence, because he thought that the trail of feelings that urged him from one place to another were his own lonely feelings and sad thoughts. After he was given a few bad events to be sad about, he was sure it was his own mood.

George woke at dawn and watched pink sunlight touch the bushes along the top of a building so they brightened up like candle flames on the top of a birthday cake. He lay with his eyes open and watched while the light brightened and the pink faded. Crickets sang and creaked in the deep grass and bending tall grass tickled against his face.

He lay still, feeling the kind of aches you get from being kicked. There were a lot of aches. The teener gang that had attacked him had even put chain bruises on his legs. They had not been trying to kill him, only to warn him against trespassing again.

But George still felt strange and without friends. Usually he could join any group. Usually he could be anybody's friend. Was he forgetting how to be buddy with strangers? The teeners had left him on the sidewalk tied in a ridiculous knot with fingers and toes hooked together by Chinese fingertrap tubes. He had worked his fingers free, and walked down to his girl friend's Brotherhood Love Commune to sleep. He felt strange and inferior, and hoped no one would look at him, when he entered the commune. The brothers in the front rooms said he was giving out bad vibes, and upsetting an important group meditation, and they gave him a cup of tea and put him out with his sleeping bag.

Four A.M., wondering what he was doing wrong, he went to

sleep in a shape-hiding shadow in the grass belt opposite the Rescue Squad midtown headquarters. Now awakened again by dawn,
he felt his bruises and felt sad and unsuccessful. He had wandered
through many places in the city the night before, but he had not
found Carl Hodges. The computerman was still an unlucky prisoner somewhere.

By the time the sun was high, George was going across George
Washington Bridge the hard way, on the understruts, clinging
with bare hands and feet, clambering up and down slopes of girders and cables, sometimes sitting and watching the sun sparkle on
the water more than a hundred feet below while huge ships went
slowly by, seeming like toys.

The wind blew against his skin, warm sometimes and sometimes
cold and foggy. He watched a cloud shadow drift up from the
south along the river. It darkened the spires of tall buildings,
became a traveling island of dark blue in the light blue of the river,
approached and widened, and then there was cool shadow across
the bridge for long moments while George looked up and watched
a dark cotton cloud pass between him and the sun.

The cloud left and the light blazed. George looked away, dots
of darkness in front of his eyes, and watched the cloud shadow
climb a giant cliff to the west and disappear over the top. He
started picking his way along a downslope of girder, moving carefully because the dazzle of sun dots was still inside his eyes, dancing between his vision and the girders. Overhead the steady rumble of traffic passing along the roadway was a faraway and soothing
sound.

A gull in the distance flapped upward through the air toward
him. It found an updraft and drifted with it, wings spread and
motionless, then paused in front of him, floating, a white beautiful
set of wings, a sardonic cynical head with downcurved mouth and
expressionless inspecting eyes.

George was tempted to reach out and grab. He shifted to the
grip of one hand on the cross strut and hooked one knee over a
bar.

The gull tilted the tips of his wings and floated upward and back, a little farther out of reach in the sky, but still temptingly close.

George decided that he was not stupid enough to let a gull trick him into falling off the bridge.

The gull slanted and slid sideways down a long invisible slope of air and squalled, "Creee. Ha ha ha ha. Ha ha ha . . ." in a raucous gull laugh. George hoped he would come back and make friends, but he had never heard of anyone making friends with a gull. He climbed on toward the New Jersey shore, going up and down slopes of girders, found a steel ladder fastened to the side and climbed it straight up to a paint locker and a telephone. He dialed Rescue Squad, and asked for Judd Oslow.

"Chief, I'm tired of taking a vacation."

"This morning Ahmed reported you walked like a cripple. How late did you work last night?"

"Three-thirty."

"Find any clues to Carl Hodges?"

"Not exactly." George looked at the far, high planes and helicopters buzzing through the blue sky. He did not feel like discussing the failure of last night.

"Where are you now?"

"In a painter's crow's nest on George Washington Bridge."

"Climbing George Washington Bridge is your idea of a rest?"

"It's away from people. I like climbing."

"Okay, your choice. You are near Presbyterian Medical Center. Report to the Rescue Squad station there and fill out some reports on what you've been doing all week. Some of the things you've been doing, we would probably like to pay you for. The information girl there will help you fill out the forms. You'll like her, George. She doesn't mind paper work. Let her help you."

Ahmed Kosavakats, George's superior and childhood friend, was ready to admit defeat. He had reasoned in trying to find Carl Hodges and reasoned well.

Any commune which had Carl Hodges could ask him how to

bias the city services computer in their favor. Ahmed had been checking the routine deliveries of repairs and improvements and rebuilding and projects to each commune, by running a comparison check against the normal deliveries through the statistics computer. Negative. There was no sign of a brilliant manipulator changing the city services.

Ahmed stood up and stretched long arms, thinking. Whoever had Carl Hodges was not using him. If Ahmed could rescue Carl Hodges and become his friend, he would not miss the opportunity to use him. If a man wanted to influence the future of his city . . .

If he could not use his own logic to find Carl Hodges, then the kidnappers were not thinking logically, and could not be predicted by logic. If they were thinking emotionally, then George Sanford could probably tune to them and locate them. But Ahmed would have to tell him what kind of people to tune to, and how they felt.

George Sanford's intuition was a reliable talent. Once, when George was a fattish, obliging kid in Ahmed's gang, Ahmed had added up how often George's simple remarks and guesses had turned out right. George had guessed right every time. But George didn't think. Half envious, Ahmed had told the others that George's head was like a radio; you could tune his brain to any station and get the news and weather and the right time in Paris, San Francisco and Hong Kong, but a radio isn't going to add anything up, not even two plus two; it works because it's empty.

George Sanford had grown up to a big silent cat of a man. Extremely strong, not caring apparently whether he ate, drank or slept, a rather blank expression, but he still tuned in on people. His goals were the simple ones of being with friends, helping out and being welcome, and he had friends everywhere.

Behind the apparent low IQ there were untapped abilities that could only be brought into action by demanding a lot of George when you asked him to help. It was not certain yet how much George could do. George did not know. He probably did not even think about it. He had no demands on himself.

The thing to do, Ahmed thought, was to keep the pressure on George. Keep him working.

Ahmed found George filling out reports by dictating them to a pretty girl. The pretty office worker had her hands poised over the typewriter and was listening to George with an expression of surprise and doubt. George, with his brow knotted, was plodding through a narrative of something he had done the day before. The girl rolled the report sheet through the typewriter opposite a different blank and asked a question timidly; a tape recorder showed its red light, recording the questions and answers. George hesitated, looking at the ceiling desperately for inspiration, his brow more knotted than before.

George always had trouble understanding the reasoning behind red tape. He did not know why certain answers were wanted. They both looked up with relief when Ahmed interrupted by turning off the tape recorder.

"They told me to team up with you this afternoon," Ahmed said to George. "They give this job priority over reports or any other job. Are you feeling okay now?"

"Sure, Ahmed," George said, slightly surprised.

"Let's go outside and see if we can tune to the subject. Okay?"

"Okay." George got up, moving easily. A bruise showed at his hairline on the side of his head, almost hidden by hair. On George's right arm were two blue bruises, and below his slacks on the right ankle was a line of red dents with bruises. A left-handed assailant with a club, or a right-handed assailant with a chain, swinging it left to right, would bruise a man on one side like that.

Walking out of the Rescue Squad office, Ahmed indicated with a gesture the bruise on George's arm.

"May I ask?"

"No," George replied and closed his mouth tightly, staring straight ahead as they went through the double doors.

George didn't want to talk about it, Ahmed thought, because he had lost that fight. That meant he had been outnumbered. But he was not dead or seriously hurt. The assailants then were not killers, or he had escaped them. Probably a trespassing problem. Probably George had trespassed onto some group's territory or Kingdom last night while searching for Carl Hodges by himself. Ahmed put the thought aside. They stopped on a walk among the bushes and trees and looked up at the towering buildings of Presbyterian Medical Center, like giant walls reaching to the sky. Helicopter ambulances buzzed around landing steps like flies.

"Let's not waste time, George, let's get you tuned into Carl Hodges," Ahmed said, pulling out a notebook and pen. "Do you have a picture of Hodges with you?"

"No." The big young man looked uneasy. "You going to do it that same way, Ahmed? If he's sick, will I get sick?"

"I've got a picture here." Ahmed reached for a folder in his pocket and passed a photo to George.

The ground jolted in a sort of thud that struck upward against their feet.

Nine miles or more away, and two minutes earlier, Brooklyn Dome, the undersea suburb, suddenly lost its dome. The heavy ocean descended upon it, and air carrying a torrent of debris that had been houses and people blurted upward through an air shaft. A fountain of wreckage flung upward into the sky, falling in a circular rain of shattered parts to float upon the sea.

All morning a mass wish to escape from the enclosure of walls had driven George happily into the heights and winds and free sky. Now that note in the blend of the mood of the city suddenly changed and worsened to panic, helplessness, defeat and pain, and then an end. The event telescoped in speed, compressed into a blow of darkness. The broadcast of many thousand minds ended and their background hum in the vibes of the city diminished.

Reaching out with his mind for information, George encountered the memory of that impact. It went by like the thunder wave of breaking the sound barrier, like a wave of black fog. He shut his eyes to tune in, and found nothing, except that the world had lightened. A burden of fear had been suddenly erased.

George opened his eyes and took a deep breath. "Something big," he said. "Something . . ."

Ahmed was watching the sweep-second hand on his watch. "Fifty-five hundred feet, one mile," he muttered.

"What are you doing?"

"It's an explosion somewhere. I'm counting the distance. Sound arrives first through the ground, second through the air. I'm waiting for the sound. I'll get the distance by the time lag."

At thirty seconds the sound of the death of an underseas city reached them, a strange sort of grinding roar, muffled, low and distant.

George shut his eyes again, and felt the world change around him to another place.

"Got something, George?" Ahmed asked alertly. "That was about seven miles."

"Someone knows what happened. I'm picking him up. Brooklyn Dome just collapsed."

"Twelve thousand inhabitants," Ahmed said, dialing his wrist radio grimly, his earphone plugged into his ear. "No one answering at headquarters, just busy signals."

George shut his eyes again, exploring the other place. "Someone's having a nightmare," he said. "He can't wake up."

"Don't flip out, George, keep in touch with facts. A lot of people just died, is all. Keep a grip on that. I'm trying to get our orders."

George stood with his eyes shut, exploring the sensation inside his head. Somewhere a man was trapped in a nightmare, half asleep in a dark prison or closet. It was some kind of delirium.

The real world was a cruel place that bright day, but the black and coiling fragments of that man's world were worse. There was something important about the man's thoughts. He had felt the explosion thud at a distance, as they had, and he had known what it meant. He had expected it.

"Can't locate where he is," George said, opening his eyes and regaining his grip on the bright sunshine world around him.

Ahmed squinted and tilted his head, listening to the obscure and rapid voices on the earplugs of his radio.

"Never mind about that case, George. That's Carl Hodges probably. He'll keep. Headquarters is broadcasting general orders for the emergency. Repair and services inspection people are ordered to make quick inspections at all danger points in the automatic services, looking for malfunction and sabotage. Repair and inspection teams are ordered into Jersey Dome, to check out every part of it and make sure it is not gimmicked to blow the way Brooklyn Dome went. They are instructed to describe it as a routine safety check."

"What do we do? What about us?"

"Wait, I'm listening. They mentioned us by name. We go to Jersey underseas and try to locate and stop a sabotage agent who might have sabotaged Brooklyn Dome and might be preparing to use the same method on Jersey Dome."

"What method?"

"They don't know. They don't even know if there is a saboteur. They're sending us to make sure."

"If there is a saboteur, he's probably working on it right now." George walked, and then ran for the subway steps down into the underground moving chair belts. Ahmed followed and they caught a brace of abandoned chairs just as they slowed and accelerated them again out into the fast lanes.

"Dirty dogs! Let me out of here. I'll kill you." Furiously Carl Hodges kicked and thrashed and bit at restraining straps, remembering at last, believing his conclusions about the group of teeners that had him prisoner. "You decerebrate lizards. Let me out of here, you fools! You killed Brooklyn Dome. I've got to get back to work and level off the exchanges before something else happens. Let me out of here!"

They backed off, their smiles fading at the barrage of his anger. The tallest one answered with a trace of resentment. "Don't get upset, Pops. They weren't real people, just technocrats and objectivists and fascists and like that."

"They were techs. This city needs techs. People with tech jobs run the city, remember?"

The tall one leaned over him, glowering. "I remember what my tapes tell me. The objectivists passed the law that the compulsory sterility of women can't be reversed without paying five hundred dollars for the operation. That means if I ever want to get married I'll have to save five hundred dollars for my woman to have a kid. They're trying to wipe us all out. Nobody has that kind of money but techs. In the next generation we'll all be gone. We're just getting back at them, wiping them out."

"But faster," chuckled a small kid. "Like *boom!*"

"The objectivists got that law through legally. Why don't your people pull enough votes to get it wiped?" Carl Hodges demanded.

"They ship us out to the boondocks. We can't vote. You're talking like an objectivist. Maybe you believe everyone without money should be wiped?"

"I believe anyone without brains should be wiped!" Carl Hodges snarled suddenly. "Your mothers wouldn't have paid ten cents to have you. Too bad the law wasn't passed sooner."

"Genocide." The tall one reached over and hit him across the mouth. "We were nice to you. To *you!*" He turned and spat in revulsion.

Others surged forward.

"Steady." The leader spread arms and leaned back against the pressure. He addressed Carl. "We don't want to hurt you. You tell us things, you're a good teacher. We'll let you have what you want. Money for rights. Lie there until you have enough money to buy your way out. It will cost you five dollars to get out. That's cheaper than five hundred dollars to be born. That's a bargain."

The kids crowding behind him laughed, and laughed again, understanding the idea slowly. After a time of clumsy humor they untied him and went off, leaving him locked in a narrow window-less bedroom.

Carl Hodges went around the room, inspecting it and thinking coldly of escaping. He had to get out and straighten up the mess the city was in after the collapse of Brooklyn Dome. He had to get out and have the kids arrested before they sabotaged anything else. According to his best logic, there was no way to get out. He was stuck, and deserved it. He pushed his mind, thinking harder, fighting back a return of weakness and tears. He reached for a happy pill, then took the bottle of white pills and poured its contents down a hole in the floor.

The two Rescue Squad men shifted their chairs through acceleration bands to the inner fast slots and passed the other chairs, each leaning forward on the safety rail of his chair as if urging it on. The people they passed were holding portable TV screens like magazines, watching in the same way that people used to read.

The voice of the announcer murmured from a screen, grew louder as they passed, and then again fell to a murmur. "Brooklyn Dome. Fifteen pounds atmosphere pressure to sixty-five pounds per square inch. Exploded upward. Implosion first, then explosion." The voice grew louder again as they approached another sliding chair in the slower lane. Another person listened, propping the screen up on the safety rail to stare into it, with the sound shouting. "Debris is floating for two square miles around the center from which the explosion came. Coast Guard rescue ships, submarines and scuba divers are converged into the area, searching for survivors."

They neared and passed a TV screen which showed a distant picture of an explosion like an umbrella rising and opening on the horizon. "This is the way the explosion looked from the deck of a freighter, the *Mary Lou*, five miles south at the moment it occurred."

George settled himself in his seat and shut his eyes to concentrate. He had to stop that explosion from happening again to the other undersea dome. Whoever had done it would be laughing as he watched on TV the explosion unfold and settle. Whoever had done it would be eager for destruction, delighting in the death and blood of a small city.

The peculiarly wide range of perceptions that was George Sanford groped out across the city.

"The police department is still investigating the cause of the explosion," said the murmur, growing louder as they passed another TV watcher in the slow lane. Someone handed the announcer another note. "Ah, here we have some new information. Bell Telephone has opened up to the investigators eight recordings taken from public phones in Brooklyn Dome. These phone calls were being made at the moment Brooklyn Dome was destroyed."

A face appeared on a screen behind the announcer, a giant face of a woman telephoning. After an instant of mental adjusting of viewpoint the woman's face became normal in the viewer eye, the announcer shrank to ant size and was forgotten as the woman spoke rapidly into the phone. "I can't stand this place another minute. I would have left already, but I can't leave. The train station is jammed and there are lines in front of the ticket booth. I've never seen such lines. Jerry is getting tickets. I wish he'd hurry." The anxious woman's face glanced sideways either way out of the booth. "I hear the funniest noise, like thunder. Like a waterfall."

The woman screamed and the background tilted as the screaming face and the booth went over sideways. A hand groped past the lens, blackness entered in sheets, and the picture broke into static sparks and splashes. The screen went blank, the antlike announcer sitting in front of it spoke soothingly and the camera rushed forward to him until he was normal size again. He showed a diagram.

George opened his eyes and sat up. Around him on the moving chairs people were watching their TV screens show the pictures he had just seen in his mind's eye. It showed a diagram of the location of the phone booths at Brooklyn Dome, and then another recording of someone innocently calling from a videophone booth, about to die, and not knowing what was about to happen, an innocent middle-aged face.

Expressionlessly, the people in the traveling subway seats

watched, hands bracing the sides of the TV screen, grip tightening as they waited for the ceilings to fall. Audience anticipation; love of power, greatness, crash . . . total force and completeness . . . admiring triumph of completeness in such destruction. Great show. Hope for more horror.

All over the city people looked at the innocent fool mouthing words and they waited, watching, urging the doom on as it approached. *This time be bigger, blacker, more frightening, more crushing.*

George shut his eyes and waited through the hoarse screams and then opened his eyes and looked at the back of the neck of the TV watcher they were passing, then turned around and looked at her face after they passed. She did not notice him; she was watching the TV intently, without outward expression.

Did that woman admit the delight she felt? Did she know she was urging the thundering waterfall on, striking the death blow downward with the descending ocean? She was not different from the others. Typical television viewer, lover of extremes. It was to her credit that when TV showed young lovers she urged them to love more intensely, and rejoiced in their kisses. Lovers of life are also lovers of death.

George slid down further in his seat and closed his eyes, and rode the tidal waves of mass emotion as the millions of watchers, emotions synchronized by watching, enjoyed their mass participation in the death rites of a small city. Over and over, expectancy, anticipation, panic, defeat, death, satisfaction.

The secretly worshiped god of death rode high.

In twenty minutes, after transfers on platforms that held air-lock doors to pass through into denser air, they arrived, carried by underseas tube train, at the small undersea city of Jersey Dome. Population: ten thousand; residents: civil service administrators and their families.

The city manager's office building was built of large colored blocks of lightweight translucent foam plastic, like children's large building blocks. There was no wind to blow it away. Inside, the colors of the light tinted the city man's desk. He was a small man sitting behind a large desk with one phone held to his ear and another blinking a red light at him, untouched. "I know traffic is piling up. We have all the trains in service that city services can give up. Everyone wants to leave, that's all. No. There isn't any panic. There's no reason for panic." He hung up, and glared at the other phone's blinking light.

"That phone," he snarled, pointing, "is an outside line full of idiot reporters asking me how domes are built and how Brooklyn Dome could have blown up, or collapsed. It's all idiocy. Well. What do you want?"

Ahmed opened his wallet to his credentials and handed it over. "We're from Metropolitan Rescue Squad. We're specialists in locating people by predicting behavior. We were sent over to locate a possible lunatic who might have sabotaged Brooklyn Dome or blown it up, and might be here planning to blow up Jersey Dome."

"He just might," replied the manager of Jersey Dome with a high-pitched trembling earnestness in his voice. "And you might be the only dangerous lunatics around here. Lunatics who talk about Jersey Dome breaking. It can't break. You understand. The only thing we have to fear is panic. You understand?"

"Of course," Ahmed said soothingly. "But we won't talk about it breaking. It's our job to look for a saboteur. Probably it's just a routine preventive checkup."

The manager pulled a pistol out of a desk drawer and pointed it at them, with a trembling hand. "You're still talking about it. This is an emergency. I am the city manager. I could call my police and have you taken to a mental hospital, gagged."

"Don't worry about that," Ahmed said soothingly, picking his wallet back off the desk and pocketing it. "We're only here to admire the design and the machinery. Can we have a map?"

The manager lowered the pistol and laid it on the desk. "If you cooperate, the girl in the front office will give you all the maps of the design and structure that you'll need. You will find a lot of technicians already in the works, inspecting wires and checking up. They're here to design improvements. You understand?" His voice was still high-pitched and nervous, but steady.

"We understand," Ahmed assured him. "Everything is perfectly safe. We'll go admire their designs and improvements. Come on, George." He turned and went out, stopped at the receptionist's desk to get a map, consulted it and led the way across the trimmed lawn of the park.

Out on the curved walk under the innocent blue-green glow of the dome, Ahmed glanced back. "But I'm not sure he's perfectly safe himself. Is he cracking up, George?"

"Not yet, but near it." George glanced up apprehensively at the blue-green glow, imagining he saw a rift, but the dark streak was only a catwalk, near the dome surface.

"What will he do when he cracks?" asked Ahmed.

"Run around screaming, 'The sky is falling!' like Chicken Little." muttered George. "What else?" He cocked an apprehensive glance upward at the green glow of the dome. Was it sagging in the middle? No, that was just an effect of perspective. Was there a crack appearing near the air shaft? No, just another catwalk, like a spiderweb on a ceiling.

Making an effort, he pulled his eyes away from the dome and saw Ahmed at a small building ahead labeled "Power Substation 10002." It looked like a child's building block ten feet high, pleasantly screened by bushes, matching the park. Ahmed was looking in the open door. He signaled to George and George hurried to reach him, feeling as if the pressurized thickened air resisted, like water.

He looked inside and saw a man tinkering with the heavy power cables that provided light and power for the undersea dome. Panels were off, and the connections were exposed.

The actions and mood of the man were those of a workman, serious and careful. He set a meter dial and carefully read it, reset it and made notes, then read it again. George watched him. There was a strange kind of fear in the man, something worse than the boxed-in feeling of being underwater. George felt a similar apprehension. It had been growing in him. He looked at Ahmed, doubtfully.

Ahmed had been lounging against the open door watching George and the man. He took a deep sighing breath and went in with weight evenly balanced on his feet, ready for fast action. "Okay, how are the improvements coming?" he asked the workman.

The man grinned over his shoulder. He was slightly bald in front. "Not a single improvement, not even a small bomb."

"Let's check your ID. We're looking for the saboteur." Ahmed held out his hand.

Obligingly the man unpinned a plastic ID card from under his lapel, and put a thumbprint over the photographed thumbprint so that it could be seen that the two prints matched. He seemed unafraid of them, and friendly.

"Okay." Ahmed passed his badge back.

The engineer pinned it on again. "Have fun, detectives. I hope you nail a mad bomber so we can stop checking for defects and go home. I can't stand this air down here. Crazy perfume. I don't like it."

"Me too," George said. A thick perfumed pressure was in the air. He felt the weight of water hanging as a dome far above the city pressing the air down. "Bad air."

"It has helium in it," Ahmed remarked. He checked the map of the small city and looked in the direction of a glittering glass elevator shaft. A metal mesh elevator rose slowly in the shaft, shining in the semidark, like a giant birdcage full of people hanging above a giant living room.

George tried to take another deep breath and felt that whatever he was breathing was not air. "It smells strange, like fake air."

"It doesn't matter how it smells," Ahmed said, leading the way. "It's to keep people from getting the bends from internal pressure when they leave here. Why didn't you okay the man, George? His ID checked out."

"He was scared."

"What of?" Ahmed asked him.

"Not of us. I don't know."

"Then it doesn't matter. He's not up to any bad business."

The two walked across the small green park, through the thick air, toward the glittering glass shaft that went up from the ground into the distant green dome that was the roof of the city. Inside the huge glass tube a brightly lit elevator rose slowly, carrying a crowd of people looking out over the city as a canary would look out above a giant room.

"Next we check the air-pump controls," Ahmed said. "They're near the elevator." People went by, looking formal and over-dressed, pale and quiet, stiff and neat. Not his kind of people. Civil servants, government administration people, accountants.

George followed, trying to breathe. The air seemed to be not air, but some inferior substitute. Glittering small buildings rose on either side of the park in rows, like teeth, and he felt inside a tiger mouth. The air smelled like lilies in a funeral parlor. The people he passed gave out vibes of a trapped hopeless defeat that made his depression worse. They passed a crowd of quiet miserable people waiting to get on the elevator, carrying fishing poles and swimming equipment.

High above them the elevator descended slowly.

"That's bad," George said. "You feel it, don't you, Ahmed?"

"Feel what?" Ahmed stopped beside a small rounded building attached to the side of the shaft. The building throbbed with a deep steady *thump, thump, thump,* like a giant heart.

"I want to get out of here," George said. "Don't you feel it?"

"I ignore that kind of feeling," Ahmed said expressionlessly, and pulled on the handle of the door to the pump room. It was un-locked. It opened. The thumping was louder. "Should be locked," Ahmed muttered. They looked inside.

Inside, down a flight of steps, two workmen were checking over some large warm thumping machinery. The two detectives went down the steps.

"Identity check, let's see your ID," George said, and looked at the two badges they handed him, in the same way he had seen Ahmed and other detectives checking them over. He took thumbprints and matched them to the photo thumbprints, he compared the faces on the photos to the faces before him. One big one with a craggy chiseled stone face and grim vertical lines on the cheeks; one short weathered one, slightly leaner, slightly more humor in the face. Both identified as engineers of Consolidated Power and Light, inspectors of electrical motor appliance and life support services.

"What are the pumps doing?" Ahmed asked, looking around.

"Pumping air in, pumping water out," replied one of the men. "There's the pump that pushes excess water up to the top, where it comes out as a little ornamental fountain in an artificial island. The pressure equalizes by itself, so it doesn't need elaborate equipment, just power."

"Why pump water out?" Ahmed asked. "The air pressure is supposed to be so high that it pushes the water out."

The man laughed. "You make it sound so simple. The air pressure is approximately the same here as up at the top surface of the dome, but the water pressure rises every foot of the way down. Down here at the bottom it is higher than the air pressure. Water squeezes in along the edges of the cement slab, up through the ground cover and the dirt. We have drains to catch the seepage and lead it back to this pump. We expect seepage."

"Why not pump in more air? Higher air pressure would keep all the water out."

"Higher air pressure would burst the top of the dome like a balloon. There isn't enough weight of water to counterpush."

George got an uncertain picture of air pushing to get out the top and water pushing to get in the bottom. "It's working all right?" He handed the ID badges back to them.

"Right," said the explanatory man, pinning on his badge. "It would take a bomb to get those pumps out of balance. Don't know why they sent us to check the pumps. I'd rather be out fishing."

"They're looking for a bomb, dummy," said the other one sourly.

"Oh." The bigger one made a face. "You mean, like Brooklyn Dome blew up?" He looked around slowly. "If anything starts to happen, we're right near the elevator. We can get to the top."

"Not a chance," said the sour one. "The elevator is too slow. And it has a waiting line, people ahead of you. Resign yourself. If this place blows, we blow."

"Why is the elevator so slow?" George asked. *Fix it!* He hoped silently. They listened to the hum of the elevator engine lowering the elevator. It was slow.

"It can go faster; the timer's right here." The sour engineer walked over and inspected the box. "Someone has set it to the slowest speed. I wonder why."

"For sightseeing," George said, "but I saw the crowd waiting. They have fishing poles. They want to get to the top, they don't want to wait in the middle of the air, just viewing."

"Okay." The talkative one walked over and firmly set the pointer over to "fast." The elevator reached the ground on the other side of the wall, rumbled to a stop and the doors whirred open.

They listened, hearing voices and the shuffle of feet as people crowded inside, then the doors rumbled shut and the elevator started for the top. The whirr was high and rapid. In less than a third of the time the trip up to the surface had taken before, the whirr stopped.

The two engineers nodded at each other. "I hope they are happy with it."

"They are getting there faster."

George said, "That makes sense," and Ahmed nodded agreement. They went out and watched the elevator return. As rapidly as falling, the great silver birdcage came down the glass shaft and slowed, and stopped, and opened. It was empty. No one who was up there was coming back in to the city.

More people got on.

"What is up there?" George asked, holding himself back from a panic desire to get in the elevator with the others and get out of the enclosed city. "I have a feeling we should go up there," he said, hoping Ahmed would misunderstand and think George was being called by a hunch.

"What do you feel?" Ahmed looked at him keenly. The doors shut and the elevator rose rapidly, leaving them behind on the ground.

"What I feel is, we shouldn't have let that elevator go without us. We've had it, old buddy. It's been nice knowing you. I didn't expect to die young."

"Snap out of it." Ahmed clicked his fingers under George's nose. "You're talking for somebody else. Hold that feeling separate from your thinking. It's not your kind of feeling. George Sanford isn't afraid, ever. You don't think like that."

"Yes I do," George said sadly. He heard the elevator doors rumble open far overhead. Somewhere above people had escaped to the top of the ocean instead of the bottom. A dock? An island? Somewhere fresh winds were blowing across ocean waves.

"Locate that feeling of doom," Ahmed said. "Maybe our mad bomber is a suicider and plans to go down with the ship. Shut your eyes. Where are you in your head?"

"On top, on an island in the daylight," George said sadly, looking at his imagination of sand and seagulls. "It's too late, Ahmed. We're dead." A few new people arrived and lined up behind him waiting for the elevator. The sound of its descent began far above. People approached through the park from the direction of the railway station, and George remembered that there had been fenced-in crowds waiting for trains, waiting to get out. Maybe some people had grown impatient and wanted to get to fresh air. The crowd behind him grew denser and began to push. The elevator doors opened in front of George.

"Get in, George," said Ahmed, and pushed his elbow. "We're going to the top."

"Thanks." George got on. They were pushed to the back of the cage and the doors shut. The elevator rose with knee-pressing speed. Over the heads of the people before him George saw a widening vision of the undersea city, small buildings circling a central park, dimly and artistically lit by green and blue spotlights on trees and vines, with a rippling effect in the light like seaweed and underwater waves. Paths and roads were lit with bead chains of golden sodium lights. On the other side of the park the railroad station, squares of soft yellow light, fenced in by lacework metal walls. Many people around it. Too many. Dense crowds. The paths across the park were moving with people approaching the elevator shaft.

The elevator reached the top of the dome and went through into a tube of darkness. For a few moments they rose through the darkness and then they felt the elevator slow and stop. The doors rumbled open and the people pressed out, hurried through a glass door and down a staircase, and were gone from the top floor.

George looked around. There was the sky and ocean spaces he had dreamed of, but the sky was cloudy, the ocean was gray, and he was looking at them through thick glass. The island viewing platform was arranged in a series of giant glass steps, and the elevator had opened and let them into the top step, a glass room that looked out in all directions through thick glass, giving a clear view of the horizon, the glass rooms below, and the little motorboats that circled the docks of an artificial island.

"How's your hunch? What do you feel?" Ahmed snapped out, looking around alertly, weight on the balls of his feet, ready to spring at some mad bomber that he expected George to locate.

"The air is faked. I can't breathe it," George said, breathing noisily through his mouth. He felt like crying. This was not the escape he had dreamed of. The feeling of doom persisted and grew worse.

"It's the same air and the same pressure as down undersea in the dome," Ahmed said impatiently. "They keep the pressure high so people can come here from under without going through air locks. They can look, take pictures and go back down. It smells lousy, so ignore it."

"You mean the air is under pressure here, as bad as all the way down at the bottom of the ocean?"

"Yes, lunk. That's what makes sense to them, so that's the way they have it set up."

"That's why the wall is so thick then, so it won't burst and let the pressure out," George said, feeling as if the thickness of the wall were a coffin, keeping him from escaping. He looked out through the thick glass wall and down through the glass roof of the observation room that was the next step down. He saw chairs and magazines, a waiting room, and the crowd of people that had come on the elevator with him lined up at a glass door, with the first one in line tugging at the handle of the door. The door was not opening. "What are they doing?"

"They are waiting for the air pressure in the room to go down and equalize with the air pressure in the stairwell and the next room. Right now the pressure in the room presses the door shut. It opens inward as soon as the pressure goes down." Ahmed looked bored.

"We have to go out." George strode over to the inside door that shut off a stair leading down to the next room. He tugged. The glass door did not open. "Air pressure?"

"Yes; wait, the elevator is rising. It seems to be compressing the air, forcing it upward." Thick air made Ahmed's voice high-pitched and distant.

George tugged on the handle, feeling the air growing thicker and press on his eardrums. "We have enough pressure here already. We don't need any more fake air. Just some real air. I want to be out of here."

The elevator door opened and a group of people, some carrying suitcases, some carrying fishing gear, pressed out and milled and lined up at the door behind George, pushing each other and murmuring complaints about pushing in tones that were much less subdued than the civil service culture usually considered to be polite.

The elevator closed its doors and sank out of sight, and air pressure began to drop as if the air followed the piston of the elevator in pumping up and down. George swallowed and his eardrums clicked and rang. He yanked hard on the handle of the stairwell door. It swung wide with a hiss and he held it open. The crowd hurried down the stairs, giving him polite thanks as they passed. With each thanks received he felt the fear of the person passing. He stared into the faces of a woman, a teener, a young woman, a handsome middle-aged man, looking for something beside fear, and finding only fear and a mouselike instinctive urge to escape a trap, and a fear of fear that kept them quiet, afraid to express the sense of disaster that filled their imaginations.

"Argh," said George as the last one went down the stairs. "Hurry up, Ahmed, maybe they are right." He gestured his friend through the door and ran down after him onto the lower step of a big glass viewing room with tables and magazines to make waiting easy. Behind him he heard the door lock shut and the whirr of the elevator returning to the top with more people.

George leaned his forehead against the thick glass walls and looked out at a scene of little docks and a buzz of small electric boats circling the platform, bouncing in a gray choppy sea, under thick gray clouds.

"What's out there?" Ahmed asked.

"Escape."

"What about the saboteur?" Ahmed asked with an edge of impatience. "What is he thinking, or feeling? Are you picking anything up?"

"One of those boats is it," George answered, lying to avoid Ahmed's duty to return to the undersea city. "Or a small submarine, right out there. The top's going to be blasted off the observation platform. Get rescue boats in here. Use your radio, hurry, and get me a helicopter. I want to be in the air to spot which boat."

It wasn't all lies; some of it felt like the truth. He still leaned his forehead against the wall and looked out, knowing he would say anything to get out. Or do anything. He tried to tune to the idea of sabotage, and open to other people's thoughts, but the urge to escape came back in a greater sickness and swamped other thoughts. "Why?" he asked the fear. "What is going to happen?" An image came of horses kicking down a barn from inside, of cattle stampeding, of a chick pecking to get out of an egg, with the chick an embryo, not ready yet to survive in air. Kicking skeleton feet broke through from inside a bubble and the bubble vanished. The images were confusing. He looked away from his thoughts and watched the outside platform.

The platform was crowded with people, shivering in a cold wind, apparently waiting their turn to enjoy a ride in the little boats. George knew that they were outdoors because they could not stand being indoors.

Ahmed tapped on his arm. He had the wrist-radio earphones plugged into both ears, and his voice sounded odd and deaf. "Headquarters wants to know why, George. Can you give details?"

"Tell them they have five minutes, seven minutes if they're lucky. Get the patrol boats here to stop it and"—George almost shouted into Ahmed's wrist mike—"GET ME THAT HELI-COPTER. Get it over here fast! We need it as soon as we get through the air locks!"

The glass air-lock door opened and people tumbled and shoved through. On the other side was another room surrounded by glass. They lined up against the glass walls like moths against a lighted windowpane, looking out.

"Why do we have to wait so long?" It was a wail, a crying sound like an ambulance siren in the night. The group muttered agreement and nodded at the woman who clutched her hands against the glass as though trying to touch the scene outside.

"I'm not worried about the bends," said a portly older man. "They adjust the waiting time for people with bad sinus and eardrum infections. Does anyone here have a sinus, or eardrum infection?"

"We don't need to wait, then," said the same man, louder when there was no reply. "Does anyone here know how to make the door open? We can go out right now."

"My son has a screwdriver," suggested a woman, pushing the teen-age young man toward the door. Ahmed moved to protest and the woman glared at him and opened her mouth to argue.

An old woman was tugging at the door. It opened suddenly and they forgot quarreling and went out through the door to the open docks and the cold salt wind, and the sound of cold choppy waves splashing against the cement pillars.

An air-beating heavy whirring sound hovered above the docks.

Ahmed looked up. A ladder fell down and dangled before them. Ahmed grabbed the rope rungs and pulled. They sagged lower. He fitted his foot into a rung and climbed.

George stood, breathing deeply of an air that smelled sweet and right and tingled in his lungs like life and energy. The clouds of panic and resignation faded from his mind and he heard the seagulls screaming raucous delight, following the small boats and swooping at sandwiches. The people clustered at the edge of the docks, beginning to talk in normal tones.

The ladder dangled before him, bobbing up and down. The rope rungs brushed against his head and he brushed them aside. What had been happening? What was the doom he had just escaped from? He tried to remember the trapped moments and tried to understand what they had been.

"Come on, George," a voice called from above.

He reached up, gripped and climbed, looking into a sky of scudding gray and silver clouds. A white and blue police helicopter bounced above him, its rotating blades shoving damp cool air against him in a kind of pressure that he enjoyed fighting. At the top the ladder stiffened into a metal stair with rails, and opened into the carpeted glass-walled platform of a big observation heli-copter.

Ahmed sat cross-legged on the floor, twitching with hurry and impatience, holding his wrist radio to his lips. "Okay, George, tune to it. *What* will blow the observation building? Who, what, where? Coast Guard is waiting for information."

Still with his memory gripped onto the strange depression he had felt inside the observation building, in the air of Jersey Dome, George looked down and tuned to it and knew how the people still inside felt, and what they wanted.

In the four-step glittering observation building, each glass room was full of people waiting at the doors. He saw the central elevator arrive and open its door and let out another crowd of people to wait and push and pull at the first door at the top. Desperation. A need to get out.

With a feeling of great sorrow, George knew who the saboteurs were. All the kids with screwdrivers, all the helpful people with technical skill who speed elevators, all the helpful people without mechanical understanding who would prop open dime-operated toilet doors for the stranger in need. They were going to be help-ful, they were going to go through the air-lock doors and leave the doors jammed open behind them. No resistance behind them to hold back sixty-five pounds per square inch air pressure forcing up from below in the compressed city, pushing upward behind the rising elevator.

He had been pretending to believe it was a mad bomber. How could he tell the police and Coast Guard that it was just the resi-dents of the city, mindless with the need to get out, destroying their own air-lock system?

George held his head, the vision of death strong and blinding. "They are jamming the air-lock system open in the observation building, Ahmed. Tell someone to stop them. They can't do that. It will blow!" The panic need to escape blanked his mind again.

"Lift," George said, making nervous faces at the view below. "Lift this damned copter."

"Is he all right?" the pilot asked Ahmed.

Ahmed was talking intensely into the wrist radio, repeating an relaying George's message. He made a chopping gesture to shu up.

The copter pilot gave them both a glance of doubt for thei sanity and set the copter to lift, very slowly.

Beating the air, the copter rose, tilting, and lifted away from th dwindling platform of glinting glass in the middle of the gra ocean.

George gripped the observation rail and watched, ashamed tha his hands were shaking.

He saw something indefinable and peculiar begin to happen t the shape of the glass building. "There it goes," he muttered, an abruptly sat down on the floor and put his hands over his face "Hang on to the controls. Here we go. Ahmed, you look. Tak pictures or something."

There was a crash, and a boom like a cannon. Something tha looked like a crushed elevator full of people shot upward at them passed them slowly, and then fell, tumbling over and over down ward.

A roaring uprush of air grabbed the copter and carried it int the sky upside down, falling in a rain of small objects that looke like briefcases and fishing rods and small broken pieces that coul not be recognized. George hung on to a railing. Suddenly th copter turned right side up, beating its heavy spinning blades i a straining pull upward away from the rising tornado.

With a tearing roar Jersey Dome spat its contents upwar through the air shaft, squeezing buildings and foam blocks an people and furniture into the shaft and upward in a hose of air upward to the surface and higher in a fountain of debris, mangle by decompression.

For long moments the fountain of air was a mushroom-shape cloud, then it subsided, raining down bits. The copter circled, it occupants deafened and awed.

With one arm and one leg still hooked around the rail, Ahme

listened intently to his radio, hands cupped over his ears to make the speaker plugs in his ears louder. He spoke.

"The city manager is alive down there and broadcasting. He says the canopy of the dome did not break, it just lowered. The air shaft sucked in everything near it and is now plugged shut with foam blocks from buildings but the blocks are slowly compressing into it, and they can hear an air hiss. Survivors are putting on scuba air equipment and finding places to survive another hurricane if the tube blows free again, but he's afraid of water leaks coming in and drowning them out from underneath because the pressure is going down. He wants the air shaft plugged from the top. Suggests bombing it at the top to prevent more air escaping."

Ahmed listened, tilting his head to the sounds in his ears.

"People in the water," George said. "Bombs make concussion. Let's get the people out."

"Affirmative," said the police pilot. "Look for people."

The helicopter swept low and cruised over the water, and they looked down at the close passing waves for a human swimmer needing help.

"There." Ahmed pointed at a pink shiny arm, a dark head. They circled back and hovered, let down the ladder, and the two Rescue Squad men climbed down and maneuvered a web mesh sling around a limp young unconscious naked woman. Her head bobbed under and came up as they slid the sling under her. The waves washed up against their knees as they leaned out from the rope ladder.

"NOW HEAR THIS, NOW HEAR THIS," proclaimed a giant amplified voice. "ALL BOATS IN THE AREA CIRCLE IN THE DISASTER AREA AND TAKE IN SURVIVORS. IN FIVE MIN-UTES, AT THE NEXT SIGNAL, ALL BOATS MUST WITH-DRAW FROM THE AIR-SHAFT CENTER TO A DISTANCE OF FIVE HUNDRED YARDS TO PERMIT BOMBING. AWAIT SIG-NAL. REPEAT. YOU HAVE FIVE MINUTES TO SEARCH FOR AND TAKE IN SURVIVORS."

Ahmed and George shouted up to the pilot, "Ready." And the

hoist drew the mesh sling with the young woman in it upward and
into the copter through a cargo door in the bottom. The door
hatch closed. They climbed back inside, dripping, and spread the
unconscious and pretty body out on the floor for artificial respiration. She was cold, pulseless and bleeding from ears, nose and
closed eyes. There were no bruises or breaks visible on the smooth
skin. George tried gentle hand pressure on the rib cage to start her
breathing again, and some blood came from her mouth with a sigh.
He pushed again. Blood came from her eyes like tears.

Ahmed said wearily, "Give it up, George, she's dead."

George stood up and retreated from the body, backing away.
"What do we do, throw her back?"

"No, we have to take bodies to the hospital. Regulations," muttered the pilot.

They circled the copter around over the choppy gray seas, wip-
ers going on the windshield. The body lay on the floor between
them, touching their feet.

They saw an arm bobbing on the waves.

"Should we haul it in?" George asked.

"No, we don't have to take pieces," said the pilot, tone level.

They circled on, passing the little electric boats of the people
who had been fishing when the dome blew. The faces were pale
as they looked up at the passing helicopter.

The corpse lay on the floor between them, the body smooth and
perfect. The plane tilted and the body rolled. The arms and legs
moved.

Ahmed seated himself in the copilot's seat, fastened the safety
harness and leaned forward with his head in his hands, not looking
at the corpse. George looked out the windshields at the bobbing
debris of furniture and unidentifiable bits, and watched Coast
Guard boats approaching and searching the water.

The copter radio beeped urgently. The pilot switched it on.
"Coast Guard command to Police Helicopter PB 1005768. Thank
you for your assistance. We now have enough Coast Guard ships
and planes in the search pattern; please withdraw from the disas-

ter area. Please withdraw from the disaster area."

"Order acknowledged. Withdrawing," the pilot said, and switched the radio off. He changed the radio setting and spoke briefly to Rescue Squad headquarters, and turned the plane away from the area of destruction and toward the distant shore.

"What's your job in police?" he asked over his shoulder.

George did not answer.

"Rescue, Detection and Prevention," Ahmed answered for him. "We were in Jersey Dome ten minutes ago." Behind them the bombs boomed, breaking and closing the air shaft.

"You sure didn't prevent this one," said the copter pilot.

Ahmed did not answer.

This is a blackmail tape. One copy of this tape has been mailed to each of the major communes and subcities in the New York City district.

We are responsible for the destruction of Brooklyn Dome. It was a warning, and demonstrated our ability to destroy. We have in our possession a futures expert whose specialty was locating and predicting accidental dangers to the city complex caused by possible simple mechanical and human failures. He is drugged and cooperative. We asked him how Brooklyn Dome could self-destruct from a simple mechanical failure, and he explained how. We are now prepared to offer his services for sale. Our fee will be fifteen thousand dollars a question. If you are afraid that your commune has enemies, your logical question would be: What and who can destroy my commune, and how can I prevent this attack? We will provide the answer service to your enemies, if they pay. They might be asking how to destroy your commune as you listen to this tape. Remember Brooklyn Dome. The name and address enclosed is your personal contact with us. No one else has this name. Keep it secret from the police, and use it when you decide to pay. If you give your contact up to the police, you will cut yourself off from our advice, your enemies will contact us through other names and buy methods to destroy you. Remember Brooklyn Dome. Act soon. Our fee is fifteen thousand dollars a question. The price of survival is cheap.

"Every police department has a copy. Want me to play it again?" Judd Oslow asked. He sat cross-legged on top of his desk like a large fat Buddha and sipped coffee.

"Once was enough," Ahmed said. "Paranoia, and war among

the communes. What do those nuts think they are doing with that tape?"

"Making money," Judd Oslow sipped his coffee, carefully staying calm. "They mailed one to each commune in the city area, and only two have turned in the entire tape, or admitted receiving it. Only one has turned in his address. The others must be keeping their addresses, planning to ask attack, or defense, questions."

"Armageddon," said Ahmed.

Judd said, "George, why don't you get off your rump and bring in Carl Hodges? These nuts can't sell his brains if we get him back."

Ahmed said, "You just gave George the job last night. He almost had him this morning, but we were reassigned when Brooklyn Dome blew, and had to get off Carl Hodges' trail to go to Jersey Dome."

"So there's some of the day left. George has spoiled me with success. I'm used to instant results. Come on, George. Carl Hodges, right here in this office, packaged and delivered."

George looked up at him, eyes round and puzzled. "I'm supposed to help people. Every time I start trying to help Carl Hodges something bad happens. It doesn't come out right. Maybe he likes being in trouble. Bodies all over the place! You don't want me helping, with my luck!"

"Snap out of it, George. This is no time for pessimistic philosophy. Get together with Ahmed and hypnotize yourself and tell me where Carl Hodges is."

"What's the use?" George ran his hands over his head in a weary gesture that was not typical of him. "Brooklyn Dome people are dead already. Jersey Dome people are mostly dead already. Everybody that ever died is still dead. Billions of people since the beginning of time. How are you going to rescue *them?* Why not let a few more die? What difference does it make?"

"Let's not have an essay on Eternity, George. Nothing makes any difference to Eternity. We don't live in Eternity, we live in now. We want Carl Hodges now."

"What's the use? My advice just makes trouble. I didn't save those people in Jersey Dome. I wasn't smart enough to understand that they'd want to break their own air locks. No, it wasn't the panic, it was the depression. The air changed its charge. Lab animals act irrational when you reverse the ground-to-air-static-charge gradient. I should have—"

Judd shouted, "George, I'm not interested in your bad conscience. If you want to help people, just answer the question."

George winced at the loudness and squinted up at him with his eyes seeming crossed. "George?"

"*Wow!*" Ahmed stepped forward. "Wait a minute. George did it already. That was Carl answering you."

Judd hesitated between confident forward and back motions. He started and stopped a gesture. His confusion reached his expression. He shouted, "Get out of here, you kooks. Go do your lunacy somewhere else. When you bring back Carl Hodges, don't tell me how you did it."

"Affirmative," Ahmed said. "Come on, Carl."

In confusion and guilt George followed and found himself on the open sidewalk, standing under a row of maple trees. The wind blew and the trees shed a flutter of green winged seeds about him. He knew he had failed his job somehow, and couldn't figure out how to get back to it. He walked to a bench and sat down.

"Do you understand what was just happening?" Ahmed asked.

"Yes." He felt in his mind and found confusion. "No."

"Shut your eyes. You seem to be on a bench in a park. It is an illusion. This is not where you are. Where are you really?"

George had shut his eyes. The voice went in deeply to a place in his mind where he knew he was in a room, a prisoner, and it was his fault. He did not like that knowledge. Better to pretend. He opened his eyes. "I want to be here in the park. Pretend you are real." He bent and touched some green vetch at his feet and felt the tiny ferns. "History doesn't matter. Sensation matters," he said earnestly. "Even these illusions are real because they are happening now. We live in now. Memory isn't real. The past doesn't exist. Why should we feel anything about the past, or care about it?"

Ahmed computed that it was a good probability that Carl Hodges was speaking through George and looking through his eyes as a form of escape. The rationalization was fluent, the vocabulary not George's. Vocabulary choice is as constant as fingerprints.

The person speaking had to be Carl Hodges.

"Carl Hodges. Do you want to get away from where you are and lie down in this park?"

"You are a questioner. I should not speak."

"Is it wrong to answer questions?"

"Yes; answers kill. People are dead. Like Susanne, they are all dead. Does mourning one person kill others? They drowned too, and floated. Saw girl in water . . . Connection . . . ?"

George had been speaking dreamily, eyes wide and round and sightless. He closed his eyes and every muscle in his face and body tightened in a curling spasm like pain. He slid off the bench and fell to his knees in the soft vetch. "Get me out of this. Make it unhappen. Reverse time. Wipe me out before I did it." The spasmed crouch—was it pain or prayer?

Watching the figure of misery, Ahmed made urgent calculations. The shame-driven need to escape memory was there to work with. Use it.

"Carl, you are in a green field in a small park on East E Avenue and Fifth Street. This is a future scene. Two hours from now, you will be rescued and free, without guilt, relaxed and enjoying being outdoors. We are the police, we are getting into a sky taxi to come and get you. What directions are we giving the driver?"

"Amsterdam Avenue and Fifty-third Street to Columbus Avenue, the wrecked blocks, one of the good cellars near the center of the flattened part of the ruins. Buzz it twice. Thanks. I think I can knock down a kid when I hear you and come out and wave. Land and pick me up fast."

"Okay," said Ahmed, straightening and stepping back from the crouched praying figure.

George took his hands from his face. "Okay what?" His voice was George's usual voice. He got up and brushed small green fronds from his knees.

"Okay, let's make a raid into another kid gang's territory," Ahmed said.

"Where's Biggy?" George looked around as if expecting to see their own gang of kids around them. "Oh, he went to the Canary Islands. And the others, they went to the Sahara. They all went . . ." He shook his head as if waking up. "Ahmed, what do you mean, raid a kid gang territory? That's all over. We're grown up now."

"We're going to rescue that kidnapped computerman. A mixed gang of teener kids are holding him in the ruins near West Fifty-third Street. We know how to handle a kid gang fight."

George was not going to let go of common sense. He settled back on the bench and looked around at the green warm comfort of the park, and rubbed one of the bruises on his arm. "Let's call the police, let them do it."

"We are the police, lunk." Ahmed still stood, smiling, depending on the force of his personality, the habit of command, to get George to obey. George looked up at him, squinting into the light of the sky, one eye half closed. Half of a bruise showed at the side of his face, most of it hidden by the hairline.

"Ahmed, don't be a nut. Logical thinking doesn't fight chains and clubs for you. I mean, your brains are great, but we need muscle against a juv army, because they don't know about thinking, and they don't listen."

"What if they are all in their cellars, lunk, and we want to drop them before they get in deeper and carry Carl Hodges away? What kind of thing could get them all out into the open where a helicopter could drop them with gas?"

George absently rubbed the dark mark on the side of his face. "They come out when somebody gets onto their territory, Ahmed.

Not an army of cops or a helicopter, I don't mean that. I mean some poor goof is crossing, looking for a shortcut to somewhere else, and they all come out and beat him up."

"That's for you."

"How did you figure . . . Oh, yeah, you don't mean yesterday. You mean strategy, like. They come out to beat me up again and the copter drops them with a gas spray, and maybe there's no one left underground to kill Carl Hodges, or take him away." George got up. "Okay, let's do it."

They came up out of the subway at Fifty-third Street and walked together on the sidewalk opposite the bombed-out shells of old buildings. A distant helicopter sound buzzed in the air.

"Separate, but we keep in touch. Leave your radio open to send, but shut it for receive so there won't be any sound coming out of it. The copter pilot will be listening. I'll circle the block and look in doorways and hallways for trouble. You cut across. We both act like we have some reason to be here, like I'm looking for an address. We're strangers."

"Okay," George said. "I've got a story for them. Don't worry about me." He turned and walked nonchalantly around the corner, across the street, past some standing ruins and into the flattened spaces and the area that had once been paved backyard, with steps down to doors that had opened into the cellars of gone buildings. Flattened rubble and standing walls showed where the buildings had been.

He stood in the middle of a backyard, near two flights of cement stairs that led down into the ground to old doors, and he walked onward slowly, going in an irregular wandering course, studying the ground, acting a little confused and clumsy, just the way he had acted the last time he had been there.

The setting sun struck long shadows across the white broken pavement. He turned and looked back at his own long shadow, and started when another person's shadow appeared silently on the pavement alongside of his. He glanced sideways and saw a tall, husky teener in a strange costume standing beside him holding a heavy bat. The teener did not look back at him, he looked off into space, lips pursed as though whistling silently.

George winced again when a short teener with straight blond hair stepped out from behind a fragment of standing wall.

"Back, huh?" asked the blond kid.

George felt the shadows of others gathering behind him.

George said, "I'm looking for a pocket watch I lost the night you guys beat me up. I mean, it's really an antique, and it reminds me of someone. I've got to find it."

He looked at the ground, turning around in a circle. There was a circle of feet all around him, feet standing in ruined doorways, feet on top of mounds of rubble, the clubs resting on the ground as the owners leaned on them, the chains swinging slightly.

"You must be really stupid," said the leader, his teeth showing in a small smile that had no friendship.

Where was Carl Hodges? The area George stood in was clean, probably well used by feet. The stairs leading down to a cellar door were clean, the door handle had the shine of use. The leader had appeared late, from an unlikely direction. He was standing on dusty, rubble-piled ground which feet had not rubbed and cleared. The leader then had not wanted to come out the usual way and path to confront George. Probably the usual way would have been the door George was facing, the one that looked used.

It was like playing hot and cold for a hidden object. If Carl Hodges was behind that door, the teeners would not let George approach it. George, looking slow and confused, shuffled his feet two steps in that direction. There was a simultaneous shuffle and hiss of clothing as the circle behind him and all around him closed in closer. George stopped and they stopped.

Now there was a circle of armed teeners close around him. Two were standing almost between him and the steps. The helicopter still buzzed in the distance, circling the blocks. George knew if he shouted, or even spoke clearly, and asked for help the copter pilot would bring the plane over in a count of seconds.

The blond kid did not move, still lounging, flashing his teeth in a small smile as he studied George up and down with the expression of a scientist at a zoo studying an odd specimen of gorilla.

"I got something important to tell you," George said to him. But they didn't listen.

"It's a kind of a shame," the blond kid said to the others. "He's so stupid already. I mean, if we just bashed out his brains he wouldn't even notice they were gone."

George faced the leader and sidled another small step in the direction of the steps and the door, and heard the shuffle of feet closing in behind him. He stopped moving and they stopped moving. For sure that door was hiding something. They wanted to keep strangers away from it! "Look, if you found my watch I lost, and if you give it to me, I'll tell you about a thing you ought to know."

If he talked long and confusingly enough, every member of the gang would come out on the surface to hear what he was trying to say. They would all be out in the open. The helicopter was armed for riots; it could spray sleep gas and get every one of them.

He didn't even feel the blow. Suddenly he was on his knees, a purple haze before his eyes. He tried to get up and fell over sideways, still in the curled-up position. He realized he wasn't breathing.

Could a back-of-the-neck karate chop knock out your breathing centers? What had the teacher said? His lungs contracted, wheezing out more air, unable to let air in. It must have been a solar plexus jab with a stick. But then how come he hadn't seen the stick? The purple haze was turning into spinning black spots. He couldn't see.

"What was it he wanted to tell us?"

"Ask him."

"He can't answer, dummy. He can't even grunt. You'll have to wait."

"I don't mind waiting," said the voice of the one carrying a chain. George heard the chain whistle and slap into something, and wondered if it had hit him. Nothing in his body registered anything but a red burning need for air.

"You don't want to trespass on our territory," said a voice. "We're just trying to teach you respect. You stay on the free public sidewalks and don't go inside other people's Kingdoms. Not unless they ask you." The chain whistled and slapped again.

George tried to breathe, but the effort to inhale knotted his chest tighter, forcing breath out instead of in.

It is a desperate thing having your lungs working against you. The knot tightening the lungs held for another second and then loosened. He drew in a rasping breath of cool air, and another. Air came in like waves of light, dispelling the blindness and bringing back awareness of arms and legs. He straightened out from the curled-up knot and lay on his back breathing deeply and listening to the sounds around him.

The helicopter motor hummed in the distance. The copter pilot is listening, he thought, but he doesn't know I'm in trouble.

He heard a clink and a hiss of breath like someone making an effort. He rolled suddenly over to one side and covered his face. The chain hit where he had been. He rolled to a crouch with both feet under him, and for the first time looked at the circle of faces of the teeners who had beaten and made fun of him when he was pretending to be drunk and making believe to be Carl Hodges, and had stumbled into this forbidden territory. He had been re-tracing Carl Hodges' actions, but he had not been sure it was working. He had been near Carl Hodges here, but he had no proof, no reason to protest when they punished him for violating their boundaries. The faces were the same. Young but cold, some faces were uncertain about punishing an adult, but gaining courage from the others. All sizes of teeners in costumes from many communes, but the fellowship and good nature he was used to seeing in groups was missing.

"I used to be in a gang like yours once" he said rapidly to inform the radio listener. "I thought you wouldn't jump me. I didn't come here to get stomped. I just want my antique watch and to tell you something."

He finished the sentence with a quick leap to one side, but the swinging chain swung up and followed, slapped into his skin and curled a line of dents around ribs, chest and arms. The magnet on the end clanked and clung against a loop of chain. The owner of the chain yanked hard on his handle and the metal lumps turned to teeth and bit in and the chain tightened like rope. George staggered and straightened and stood wrapped up in biting steel chain.

He stood very still. "Hey," he said softly. "That ain't nice."

"Tell us about your news." The circle of teeners and juvs around him were curious about the message he wanted to deliver to them.

George said, "A friend of mine was figuring from my lumps that I got here last time that you've got something important you want me to keep away from. He figures you got the missing computer-man. The one who blew up Brooklyn Dome. There's a reward out for him."

A ripple of shock ran through the group surrounding him but the blond kid did not need time to assimilate the threat. Without change of expression he made a gesture of command. "Three of you check the streets. Maybe he brought somebody with him." Three ran silently in different directions.

"I'm just doing you a favor telling you what people say," George said in stupid tones. "Now you gotta do me a favor and help me get my watch back."

"Favor?" screamed the tall, misproportioned one with the chain. "Favor? You stupid fink, you should have kept your stupid mouth shut." He yanked hard on the chain to make its teeth extend more sharply.

An outraged force had been expanding in George's chest. He stood still, looking meek and confused one more second, watching his captors snarl and hate him for having "told his friend." Then he bent forward and butted the chain holder down, rolled over his form to the cement and rolled rapidly down three small cement steps, unrolling the chain behind him. He came up on one knee, reaching for the chain as a weapon. It was a seven-foot chain with a handle at each end. A heavy chain is a terrible weapon in the hands of a strong man. If it had been behind him at the moment of impulse, he would have swept it around and forward and cut them down like grass. He gathered it looped into his hands, eyeing the crowd of oddly dressed teeners that was his target. His speed was too fast to intercept, his motions too smooth to look fast. He threw the chain up into the air behind him, then arched back with every muscle tight and bent forward with a grunt of effort, ignoring two clubs that bounced off his shoulders, bringing the chain forward with a tremendous released surge of force that was rage. The teen gang scattered and fled and the chain swung its cutting deadly circle through the air where they had been.

"Dumb punks." George breathed noisily with the effort. "Whyncha act like brothers? Can't let anybody be your friend. Trying to be smart, not knowing . . ."

He stopped and let the swinging chain drag along the ground, slowing. He rippled it in and let it wrap around his arm, with a short murderous loop of it in his hand. The sun had set and it was growing darker in the corners and harder to see. George fended off a flung stick by deflecting it with the chain, then grabbed a club for his other hand. Something whistled by and clanged against a wall. Probably a knife. The teener leader would see that George knew too much, and instruct the gang to kill him. The boy was logical and ruthless and would decide a stranger's life was less important to him than the million he hoped to gain from selling the computerman's answers.

"Carl Hodges," George bellowed. "Ally ally infree. I need help. Computerman Carl Hodges, come out." The police riot control man in the circling copter would at last hear a request for help, and bring his plane in fast. The teeners would only hear him yelling Carl Hodges' name and still not be sure the police were near.

The cellar door gave two thumps and a crash and fell forward off its rusty hinges across the steps. A man fell out on top of it and scrambled across the door and up the steps without bothering to straighten from all fours.

At the top he stood up. He was thin and balding, wiry and a little under average in size, totally unlike George in either shape or face, but the impression of lifetime familiarity was overwhelming. His own eyes looked out of the strange face.

George handed him a club from the ground. "Guard my back. They are going to try to take you alive, I think, but not me." He spun slowly, looking and listening, but all was quiet. Teeners lurked in a distance along the routes George would use if he tried to escape.

George looked back at Carl Hodges and saw the thin computerman inspecting George's appearance with a knot of puzzlement between his brows. Looking at him was like looking into a mirror.

"Hello, me over there," George said.

"Hello, me over there," the man said. "Are you a computerman? When I get back on the job do you want to come play City Chess with me? Maybe you could get a job in my department."

"No, buddy, we are us, but I don't play City Chess. I'm not like you."

"Then why—" Carl Hodges ducked a flung club and it clattered against the cement. *Then why do I have this impression of two people being the same person?* he meant.

"We have an empathy link in our guts," George said. "I don't think like you. I just feel what you feel."

"God help anyone who feels the way I feel," Hodges said. "I see some kids advancing on my side."

"Hold them off. Back to back. All we need is a little time." George turned away from him again, and searched the corners with his eyes, ready for a rush. "About the way you feel. It's not all that bad. I'll get over it."

"I did it," Carl Hodges said. "How do I get over it? I feel . . . I mean, I have a reason for feeling . . . I got drunk and the egg hit the fan. How do I get over *that?*" His voice was broken by grunts of effort, and things clattered by, deflected, missing them and hitting walls and cement flooring.

They stood back to back and fended off bricks, sticks and glittering objects that he hoped were not knives. "We can get killed if we don't watch it. That's one way," George said. A stick came through the air and rapped George's ear as he met it with his club. The attackers advanced, silhouettes against the dimming view of stone walls. Another attacker shadow picked up the clattering stick from the ground and threw it back as he advanced.

"Ouch," said Carl Hodges. "Duck." They both ducked and a flung net went by. "We fight well together. We must get together and fight another teen gang sometime. Right?" said his brisk voice. "Ouch, damn."

George received a rush by the tallest of the gang, caught at the outstretched staff and yanked the enemy past. He tried to trip the teener as he hurtled by, but missed and turned to see him neatly tripped by a stick between the ankles by Carl. The teener went face forward to the ground and rolled, getting out of range.

"Good pass!" Several new and heavy blows on head and shoulders reminded George to watch his own side. Dizzied, he spun, bracing the staff for a pushing blow with both hands, and felt it strike twice against blurred forms. He reversed it and struck down at an attacker with a contented growl.

With a heavy thrumming and a push of air the police helicopter came over a wall, swooping low, like an owl settling over a nest of mice, and released a white cloud of gas.

George took a deep breath of the clear air before the cloud reached him. Beside him Carl Hodges took a deep startled breath of the white cloud and went down as suddenly as if a club blow had hit.

Still holding his breath, George straddled him and stood alert, peering through the fog at shapes that seemed to be upright and moving. Most of the teeners had run away, or gone down flat on the ground. What were these shapes? Eighteen seconds of holding his breath. Not hard. He could make two minutes usually. He held his breath and tried to see through the white clouds around him. The sound of the helicopter circled, in a wider and wider spiral, laying a cloud of gas to catch all the running mice from the center of the area to its edges.

The shapes suddenly appeared beside him, running, and struck with a double push, flinging him back ten feet so that he skidded on his back on the sandy concrete. He remembered to hold his breath after one snort of surprise and silently rolled to his feet and charged back.

Carl Hodges' unconscious form was missing. George saw movement through the white fog ahead, heard feet scuffing cement and hollow wood, and he charged in pursuit of the sounds. He half fell, half slid down the cement steps, across the wooden door on the ground and into a corridor, and glimpsed motion ahead, and heard a closet door shutting. Holding his breath, groping, he opened the door, saw broken wall with an opening, smelled the wet smell of cement and underground drafts, and leaped over a pile of ancient trash brooms into the opening.

Safe to breathe here. As he took a deep breath a brilliant flashlight suddenly came on, shining blindingly in his face from only two feet away. "I have a gun pointed at you," said the precise voice of the blond short teener. "Turn left and walk ahead in the directions I tell you. I could kill you here, and no one would find your body, so try to keep my good will."

"Where is Carl Hodges?" George asked, walking with his hands up. The flashlight threw his shadow ahead of him big and wavering across the narrow walls.

"We're all going to be holing down together. Turn left here." The voice was odd.

George looked back and saw that the short teener was wearing a gas mask. As he took a breath to ask why, the white fog rolled down from a night-sky crevice above them. It smelled damp and slightly alcoholic.

"Keep moving," said the teener, gesturing with his gun. George turned left, wondering what happened next when you breathed that fog. A busy day, a busy night. An experience of symbolic insight was often reported by people who had been flattened by police anti-riot gas. What had the day meant? Why were such things happening?

Floating in white mist, George floated free of his body over the city and saw a vast spirit being of complex and bitter logic who brooded over the city and lived also in its future. George spoke to it, in thoughts that were not words. "Ahmed uses the world view of his grandmother, the gypsy. He believes that you are Fate. He believes you have intentions and plans."

It laughed and thought: *The wheels of time grind tight. No room between gear and gear for change. Future exists, logical and unchangeable. No room for change in logic. When it adds up, it must arrive at the same concluding scene. The city is necessity. The future is built. The gears move us toward it. I am Fate.*

George made a strange objecting thought. "The past can change. So everything that adds up from the past can change."

There was a wail from the atmosphere. The vast spirit that brooded over the city vanished, destroyed, dwindling to nowhere, uncreated, never true, like the Wicked Witch of the West when Dorothy poured a bucket of water over her, leaving behind the same dwindling wail. "But all my beautiful disasters, the logic, the logic . . ."

"No arithmetic," George said firmly. "If you can see the future, you can change it. If you can't see the past, it can change by itself and be anything. It won't add up the same twice."

All the crystallized visions of the city of the future shattered and dissolved into white fog, a creative fog that could be shaped to anything by thought. George stood at the center of creation and felt stubborn. They were tempting him again, trying to get him into the bureaucratic game of rules and unfreedom. "No," he said. "I won't fence anyone in with my idea. Let them choose their own past."

He came to consciousness lying on the floor in a small tight room with the blond kid sitting on a bed pointing a gun at him.

"They got Carl Hodges back," the kid said. "You ruined everything. Maybe you are a cop. I don't know. Maybe I should kill you."

"I just had a wild dream," George said, lifting his head, but not moving because he did not want to be shot. "I dreamed I talked to the Fate of New York City. And I told Fate that the future can change anytime, and the past can change anytime. In the beginning was the middle, I said. And Fate started crying and boohooing and vanished. I mean, no more Fate. Vanished."

There was a long pause while the short blond kid held the pistol pointed at George's face and stared at him over the top of it. The kid tried several tough faces, and then curiosity got the better of him. He was basically an intellectual, even though a young one, and curiosity meant more to him than love or hate. "What do you mean? The past is variable? You can change it?"

"I mean, we don't know what happened in the past exactly. It's gone anyhow. It's not real anymore. So we can say anything happened we want to have happened. If one past is going to make trouble, we can change it just by being dumb, and everything will straighten out. Like, for example, we just met, right now, right here, we just met. Nothing else happened."

"Oh." The kid put away his gun, thinking about that. "Glad to meet you. My name's Larry."

"My name's George." He arranged himself more comfortably on the floor, not making any sudden moves.

They had a long philosophical discussion, while Larry waited for the police outside to finish searching and go away. Sometimes Larry took the gun out and pointed it again, but usually they discussed things and exchanged stories without accepting any past.

Larry was serious and persuasive in trying to convince George that the world had too many technicians. "They don't know how to be human beings. They like to read about being Tarzan, or see old movies and imagine they are Humphrey Bogart and James Bond, but actually all they have the guts to do is read and study. They make money that way, and they make more gadgets and they run computers that do all the thinking and take all the challenge and conquest out of life. And they give a pension to all the people who want to go out into the woods, or surf, instead of staying indoors pushing buttons, and they call the surfers and islanders and forest-farmers Free Loaders, and make sure they are sterilized and don't have children. That's genocide. They are killing off the real people. The race will be descended from those compulsive button pushers, and forget how to live."

It was a good speech. George was uneasy, because it sounded right, and he was sure no man was smart enough to refute the killer, but he tried.

"Couldn't a guy who really wanted children earn enough money to get a breeding permit for himself and an operation for his wife?"

"There aren't that many jobs anymore. The jobs that are left are button-pusher jobs, and you have to study for twenty years to learn to push the right button. They're planning to sterilize everyone but button pushers."

George had nothing to say. It made sense, but his own experience did not fit. "I'm not sterilized, Larry, and I'm a real dope. I didn't get past the sixth grade."

"When did your childhood support run out?"

"Last year."

"No more free food and housing. How about your family—they support you?"

"No family. Orphan. I got lots of good friends, but they all took their pensions and shipped out. Except one. He got a job."

"You didn't apply for the unemployable youth pension yet?"

"No. I wanted to stay around the city. I didn't want to be shipped out. I figured I could get a job."

"That's a laugh. Lots of luck in getting a job, George. How are you planning to eat?"

"Sometimes I help out around communes and share meals. Everyone usually likes me in the Brotherhood communes." George shifted positions uneasily on the floor and sat up. This was almost lying. He had a job now, but he wasn't going to talk about Rescue Squad, because Larry might call him a cop and try to shoot him. "But I don't bum meals."

"When's the longest you've gone without meals?"

"I don't feel hungry much. I went two days without food once. I'm healthy."

The kid sat cross-legged on the bed and laughed. "Really healthy! You got muscles all over. You've got muscles from ear to ear. So you're trying to beat the system! It was built just to wipe out muscleheads like you. If you apply for welfare, they sterilize you. If you take your unemployable support pension, they sterilize you. If you are caught begging, they sterilize you. Money gets all you muscleheads sooner or later. It's going to get you too. I'll bet when you are hungry you think of the bottle of wine and the big free meal at the sterility clinic. You think of the chance of winning the million dollar sweepstakes if the operation gives you the right tattoo number, don't you?"

George didn't answer.

"Maybe you don't know it, but your unemployable pension is piling up, half saved for every week you don't claim it. You've been avoiding it a year almost? When it piles high enough, you'll go in and claim your money and let them sterilize you and ship you out to the boondocks, like everyone else."

"Not me."

"Why not?"

George didn't answer. After a while he said, "Are you going to let them sterilize you?"

Larry laughed again. He had a fox face and big ears. "Not likely. There are lots of ways for a smart guy to beat the system. My descendants are going to be there the year the sun runs down and we hook drives to Earth and cruise away looking for a new sun. My descendants are going to surf light waves in space. Nobody's going to wipe me out, and nobody's going to make them into button pushers."

"Okay, I see it." George got up and paced, two steps one way, two steps the other way in the narrow room. "Who are you work-ing for, Larry? Who are you crying over? People who let them-selves be bribed into cutting off their descendants? They're differ-ent from you. Do they have guts enough to bother with? Are they worth getting your brain wiped in a court of law? You're right about history, I guess. I'm the kind of guy the techs are trying to get rid of. You're a tech type of guy yourself. Why don't you be a tech and forget about making trouble?"

At the end of the room, faced away from Larry, George stopped and stared at the wall. His fists clenched. "Kid, do you know what kind of trouble you make?"

"I see it on television," Larry said.

"Those are real people you killed." George still stared at the wall. "This afternoon I was giving artificial respiration to a girl. She was bleeding from the eyes." His voice knotted up. Big muscles bulged on his arms and his fists whitened as he tried to talk. "She was dead, they told me. She looked all right, except for her eyes. I guess because I'm stupid." He turned and his eyes glittered with tears and with a kind of madness. He glanced around the small room looking for a thing to use for a weapon.

Larry took out his gun and pointed it at George, hastily getting off the bed. "Oh oh, the past is real again. Time for me to leave!" Holding the gun pointed steadily and carefully at George's face, he used his other hand to put on black goggles and slung the gas mask around his neck. "Hold still, George, you don't want a hole through your face. If you fight me, who are you working for? Not your kind of people. Think, man." He backed to the door. George turned, still facing him, his big hands away from his sides and ready, his eyes glittering with a mindless alertness.

Larry backed into the dark hall. "Don't follow. You don't want to follow me. This gun has infrasights, shoots in the dark. If you stick your head out the door, I might shoot it off. Just stand there for ten minutes and don't make any trouble. The gun is silenced. If I have to shoot you, you don't get any medal for being a dead hero. No one would know."

The short teener backed down the dark corridor and was gone.

George still stood crouched, but he shook his head, like a man trying to shake off something that had fallen over his eyes.

He heard Larry bump into something a long way down the corridor.

"I would know," a voice said from the ceiling. Ahmed let himself down from a hole in the ceiling, hung by both long arms and then dropped, landing catlike and silent. He was tall and sooty and filthy and covered with cobwebs. He grinned and his teeth were white in a very dark face. "You just missed a medal for being a dead hero. I thought you were going to try to kill him."

He twiddled the dial of his wrist radio, plugged an earphone into one ear and spoke into the wrist radio. "Flushed one. He's heading west on a cellar corridor from the center, wearing a gas mask and infragoggles, armed and dangerous. He's the kingpin, so try hard, buddies."

George sat down on the edge of the bunk, sweating. "I get too mad sometimes. I almost did try to kill him. What he said was probably right. What he said."

Ahmed unplugged the speaker from his ear. "I was mostly listening to you, good buddy. Very interesting philosophical discussion you were putting out. I kept wanting to sneeze. How come you get into philosophical arguments today and I just get beat up? Everything is backward."

"You're the smart one, Ahmed," said George slowly, accepting the fact that he had been protected. "Thanks for watching." He looked at his own hands, still worrying slowly on an idea. "How come everything the kid said made sense?"

"It didn't," Ahmed said impatiently. "*You* made sense."

"But Larry said that techs are wiping out nontechs."

"Maybe they are, but they aren't killing anybody. The kid kills."

George pushed his hands together, felt them wet with sweat and wiped them on his shirt. "I almost killed the kid. But it felt right, what he was saying. He was talking for the way things are and for the way they're going to be, like Fate."

"Killing is unphilosophical," Ahmed said. "You're tired, George. Take it easy, we've had a long day."

They heard a police siren wail and then distant shots. Ahmed plugged the earphone into his ear. "They just dropped somebody in goggles, gas didn't work on him. They had to drop him with hypo bullets. Probably Larry. Let's try to get out of here."

They put a wad of blankets out into the corridor, head high. No shots, so they went out cautiously and started groping down the long black hall, looking for an exit.

Ahmed said, "So you think Larry was the fickle finger of Fate on the groping hand of the future. No power on Earth can resist the force of an idea whose time has come, said somebody once. But, good buddy, when I was listening to you whilst lying in the ceiling with the spiders crawling on me, I thought I heard you invent a new metaphysics. Didn't you just abolish Fate?"

The corridor widened, and George felt a draft of fresh air without dust, and saw a glimmer of light through a hole. They climbed through and saw a doorway, and a broken door. "I don't know, Ahmed," he said vaguely. "Did I?"

They climbed up the broken door and a flight of stone steps and found themselves in a deserted yard at the center of the ruin. It was very quiet. In the distance around the edges of the block police copters buzzed, landing in the streets.

"Sure you did," Ahmed said. "You abolished Fate. I heard you."

George looked up at the moon. It was bright and it shone across the entire city, like the evil Fate in his dream, but it was only the moon, and the city was quiet. Suddenly George leaped into the air and clicked his heels. "I did. I did." He bellowed. "Hey, everybody! Hey, I did it! I abolished Fate!"

He landed and stopped leaping, and stood panting. The red glow in the sky over New York blinked on and off, on and off from the giant sign they could not see.

"Congratulations," said Ahmed, and rested an arm briefly across his shoulders. "May I offer you a tranquilizer?"

"No, you may offer me a meal," George said. "No, cancel that too. Judd gave me money yesterday. Steaks, hot showers, hotel room. *Wow.* I've got a job." He turned abruptly and walked away. "See you tomorrow."

Left alone, tall and tired, smeared with dirt and itchy with cobwebs, Ahmed stared after him, feeling betrayed. Where was all the respect George used to give him? George was a short fat kid once, and treated Ahmed like a boss. Now he was beginning to loom like a Kodiak bear, and he walked away without permission.

Ahmed looked up at the lopsided moon. "Mirror, mirror, on the wall, who's the smartest guy of all? Don't answer that, lady. It's been a long day. I'm tired."

NEBULA AWARD
SCIENCE FICTION, 1965–1970

POUL ANDERSON

The Science

Never mind what science fiction is. It has as many definitions as it has definers. For that matter, there's no universal agreement on the meaning of "science" and "technology." Having been asked to discuss the status of those elements in current sf, I won't stop to wrestle with the words, but will simply use them in their ordinary senses. In fact, sometimes I'll be using "science" as shorthand for "science and technology"; Newspeak like "scitech" (or "sci-fi"!) is just too ugly. It's worthwhile bearing the distinction in mind, if only because much sf has not been about science at all, but rather about technology. However, today they are so closely intertwined that my looseness of language ought not to confuse the question.

That question can be put: "Is science on its way out of sf? Is the scientific element being reduced to a few gimmicks and catchwords in a literature which is really about something else, such as depth psychology, social protest or mysticism, when it isn't mere taletelling with no intellectual content?" My assignment is not to say whether this would be good or bad. I'm supposed to find out which way the wind is blowing, if that can be done.

In this study, for the record, my principal sources have been: the Nebula Award anthologies, numbers one through six; winners and runners-up among novels on the final Nebula ballots, 1965–1970; the two volumes of Hugo winners which Isaac Asimov has edited;

the MIT index to the magazines; the brains of my wife, Karen, and our own bookshelves and memories.* In what follows, I will for your convenience identify Nebula runners-up by a single asterisk in parentheses, winners by two.

I decided that an analytical approach offered the sole hope of getting anything like a meaningful answer to the problem. What I did was divide sf into four types with three attitudes, twelve sorts altogether, and compare how well they have been faring.

I make no extravagant claims. The method remains subjective, arbitrary and full of ambiguities. My classifications do not correspond to the real skeleton of sf; reality is always too big and various to fit into any neat scheme. I have nothing here except temporary scaffolding on which to walk around and look at the subject.

My concern is not with plot, character, philosophy, literary values—though my illustrative examples will mostly be good stories —but with motifs relevant to the scientific content of sf. The names hung on the different classes are not very precise, but then, neither are the classes themselves. After these caveats, let's get started on the four species.

1. *Hard science.* This includes "hard technology." Stories employing it are what the public to this day tends to identify with sf as a whole. Actually, that always was a mistake.

A hard science story bases itself on real, present-day science or technology, and carries these further with a minimum of imaginary forces, materials or laws of nature. Among Jules Verne's works are classic examples of technological extrapolation, while Hal Clement's—e.g., his novel *Mission of Gravity* and its sequel *Star Light*—represent perfect scientific extrapolation, where known facts of physics, chemistry, biology and astronomy go into the construction of fascinatingly strange worlds and creatures.

Of course, science includes theories, and way-out minority-opin-

*Although they modestly asked not to be mentioned in the text, dammit, I do want to thank Lloyd Biggle, Jr., and Dean McLaughlin for vital assistance in getting certain materials.

ion hypotheses, advanced by practicing scientists. A clearcut instance of an author's exploring at the very frontiers of knowledge, and beyond, is Larry Niven's novel *Ringworld* (**), an awesome vision of a vast, artificial, annular planet.

This sort of story offers a unique thrill. Those who know enough about the scientific subject can have their eyes opened to some astounding possibilities. They can also have fun playing what Clement calls The Game: trying to find errors, explicit or implicit, in the author's development.

The hard science does not have to be all or even most of what the *story* is about. Thus, Bob Shaw's "Light of Other Days" (*) and James Gunn's "The Listeners" (*) concentrate on human problems, while Kate Wilhelm's "The Planners" (**) begins with research on the DNA-RNA complex in order to deal almost entirely with the interior world of her protagonist. Other hard science works of high philosophical as well as literary value include Ursula K. Le Guin's "Nine Lives" (*) and *The Left Hand of Darkness* (**) —firmly grounded biological speculation—and Frank Herbert's *Dune* (**)—ecology.

Both these novels contain, in addition, a lot of anthropology. This may lead you to ask what I mean by "hard science." The linguistics in it may justify putting Samuel R. Delany's *Babel 17* (**) here, but what about John Brunner's *Stand on Zanzibar* (*)? I'd say yes to it too, if only because of the sociometrics the author used in his thinking. On the other hand, *1984* doesn't belong in this category.

Now, no story will fit entirely into any of my classes. Quite often a writer makes certain assumptions which go altogether beyond existing science, or directly contrary to it. For instance, to get his characters to one of his meticulously detailed extrasolar planets in reasonable time, Clement must suppose that man in the future will find a way to travel faster than light . . . regardless of what twentieth-century physicists think. Classification is basically dependent on where the emphasis lies: which brings us to our next species.

2. *Imaginary science*. I avoid calling this "pseudoscience" because that would look pejorative. Many fine and intellectually stimulating stories have turned on the development of an idea for whose reality we have no evidence, or which the evidence is actually against. Examples are H. G. Wells's *The Time Machine* and Robert Heinlein's "By His Bootstraps." The first set forth the notion of deliberately using the (almost certainly impossible) phenomenon of time travel, which earlier writers like Mark Twain had postulated. The second worked out, with marvelous ingenuity, several implications of such use.

The employment of chronokinesis, or whatever, does not automatically make a story type 2. Thus, I'd put L. Sprague de Camp's "A Gun for Dinosaur" under "hard science" because it's mainly about paleontology, the time machine being a mere device for getting people onto the scene.

On the other hand, I'd take what most people think of as the granddaddy of hard science stories, Hugo Gernsback's *Ralph 124C41+*, and set it very firmly right here. Aside from a vague mention of something like radar, which Hertz had already forecast, nearly the whole of its "technology" consists of words and has no relationship to real engineering—except in its spirit of technical man triumphant.

Besides time travel and faster-than-light travel, common imaginary science ideas include psionics, parallel universes, etc. I'd classify most of James Blish's work under the present heading, though of course he writes topflight hard science whenever he wants to. So does Theodore Sturgeon; but stories of his like "The Man Who Learned Loving" (*) and "Slow Sculpture" (**) assume things quite unknown to science.

To be sure, science may one day discover them, or something like them. We would be foolhardy to suppose that we, today, have any final answers. Hence my second class differs from my first more in degree than in kind. Further specimens are Delany's *The Einstein Intersection* (**), Anne McCaffrey's "Dragonrider" (**) and Joanna Russ's *And Chaos Died* (*):

which shows how vital a part of sf imaginary science is.

I repeat, a story belongs here only if the exploration of such an idea is integral to it, not if the author has simply found it convenient to make certain postulates. That brings us to our next class.

3. *Quasiscience.* I can't find a better name for this species. It comprises those stories wherein the real or imaginary science is principally background or incidental material.

I do not mean they are costume Westerns or the like. The future civilization's far-advanced knowledge, or the extraterrestrial setting, or the telepath, or any similar sf appurtenance, is (or should be) quite essential. But these concepts are not what the author *develops.* His focus is entirely elsewhere.

Examples include Jack Vance's "The Last Castle" (**) and Gordon Dickson's "Call Him Lord" (**), both conspicuous for color and adventure as well as presenting societies different from our own; Richard Wilson's "Mother to the World" (**) and Alexei Panshin's *Rite of Passage* (**), which concentrate on interpersonal relationships; Robert Silverberg's horror story "Passengers" (**); Norman Spinrad's vatic *Bug Jack Barron* (*).

Sometimes it's hard to know where to put a work—which demonstrates once more the artificiality of categories. Is Isaac Asimov's "Foundation" series quasiscience, using a galactic background to treat of history and politics; or is it about the imaginary science of psychohistory; or is it an extrapolation of historiography, which is a real science? I call it quasiscience, because it seems to me that the "psychohistory" is flatly postulated for story purposes rather than elaborated for its own sake. You—or the Good Doctor—may disagree. Similarly controversial may be my placing here Philip José Farmer's "Riders of the Purple Wage" (*).

These, and many more, prove that quasiscience is a valuable part of sf. Indeed, it includes the majority, probably the large majority, of all the sf ever published. When its authors are honest craftsmen, they make every effort to get straight their scientific facts and the logic of their imaginary phenomena.

We have a final class to which that requirement does not always apply.

4. *Counterscience.* Again, I have no good name. "Fantasy" isn't right, though fantasies can be placed here, e.g., Fritz Leiber's "Ill Met in Lankhmar" (**). But many stories wear some of the trappings of sf while ignoring the standards of accuracy or logic which I have mentioned. This does not—repeat, not—mean that they are bad stories. On the contrary, their approach can be legitimate and necessary to the authors' purposes.

A case would be Roger Zelazny's "The Doors of His Face, the Lamps of His Mouth" (**), wherein he used a model of the planet Venus which had already been disproved in order to tell a hell of a fine yarn. Obviously this is the rubric for Blish's *Black Easter* (*), Keith Laumer's Kafkaesque "In the Queue" (*) and much of the work of Brian Aldiss, J. G. Ballard, Philip K. Dick and R. A. Lafferty. Proof enough that counterscience can inspire good writing!

Still, only in recent years has it become conspicuous in sf This is doubtless one reason why certain commentators think the field is changing its whole character.

Another reason is that there *seems* to be a new attitude taken by many writers, especially younger ones: a wariness of or outright hostility toward science and technology, a turning to "inner space" or actual mysticism. How important is this trend? In an effort to understand, I found myself defining three classes of attitude, philosophy or what-have-you. They cut across the four classes of motif, are equally arbitrary and blurry, but will perhaps be useful.

(a) *Technophilia.* This is the viewpoint which the popular mind associates with sf. Science, discovery, material achievement and the rest are basically good. In them lies a necessary if not sufficient condition for the improvement of man's lot, even his mental and spiritual lot.

Gernsbackian sf (usually) expressed this in its most primitive exuberance. A more mature version, admitting that technology can be misused though still finding man's best hope in it, is exemplified by Heinlein's *The Moon Is a Harsh Mistress* (*). Frederik Pohl's "Day Million" (*) says technology will change our inmost nature . . . and approves. Ursula K. Le Guin sees mind expansions and changes so subtle that you, or she herself, may not agree with me that her writing is technophilic.

Do not confuse technophilia with technolatry! We today have learned, the hard way, what Thoreau and Henry Adams knew, that in blind expansionism lies doom. The modern technophile says, "What we need is not less science and technology, but more, of the right kinds: a science which sees man in perspective, a technology which will let him treat his world and his fellows with reverence. The gains of moving onward are worth the risks and costs."

(b) *Neutrality*. In most sf, the issue hardly arises. The science and technology, at whatever level is postulated, are simply there. They may have been used well or ill, but the story does not suggest that this was an inevitable consequence of their very existence. Gary Wright's "Mirror of Ice" (*) and Michael Moorcock's "Behold the Man" (*) both give me this impression, although one is essentially upbeat, the other tragic. I would likewise call neutral those stories which, examining alternatives, call for us to choose the better ones but do not say we have already taken a wrong turning.

In this science-dominated age, it would seem that nominally neutral stories are, by and large, pro-science. "He who is not against us is with us." However, being a technophile myself, I felt it best to demarcate a middle ground.

(c) *Technophobia*. It is an oversimplification to speak of "anti-science sf." For one thing, many stories involving a green utopia suppose that what has made it possible is a superior technology (be this improved engineering, a rationalized society, psionics or whatever) and hence are technophilic. So is, say, Walter Miller's *A Canticle for Leibowitz*. In this famous book, though sinful man destroys his own works again and again, it is right that he strive to rebuild.

For another thing, our dangers are real enough, and the author may just be reminding us of how late the hour has grown: like Harlan Ellison when he shows a hopelessly devastated and degraded world in "A Boy and His Dog" (*). Or he may be telling a horror story, like Delany's "Aye, and Gomorrah" (*) or Dickson's grimly humorous "Computers Don't Argue" (*)—using radiation or computers where his Victorian forebears would have used ghosts. (Remember, Victorian ghosts were not necessarily evil. See Kipling's beautiful "They.") I must classify these narratives as technophobic, but do not regard them as indicating any trend.

In contrast, some tales do depict the rationalism of science, the artifices of technology, as inescapably destructive and dehumanizing. If we are to be saved, they say, we must declare a moratorium; or we must revert to an earlier level; or we must take off in a totally different direction, perhaps abandoning rationalism—even rationality—altogether. Other stories intimate we've gone beyond redemption.

Though disagreeing, I admit that such viewpoints are philosophically respectable and that we technophiles have something to learn here too. In any event, technophobia can lead to good writing. The most notable example must be *Brave New World*, but one could also name Thomas Disch's *The Genocides* (*), Wilson Tucker's *The Year of the Quiet Sun* (*), and Kurt Vonnegut's *Slaughterhouse-Five* (*)—to pick three out of a fairly large bag.

The authors may deny that these works are technophobic. Again I remind you that subjectivity is built into literary analysis. Certainly the authors need not be technophobic in their opinions about the real world. I know for a fact that some are not.

Obviously, hard science stories will be mostly technophilic; but *Brave New World* is about as hard-science as they come. One suspects the highest percentage of technophobia will be found in the counterscience group; but I'd call Niven's "Not Long Before the End" (*) technophilic, even if the technology is the dying art of magic. This illustrates how the classifications of theme and attitude intercut each other.

And now, having established them, let's use them to try to find out what the facts of the case are.

To those critics who see in counterscience, imaginary science or technophobia an overwhelming wave, I can say a blunt "Nonsense!" Counterscience is as old as fantasy, which is probably the oldest literary form in the world. Imaginary science we have long had with us, as in E. E. Smith's influential "Skylark" and "Lensman" series, not to speak of Wells, Stapledon & Co. Both of the latter expressed reservations about the idea that engineers are infallible guides to paradise. As for overt technophobia, early sf was full of Mad Scientists, Absent-minded Professors, Ravenous Monsters and Things Man Was Never Meant to Know. It was largely the editorial influence of the late John W. Campbell which eliminated these clichés and, indeed, brought the four species of sf toward full development. Neither he nor any of his competent colleagues tried to impose a particular attitude on the writers.

To be sure, the mix has varied from place to place and time to time. All my twelve sorts are still around and doing quite well, thank you, provided the individual stories are good. The question I was set to answer therefore boils down to: "What has the characteristic mix been in the last several years, and what has been the relative success—in sales or critical recognition—of each sort of sf?"

The reply depends largely on personal judgment and gut reaction. How would *you* describe a given work? To get an overview of my own feelings, I made a table of my assessments. The items were the Nebula-winning novels and runners-up since the award was instituted, and those shorter stories which have appeared in the Nebula anthologies. (Lacking copies of the final ballots, I had to leave out the remaining nominees in the latter category.) Because of the difficulty and frequent arbitrariness of every assessment, I shan't reproduce my table here. The illustrations given ought to tell you the general style of my thinking. Why not make up your own chart and see how it compares? I'll simply report my results.

In the anthologies:

1. *Hard science:* 10 stories, 2 winners. Technophilic, 5; neutral, 4 (including both winners), technophobic, 1.

2. *Imaginary science:* 10 stories, 1 winner. Technophilic, 5 (including the winner); neutral, 4; technophobic, 1.

3. *Quasiscience:* 11 stories, 7 winners. Technophilic, 3 (all winners); neutral, 3 (1 winner); technophobic, 5 (3 winners).

4. *Counterscience:* 14 stories, 2 winners. Technophilic, 1; neutral, 9 (including both winners); technophobic, 4.

This looks fairly well balanced between the different sorts. Remember, though: the editors were required to print the winners, but made their choices among the runners-up since it was impossible to include every one of these. So the anthology contents are bound to reflect individual preferences, as well as the desire to produce a variegated volume.

This is borne out by the noticeably different outcome for novels:

1. *Hard science:* 12 entries, 5 winners. Technophilic, 8 (including 4 winners); neutral, 4 (including 1 winner); technophobic, none.

2. *Imaginary science:* 8 entries, 1 winner. Technophilic, none; neutral, 5 (including the winner); technophobic, 3.

3. *Quasiscience:* 12 entries, 1 winner. Technophilic, 3; neutral, 5 (including the winner); technophobic, 4.

4. *Counterscience:* 7 entries, no winners. Technophilic, none; neutral, 3; technophobic, 4.

Thus, if my assessments are correct, hard science and technophilia are flourishing—maybe more than ever! The impression gets reinforcement from the awards bestowed by fans rather than writers: yesterday's International Fantasy Awards, today's Hugos. This table says:

1. *Hard science:* 14. Technophilic, 9; neutral, 5; technophobic, none.

2. *Imaginary science:* 11. Technophilic, 3; neutral, 8; technophobic, none.

3. *Quasiscience:* 14. Technophilic, 9; neutral, 3; technophobic, 2.

4. *Counterscience:* 3. Technophilic, none; neutral, 3; technophobic, none.

Evidently readers continue to go for "traditional" sf. A study of the MIT index, to check up on my recollection of what the magazines have been publishing, lends confirmation, as does the fact that *Analog,* long identified with that tradition, continues to enjoy much the highest circulation. It would be interesting to have sales figures on the novels; but at least the bulk of those which are appearing fit into my first three classes of theme and my first two of mood. This seems to indicate that those types sell best.

Let me reemphasize that if you go through the same exercise of evaluating and tabulating, you will doubtless get different figures. However, I bet you'll find the same basic pattern.

And let me finish by reiterating the most important point of all. Every sort of sf is valuable. None threatens any other. They are not only complementary, they blur together; to the extent that they are distinct, they keep cross-fertilizing; in their vigorous diversity, we can hope that the reader will find delight.

POUL ANDERSON

THEODORE STURGEON

The Fiction

In the best scientific tradition, we should define our terms. According to the Random House Dictionary, fiction is "the class of literature comprising works of imaginative narration, esp. in prose form." That will do, I suppose, though the temptation to apply it to advertising, political speeches, legal briefs, certain history books, some sermons and Form 1040 is overwhelming.

The same dictionary, in the process of distinguishing among fiction, fabrication and figment, says fiction "suggests a story invented and fashioned either to entertain or to deceive." One might say that is a better definition for the kind of fiction we are talking about than the primary one—except for that "either/or." The stories designed *both* to entertain and to deceive would make a bibliography five feet thick.

If by these remarks you deduce that I find the definitions unsatisfactory, you deduce rightly; I find, however, that I cannot quote any sole source for my definitions, intuitions and working parameters for the concept "fiction." Yet cite these subjective parameters I must, for it is within these that I write, teach, review* and occasionally criticize fiction.

It comes down to this: fiction is people.

Good fiction cannot be wrought from ideas. Idea pieces can be fascinating and important and moving and provocative, but they can also be (and often are) tracts, fulminations, pedantries and muddy blasterpieces. Fiction (in my very personal operating definition) is people; the action and reaction and interaction of people on people, of ideas and events and growth and change on people. People read fiction, and fiction is at its most successful when the reader identifies with someone or some-several in the narrative, so that the narrative happens to the reader and is recalled as his own experience.

Good science fiction is perforce good fiction . . . and at the risk of colliding with a man I respect most highly, I shall swerve into the "science" area just this much: "Science," in its most radical etymological significance, does not mean "method" or "technology" or "discipline" or anything else remotely like these. It means *knowledge*. Science fiction is knowledge fiction, and a murrain on those who would exclude from it stories of the inner spaces, of mind and its convolutions, and feelings, and permutations in and around the spectra of "soul," for all these are legitimate areas of extant and extrapolated knowledge. If ever the emphasis turns on self-knowledge, this should not disqualify it—most especially if in other ways the fiction achieves that sharing, that participative quality of "it happened to *me*."

Too much—painfully and infuriatingly too much—is made of the game of categorization. It is, I think, the intrusion of what I refuse to call the scientific method, saying rather the technological method, into art. Categorization has its uses, of course. When analyzing an amorphous mass, it can be helpful to break it into parts so the parts can be examined separately. We have, however, nearly reached a point at which it is impossible to think, to ana-

---

*The author regularly reviews science fiction in *Galaxy, National Review* and *The New York Times Book Review.*

lyze, even to enjoy unless and until the right-sounding categorization has been made. Mostly we don't read anything—perhaps
even *can't* read it—unless we are told beforehand what it's about!
What ever happened to a reader who could say to a closed book:
"Tell me a story!"—not caring what the story was about? He's gone
the way of the general fiction magazine, and all we have left are
specialists. A writer makes a new phrase, a new way, and the
response is immediate: "This is New Wave." Thereupon the preju-
dices assert themselves and the category of reader in which I have
placed myself immediately reacts (pro or con) to the category to
which I have assigned "New Wave."

On careful examination, New Wave shows itself to be no one
thing. It is many things; at its worst a self-conscious, infantile defiance of the rules by a writer who has never properly learned
them, like an artist who is nonobjective because he has never
learned to draw, or a second-semester student of music who ardu-
ously goes through a composition removing harmonies and insert-
ing discords. At its best, the so-called New Wave is the expression
of growth and change, and that is no less than the expression of
life itself. Your hard-core purist is anything but life-oriented;
heaven preserve us from those who would devitalize science
fiction, who would keep it from maturing and evolving.

Increasingly, the Nebula Award stories are good—really good—
fiction. They have to be, for they are chosen by the people who
know the field best and love it most. No one can ever know how
much envy, how much rue, how much agonizing honesty goes into
those votes, for the voters, each one of them, had reason to hope
(he is, way down deep, sure) that his work would be selected. No
one can know how often a writer with a good chance of winning
the honor cast his vote for someone else when sheer honesty
demanded it, only to see that other win by that one vote. It is a
fine thing to win a "Hugo"—but the qualification to vote for a
Hugo is to buy a ticket to the annual World Convention, and (it's
been done) a man can buy ten votes by buying ten memberships.
To qualify for the Nebula voting, you have to be a working writer,

and the winners have been selected by their peers.

Increasingly, too, the distaff shows its strength. Women were libbed in science fiction a long time ago, and are judged now as writers—just that.

It was my plan to climax this effusion with a list of my favorites, with a word about how far so-and-so has come, and how close what's-his-name has come so many times, and how sure I am he'll make it within the year. And to do this I shall reveal to you that I have spent a lot of hours with all the Nebula collections. A heady experience.

And in its way a frightening one too. I have had the horrid thought that perhaps the Hugo, essentially a reader's award, is after all more significant than a writer's one like this. How close can a professional get to being boxed in by his own professionalism? And really, can one be coldly separate from the fact that one knows some of these people, and that A's story is after all better than B's, but then B is such an incredibly wonderful person and A is such a nothing. . . .

No, I won't chance it. You decide. If these stories move you, write to those authors and tell them so. You bear more weight with them than I do . . . you can, perhaps, react more fairly.

I'll settle for this: from where I sit, this is the most remarkable and informative series in the field.

THEODORE STURGEON
Los Angeles

In Memoriam

This information has been compiled from several sources, among them two science fiction news publications, *Luna Monthly* (655 Orchard Street, Oradell, New Jersey) and *Locus* (3400 Ulloa Street, San Francisco, California). The major source was *The Encyclopedia of Science Fiction and Fantasy,* by Donald H. Tuck. The 1959 version of this truly monumental reference work will soon be replaced by a three-volume revised, expanded and updated edition, to be published by Advent: Publishers (P.O. Box 9228, Chicago, Illinois) beginning in 1973. With the kind cooperation of Advent: Publishers I was able to consult the unpublished 1973 edition.

—Lloyd Biggle, Jr.

ROBERT ARTHUR (November 1, 1909–April 28, 1969)
Born Robert Arthur Feder, he worked as an oil operator before he joined MGM as a screenwriter in 1937. He became a prominent Hollywood writer and subsequently produced radio and TV programs. He wrote a number of science fiction stories for the magazines of the early 1940s, and his series about Murchison Morks was later featured in *Argosy*. He published a collection of stories for juveniles, *Ghosts and More Ghosts* (1963), and two anthologies, *Davy Jones' Haunted Locker* (1965) and *Monster Mix* (1968). His wife was Joan Vatsek (b. 1916), likewise an author of science fiction.

279

JOHN W. CAMPBELL (June 8, 1910–July 11, 1971)

Born in Newark, New Jersey, where his father was an electrical engineer for Bell Telephone, he himself studied engineering and science at MIT and Duke University, but the direction his career was to take had been determined when he sold his first science fiction at the age of seventeen. Writing under his own name and the pseudonyms Arthur McCann, Don A. Stuart and Karl van Campen, he quickly established himself as a leading science fiction author. His later phenomenal success as an editor has tended to eclipse his own writing achievements, but two of his stories, "Twilight" (1934) and "Who Goes There?" (1938), are included in *The Science Fiction Hall of Fame* collections, the honor roll of all time great science fiction stories selected by members of Science Fiction Writers of America; and when a list was recently compiled of the best short science fiction written before 1940, four of the six stories were by John W. Campbell.

In 1937 he began editing *Astounding Stories* as an assistant to F. Orlin Tremaine, and in 1938 he succeeded Tremaine as editor. As *Astounding Science Fiction,* the magazine moved to the head of the field and remained there, and the list of writers Campbell discovered and developed reads like a science fiction honor roll: Heinlein, del Rey, Asimov, Sturgeon, de Camp, van Vogt, Leiber, Simak, Anderson, Budrys . . . the list goes on and on. He edited *Astounding Stories,* later *Analog,* for thirty-four years and two months, and during that time he was the only reader the magazine had. He read every manuscript submitted.

His fiction is widely anthologized, and paperback collections of his stories are still reissued. Nonfiction writings include a collection of his editorials from *Analog* (1968) and one of the first books on atomic energy, *The Atomic Story* (1947). As editor, he compiled a series of anthologies of stories from his magazine, *Astounding Science Fiction Anthology* (1952), *Prologue to Analog* (1962) and the series beginning with *Analog 1* (1963).

"And now that he is dead, where can we find ten people who by united effort might serve as a pale replacement for the man who, in the world of science fiction, lived a super-story more thrilling than any even he ever wrote." —Isaac Asimov

"John Campbell began an era in science fiction. He found it a literature of gimmicks and stage effects and made it a literature of ideas." —P. Schuyler Miller

"He . . . stood as its most massive and central pillar for over three decades; and the development of science fiction itself had literally been dominated by his ideas and his presence." —Gordon R. Dickson

". . . the greatest editor science fiction ever had." —Frederik Pohl

"John was the great discoverer, the knower, the teller and teacher. He was uncompromising in his wants and demands, but you couldn't fault him for that; he was always willing to work harder than you to get it out of you. Once I got seven thousand words of comment from him on a five-thousand-word story." —Theodore Sturgeon

"Of course you can give me whatever I want. I know *that!* And if I tell you what I want, that's exactly what you'll give me. Un-uh! Go home and do me something I won't know I want until I see it!" —John W. Campbell, quoted by artist Kelly Freas

"He was the only man I know who could say 'Good Morning,' and make it an order." —Bjo Trimble

"Science fiction, to which he devoted his life, forever will bear the hallmark of his greatness." —Clifford D. Simak

"Losing him now is very much like having Jupiter or Saturn ripped from the solar system: it leaves a huge empty place and sets up all sorts of cosmic perturbation and reverberations." —Robert Silverberg

"As an editor, he was so large a man that he made a tiny and seemingly unimportant field grow to fit his vision and his stature. As a man and a friend, he was much greater." —Lester del Rey

AUGUST DERLETH (February 24, 1909–July 4, 1971)
   Author, anthologist, editor, publisher, he was born, lived and died in Sauk City, Wisconsin. He wrote his first story at the age of thirteen, and at sixteen he sold a story to *Weird Tales*. At the University of Wisconsin he wrote his B.A. thesis on "The Weird Tale in English Since 1890."
   He personally produced more than one hundred books, ran three publishing houses and was a regular contributor to newspapers and magazines. An ardent disciple of H. P. Lovecraft, he founded Arkham House with Donald Wandrei in 1939 when he was unable to persuade any publisher to bring out an omnibus volume of Lovecraft's works. He became executor of Lovecraft's estate and continued to publish his works and correspondence.

His own writing ranged from weird and detective stories to poetry, biography and history. In 1938 he received a Guggenheim Fellowship to enable him to continue his *Sac Prairie Saga*, books about the prairie country. Derleth edited nine anthologies of science fiction stories and six of supernatural stories.

GUY S. ENDORE (July 4, 1900–February 12, 1970)
Novelist, biographer and screenwriter, he was born in New York City and attended Carnegie Institute of Technology before graduating from Columbia University. His short story "Men of Iron" appeared in the *Magazine of Fantasy and Science Fiction* in 1949. Fantasy novels were *Methinks the Lady* (1945) and *The Werewolf of Paris* (1933).

JOHN BEYNON HARRIS [JOHN WYNDHAM] (July 10, 1903–March 11, 1969)
Although his occupations ranged from farming to advertising, with an interval of reading for the bar, Harris was the dean of British authors in the science fiction and fantasy fields, where he was active for almost forty years. He began writing in the 1930s under his own name; later he used the pseudonym "John Beynon." After service in World War II, he adopted the pseudonym "John Wyndham," under which he became one of the foremost science fiction authors, with a large following outside the field.

The Day of the Triffids (1951) appeared in *Collier's*, was widely reprinted and translated, received the International Fantasy Award in 1952, was serialized on BBC Radio, and was released as a feature film in 1963. *The Midwich Cukcoos* (1957) was produced as a film entitled *Village of the Damned*, released in 1960. Other novels were *Out of the Deeps* (British title, *The Karken Wakes*, 1953), *Re-Birth* (British title, *The Chrysalids*, 1955), *Chocky* (1968), *The Outward Urge* (1959), *Planet Plane* (1936), *The Secret People* (1956), *The Trouble with Lichen* (1960). Some of his numerous short stories were collected under the titles *Consider Her Ways* (1961) and *Tales of Gooseflesh and Laughter* (1956).

WILLY LEY (October 2, 1906–June 24, 1969)
One of the most popular science fiction personalities of this era, paradoxically Willy Ley was not (except for three stories published under the pseudonym Robert Willey) a writer of science fiction. He was born in Berlin, and his early ambition was to be a paleontolo-

gist. He was one of the founders of the German Rocket Society, was the author of the first book about rockets and space travel for the layman, and collaborated with Fritz Lang on a famous science fiction film, *The Girl in the Moon*. When the Nazis ordered him to stop writing articles on rocketry, he came to the United States with the help of the American Rocket Society. He became a naturalized U.S. citizen in 1944.

He called himself an historian of science, and in America he became a foremost writer of popular books on scientific subjects. He wrote voluminously about rocketry, space travel, astronomy, historical zoology and the many fascinating byways of science and science history his inquiring mind had touched. *Conquest of Space* (with Chesley Bonestell, 1949) won the International Fantasy Award.

Ley was a popular lecturer on science subjects, and he attended and addressed many of the World Science Fiction Conventions, beginning with the first, in New York City, in 1939. He died just four weeks before his dreams of a lifetime were realized in the first moon landing.

NOEL M. LOOMIS (April 3, 1905–September 7, 1969)
A linotype machinist by trade, he was born in Wakita, Oklahoma, attended Clarendon College and the University of Oklahoma, and worked as a printer, editor and newspaperman in several western cities. He wrote fiction in many fields, often under the pseudonym "Benj. Miller." He was best known as a writer of Western and mystery stories, and he held offices in Western Writers of America. His most prominent science fiction books were *City of Glass* (1942), its sequel, *Iron Men* (1945) and *Man with Absolute Motion* (1955).

SEABURY QUINN (January 1, 1889–December 24, 1969)
Born in Washington, D.C., he graduated from the National University in 1910 and was admitted to the District of Columbia bar. He alternated between law and journalism throughout his life. He edited trade papers, taught medical jurisprudence and worked as a government lawyer while authoring some five hundred stories, many of which appeared in *Weird Tales*, where Quinn was a noted writer. Best known are stories of the Jules de Grandin series, which . were published in *Weird Tales* from 1925 to 1951.

SEWELL PEASLEE WRIGHT (August 7, 1897–March 31, 1970)

Though born in Butler, Pennsylvania, Wright spent the early years of his life in Toledo, Ohio, and graduated from the University of Toledo. In World War I he served in the Chemical Warfare Section, and subsequently he worked on newspapers in Toledo, Portland and Tulsa. In 1920 he joined an advertising agency in Springfield, Illinois, which he later purchased and named S. P. Wright and Co. He was a radio ham and proud of the fact that he described radar in a science fiction story before it was invented. He wrote in several fields, and his books include a text on advertising. His first science fiction story was sold in 1923, and in the 1930s he became a well-known science fiction writer. His best remembered stories are those of his John Hansen series.

PHILIP WYLIE (May 12, 1902–October 25, 1971)

Born in Beverly, Massachusetts, Wylie attended Princeton University for three years. He subsequently worked as a press agent, advertising manager and screenwriter, and he collaborated on the script for the screen version of H. G. Wells's *Island of Doctor Moreau*, released as *Island of Lost Souls*.

Wylie was a leader and prophet in the fight against pollution and for environmental protection, and he wrote numerous magazine articles in these causes. He helped to establish the Everglades National Park. Though best known as a critic of contemporary man and society, especially through his nonfiction book *Generation of Vipers* (1942), he wrote a number of science fiction novels: *Gladiator* (1930), *The Disappearance* (1951), *Tomorrow* (1954) and *Triumph* (1963). *Los Angeles 2017* was written first as a television motion picture (1970). His final novel, *The End of the Dream*, is also science fiction and was published posthumously (1972).

When Worlds Collide and its sequel, *After Worlds Collide*, both written in collaboration with Edwin Balmer, were considered science fiction classics when they first appeared, 1932–1933. A film version of *When Worlds Collide* was released in 1951.

Award-Winning Science Fiction, 1965–1971

NEBULA AWARDS

Winners of the Nebula Award are chosen by the members of Science Fiction Writers of America. Throughout the year SFWA members nominate the best science fiction stories and novels as they are published. At the end of the year there is a final nominating ballot and then an awards ballot to determine the winners. Nebula Trophies are presented at the annual Nebula Awards Banquets, held simultaneously each spring in New York City, New Orleans and on the West Coast.

Science Fiction Writers of America was organized in 1965, and the first Nebula Awards were made in the spring of 1966 for 1965 publications. The Nebula Trophy was designed by Judith Ann Lawrence (Mrs. James Blish) from a sketch by Kate Wilhelm (Mrs. Damon Knight). Each trophy is an individual creation, consisting of a block of lucite four inches square by nine inches high, into which a spiral nebula made of metallic glitter and a specimen of rock crystal are embedded.

The categories in which the awards are made have remained unchanged from the beginning. In the following list, the year given is the year of publication for the winning entries.

1965

Best Novel: DUNE *by Frank Herbert*
Best Novella: "The Saliva Tree" *by Brian W. Aldiss*
  "He Who Shapes" *by Roger Zelazny* (tie)
Best Novelette: "The Doors of His Face, the Lamps of His Mouth" *by Roger Zelazny*
Best Short Story: " 'Repent, Harlequin!' Said the Ticktockman" *by Harlan Ellison*

1966

Best Novel: FLOWERS FOR ALGERNON *by Daniel Keyes*
  BABEL-17 *by Samuel R. Delany* (tie)
Best Novella: "The Last Castle" *by Jack Vance*
Best Novelette: "Call Him Lord" *by Gordon R. Dickson*
Best Short Story: "The Secret Place" *by Richard McKenna*

1967

Best Novel: THE EINSTEIN INTERSECTION *by Samuel R. Delany*
Best Novella: "Behold the Man" *by Michael Moorcock*
Best Novelette: "Gonna Roll the Bones" *by Fritz Leiber*
Best Short Story: "Aye, and Gomorrah" *by Samuel R. Delany*

1968

Best Novel: RITE OF PASSAGE *by Alexei Panshin*
Best Novella: "Dragonrider" *by Anne McCaffrey*
Best Novelette: "Mother to the World" *by Richard Wilson*
Best Short Story: "The Planners" *by Kate Wilhelm*

1969

Best Novel: THE LEFT HAND OF DARKNESS *by Ursula K. Le Guin*
Best Novella: "A Boy and His Dog" *by Harlan Ellison*
Best Novelette: "Time Considered as a Helix of Semi-Precious Stones" *by Samuel R. Delany*
Best Short Story: "Passengers" *by Robert Silverberg*

1970

Best Novel: RINGWORLD *by Larry Niven*
Best Novella: "Ill Met in Lankhmar" *by Fritz Leiber*
Best Novelette: "Slow Sculpture" *by Theodore Sturgeon*
Best Short Story: No award

1971

Best Novel: A TIME OF CHANGES, *by Robert Silverberg*
Best Novella: "The Missing Man" *by Katherine MacLean*
Best Novelette: "The Queen of Air and Darkness" *by Poul Anderson*
Best Short Story: "Good News from the Vatican" *by Robert Silverberg*

HUGO AWARDS

The Science Fiction Achievement Awards, a title rarely used, became known as "Hugo" Awards shortly after the first such awards were presented, in 1953. The "Hugo" is after Hugo Gernsback, author, editor and publisher and one of the "fathers" of modern science fiction. The Hugo Awards have been made annually since 1955, and their winners are determined by popular vote. Because each year's awards have been under the administration of a different group, the committee in charge of the year's World Science Fiction Convention, rules and categories have fluctuated from year to year, sometimes drastically.

From their inception, the Hugo Awards have been made for amateur as well as for professional achievement. Thus there are usually awards for Best Fanzine (the initiate's term for amateur magazine), Best Fan Writer and Best Fan Artist as well as the awards for professional writing, for Best Professional Magazine, and for Best Professional Artist. Only the more standardized awards for professional writing are listed here.* In recent years voting on both the nominating and final ballot has been limited to those who have purchased memberships in the World Science Fiction Convention. The Hugo Trophy is a miniature rocket ship poised for takeoff, though details of design and materials have varied from year to year. In the following list, the year given is the year of publication for the winning entries, and this is followed by the name, place and year of the World Science Fiction Convention at which the awards were made.

1965 ("Tricon," Cleveland, 1966)

Best Novel: . . . AND CALL ME CONRAD *by Roger Zelazny*
          DUNE *by Frank Herbert* (tie)
Best Short Fiction: " 'Repent, Harlequin!' Said the Ticktockman" *by Harlan Ellison*

1966 ("NYCon III," New York City, 1967)

Best Novel: THE MOON IS A HARSH MISTRESS *by Robert A. Heinlein*
Best Novelette: "The Last Castle" *by Jack Vance*
Best Short Story: "Neutron Star" *by Larry Niven*

1967 ("Baycon," Oakland, California, 1968)

Best Novel: LORD OF LIGHT *by Roger Zelazny*
Best Novella: "Riders of the Purple Wage" *by Philip José Farmer*
          "Weyr Search" *by Anne McCaffrey* (tie)
Best Novelette: "Gonna Roll the Bones" *by Fritz Leiber*
Best Short Story: "I Have No Mouth, and I Must Scream"
          by Harlan Ellison

*The reader is referred to *A History of the Hugo, Nebula and International Fantasy Awards,* published by Howard DeVore, 4705 Weddel Street, Dearborn, Michigan, for the history of the awards and a detailed listing of Hugo winners and nominees in all categories. The book also contains a complete listing of Nebula Award nominees.

1968 ("St. Louiscon," St. Louis, 1969)

Best Novel: STAND ON ZANZIBAR *by John Brunner*
Best Novella: "Nightwings" *by Robert Silverberg*
Best Novelette: "The Sharing of Flesh" *by Poul Anderson*
Best Short Story: "The Beast That Shouted Love at the Heart of the World" *by Harlan Ellison*

1969 ("Heicon," Heidelberg, Germany, 1970)

Best Novel: THE LEFT HAND OF DARKNESS *by Ursula K. Le Guin*
Best Novella: "Ship of Shadows" *by Fritz Lieber*
Best Short Story: "Time Considered as a Helix of Semi-Precious Stones" *by Samuel R. Delany*

1970 ("Noreascon," Boston, 1971)

Best Novel: RINGWORLD *by Larry Niven*
Best Novella: "Ill Met in Lankhmar" *by Fritz Leiber*
Best Short Story: "Slow Sculpture" *by Theodore Sturgeon*

1971 ("L.A. Con," Los Angeles, 1972)

Best Novel: TO YOUR SCATTERED BODIES GO *by Phillip José Farmer*
Best Novella: "The Queen of Air and Darkness" *by Poul Anderson*
Best Short Story: "Inconstant Moon" *by Larry Niven*

73 74 10 9 8 7 6 5 4 3 2 1